ODDS AGAI

Young Delgado Mc into Turley's Mill through the ring of death around it. "How many are in here?" he asked, trying to ignore the pain of his twisted ankle.

"Well, let's see," Simon Turley said. "There's Tom Tobin, Ike Claymore, Billy Russell and that breed partner of his, Stump Willis and Amos Marsh. Then there's me and Falconer. You're the ninth man, Del."

"Nine men," said Delgado. "Against a hundred."

"I wish you hadn't come, Del," Falconer said.

"We have no chance, do we?" Delgado said.

"Anything can happen," said Falconer.

"No. You're lying," Delgado said. "You know we're finished. There is no hope. Aren't you afraid, Hugh? Afraid to die?"

"We all die," Falconer said. "Guess that's the price we pay for getting to live."

Delgado looked around him. Maybe they would die, but not like rats in a trap. They would die like men—mountain men. . . .

Jason Manning

AMERICAN BLOOD

A SIGNET BOOK

SIGNET
Published by the Penguin Group
Penguin Books USA Inc., 375 Hudson Street,
New York, New York 10014, U.S.A.
Penguin Books Ltd, 27 Wrights Lane,
London W8 5TZ, England
Penguin Books Australia Ltd, Ringwood,
Victoria, Australia
Penguin Books Canada Ltd, 10 Alcorn Avenue,
Toronto, Ontario, Canada M4V 3B2
Penguin Books (N.Z.) Ltd, 182–190 Wairau Road,
Auckland 10, New Zealand

Penguin Books Ltd, Registered Offices:
Harmondsworth, Middlesex, England

First published by Signet, an imprint of Dutton Signet,
a division of Penguin Books USA Inc.

First Printing, November, 1996
10 9 8 7 6 5 4 3 2 1

Printed in the United States of America

Author's Note

When people first become aware that I have devoted my professional life to the study of the history of the United States between the creation of the Constitution and the outbreak of the Civil War, many of them give me a blank or bewildered stare, sometimes seasoned with pity. How could someone waste so much time on such a dull subject? What, they might ask, transpired in that three-quarters of a century that could be of much relevance to people today?

As to the second question—what happened?—I take great pleasure in telling them.

The War of 1812 happened. The Mexican War, too. The Aroostook War and the war with the Barbary Pirates. Let's not forget the "Quasi-War" with France. The Black Hawk War. The Alamo and the Battle of San Jacinto. The First and Second Seminole Wars.

Great men strode the American stage, Andrew Jackson, Thomas Jefferson, Henry Clay, Daniel Webster, John C. Calhoun, Thomas Hart Benton, Jim Bridger and Kit Carson, Davy Crockett and Jim Bowie, Lewis and Clark, Madison and Monroe, Hamilton and Burr, Martin Van Buren, Sam Houston, Tecumseh, Ralph Waldo Emerson, and Washington Irving. James Fenimore Cooper wrote

The Leatherstocking Tales. Hawthorne wrote *The Scarlet Letter.* Thoreau retired from the human rat race to Walden Pond and penned *Civil Disobedience.* Great women also strode that stage. Harriet Beecher Stowe wrote *Uncle Tom's Cabin.* There was Ann Lee of the Shakers, the abolitionist Grimke sisters, Margaret Fuller, Dorothea Dix, and Harriet Tubman of Underground Railroad fame.

What happened, you ask? The Louisiana Purchase happened. The Monroe Doctrine. The Missouri Compromise, the Tariff of Abominations, the ill-advised Embargo Act, the Nullification Crisis, the Gadsden Purchase, the Second Great Awakening, the Oregon Trail and the Trail of Tears, the Panic of 1837, the yellow fever epidemic of 1832 in New Orleans (in which one-sixth of the city's population fell victim in twelve days.) The Lincoln-Douglas Debates happened, and Bleeding Kansas, and the Bank War, and Eli Whitney and his cotton gin, Colt's revolver and Winchester's rifle, and inventions by McCormick and Goodyear and Singer.

Mountain men and the fabulous fur trade happened. Nat Turner and Denmark Vesey and slave rebellions, the great Webster-Hayne Debate, the notorious Burr-Hamilton duel, the Erie Canal and Robert Fulton's steamboat, the Santa Fe Trail and Pikes Peak and the Bear Flag Republic, "Fifty-Four Forty or Fight," "Tippecanoe and Tyler Too," the Spanish Conspiracy and the Corrupt Bargain, the Fugitive Slave Law and the Dred Scott Decision, *Marbury* v. *Madison, McCulloch* v. *Maryland,* William Lloyd Garrison and the *Liberator,* Transcendentalists and Millerites and Utopians, Brigham Young and the Mormons, Manifest Destiny and States' Rights, War Hawks and Whigs and Anti-masons and Locofocos, Jean Lafitte and the Reverend Devil, Tammany Hall and the Know-Nothings.

In short, what happened between 1787 and 1861 was the growth of our nation, the seed of a great democratic experiment, unlike anything the world had seen before, sprouting into a sapling buffeted by the storms of political and cultural change in a vibrant and exciting age. It was a time when a polyethnic people defined what it meant to be an American—a definition of principles based on ideals which, though even now buffeted by winds of change, yet holds true.

This novel is the story of one man's struggle to come to terms with what it meant to be an American in those tumultuous times.

Chapter One

"These are the facts which insult you . . ."

1

Delgado McKinn was awakened by the shrill keening of the riverboat's steam whistle.

Sitting up too quickly, he winced at the stabbing pain in his head. It felt as though a stiletto of white hot steel had been thrust through his temples. Too much cognac. He smiled ruefully. Ten dollars a bottle, imported from France. How much had he consumed? He could not remember—but obviously more than he should have.

Guilt promptly insinuated itself, made him feel worse still. His father would have sternly disapproved of his actions last night. Angus McKinn was descended from Scottish Covenanters who made Quakers look like libertines. He viewed any form of recreation as a sign of moral weakness, indicative of a shameful proclivity toward self-indulgence. Ceaseless work was the only justification for man's presence on earth. Delgado admired his father, and the last thing he ever wanted to do was disappoint him. And Angus McKinn would most certainly have been disappointed had he known of his son's promiscuity. Getting drunk and gambling at cards! The Devil's work!

Delgado swung long legs off the bed and groaned as the well-appointed stateroom began to spin. He closed his eyes and ran long fingers through tousled hair as black as a crow's wing, kneading his scalp. If a man took his pleasure, he had to endure the pain. There was always a price to be paid. At least, mused Delgado, I did not lose at cards.

Fortunately, from his standpoint, the game had been whist. He would not have fared so well, perhaps, at poker or keno. Three gentlemen had been looking for a fourth, and Delgado had just happened to be passing by their table in the grand saloon. They were Messrs. Horan, Wheeler, and Sterling. Horan, the planter's son. Pale, angular features. A full, selfish mouth. Pale blue eyes. Pale hair that curled down over his forehead in stubborn resistance to a generous application of pomatum. Wheeler, stocky, with a pleasant kind of bluff pugnacity, a jowly face framed by prodigious muttonchop whiskers, a loud, braying voice, a St. Louis merchant with an expert's grasp of the Mississippi River commerce down to its most intimate and obscure details, and a wealthy man as a consequence of this expertise. Sterling, thin as a rapier's blade, and with a wit as sharp as the tip of a duelist's sword, cool and collected at all times, impeccable in dress and manners, although early on Delgado had detected in him a streak of misanthropy. A newspaper editor. Delgado could not recall the name of the newspaper.

He had been fortunate, too, in being paired with Sterling, a polished and utterly ruthless player. Wheeler proved too predictably straightforward in his play—whist was a game best played with guile. Horan was a daring player and had fared well enough in the early going, but he hated to lose, which he had begun to do as the night wore on. The more he lost, the more reckless and erratic became his game.

One thing Delgado could remember with crystal clarity was the final round. A true masterpiece. Wheeler had dealt, turning up a heart as trump. Delgado had led with the king of hearts, a thoughtless opening on the face of it, and he had seen the dismay flash fleetingly across Sterling's features. But the king of diamonds followed, taking the trick, and then the ace of hearts, and the seven, and Sterling took the next trick with the queen, returning a diamond, as eleven hearts had by that time been expelled. Delgado passed the queen of diamonds. It was followed by the ace. Their opponents lost small spades to a seemingly endless onslaught of diamonds, and when the time was right, Delgado played his ace of spades, followed by the four. Sterling knew now that his partner had played a good hand with great skill. He finessed his knave, played the king of spades, upon which Delgado disposed of his singleton. The last two tricks were then Delgado's for the taking. Wheeler and Horan had held every trick in spades, and yet Delgado and his partner had made a slam.

Of course, gentlemen usually indulged in a friendly wager over cards. During his leisurely jaunt across the United States, Delgado had come to the conclusion that Americans had an insatiable appetite for gambling. Risk taking was deeply ingrained in the national character. Games of chance, horse races, cock fights, wrestling matches—Delgado had even seen two men bet heavily on which of a pair of raindrops would reach the bottom of a windowpane first.

Wheeler and Horan lost a hundred dollars on the final round, Sterling had been the one to raise the ante all night, to and even beyond the point where Delgado began to feel butterflies in his stomach. After all, this was his father's money, and Angus McKinn had not given it to his son to lose in a card game. Then, too, Delgado had the distinct impression that Sterling, for whatever reason, derived immense satisfaction from taking Brent Horan's money. It was more than a friendly wager for the newspaperman. He had used his wit, like sharp steel wrapped in silk, to cunningly and mercilessly prod Horan into ever higher bets. A dangerous game, since Horan was a Southern aristocrat, and Delgado knew such men were quick to take offense at even the most innocuous slight. Yet Sterling played his needling barbs with as much finesse as he did the pasteboards, enticing Horan into further costly flirtation with Lady Luck, pricking his pride and vanity, goading him to renewed recklessness. His senses dulled by strong spirits, Horan had been led like a lamb to slaughter, and by the end of it all had lost several hundred dollars.

"I was at first concerned," Sterling admitted to Delgado as they split their winnings over one last drink, after Wheeler and Horan had departed the grand saloon. "I thought you might be an amateur when it came to whist. But you have a masterful command of the game, sir. You play a good hand well and, even more important, a losing hand even better."

Delgado thanked him. "I had excellent teachers. I played whist every Saturday night for three years at Oxford, almost without exception."

"Oxford? I didn't think you were an American, sir. English, then?"

Delgado smiled. "Not quite. My father is a Scotsman. My mother is the daughter of a Spanish grandee."

He left it at that, for by that time the cognac

had the better of him, and he wanted nothing more than to retire to his stateroom and lie down and close his eyes. Sterling was intrigued, one look at Delgado McKinn and you could tell his was no ordinary pedigree. His black hair was wavy and unfashionably long, by American standards, to the shoulder. His clean-shaven features were aquiline, the eyes brooding and almost black. He was tall at two inches over six feet, and so slender in build that he seemed taller still. He spoke with a definite accent, but it was not obtrusive. One thing was clear—Delgado McKinn was endowed with a gentleman's grace, and had a gentleman's grasp of manners and vocabulary, and yet strong, almost reckless, passions surged just beneath that polished exterior. Finally, and with perfectly natural envy, Sterling conceded that Delgado McKinn was an extraordinarily handsome fellow. No young woman—and probably no woman of any age—no matter how well brought up, would be able to resist letting her gaze linger in speculative wonder upon this dark and rather mysterious stranger.

For his part, Delgado had learned to be vague about his citizenship. His home, Taos, was still part of the Republic of Mexico, and Mexico, as of May 13, 1846, only eight weeks ago, was at war with the United States. Technically, then, Delgado McKinn was traveling through enemy territory.

2

The side-wheeler's whistle shrilled again, and Delgado rose from his bed. Though it took considerable effort to do so, he was determined to demonstrate to the Fates that he still had a will of his own. He had slept in his clothes, so he changed into a clean white cambric shirt and donned a fresh waistcoat, fitted dark blue frock coat, and a fresh cravat, skillfully knotted to create an impression of deliberate negligence, which was the fashion of the day. He made certain to transfer his wallet from last night's rumpled coat to the one he now wore. One did not leave one's valuables lying about in a steamboat stateroom. Even on a boat as reputable as the *Sultana*. On the river packets you met the wealth, the wit, and the rascality of the land. The passengers included ladies and gentlemen of unassailable propriety: businessmen, cotton planters, Creole lawyers, bankers, and commission merchants. But there were plenty of scoundrels riding the river, as well. Gunmen and gamblers, courtesans and common thieves.

The Mississippi River was the carotid artery of Trans-Appalachian America. And dozens of lines branched off to service her many tributaries: on the Ohio System, the Cumberland up to Nashville, the Kanawha up to Charleston, the Allegheny and the Muskingum. Steamboats struggled against the wild Missouri as far as Fort Benton these days, carrying supplies to military outposts strung all along the Big Muddy. On the "Lower River," the packets steamed up and down the Red, Arkansas, Ouachita, Black, and Yazoo rivers. Smaller boats made their way along the numerous bayous of Louisiana and to the very steps of the plantation houses to load thousands of bales of cotton each year and carry them to the docks of New Orleans for shipment overseas or to the New England mill towns. But cotton was not the only freight of the riverboat—corn, wheat, hemp, tobacco, and livestock came down the river from the young nation's heartland, while manufactured goods and luxuries were carried upriver from the great port of New Orleans.

Delgado remembered to pocket the pearl-handled derringer his father had presented him on the day he left home three years ago. Angus McKinn was of the firm opinion that a wise man trusted no one, and he would not permit his son to venture forth into the world unarmed. Delgado considered the short-barreled, large-bore, "over and under" hideout a useless encumbrance, he had never had cause to resort to it and never expected to. But he did not want the gun to fall into the hands of a sneak thief. The derringer was a gift from his father, and he cherished it for that reason, if for no other.

With one last glance about the stateroom, Delgado stepped out into the long, gilded, grand saloon, off which all the staterooms were aligned. Two rows of fluted columns, ten prism-fringed chandeliers, an oil painting—a misty and eye-pleasing pastoral scene—on every stateroom door, a blue-and-gold rug, custom-made in Belgium, two hundred feet in length, extending from one end of the ornate room to the other. In stark contrast to the previous night, the saloon was nearly empty this morning. A platoon of cabin boys, looking natty in their plum-colored livery, were busy sweeping, wiping, and polishing up. The *Sultana* was no cheap, gaudy packet, but rather a genuine "floating palace," and it was Delgado's opinion that the saloon, as well as the adjoining staterooms with their brass and porcelain and velvet accouterments, were as splendid as the court of any Persian potentate.

He found the spacious gallery, forward of the saloon on the boiler deck, already crowded, as ladies and gentlemen took advantage of the cool morning air. Finding a spot at the railing, Delgado glanced down the starboard length of the boat, admiring the graceful sheer of the three-hundred-foot vessel. Though she sat on an even keel, her decks—main, boiler, hurricane, and texas—all followed the same pronounced curve, for the boat rode high at bow and stern. The upper three decks were fenced and ornamented with white railings. The paddleboxes were adorned with the *Sultana*'s crescent moon emblem. A similar device dangled between the pair of soaring smokestacks capped with filigree crowns done in the likeness of oak leaves. At the base of the smokestacks on the texas deck stood the pilothouse, with glass and exquisitely wrought "gingerbread" all around.

Black smoke bellowed from the smokestacks, pluming behind the *Sultana* as she splashed resolutely against the strong current, making eight miles an hour. Delgado felt the rhythm of the wheels as they smote the shimmering surface of the mighty river and heard the muted roar of the inferno in the boilers through the open furnace doors. A half mile to the east a line of trees, solemn old woods, marked the Illinois shore. Kaskaskia was behind them; today they would reach St. Louis.

St. Louis marked an ending of sorts for Delgado, and he contemplated his imminent arrival there in a melancholy light. Another eight hundred miles lay between him and his Taos home—long, arduous miles across the southern plains. Thus far he had enjoyed the trip immensely. Having dutifully applied himself to his studies at Oxford for the better part of three years, he had viewed his leisurely return via New York and New Orleans as a well-earned vacation. At the time of his departure from England the United States and the Republic of Mexico had still been at peace.

This had been his first exposure to the United States. The vibrant new nation had many wonders for a young man who had spent his twenty-three years in the insulated environment of Taos. He had been particularly impressed by New York City, where he had arrived three months ago aboard a steamship of the Royal Mail Steam Packet Company, founded six years before by Sir Samuel Cunard. The voyage across the Atlantic had taken only a fortnight. The steam engine was revolutionizing sea travel and doomed the sailing ship to eventual extinction, and in a way Delgado regretted that. His voyage to England had been as a passenger aboard the *Flying Cloud*, one of the most famous of the clipper ships, and the experience had been an exciting one. Sadly, he predicted that in ten years the clipper ship would be but a memory.

No question but the times were a-changing, almost faster than the mind could assimilate. In Taos all things moved at a languorous and well-structured pace. In many ways Taos was little changed from the way it had been a hundred years ago. The society was steeped in time-honored tradition. Life was to be savored. In the United States life was to be spent—in a hurry, and in the pursuit of prosperity. Only recently were Americans learning to indulge in leisure.

New York City was a case in point. No one who saw the metropolis in all its vitality and magnitude could fail to be inspired by a sense of raw power and magnificent destiny. A forest of masts and spars rose from the hulls of hundreds of ships packed like sardines in the East River. The merchants and warehouses at the southern end of Manhattan Island handled half the imports and a third of the exports for the entire nation. Though London was still considered the financial capital of the world, Wall Street was coming on fast and could already boast the greatest concentration of wealth in America. Forty-six years ago, at the turn of the century, New York's population had not exceeded 125,000, now almost 400,000 souls resided there, with hundreds more arriving every week, most of these refugees from the political unrest in Europe, or, as in the case of the Irish, fleeing the grim prospect of famine.

Once Boston and Philadelphia had rivaled New York City as commercial centers, but no longer. The latter enjoyed too many natural advantages. Its harbor was broad and sheltered. It enjoyed ready access to a busting, industrialized New England. To the north the Hudson River linked the city with the Erie Canal, which in turn connected New York with the fast-growing regions beyond the formidable barrier of the Appalachians. The decade of uncertainty, deflation and, in some cases, ruination, which had marked the worldwide depression following the Panic of 1837 had been but a temporary setback.

New York City was symbolic of American power and progress. The city was brash, barbaric, hustling, arrogant, ostentatious, confident, unrefined. Delgado had visited the Astor Place Opera, and at the Chatham he had been entertained by a "grand national drama" entitled *The March to*

Freedom, which featured General Taylor and the Goddess of Liberty vanquishing Mexican tyranny. He had dined at the Milles-Colonnes, sampled ice cream—the newest rage—at Contoit's, been accosted by a lady of dubious virtue as he strolled the enchanting woods of the Elysian Fields in Hoboken, seen the magnificent town homes of the gentry in Park Place and Washington Square.

He had seen the darker side of the city, too—the squalid ghettos near Five Points, the ragpickers, hot corn girls, and apple peddlers who exemplified the thousands of unseen poor. Many better-off New Yorkers ignored these suffering masses or contemptuously considered them the degraded overflow of European society. But many more, feeling it their duty to extend a helping hand to those less fortunate, contributed time and money to a host of benevolent charities like The Society for the Relief of Poor Widows and the New York Orphan Asylum. Delgado had concluded that while sometimes Americans could be small-minded, they were more often than not big-hearted.

After experiencing New York, he could not help but wonder what fate held in store for Taos. The Americans believed they were destined to own the continent, and Delgado did not believe the strife-torn Republic of Mexico could stand against the irresistible Yankee tide. Though Angus McKinn had never said so, Delgado suspected his father of sending him off to England to place him well out of harm's way, knowing that a clash was inevitable. This had suited Delgado, he was no warrior, and he could muster no allegiance, no patriotic enthusiasm, for any flag. Now a war was being fought, and territory would change hands.

Taos would soon be a part of the United States. The Stars and Stripes would fly above the old Cabildo in the provincial capital of Santa Fe.

By virtue of conquest, whether he liked it nor not, Delgado McKinn was destined to become an American. On that score he was ambivalent. Americans and their ways were fascinating, but remained strange to him. He wondered if he would fit in, or forever feel like an outcast.

3

The *Sultana* was putting in to shore on the Missouri side, where a small village in a quick-cut clearing was coming to sudden life with the arrival of the "floating palace." In such a frontier settlement, drowsy in the summer sunshine, the day was a slow and dreary thing, yesterday's mirror image and a blueprint for tomorrow. But even as Delgado watched, the levee came alive with people as the cry *"Steamboat a'comin'!"* rang out. From every rough-hewn log and raw clapboard structure the denizens poured to gaze in awe at the wondrous sight of the side-wheeler, so long and trim and resplendent.

The whistle blasts that had awakened Delgado served to alert crew and passengers of imminent landfall. Now, as the *Sultana* veered nearer the western shore, the big bell above the pilothouse rang out, two mellow notes. From the hurricane deck, almost directly above Delgado, the watchman called out, *"Labboard lead! Starboard lead!"*

The leadsmen rushed to their places near the bow, on the main deck. When the pilot rang the bell once, the starboard leadsman tossed out his knotted and weighted line to measure the river's depth and called out, "Mark three!" At two bells the man on the other side performed the same ritual "Quarter less three!" And soon, "Half twain! . . . Quarter twain! . . . Mark twain!" The pilot hailed the engine room, and the *Sultana* slowed perceptibly. Steam whistled as it escaped through the gauge cocks.

Having visited the pilothouse earlier, Delgado could picture in his mind's eye what was occurring there at this moment. The pilot would be putting the wheel down hard to swing the boat into her marks. The cries of the leadsmen indicated that the water was becoming "shoal." "Eight and a half!" "Eight!" *"Seven and a half!"* Delgado felt a tingle at the base of his spine and glanced about him surreptitiously to see if any of the other passengers presently occupying the deck realized that now the steamboat's hull was less than two feel from the bottom. *"Seven feet!"* Would they run aground? Surely not. A boat like the *Sultana* would merit the services of the best "lightning pilot" money could hire. At this speed, if they did run aground, the impact would be violent, and Delgado imagined himself hurled through a shattered railing into the murky brown water below. But he did not move, or betray in any way his apprehension. Suddenly, the engines stopped—he could no longer feel their pulse through the decking beneath his feet. The agile *Sultana* swung its stern sharply toward the shore as the pilot rolled the big wheel faster than the human eye could follow.

"Eight feet!" called the starboard leadsman, and Delgado breathed again.

Nice as you please, the side-wheeler came

alongside a ramshackle wharf of gray, weathered timber. The mate, a big, burly, and profane man, took charge of the deck hands responsible for running out the gangplank. "Start the plank forward! Look lively now! Damn your eyes, are you asleep, boy? Heave! Heave! You move slower than a damned hearse! Aft again! Aft, I say! Are you deaf as well as daft?"

Delgado watched four men with rifles tilted on their shoulders come up the gangplank. They halted before stepping foot on the packet and looked up at the captain who stood in his most imposing fashion by the big bell on the texas deck.

"Ahoy, Cap'n!" called the foremost of the quartet. "We be bound for St. Looy to join Doniphan's Volunteers. Will you take us free of charge? Our pockets are full of dust and not much else."

"Come aboard, boys," answered the *Sultana*'s captain with a sweeping and magnanimous gesture. "I would not accept so much as a redback dollar from brave men who are marching off to strike a blow for liberty."

The volunteers grinned and tipped their hats and came aboard, seeking some small space on the already overcrowded main deck, where those who could not afford the first-class comfort of the staterooms were packed in amongst the freight: sacks of rice, barrels of molasses, casks of rum, crates of imported goods, and a variety of livestock.

The four rifle-toting young men intrigued Delgado. Where were they bound? Surely St. Louis was not their final destination. Who was Doniphan? No doubt it had something to do with the war.

A man appeared at the railing beside him. It

was Sterling, a newspaper rolled under one arm and a twinkle in his eye.

"Good morning, McKinn. No ill effects from last night's excesses, I trust?"

"I've never felt better," lied Delgado. The sharp, stabbing pain in his head had subsided into a dull, persistent ache behind the eyes. "Tell me, Sterling, about Doniphan's Volunteers."

"You mean the First Missouri Mounted Rifles. They are to join Colonel Stephen Kearny and his dragoons at Fort Leavenworth. Kearny is being dispatched to Santa Fe to protect U.S. citizens and property there. In other words, to occupy New Mexico and—who knows?—California, too, in all likelihood. Alexander Doniphan is an acquaintance of mine, a young lawyer, who was one of the first to answer Governor Edwards's call for volunteers. He enlisted as a private, but, as is the custom in our volunteer forces, the men elected him their commander. Whereupon the State of Missouri has honored him with the rank of colonel."

"I see. Santa Fe, you said?"

"Yes. They are calling Kearny's command the Army of the West. Have you not been keeping up with news of the war?"

Delgado flinched. "I have made it a point not to."

"May I speak bluntly?"

"By all means."

"You struck me at first as something of a ne'er-do-well. Someone who would not bother himself with the intricacies of current affairs, who would instead interest himself solely in the sporting life. Not unlike our young friend, Horan. But, upon further reflection, I've changed my mind about you, McKinn. This war with Mexico *is* of grave concern to you, isn't it?"

"Yes," said Delgado, deciding on the spur of the moment that he could confide in Sterling. "Taos is my home. My father is a trader. His name is Angus McKinn. He is Scottish-born, a Highlander, but thirty years ago he established himself in Taos and became a Mexican citizen in '24. The new Republic of Mexico required all foreign-born residents to convert to Catholicism and swear allegiance to the republic and its constitution. My father was quite happy to do both."

"Even forsake his religion? I assume he was a Protestant."

"Even that. He had fallen in love with my mother, the daughter of a Spanish grandee. In order to marry her, he had to convert. She could not have become his bride otherwise. At any rate, after the Texas expedition to seize Santa Fe, my father decided to send me off to England. He wanted the best possible education for me, and that meant Oxford."

"We have a few good institutions in this country," said Sterling. "Yale, for instance, and Brown, to name but two."

Delgado smiled. "My father had an ulterior motive. To place me as far away as possible from the war he knew was coming."

"I see. That explains England. But your return is a little premature, my friend. War broke out only two months ago. Mexican soldiers crossed the Rio Grande and killed some of our brave soldiers. American blood shed on American soil, as President Polk described it to Congress. Of course," added Sterling with a wry smile, "Northern Whigs take issue with the 'American soil' part of that equation. As you must know, there is still some debate regarding which country holds legitimate title to the territory that lies between the Rio Grande and the Nueces River."

"War or no," said Delgado flatly, "I must get home."

Sterling leaned forward. "I may be presuming a friendship where none exists," he said, "but I ask you this solely out of concern for your welfare, which I value if only because your skill at whist provided me with the opportunity to best that pompous Brent Horan. Where does your allegiance lie, sir?"

"With my father," was Delgado's prompt answer. "To no one and nothing else."

"And your father's allegiance?"

"He is a businessman."

"He swore an oath to the flag and constitution of the Republic of Mexico, did he not?"

"That he did," conceded Delgado. "But he will always put my mother and me, and his business affairs, before all else. I am not implying that he is without honor, of course."

"Of course not."

Delgado drew a deep breath. "He has a long-standing commercial relationship with a man named Jacob Bledsoe in St. Louis. Perhaps you have heard of him?"

"Indeed I have. I am well acquainted with Bledsoe. He is one of the leaders of the community, a highly respected gentleman."

"At my father's request I have come to St. Louis to visit Mr. Bledsoe. Perhaps he will have some ideas regarding how I am to get home, now that it appears that there is a war in my way."

A sudden commotion drew their attention. A

stateroom door burst open and several men, locked in fierce combat, tumbled out across the threshold. A young lady shrieked. The knot of men careened off the railing, and Delgado was amazed that the railing did not give way and pitch all of the combatants into the river or onto the ramshackle wharf.

"Look!" exclaimed Sterling. "It's Horan."

So it was. Horan emerged from the melee, hat missing, cravat askew, an expression of savage elation on his features. He brandished a pamphlet over his head.

"We caught him!" he cried to one and all. "Caught the scoundrel red-handed. A damned abolitionist, come to stir up our Negroes into insurrection. I say we teach the blackguard a lesson he won't soon forget."

"Tar and feather him!" came one bellicose suggestion.

"No," said Horan, his eyes blazing with a lurid fever. "Get a rope. We will hang him, here and now, and be done with it."

4

Sterling stepped forward. "Let me see that pamphlet, Horan," he said sternly. It was more an order than a request.

Smirking, Horan surrendered the damning evidence. "Have in mind defending this rascal, *Mister* Sterling?"

Delgado had no doubts now—deep animosity ran like a river of black bile between these two men. What had transpired to set these two strong wills at odds?

Sterling studied the pamphlet. "The American Antislavery Society." He fastened a cold, piercing gaze upon the stout, disheveled man now held firmly in the grasp of two others. "Your name, sir?"

"Rankin. Jeremiah Rankin." He was afraid, but though his voice trembled, he managed to conjure up a little defiance. Under the circumstances, mused Delgado, that was quite commendable.

"You are either a very courageous man, or a very foolish one, sir," said Sterling. "Were your intentions to distribute this material among the slaves?"

"I have already done so, sir, in New Orleans, Natchez, and Vicksburg."

A man emerged from Rankin's stateroom with a carpetbag. When opened, it could be seen that the valise was half full of pamphlets identical to the one in Sterling's possession.

"And these?" asked Sterling. "Bound for St. Louis, no doubt."

Rankin did not answer.

"What do we do with them?" asked the man holding the carpetbag.

"Burn them," growled Horan. "Consign them to the flames of the furnace. Perhaps our abolitionist should meet the same fate. Give him a taste of the Hell to which a just God will send him for daring to instigate our servants to revolt—to murder, rape, and pillage."

Delgado thought at first that Horan had to be joking. But there was nothing to his tone or expression to suggest that he was not in deadly earnest.

"Sterling," said Delgado. "May I see that pamphlet?"

"Certainly."

"Read it aloud, sir," insisted Horan, "so that these people may have no doubt as to the man's guilt."

Delgado glanced at the crowd of gentlemen and ladies who had congregated on the deck. He opened the slim pamphlet to a random passage and read aloud.

"We view as contrary to the Law of God, on which hang the Unalienable Rights of Mankind, as well as every Principle of revolution, to hold in deepest debasement, in a more abject slavery than is perhaps to be found in Any part of the World, so many souls that are capable of the image of God."

He paused to scan the circle of intent faces. No one seemed to be breathing. Clearly, the pamphlet and what it contained fascinated even while it repulsed them. Delgado felt like a snake handler. Turning a page, he read on:

"What is meant by IMMEDIATE ABOLITION? It means every Negro husband shall have his own wife, united in wedlock, protected by law. It means Negro parents shall have control and government of their own children, and that these children shall not be taken away from their parents. It means providing schools and instruction for the Negro. It means right over wrong, love over hatred, and religion over heathenism."

"Immediatism," said Sterling with a hard look at Rankin. "Gradual emancipation is out of fashion these days, isn't it?"

"This all seems rather harmless," said Delgado.

Horan snatched the pamphlet from his grasp. Fuming, the Southerner turned to the last page of the document.

"Voluntary submission to slavery is sinful," he read triumphantly. "It is your solemn and imperative duty to use every means—moral, intellectual and physical—that promises success in attaining your freedom. You must cease toiling for tyrants. If you then just commence the work of death, they and not you are responsible for the consequences. There is not much hope of redemption without the shedding of blood."

A murmur of shocked outrage rippled through those gathered near.

Horan raised a clenched fist. "Tyrants? Physical means? The work of death?" Infuriated, he slapped Rankin across the face with the pamphlet. "Defend that, Sterling. If you dare."

"But," said Delgado, "you've seen to it that your slaves are illiterate. Since they cannot read, those words are harmless."

"A few of the ungrateful wretches flaunt our codes and *have* learned to read," said Horan. "They will spread this vile poison to others, sowing the seeds of discontent. They think they want their freedom? They will suffer and starve as freedmen. Our Negroes are well cared for. They are clothed, fed, and housed. They are nursed to health when they fall prey to sickness. They want for nothing. Compare their condition to the plight of the poor in Northern cities, who labor sixteen hours a day in mill and factory, are paid starvation wages, and struggle to survive in plague-infested slums!"

Horan stabbed an accusing finger at Rankin. "This man is not concerned with the well-being of the Negro. The abolitionist is the tool of the Northern industrialist, who fears the political power of the South, and seeks to destroy our society by removing the cornerstone of its foundation. The South cannot survive without the institution of slave labor, sir. You should understand that, Sterling. You were, after all, born a Southerner."

"I am a Westerner," said Sterling.

"A Westerner, opposed to expansion."

"I favor the expansion of republicanism, sir, but not the peculiar institution with it. And I will not allow you to hang this man. I may not agree with his ideas, or especially his tactics, but I will not stand by and let the fate which befell Elijah Lovejoy repeat itself here."

Delgado knew the story of Lovejoy, the abolitionist editor. Ten years ago, the man had been hounded out of Missouri. Moving to Illinois, he continued his crusade against slavery. After his printing presses were destroyed on three separate occasions, his house invaded by an unruly mob, and his wife pushed to the verge of hysterical collapse, Lovejoy had armed himself, vowing to protect his family and property. When a mob came to wreck his fourth printing press, Lovejoy confronted them with pistol in hand, and was gunned down in the process. He had become a martyr to the abolitionist cause.

A boy broke through the press of passengers. By the condition of his dirty linsey shirt and ragged dungarees, Delgado took him for one of those less fortunate souls who were berthed on the main deck with the cargo. In his white-knuckled grasp was a length of braided hemp, and on his face was stamped the same mad lust for blood Delgado had seen on Brent Horan's patrician features.

"Here's your rope!" exclaimed the youth. "Stretch the damn Yankee's neck!"

Horan gave Sterling a look of defiance as he

snatched the rope from the boy. Making a slip knot loop at one end, he put it over Rankin's head and pulled the loop closed around the abolitionist's neck. Rankin renewed his struggle to free himself, but to no avail. The pressure of the rope seemed to make his eyes bulge in their sockets. Cold sweat beaded his forehead, and he began to mumble the Lord's Prayer. He could no longer deny his fate.

Seeing that Horan was prepared to go through with the lynching, some of the men in the crowd turned their backs, leading the women away from the scene. But no one stepped forward to intervene—except Sterling, who clutched Horan's arm.

"Don't be a fool," rasped the newspaperman. "By his own admission, this man has broken the laws of several states. Turn him over to the authorities, Horan, for the love of God."

Horan grinned like a wolf. "Let go of me, Sterling, or I'll hang you right alongside him."

Sterling removed his hand. The slump of his shoulders told Delgado that he would go no further to try to save Rankin.

As he stepped forward, Delgado reached into the pocket of his frock coat and extracted the derringer. He acted almost by reflex, without giving any thought to the consequences of his actions. Angus McKinn had always claimed his son was too impetuous for his own good.

"Pardon me," he said.

Horan looked at him, saw the pocket pistol, and froze.

"I was under the impression," said Delgado coldly, "that this nation was built upon certain unalienable rights. Are you acquainted, Horan, with the first ten amendments to the Constitution?"

Horan just stared at him, rendered speechless by astonishment more so than fear.

"I refer specifically," continued Delgado, "to the right of free speech, not to mention the right to a public trial with an impartial jury and the assistance of counsel."

Horan was quickly recovering. "Stay out of this, sir," he warned, his words like cold steel. "This is none of your affair."

"I disagree. Is this a republic, or a monarchy? The former is antithetical to the latter. Yet, in recent weeks, during my sojourn in the South, I have begun to wonder if the United States of America is a republic at all. I have seen tyranny, aristocracy, hereditary privilege, restrictive land tenure, and servile obedience enforced by repressions. And you, sir, you must be a prince of this aristocracy, since by your whim a man can lose his life."

Horan darkened. "I find your words insulting, McKinn."

"These are the facts which insult you." Delgado took a step closer and planted the derringer's double barrel in Horan's rib cage. "If this man hangs, Horan," he said, pitching his voice so low that only Horan could hear him, "you won't be alive to see it."

For a moment Horan made no move. He searched Delgado's face for any clue that this might be a bluff. There was no such clue. Delgado knew he might very well have to kill Horan. The man's towering pride might not permit him to back down, especially in the presence of so many witnesses. But Delgado realized that he could not back down either, if for no other reason than that Jeremiah Rankin's life depended on him. So he kept his nerve and did not flinch from the malevolence in Horan's gaze.

"Let the man go," Sterling told the two men who were restraining the abolitionist. "Let him go, or Horan's blood will be on your hands."

It was a clever stratagem. If Horan died, they would be responsible, because Sterling suspected, as did they, that Horan would not submit, preferring death to dishonor. This was a code they understood and strove to live by. The honorable course for them would be to release Rankin and save the life of their friend.

They let Rankin go. One of them removed the rope from around the abolitionist's neck. "I will turn him over to the authorities in St. Louis," he told Sterling curtly as he flung the rope over the railing.

The second man turned to Horan. "Come on, Brent," he said softly with a wary glance at Delgado and his pistol.

"This is not the end," Horan told Delgado and turned briskly away.

Delgado pocketed the derringer and went to the railing, feeling suddenly nauseated, hoping only that he did not show it. Below him in the brown water between the hull of the *Sultana* and the old wharf, the rope slowly squirmed in the river's current like a long snake. Delgado stared at the rope, unaware of all else about him. When Sterling put a hand on his shoulder he flinched.

"That was a brave act, McKinn," said the newspaperman. "And it just may yet get you killed."

"Something had to be done. We have to live with ourselves. I think that would have been a difficult proposition had we stood by and watched a man hanged for no good reason."

"Slavery." Sterling shook his head. "It is an issue tearing at the very fabric of our nation. But Horan will not forget, or forgive, what you did. I thought for a moment he might issue a challenge."

"A duel?"

Sterling nodded. "It is still quite possible he will have his representative pay a call on you."

Delgado laughed sharply. "I am no duelist and refuse to become one."

"Well, perhaps nothing will come of it. Cooler heads may yet prevail. You are an unknown quantity, and that works in your favor. I hope we will meet again in St. Louis, before you leave for Taos. Perhaps you will be in the mood for another game of whist. Here is my card."

Sterling handed him the newspaper he had been carrying and walked away.

Delgado opened the newspaper. It was the *St. Louis Enquirer,* yesterday's edition. A few copies had come up the gangplank at this landing. The banner headline jumped out at him. Men from Commodore Sloat's naval squadron had seized the California ports of Monterey and San Francisco. Mexican troops were reported to be massing in the Los Angeles area, preparing to march against the American interlopers. A great and decisive battle was expected.

Delgado grimly folded the newspaper, put it under his arm, and returned to his stateroom, wondering what the future held for Taos, his home, and his family.

Chapter Two

"If there is no cure, one must endure . . ."

1

St. Louis was a thriving city of more than seventy thousand souls on that summer day in 1846 when Delgado McKinn arrived on the magnificent *Sultana.* The town was both cosmopolitan and frontier, American as well as French in character. At least fifty steamboats were moored to its mile-long docks, taking on or discharging cargoes and passengers, the serried ranks of their ornamented smokestacks looming against the azure sky. The levee was covered as far as the eye could see with merchandise just landed or ready to be shipped—hundreds of barrels of flour, hogsheads of tobacco, piles of lead harvested from nearby mines, hundreds of head of livestock of every description. Boatman, draymen, factors, and laborers went about their business with that hustle and bustle that seemed, to Delgado, so American. Beyond the levee, the vigorous and ever-expanding city sprawled across a long limestone bluff and spilled onto the plateau beyond.

In thirty short years St. Louis had grown a thousandfold. It had been founded in 1764 by a French soldier and adventurer named Pierre Laclede Ligueste, leader of a commercial enterprise that enjoyed the royal monopoly of trade with the Indians along the Missouri and upper Mississippi.

Where these two mighty rivers met, Laclede established an outpost, named St. Louis in honor of the enterprise's patron, Louis XV, King of France. Early on, St. Louis became the jumping-off point of most expeditions into the uncharted western country, as well as the center of the fur trade.

Even after France ceded all of the Louisiana Territory to Spain, St. Louis remained predominantly French. But when Louisiana was purchased by the United States in 1803, numerous New England speculators materialized. With the advent of the steamboat, St. Louis boomed, her wealth and population and importance soaring, and she was soon the undisputed river capital of the West. The fact that she stood at one end of the Santa Fe Trail only added to her phenomenal growth.

Delgado had never visited St. Louis before, although the city had played a pivotal role in his life. His father had embarked from here on his first bold venture down the Santa Fe Trail. In 1822 Angus McKinn had outfitted in the Vide Poche district, the old, French section of town, putting every penny he had to his name into all the merchandise that two dozen Missouri mules could carry, and which he subsequently sold at a tremendous profit in Santa Fe. Though rich in silver and wool, Santa Fe was starved for the simplest manufactured goods, since vast deserts separated it from the metropolitan centers of Mexico proper. On his third trip Angus met Delgado's mother, married her, and made his home in Taos. Yet he still maintained his St. Louis connections and prospered as a result of them. The Santa Fe trade was still going strong. Angus had written his son that in the year 1843, by his calculations, a half million dollars worth of goods had been transported from St. Louis to Santa Fe.

Delgado still vividly remembered his father's description of St. Louis in the old days. A raw frontier village of less than ten thousand back then, just beginning to flex her muscles and contemplate her prospects. Already the warehouses of gray and yellow stone, erected on a flat bench between the levee and the limestone bluff, were filled with the pelts for which the fur trappers had risked life and limb in the great unknown of the Shining Mountains—pelts bound for New York, London, Paris, Canton, Athens, and Constantinople. Today, the fur trade was in decline. The silk hat had replaced the one made of beaver, and the China trade had surpassed the fur trade. But the sturdy old warehouses still stood, along with others of more recent construction, all chock full of merchandise hauled by riverboat, or about to be.

Back in the days when Angus McKinn had stepped off an Ohio River flatboat and swept this very scene with his flinty gaze, French had been spoken on every hand, and the narrow unpaved streets were lined with the shabby dwellings built in the way of the *voyageur*—logs or planks driven vertically into the ground with the interstices daubed with mud—interspersed by a few more stately abodes of brick and stone. One of these, still standing in '46, and which, for nostalgic reasons, Delgado wanted to see, was the home of Auguste Chouteau, one of the stalwart band who had come here with Laclede. The Chouteau home and outbuildings occupied a square near the center of town, between the Rue de la Tour and the Rue de la Place.

Chouteau's son and grandson had made their

fortunes in the fur trade, Pierre Chouteau, Sr. had partnered with Manuel Lisa, William Clark, and Andrew Henry to form the Missouri Fur Company in 1809. Pierre, Jr. had carried on the family tradition and allied himself with John Jacob Astor in the formation of the American Fur Company twenty years later. The Chouteau family had shown Angus McKinn every kindness.

In the new West a fluid society provided a forum where any immigrant, regardless of his ancestry, could command respect, so long as he demonstrated ability and ambition. Personal drive and self-reliance were virtues to be admired in a man of talent and personality. Angus McKinn fit that bill in every particular, and the Chouteaus had warmed to him immediately.

Today, the southern part of St. Louis, called the Vide Poche, was still the stronghold of the French Canadian trappers and traders. It was considered the rough side of town, and for good reason. By way of contrast, there was Washington Square, where the affluent—people like Jacob Bledsoe—lived in palatial homes. High society was comprised of old French families who had made their fortunes in the fur trade, and southern slaveholders, relative newcomers, who had found the rich black soil of the area conducive to the growing of money crops. Great plantation homes and lavish town manors were now commonplace. Two renowned hostelries, the Planters House and the Union Hotel, vied for the custom of the well-heeled visitor. Some of the major thoroughfares were paved now, and a few were even lighted. There were churches side by side with cathedrals, an opera house, business establishments of all persuasions, a typically American epidemic of lawyers, the famous Market House, a notorious slave auction, a good many mills on the outskirts, numerous taverns and gambling dens, and Bloody Island, the city's designated dueling ground.

One thing, though, hadn't changed since Angus McKinn's days here. Regiments of pigs roamed the streets, growing fat on the refuse. Delgado had learned that even a metropolis as sophisticated as New York tolerated these porcine "street cleaners"—one had to take care not to trip over them while emerging from private club or theater house.

In the melee of white and black, gentleman and common laborer, with the tumultuous babble of French, English, and German ringing in his ears, Delgado paused at the bottom of the gangplank, burdened with a bulging valise in either hand, momentarily at a loss. Jacob Bledsoe, his father's business partner, was expecting him. He had forwarded a letter to Bledsoe from New Orleans in advance of his six-day, twelve-hundred-mile journey upriver. But, having never before met Bledsoe, they would have no way of recognizing one another, slender and dark-haired, Delgado resembled his Castilian mother, not the stocky, ruddy-complected Angus McKinn.

"Delgado!"

A big man was coming toward him, cleaving the stream of humanity on the levee.

Delgado grinned broadly. Here was a familiar face in a sea of strangers. He set the heavy valises down and stuck out a hand. The man clasped it with an iron grasp and an easy grin of his own.

"Hugh Falconer!" said Delgado, delighted. "You are the last person I expected to see here."

"Jacob asked me to meet you. You're looking well, my friend."

"As are you. But I must confess, I almost didn't recognize you."

"Times change," said Falconer, rueful. "A man must change with them."

Delgado had met Hugh Falconer on two previous occasions. The first one he did not remember, as he had been but two years of age. Falconer had come down the Santa Fe Trail on his way to the Shining Mountains and the life of a trapper. Angus McKinn had outfitted him and introduced him to several other buckskinners, including Wolf Montooth, who was about to lead a brigade into prime beaver country.

What had happened next became mountain legend. The trappers had run afoul of Blackfoot Indians, and one of the men was mortally wounded. Montooth had abandoned the man, but Falconer had refused to do the same. Only when the man had breathed his last did Falconer leave his side, miraculously escaping the Blackfeet. Later, he hunted Montooth down and killed him. Or so went the story. There had been no witnesses, and Falconer was tight-lipped about the whole business.

The last time Delgado had met Falconer was three years ago, just weeks prior to Delgado's departure for England and the ivy-colored halls of Oxford University. Falconer had been hunting two men who had robbed Oregon-bound emigrants of their grubstakes. These two men were also fugitives from Santa Fe justice. One of them had killed a prominent local man. Falconer had ventured alone into Comanchero country and slain one of the men, bringing the other back to Santa Fe to collect the reward, which he in turn passed on to the luckless emigrants. This had made of Falconer something of a hero in Santa Fe, at a time when all Anglo outsiders were suspect; Mirabeau B. Lamar, the president of the Republic of Texas, had recently dispatched a military expedition with orders to seize Santa Fe for the new republic. Lamar's grandiose scheme to extend Texas to the Pacific had been stymied, and bred animosity among Santa Feans toward the land-grabbing Anglos. Falconer's subsequent exploits had somewhat improved that situation.

Wounded in the fray, Falconer had spent a few days with the McKinns, until Angus could expedite the payment of the bounty. Against a doctor's advice, Falconer had promptly taken his leave once the gold was in hand. He had left the emigrants to winter in the high country, and he was anxious to get back to them. Delgado remembered being impressed by the buckskinner's toughness. To venture into the mountains in the dead of winter while suffering from a gunshot wound seemed foolhardy, perhaps even suicidal. But then Hugh Falconer was no ordinary man.

He was in his mid-forties now, but looked ten years younger, in spite of a life of tragedy and travail. He was tall, broad in the shoulders, whipcord lean, with brown eyes and yellow hair. His beard, darker than his shoulder-length locks, was close cropped now. In place of buckskins he wore a kersey shirt and stroud trousers tucked into mule-eared boots. A Bowie knife with staghorn handle rode on his right hip in an Indian sheath. His left arm was nestled in a sling.

"I never thought you would forsake the mountain life," Delgado told him.

"I have responsibilities now, to others than myself." Sensing that this answer did not satisfy Delgado's curiosity, Falconer added, "A wife and son."

"Congratulations. I see you've been wounded. Again."

Falconer grimaced. "I guess I'm slowing down in my old age, Del, I didn't duck quick enough. Jacob's son had joined up with the United States cavalry. Led his own squadron of dragoons into battle. You haven't made Jeremy Bledsoe's acquaintance, have you? Well, he's a good lad, but reckless to the extreme. At his father's behest, I went along to make sure no harm came to him. But I failed in my mission at Resaca de la Palma."

"He was killed?"

"No. But it was a near thing. As for this"—Falconer indicated the arm in the sling—"the bullet missed the bone. I'll be free of this damned contraption in a few days. My wife insists I follow the doctor's orders to the letter. I've worn it this long only out of deference to her wishes."

Delgado was intrigued. This man, this legend of the frontier, who had lived a wild and untrammeled existence in the most remote reaches of the high country, and who had answered to no man, seemed to have fallen prey to an affliction common to the male of the species—he had taken a wife and surrendered his sovereignty by so doing.

"Come along," said Falconer, taking up one of the heavy valises with which Delgado had been struggling, and he did so with such ease that one might have thought the bag filled with goose down. "I have a surrey yonder."

They began to cross the levee, Delgado following closely in Falconer's wake as the bigger man resolutely blazed a trail through the polyglot crowd. Between the levee and the row of warehouses was a narrow lane, and here stood the conveyance of which Falconer had spoken. A single horse stood patiently in the shafts. The two padded seats were covered by a calash folding top of leather, with an isinglass light in the rear. Falconer tossed one valise onto the backseat and turned to relieve Delgado of the other one—but Delgado wasn't paying attention. He was staring at eight Negroes marching single file down the lane toward them. They were bound together by a length of rope to which their leather collars were attached. A brutish-looking man, a Collier pistol in his broad belt and a cudgel in his hand, was walking alongside, keeping a wary eye on the slaves. Behind him came a smaller man in a black broadcloth frock coat and a straight-brimmed hat.

"They're being sold down the river," said Falconer.

"That has an ominous sound to it."

Falconer nodded. "Bodes ill for them, that's certain. In some way each one of them has drawn his master's wrath. Made trouble. So they'll end up in Louisiana, or maybe even Cuba, where they're likely to be poorly treated."

"There is a woman among them. A white woman."

At the end of the line walked a dark-haired beauty with skin as pale as Delgado's own.

"She's got Negro blood in her, or she wouldn't be there," replied Falconer. "Octoroon, maybe. With her looks she might wind up in a New Orleans brothel. Or, if she's real lucky, the mistress of a young Creole blade."

Falconer's delivery of these facts was meticulously devoid of emotion, and Delgado studied the frontiersman's features for any indication of his true feelings. But Falconer was as stoic as a statue.

"I don't think I care for the 'peculiar institution,' " decided Delgado.

"What is there to like about it?"

"Hold there!"

Delgado's stomach muscles knotted. He recognized that voice as belonging to Brent Horan. But Horan, coming down the backside of the levee, was paying no attention to him, but rather was hurrying to intercept the slave dealer and his merchandise.

2

"Sir," said Horan, addressing the man clad in black, "have these niggers been sold?"

"Why, no indeed, sir," replied the dealer. "They are bound for points down the river. I intend to auction them off in New Orleans."

"I am interested, then, in buying the wench." Horan was staring at the octoroon. In fact, he could not seem to take his eyes off her. For her part she kept her eyes cast down. Just as well, mused Delgado. The naked lust on Horan's face was revolting.

"Well, I . . ." The dealer looked about him with a nervous air. "This is not really the ideal place to carry out such a transaction, sir."

"How much?"

"Beg pardon?"

"How much for the girl?"

"I . . . I would expect to get at least a thousand

dollars in New Orleans. Perhaps as much as fifteen hundred . . ."

Horan stepped closer to the octoroon and began to lift her calico skirt. Aghast, the dealer clutched at his arm.

"Sir! This is a public place."

"Just want to see what I'm buying. She has a finely turned ankle, doesn't she?"

"There are ladies about. We must consider their tender sensibilities."

Upon hearing this, Delgado scoffed. The slave dealer was one to be concerned about the feelings of others!

"I'll give you fifteen hundred for her," decided Horan.

"Fifteen? Well, I . . ." Things were moving far too fast for the dealer.

"Very well then. Two thousand dollars."

"Two thousand!" Avarice gleamed in the dealer's eye.

"Do you know who I am?"

"I do not enjoy the privilege of your acquaintance, sir, but yes, I know who you are. Of course."

"Then you know that any bank in St. Louis will honor my draft." Horan brandished a wallet. "I do not have quite enough cash on me. But I will write a note, payable upon receipt. In return, you will write out a proper bill of sale."

The dealer was beginning to have second thoughts. "Mr. Horan, this one is a troublemaker. Her former master virtually gave her away, which should instruct you as to her—"

Horan waved all that away with a dismissive gesture. "Then you will realize a particularly handsome profit, sir. How is she called?"

"Her name is Naomi."

"Naomi. If you cause me any trouble, girl, you will regret it. I will flay every inch of skin off your back. What a shame that would be, too, for you have very smooth and seductive skin." He stroked her cheek with two fingers. Naomi flinched, but did not move.

"I can't let this happen," muttered Delgado to no one in particular. He started forward.

Suddenly Falconer blocked his path. "Son, it's generally been my rule to let others make their own mistakes. But I'm obliged in this instance by my liking for you and my friendship with your father to interfere."

"Stand aside," said Delgado rashly.

"Let me ask you this, Del. Do you have the funds to buy the woman?"

The question was like a dash of cold water, and Delgado faltered in his resolve.

"Under the circumstances," continued Falconer, seeing that he was making headway, and desiring to press his advantage, "I doubt anyone here would honor a draft on a Santa Fe bank. And, say you made your purchase. How would you explain to your father that you had become a slaveholder?"

"I would set her free straightaway," replied Delgado.

Falconer glanced over his shoulder. Horan and the slave dealer stood less than a hundred feet from them, and Delgado, in his impulsive fervor, was speaking loudly, with no thought to the consequences of being overheard. But Horan and the dealer were engaged in their own conversation and seemed not to hear.

"I admire your motives," said Falconer softly,

"but not your means. Your father's commerce in this city would likely suffer if you go through with this deed, no matter how noble. This issue of slavery is tearing at the guts of this republic, Del. Feelings run high. The smallest spark can set off an explosion."

"I've had a taste of it already," said Delgado. "That fellow, Horan, came close to hanging an abolitionist on board the *Sultana* this morning."

"Came close? Knowing what I do of Brent Horan, I am surprised he didn't see it through."

Practicing discretion, Delgado decided not to tell Hugh Falconer just how Horan had been dissuaded from committing cold-blooded murder.

"I hate to think of her at Horan's mercy," he said, turning back to the subject at hand. But the rash impulse had run its course and subsided. He knew Falconer was talking perfect sense. Keen regret left a bitter taste in his mouth. He was powerless to help the slave girl.

Falconer put a big, scarred hand on Delgado's shoulder. "It's likely you'd be doing her no service by setting her free. With her looks, manumission papers would not save her, unless you were willing to take her north yourself and hand her over to someone like William Lloyd Garrison or the Tappan brothers, who could protect her from the slave catchers."

Sickened, Delgado climbed into the surrey. Falconer got in beside him, took up the reins, and with a flick of the leathers put the horse into motion, without resorting to the whip, which remained in its stock.

As they passed by on the lane, Brent Horan seemed to notice them for the first time. Recognizing Delgado, his expression turned ugly. Perfectly miserable, Delgado saw that the octoroon called Naomi was watching him, too, as though in some extrasensory way she knew what was in his heart, and he only prayed that he was imagining the hopelessness in her eyes as she watched her salvation pass by.

3

The Bledsoe house stood at the corner of the Rue St. Eglise and Laurel Avenue, a spectacular house set in the midst of immaculately groomed grounds, and built in the popular Greek Revival style. Fluted Doric columns flanked the door, which, with pilasters on either side, supported a broad, flat entablature. A full three stories above ground, the structure lacked the pitched roof and dormer window arrangement common of the Federal style. The simplicity of its form gave the residence added dignity. The exterior was composed of superbly cut and fitted native limestone. The iron perimeter fence, set in limestone columns crowned with whitewashed lintels, was adorned with the fashionable anthemiom, a stylized honeysuckle motif.

Inside, the high basement housed a huge kitchen and the servants' quarters. A formal dining room, study, and two parlors occupied the first floor, while bedrooms were found on the two upper floors. The first-floor rooms that met Delgado's admiring gaze had wall-to-wall carpeting and twelve-foot ceilings augmented by boldly detailed cornices and centerpieces. More fluted columns flanked the double doors of dark paneled wood, which gave access to each room off the wide central hall. In the rear of the house an open gallery, three stories high, accommodated the stairwell. In the same area was a windowed porch, commonly called a tearoom, filled with potted plants. As soon as he stepped inside this American palace, as stately as any private residence he had seen in New York City, Delgado felt far removed from the wild and woolly frontier that lingered, not a mile away, on the outskirts of St. Louis.

Delgado and Falconer were admitted by a Negress wearing a white apron over her calico dress. She smiled pleasantly and escorted them to the front parlor, exiting soundlessly to find the master of the house and announce that his guests had arrived.

"Is she a paid servant or a slave?" Delgado asked Falconer as soon as the parlor doors had closed behind her.

"I guess you'd call her a slave," replied Falconer. "But in truth, Clarisse is much more than that. She's got Creole blood in her veins and speaks French better than she does English. She's well-mannered and highly educated. She was the showpiece on a Louisiana sugarcane plantation before Jacob bought her. That was shortly after Jacob's wife died, giving birth to his daughter, Sarah. Jacob needed someone to care for his two children. Clarisse has done a handsome job of that. She's more like a member of the family. But she's still a slave."

"Good Lord," said Delgado, slumping, slack and weary, onto a velvet sofa. "I didn't know Jacob Bledsoe was a slaveholder. I see now why you advised me against buying and freeing the octoroon. I thought he was a Northerner . . ."

"Doesn't necessarily mean he's against slavery.

There are quite a few Southerners who don't like the business at all. Jacob's not really for it or against it, far as I can tell. He just wishes the problem would go away. Bad for business, you see."

"How, I wonder, does he feel about the war with Mexico?"

Even as Delgado posed the question, the parlor doors swept open and their host entered the room. "The war with Mexico?" echoed Jacob Bledsoe, striding forward with beaming face and outstretched hand. "Regrettable, but unavoidable. Welcome, young man! Welcome! My word, but Angus is right. You are your mother's spitting image, and you cut a fine figure, son. How is she? How is your father?"

"Quite well, sir." Standing, Delgado found his hand pressed vigorously by the effusive Jacob Bledsoe. "I bring their warmest regards."

"Of course you do! Of course you do! Hugh, thanks for fetching him at the levee. Stay and have a drink."

"Don't mind if I do. Thank you, Jacob."

"Good, good." Bledsoe strode to a sideboard strewn with decanters and glasses. "Gentlemen, name your poison."

Falconer opted for good Kentucky bourbon. Having acquired a taste for port during his years in England, Delgado indulged it. Bledsoe poured himself a dollop of an expensive claret. As the St. Louis merchant performed the honors, Delgado had a moment to study his host.

Bledsoe was a short, stocky man. The thinness of hair on the top of his head was compensated for by a magnificent set of muttonchop whiskers. His nose and chin were pugnacious, but that was offset by the merry twinkle in his eye. Here was a man who enjoyed life. A self-made man pleased with his accomplishments. Bledsoe was living proof that money could make one happy. Delgado's father had portrayed Bledsoe as a hard-nosed Yankee trader.

It would be overstating the facts to say that Angus and Jacob Bledsoe were friends, but their business association of twenty years had been a mutually profitable one, and both trusted the other's integrity. Angus sold all the goods Bledsoe transported down the Santa Fe Trail: largely textiles—broadcloth, muslin, taffeta, calico, and velveteen, with buttons, razors, thread, writing paper, knitting pins, and scissors thrown in. In exchange, Bledsoe enjoyed exclusive rights to the wool, furs, silver, and gold that Angus shipped back up the trail, gladly paying the export duty levied by the Mexican government on all specie taken into the United States.

Once they were all seated, drinks in hand, Bledsoe asked Delgado about his journey, and Delgado obliged with a blow-by-blow account of his adventures since departing the hallowed halls of Oxford.

"I think I should have sailed directly to Tampico, however," he concluded. "These excursions of mine have been pleasant, but costly for my father. Still, it was he who insisted I visit the United States and, specifically, to come see you, sir."

"Angus has your best interests at heart, my boy," replied Bledsoe. "No doubt he was aware that for some time now there has been a debate in this country regarding the seizure of the port of Veracruz, or Tampico, as a jumping-off point for a strike overland at Mexico City. Already, Commodore Connor's squadron is patrolling Mexico's gulf coast. I expect just such an expedition to become a reality by the end of the year, and I suspect General Winfield Scott will be at its head."

Delgado did not care to dwell on the subject of the war, so he changed the subject.

"I wonder, Mr. Bledsoe, if you could give me some advice. It concerns a subject with which I believe you are familiar."

"By all means," said Bledsoe, beaming. "By all means."

"Though I doubt my father would approve, I won some money at cards aboard the *Sultana* . . ."

Bledsoe chuckled. "Tell him you did it to defray some of the expense of your travels."

"Yes, sir. But the currency situation here in your country is somewhat confusing."

"True, true. This is the heyday of wildcat currency, my boy, there being no stable system in place for the issuance of government paper since Andy 'By God' Jackson dealt the Bank of the United States its death blow. Every state, county, and bank now issues its own notes, and much of it is practically worthless, or, at the very least, depreciates drastically the moment you are a stone's throw from the establishment which issued it. There is one bank, however, that enjoys a record of unblemished integrity and soundness, which imparts upon its paper the merit of full value even so far away as New York and Philadelphia. I refer, sir, to the Banque des Citoyens de la Louisianne, of New Orleans. I can only hope your winnings are comprised of that institution's dixies."

"Dixies?"

"Ten-dollar notes. Printed in English on one side and French on the reverse. *Dix* is French for ten, as I am sure you know. A dixie, as our Creole friends downriver would say, is *bon-bon.*"

"Why, yes," said Delgado. "Most of them happen to be ten-dollar notes from that bank."

Bledsoe slapped his knee. "Fine! Just fine! They are as good as gold. Lucky for you your opponent did not fill the pot with Illinois or Tennessee paper. I would have to consult *Paddick's* to be certain, but I believe Illinois and Tennessee state currency is redeemable at no less than a ten percent discount these days."

"*Paddick's?*"

"*Paddick's Bank Note Detector.* A New York publication, which tries to keep track of fluctuations in currency values. No easy task in this day and age, I assure you."

"Would you see your way clear to exchange gold for the dixies in my possession, sir? Under the circumstances, I don't know that any American paper would be acceptable in Santa Fe."

"Of course, my boy. Of course. Glad to be of service. We will stroll down to my bank in the next day or two—"

"As soon as possible, please. I cannot stay long. In fact, I feel as though I should get home as soon as possible."

Bledsoe's smile faded. He cleared his throat, then glanced across at Falconer with troubled eyes beneath knitted brows.

"I recently received a letter from your father, Delgado."

Bledsoe's tone of voice alarmed Delgado. He leaned forward.

"Is something wrong?"

"No, no. Rest assured, your mother and Angus are quite well. But . . . well, as much as he misses you after your long absence overseas, Angus desires that you remain here as my guest for a time."

"A time?"

"Until the war is over."

Delgado was momentarily at a loss for words.

"He has only your best interests at heart, my boy. These are perilous times in the Southwest."

Delgado made up his mind on the spot. "I am grateful for your hospitality, Mr. Bledsoe, and your concern. But I intend to go home."

"Hmm." Bledsoe eyed Delgado keenly. An astute judge of character, he could tell there would be no dissuading this young man once his course had been set. "Well," he said, "if you are anything like your father, I would be wasting my time trying to talk you out of returning to Taos. As the best way to realize your safe return, well, that will require some planning."

"I do not care to be a burden to you. I can purchase a horse and provisions and make the trip alone."

Bledsoe was aghast. He looked to Falconer for help.

"Not wise," obliged the mountain man. "The trail is a dangerous one, Del. Always has been, but especially now. A man alone would have a poor chance of reaching the other end."

"Hugh speaks from experience, lad," said Bledsoe. "He knows the plains as well as anyone. That is why I retain him as my wagonmaster. He has taken two of my caravans safely through to Santa Fe. No, no, Delgado. We will have to devise a better means to get you home. At least honor us with your presence for a few days. Say a week. Tomorrow, my son, Jeremy, should be back from Fort Crawford. I would like very much for you to meet him. The two of you may well discover that you have a lot in common. And I am also expecting my daughter, Sarah, two days later. She has been in the East, living for a time with her aunt, and attending an academy in Pennsylvania. The evening of her arrival I have arranged a dinner to celebrate her return. I believe you will find the guests I have invited to that affair very interesting. No less a personage than Senator Thomas Hart Benton will attend. And I have taken the liberty of announcing your presence at a ball to be held this coming Friday at Blackwood, the Horan plantation."

"Horan?" Delgado was dumfounded.

"Yes. Another affair to honor Sarah's homecoming. You see, I fully expect in time that she will become the bride of Mr. Brent Horan."

Poor woman, thought Delgado.

"You know Brent Horan, I believe," remarked Falconer.

Delgado grimaced. Falconer had seen the look Horan had given him on the levee road.

"We've met," replied Delgado. It would be unconscionably rude to refuse Jacob Bledsoe's cordiality, so he nodded and added, "A week, then, and I thank you, sir."

"Splendid!" said Bledsoe, beaming. "Absolutely splendid!"

4

Jacob Bledsoe was right—Delgado took an immediate liking to Jeremy, who returned to St. Louis as expected on the following day. He had journeyed to Fort Crawford, headquarters of the

Northwest Military District, located at Prairie du Chien in the Michigan Territory. Due to the wound he had received at the battle of Resaca de la Palma a few months earlier, Jeremy had been rendered officially inactive. Now that he was fully recovered—or rather as fully as he could ever expect to be with fragments of Mexican lead in his leg that, at times, caused him to limp—Jeremy had been striving to have his name placed back on the active rolls. He did not need to go as far as Fort Crawford to plead his case, but Delgado learned that he had friends there, and he had hoped those acquaintances would use their influence to assist him in his quest.

Apparently unhappy with the results of his trip, Jeremy announced upon his arrival that he intended to resign his commission as a lieutenant in the Regular Army so that he could enlist in a volunteer unit. His overriding ambition was to get back into the war. He simply could not sit by and rest on his laurels in the safety of his own home while fellow countrymen fought and died for a cause that was just. Jacob Bledsoe voiced the opinion that his son had done more than anyone could expect of a patriot. Had he not come within a hair's breadth of giving up his life for his country? What more could his country ask of a man?

But Jeremy was as determined to rejoin the war as Delgado was to get home *because* of the war. Jacob Bledsoe was keenly disappointed in his son's decision. Delgado assumed that the merchant would have preferred that Jeremy show as keen an interest in commerce and finance as he did in the martial pursuits. This, however, was simply not to be.

Jeremy Bledsoe was different from his father in

many ways. Jacob was a product of the old Eastern establishment—settled, urbane, and traditional. His son, born in St. Louis twenty years ago when the settlement had been quite a bit more rough and tumble than it was nowadays, reflected the frontier with all its virtues and vices. He was brash, sometimes boisterous—though his father believed that his going off to war had matured him considerably. He was a doer, and though he did not lack a gentleman's graces, they had a raw edge. His marks as a cadet at the Military Academy at West Point proved he was more the man of action than a profound thinker, top of his class with the horse and saber, near dead last in mathematics and chemistry. Poor marks, which had rendered him ineligible for a posting in the coveted Corps of Engineers, and fit only for the cavalry. This, though, had suited Jeremy just fine.

He was a tall and slender young man, with green eyes and light brown hair, as agile as a man with a damaged leg could be. Clad in the uniform of a dragoon, he was the picture of a dashing *beau sabreur*. But on the day that he and Delgado went riding, he exchanged the uniform for a suit of brown broadcloth and a pair of brown blucher boots. In place of an officer's shako he wore a plain visored cap. "I will never again wear that uniform," he said with a blend of conviction and regret.

Delgado had wondered how Jeremy would handle the fact that his father's house guest was a citizen of the Republic of Mexico, since another citizen of that same republic had been responsible for shooting the bullet into his leg. But Jeremy, if he made any such connection, displayed no prejudice.

An accomplished horseman in his own right, Delgado had forgotten how much he missed riding until he settled into the saddle cinched to the back of a tall, stockinged bay; he had selected the horse himself out of the for-hire corral at the livery.

"Don't you know that old saying about horses with four stockings?" asked Jeremy, half in jest. "One white foot, buy her. Two white feet, try her. Three white feet, be on the sly. Four white feet, pass her by."

"A quaint saying," replied Delgado, "but there is no truth in it."

The bay proved him right. As soon as they had put St. Louis behind them, Jeremy challenged him to a race—across an open field to a distant line of trees and back to the road. Jeremy's sorrel hunter leaped into an early lead, but Delgado had caught up at the halfway mark, and was a full two lengths out in front by the time they were once again on the road.

Jeremy was gracious in defeat. "I thought about making a little wager on the outcome," he said, laughing. "Glad I didn't. To be honest, I don't put much faith in the old sayings, either."

A mile farther down the lane the forest began to close in—for several miles around, the insatiable appetite of a fast-growing city for timber had virtually denuded the landscape. Delgado wondered aloud why this virgin growth had remained untouched when all else around had fallen prey to the woodsman's axe or double-cut saw.

"This is Blackwood," replied Jeremy. "The Horan plantation. Or, at least, the edge of it. A mile or farther on you will find the fields, and then the main house."

There seemed, mused Delgado wryly, no escaping Brent Horan.

As they rode through the tunnel of sun-speckled green, Jeremy proceeded to tell him what he knew about the Horans, which turned out to be quite a lot. Daniel Horan, Brent's father, had been but one of many Virginian gentlemen to abandon the overcropped land of the Old Dominion for the rich black soil of the Missouri bottomlands. In a caravan of wagons, trailed by a small herd of livestock, he had brought his wife and two little boys west, along with more than forty slaves and many fine furnishings.

The site Daniel Horan chose for his new beginning was on the bank of a navigable tributary of the Big Muddy, with abundant timber for building and for fuel. Despite the fertility of the land and being financially better off than many of his fellow pioneers, the first years for Daniel Horan had been difficult ones. Even basic supplies had proven hard to get in this as yet untamed land. Fortunately, the forests teemed with game—elk, deer, wild turkey, squirrel, and duck. They were also home to bears, wolves, and panthers, which preyed mercilessly on Horan's livestock.

"Finally," said Jeremy, "one of Horan's field hands was killed by a panther. That put Horan out of pocket eight or nine hundred dollars, so he declared war on the woodland predators. He offered a bounty on animal scalps. Times were hard, and many a frontiersman made ends meet by collecting on that bounty. Naturally, folks in these parts became beholden to Daniel Horan. The buckskinner and the dirt farmer consider him a great man still and won't brook anyone saying otherwise."

Gradually, the wilderness had been subdued. The forest fell to broadax and fire. The ground was broken by the bull plow. The yeoman farmer planted his corn or rye and sometimes even tried his luck with a few acres of tobacco for a little extra cash, while Horan and a handful of other slaveholders, with the benefit of slave labor, cultivated much larger amounts of tobacco, wheat, and hemp. With the profits from his first good year, Horan built a grand manor, importing experienced masons to work the limestone from a nearby quarry. When the manor was finished, he moved his family out of the log blockhouse in which they had been living. But Horan's wife had precious little time to enjoy her newer, more elegant surroundings. A few weeks later, she was bitten by one of the rattlesnakes that infested this country and died the following day.

"His wife's death changed Daniel Horan," said Jeremy grimly. "He became a recluse and a brutal master. Brutal father, too, by all accounts. His eldest son finally could not stand it any longer. He ran away. No one knows for certain what became of him, though I have heard rumors that he is living in Paris now. But the second son stuck it out."

"That would be Brent."

"Right. Do you know him?"

"We've met. On the packet up from New Orleans."

Jeremy smirked. "Brent enjoys his little jaunts to the Crescent City, ostensibly to attend to his father's business affairs. But I think the brothels of the Vieux Carré attract him most of all."

"I would have to say that the son has learned

the art of brutality from the father," remarked Delgado.

"Ah, so you *do* know Brent. Yes, he is a dangerous man to cross."

"You don't care for him."

"I have never pretended to."

"Yet your father suggests that he may marry your sister."

"Sarah has better sense."

Delgado thought that Jeremy sounded more hopeful than convinced.

"She used to be infatuated with Brent," continued Jeremy. "Young, foolish girls sometimes like to flirt with danger. If her letters are any indication, though, she has grown up in her absence. Now she flirts with dangerous ideas."

"What kind of ideas are you talking about?"

"Those New England reformers have bent her ear, I'm afraid. She pounces with complete abandon on every new fad. Women's suffrage, temperance, even abolitionism. Now the latter certainly wouldn't sit well with Brent Horan."

"I saw him buy a slave girl, an octoroon, on the levee. And I don't think she was destined for the fields, either."

"If she was pretty enough, I'm sure not." Jeremy rode in silence for a moment, brows knit, deep in thought. Then he flashed a sly grin at Delgado. "Of course, it's entirely likely my sister will find you even more irresistible than she did Brent Horan. You strike me as a decent sort. A man who knows the meaning of honor. Which is more than I can say for Brent."

"I thought he and his kind put great store in honor."

"That's not honor you're talking about. That's

pride, and vanity. Honor means doing the right thing regardless of the consequences."

"I doubt if Brent Horan would define honor any differently."

"By 'right thing' I mean abiding by the laws of God and man. But you're correct, Del. Brent is very jealous of what he calls his honor. You see, he is a violent man, a man ruled by his passions. He uses the defense of his honor as his excuse to vent that violence upon others. Folks think he is a gentleman because of it. The irony is that he has no real honor."

They rode on as Delgado mulled this over. He could hear, deep in the woods, the baying of hounds, but paid little attention to the sound—until it was accompanied by the blast of a shotgun, surprisingly close to the road. He peered into the verdant gloom of the forest, trying to locate the source of the sound. Around a bend in the lane they came upon a horse tied to a tree, its saddle empty. As they curbed their own mounts, a lanky hound emerged from the forest, barked at them, tail wagging slowly. Several more hounds appeared, milling about, tongues lolling; clearly they had just had a long, hard run.

A moment later, a bearded, rough-looking individual appeared. Another man, a Negro, was draped over his shoulder. Delgado knew immediately that the black man was dead, and he looked at the shotgun in the bearded one's grasp.

With a cold, indifferent glance at Delgado and Jeremy, the bearded man heaved the corpse across the saddle of his horse, demonstrating his herculean strength by the ease with which he effected the transfer. Here, thought Delgado, was a man who could be extremely dangerous even when completely unarmed.

"Mr. Talbott," said Jeremy, cool dislike evident in his tone of voice. "Hard at work, I see. Del, allow me to introduce John Talbott. He is employed by Daniel Horan as overseer and, as you can see, slavehunter, as well. One of Horan's runaways, Mr. Talbott?"

"That's right," was Talbott's gruff, barely civil reply. "If it's any of your business." He obviously did not think it was.

"He didn't get very far, did he?" asked Jeremy.

"They never do," said Talbott as he proceeded to lash the corpse down with a length of rope.

"Talbott always gets his man," Jeremy told Delgado. "Usually brings them back in this condition."

"That must cost Horan dearly," observed Delgado. The dead man had been young and muscular, a prime field hand.

"Mistuh Horan don't mind," said Talbott. "Serves as a warnin' to them other darkies."

One of the hounds was snarling as it mauled one of the dead Negro's dangling arms. Cursing, Talbott kicked the dog in the ribs. The dog slunk away, baring bloody fangs.

"Come on, Jeremy," said Delgado, disgusted. He turned the bay with a sharp pull on the reins.

As they rode back the way they had come, Delgado looked over his shoulder once. Talbott was leading the corpse-burdened horse in the other direction, surrounded by his dogs. Delgado felt sick to his stomach.

"My God," he said. "I've seen enough of your peculiar institution to last me a lifetime, Jeremy."

Jeremy nodded. "It is a brutal business."

"You don't approve. You couldn't possibly."

Wearing a troubled frown, Jeremy did not reply.

"Why don't you do something?" persisted Delgado.

"Such as?"

"Well, I don't know . . ."

"If there is no cure," said Jeremy grimly, "one can only endure."

He kicked the sorrel hunter into a gallop, and Delgado quickened the bay's pace, and was glad when they emerged from the gloomy old woods into the sunshine of the clearings.

Chapter Three

"I will always cherish this acquaintance."

1

Delgado spent much of his free time exploring St. Louis. Gateway to the frontier, the city pulsated with life, and proved fascinating to a young man with Delgado's highly developed curiosity. But he was present at the Bledsoe house on the morning of Sarah's arrival, as any good guest would be—and he was forever glad of it.

She had come by coach from Philadelphia to Cincinnati and taken passage aboard an Ohio River packet at the city they called the Queen of the River. Twenty years earlier the Falls of the Ohio, located near the town of Louisville, had posed in certain seasons an insurmountable obstacle to riverine traffic, but a canal had been recently excavated around the falls on the Kentucky side. This was the route that Delgado would have taken to reach St. Louis from New York City, had he not opted for a succession of coastal steamers in order that he might experience the unique ambience of legendary New Orleans.

Since his arrival in St. Louis, Delgado had been chafing at the bit to embark for Santa Fe and Taos, but when he saw Sarah Bledsoe, that sense of urgency immediately melted away. She was the most beautiful woman he had ever seen. Her eyes were limpid pools of hazel, her lips as shapely and red as the blossom of a rose. A heart-shaped face was framed by chestnut brown curls. Her figure was petite, but well-rounded. She wore a gray serge traveling outfit consisting of a long skirt and a short jacket over a pale yellow muslin blouse, pleated and tight. Her hat was adorned with a wide yellow silk band and peacock feathers. She wore pale gray kid gloves on her delicate hands and high laced black shoes on her tiny feet.

Jeremy had gone to wait for her boat at the levee. He had invited Delgado to accompany him, but Delgado had declined, not wishing to impose upon the reunion of long-separated siblings. Now he stood unobtrusively to one side as Sarah greeted her father, who had just returned to the house from a day of business. If anything, Sarah's reunion with Clarisse was the most touching of all. The two women embraced and wept with joy. Only when Sarah had composed herself did Jacob Bledsoe introduce his daughter to his guest.

"Sarah, may I introduce Mr. Delgado McKinn. Del, my daughter, Sarah."

Delgado took the proffered hand and, with a very supple, continental bow, brushed her glove-encased fingers with his lips.

"Miss Bledsoe," he said almost reverently, "I will always cherish this acquaintance."

She smiled, both flattered and amused by his suave gallantry. "Mr. McKinn, I am thoroughly delighted to meet you." Her hand lingered in his, and her smile lingered, too, as she gazed at him, and Delgado felt a blush of warmth in his cheeks. In the magic of that moment he forget all about going home.

"You must be exhausted, my dear," said a solicitous Jacob. "Perhaps you would like to retire to your room. I hope you don't mind, but I have invited a few close friends to dinner this evening in honor of your safe return."

"Of course I don't mind, Father." To Delgado's chagrin, Sarah finally took her hand away. "Come with me, Clarisse. I have so much to tell you!"

Delgado spent the rest of the day loitering about the house, idle and restless, no longer the least bit interested in the sights of St. Louis, waiting only for the next opportunity to gaze at Sarah. He had to bide his time until dinner, because she did not come downstairs until all the guests had arrived.

These included Dr. John J. Lowry, the banker, president of the Bank of Missouri, and Montgomery Blair, the mayor of St. Louis, son of the famous Francis P. Blair, editor of the *Washington Globe* and erstwhile member of Andy Jackson's "Kitchen Cabinet." Also present was Joshua Pilcher, who had to come to St. Louis during the War of 1812 and made his fortune in merchandising, and was now Superintendent of Indian Affairs in Missouri. To Delgado's pleased surprise, Sterling, his whist partner aboard the *Sultana,* and editor of the *Enquirer,* had accepted Jacob Bledsoe's invitation. Falconer showed up, too. He looked uncomfortable in a brown frock coat and, compared to the sartorial perfection of Lowry and Pilcher and Blair, appeared rather rustic. His wife could not attend, occupied as she was with the care of a very sick friend. Pilcher and Lowry were accompanied by their wives.

Last but by no means least on the guest list was Thomas Hart Benton, U.S. Senator from Missouri. "Old Bullion" was one of the giants currently straddling the stage of American politics, an accomplished orator who could hold his own against the likes of such notables as Henry Clay and Daniel Webster, a man of remarkable powers as well as seething passions, a highly influential gentleman who saw himself as the leading spokesman for the West. "Calhoun represents the interests of the Southern slaveholder and nullifier," he said at one point during dinner. "Webster stands for the commercial interests of the Northeast—a great talent gone to waste. I speak for the hardy pioneer, the free man who breathes deep into his lungs the unfettered air of the frontier. Henry Clay? That strutting gamecock represents only himself and his overweening ambition."

Benton's wife of many years, Elizabeth, was a semi-invalid, a victim of epilepsy, and could not attend. In her stead was Jessie, Benton's pretty, brown-haired, effervescent daughter of twenty-two years, who had married a young Army officer named John Charles Frémont. At the time she had been only seventeen, and the Bentons had strongly disapproved of one so young marrying one so low on the ladder of Army advancement, but these days Benton was proud of his son-in-law, who at present was in California, one of the leaders of the attempt to wrest that valuable province away from the Republic of Mexico.

The meal was a feast fit for kings. But Delgado discovered that he lacked any kind of appetite. All he wanted to do was stare, enraptured, at Sarah Bledsoe, who by happy chance sat directly across the long mahogany dining room table from him. She was so radiantly beautiful that the setting—the polished red oak floor, the velveteen draperies on the windows, the burgundy damask on the walls, the ornately framed oils, the gleaming brass wall sconces, the snowy white linen table cloths, the gold-rimmed china, the sparkling crystal, the Rogers silverware—all of it paled to nothingness by comparison. She wore a rose organdie dress with a long pink sash, and it was quite becoming in contrast to her honey-and-cream complexion and her chestnut hair that flared with fiery scintillas as it captured the candlelight.

Delgado's problem was that, bracketed between Jeremy and Jacob Bledsoe, the latter in his customary place at the head of the table, he had to be extremely circumspect in his staring, and he tried his best to be, for that reason and because it was not gentlemanly to allow one's eyes to rest so boldly and so long upon a young lady. Of course, she caught him red-handed early on, and though she smiled tolerantly, he looked quickly away, mortified, and tried to exercise his will and avoid looking at her for the remainder of the meal, only to find that he was not in command of his own will, after all. She was waiting with a sweet and slightly sultry smile when he finally gave up and glanced her way again, and Delgado realized, elated, that his inordinate interest was not, apparently, the least bit offensive to her. Throughout the dinner they exchanged surreptitious smiles. Delgado was thrilled, and pleased that no one at the table seemed to notice all this eye contact. He paid absolutely no attention to the lively conversation taking place around him—until he heard his name spoken. To his horror he realized that Jacob Bledsoe had asked him a question.

"I beg your pardon, sir?"

"I am concerned that the subject of our discussion might be offensive to you, Del."

Delgado glanced around the table and nervously saw that all eyes were on him. He had no idea to what subject Bledsoe was referring. So, in a flash of inspiration, he hedged magnificently.

"Why should it be?" It was, he decided, infinitely better than admitting he had been rudely ignoring the talk.

"You are, sir," said Thomas Hart Benton, "are you not, a citizen of the Republic of Mexico?"

"I suppose I am, technically."

"Do you not support your country in the present conflict?" asked Pilcher bluntly.

"Really, Joshua," scolded Bledsoe. "Perhaps we should talk about something else entirely."

"No," said Delgado, his pride pricked. He had no desire to be mollycoddled. "Mr. Pilcher, my home, Taos, is isolated by hundreds of miles of desert waste from the rest of the republic. The tumult of war and politics rarely touches us there. And besides, while I support the Constitution of 1824 and all it represents, Mexico has suffered under the heel of a succession of tyrants, the worst of which is Antonio Lopez de Santa Anna."

"Here, here," said Dr. Lowry, in full accord with Delgado's last sentiment.

"My father is a Scot," continued Delgado, "who is only concerned with politics as they may affect his commerce. My mother is an Arredondo, a *peninsular.* This means she was born in Spain, of a distinguished family of pure Spanish blood, who happens to reside in Mexico. During the revolution her father and her brother were killed by the *mestizos.* Needless to say, you will not find her supportive of the republic. She has no respect for Santa Anna, for he is a *criollo,* a creole, of Spanish blood but born in Mexico; she feels he has betrayed his own kind."

"It would be very unfair," remarked Sterling,

"to suggest that my friend Delgado is any less a patriot to his country because he does not support its present government than are our own Whigs, who decry 'Mr. Polk's War.' "

"I certainly did not mean to suggest any such thing," said Pilcher hastily.

"Our young friend has hit the mark," said Benton. "Tyrants rule Mexico. They are concerned only with their own aggrandizement. As everyone knows, I deplore the outbreak of war. I have consistently spoken for peace. It was my most fervent desire that our two nations might negotiate a mutually satisfactory settlement of the boundary disputes, as well as the rightful claims of our citizens against Mexico, which, I might add, are grossly inflated by President Polk. But, as you are aware, Mexico refused to even receive our envoy, Mr. John Slidell. And she broke off all diplomatic relations subsequent to our annexation of Texas."

"Yet you voted in the affirmative for the president's declaration of war and the appropriations bill for raising a volunteer army," said Sterling.

"I did indeed, and I was not the only member of Congress who voted yes in spite of an aversion to war. As chairman of the Military Affairs Committee, I had a long discussion with the president. I told him I would vote men and money for defense of our territory, but not for open aggression against the Republic of Mexico. I also informed him that I strongly disapproved of marching Zachary Taylor's army to the left bank of the Del Norte, since I do not believe for a moment that the territory of the United States extends beyond the Nueces. Since I feel that way, how could I accept the president's contention that Mexico, by crossing the Del Norte and attacking our troops on the left bank, had invaded our territory and shed American blood on American soil?"

While in New York City, Delgado had learned of the Del Norte fight—details had been plastered over the front pages of every penny press edition in town. The trouble had started with Texas winning her independence from Mexico in 1836. Captured at the Battle of San Jacinto, Santa Anna had obliged the Texans with a pronouncement, given under duress, that the Del Norte, otherwise, known as the Rio Grande, marked the legitimate southern border of the new republic. With this, Santa Anna earned his release, and the pronouncement was promptly repudiated, not only by him but by the Mexican congress. As a Spanish and then a Mexican province, the boundary of Texas had never extended beyond the Nueces, much less to the Del Norte.

American expansionists ardently asserted that both Jefferson and Madison had claimed that Texas did extend to the Del Norte, by virtue of the disputed territory's inclusion in the Louisiana Purchase. Those opposed to expansion pointed out that even if this were so, the United States had relinquished any claim it might have had to any part of Texas by the 1819 treaty in which Spain, in return, ceded East Florida.

Even when, by joint resolution, Congress had voted to approve annexation of Texas, its language had been circumspect regarding the boundary, which was subject to "adjustment." Such diplomatic niceties were lost on President James Knox Polk. When Mexico made belligerent noises following the annexation, Polk promptly dispatched General Zachary Taylor to the vicinity of the Del Norte with orders to repel any "invasion" by Mexican forces.

In this Polk was right or wrong depending on which paper a person happened to have on hand. The *New York Herald* applauded the president for such bold leadership, while the *Tribune* roundly denounced his actions as bald-faced aggression, and likened the chances of a Mexican invasion to that of a sparrow flying into the territory of a hawk to hold it in adverse possession. Mexico would have no better chance than the sparrow; that republic was rent by internal disorders. Great Britain, whose loans were keeping the Mexican government afloat, advised against war in the strongest possible terms.

But the Mexican people were disgruntled; they disliked the passive stance of the Herrera government. A defiant army led by General Mariano Paredes threatened to take over if Mexico conducted any further negotiations with the land-hungry Yankees. Polk's minister plenipotentiary, John Slidell, carrying a portmanteau full of papers describing the grandiose ambitions of the United States, was rudely spurned in Mexico City. Finally, last April, a Mexican force had indeed crossed the Del Norte, attacking a patrol of American dragoons, killing three and taking the rest prisoner.

"So why," persisted Sterling, addressing Thomas Hart Benton, "did you finally vote in the affirmative, Senator?"

Benton grinned down the table at Jacob Bledsoe. "Shame on you, Jacob, for inviting a Whig newspaperman to a gathering of good ol' Democrats."

Smiling, Bledsoe shrugged. He could tell Old Bullion was only half joking.

"In answer to your question, sir," said Benton, "I voted for the appropriations because the president was determined to have a war, and I would not be responsible for denying our boys in uniform the provisions and reinforcements they required."

"I suppose I must be a Whig, then," said Sarah Bledsoe, "because I agree with Mr. Sterling. Mr. Polk provoked this war. He is a Southerner, and he wants to create a slave empire. He will seize all of Mexico if given the chance, and Cuba, as well."

Thunderstruck, Jacob Bledsoe stared open-mouthed at his daughter. Then, with an apologetic glance at his gentlemen guests, he cleared his throat and said, "Perhaps the ladies would like to retire to the parlor, since it seems we have all finished with our meals."

"I would prefer to stay," said Sarah, even as Mrs. Pilcher and Mrs. Lowry began to rise from their chairs accompanied by a rustling of petticoats.

"Really, my dear," said Bledsoe, discomfited. "What has come over you?"

"Oh, I see," replied Sarah, archly. "You gentlemen persist in thinking that women are merely brainless porcelain dolls, pretty adornments for your arms, and pleasant company in your beds, but not worth much else—"

"Sarah!" Bledsoe turned white as a sheet before a storm cloud of anger threw its dark shadow across his features. "Gentlemen, ladies, I beg your forgiveness and extend my most heartfelt apologies for my daughter's outrageous conduct. I can make no excuse for her other than to say that she has been away for more than a year, attending an academy near Philadelphia where I *thought* she was receiving instruction on how to be a proper young lady."

"I have learned that I am a human being," retorted Sarah with, in Delgado's opinion, a very fetching blush to her cheeks, "as well as a citizen of this republic, and that I am endowed with certain rights. Do you know that hundreds of women like Elizabeth Cady Stanton and Lucretia Mott are planning to meet soon to adopt resolutions patterned on the Declaration of Independence—resolutions which will demonstrate beyond a shadow of a doubt to any thinking person that men and women are created equal? The history of mankind is the history of the male's absolute tyranny over the female, and—"

"Enough!" roared Jacob Bledsoe, apoplectic. "I will not tolerate such talk at my table."

Sarah smiled frostily. "A perfect case in point."

"Leave this room this instant, young lady."

"I shall not." Sarah settled sulkily in her chair, as though prepared to resist any attempt to physically remove her.

Impulsively, Delgado rose from his chair. "Perhaps Miss Bledsoe would be kind enough to honor me with a stroll in the garden. It is too pleasant an evening to waste and would be made infinitely more pleasurable by her company."

As he made the invitation, he moved around the table, so that when he was done he stood beside her chair with extended arm.

Sarah hesitated, stubbornly inclined to stand her ground, and Delgado realized how foolish he would look if she refused.

"I think these gentlemen could speak more freely what is in their hearts concerning the war if I was absent," he told her, bending close to her ear and speaking in a conspiratorial whisper.

In this way he addressed her as one undesirable to another. Sarah smiled and placed her hand lightly on his proffered arm.

"If you will excuse us, ladies and gentlemen," said Delgado.

"A bold move," murmured Jeremy approvingly as Delgado escorted Sarah from the dining room.

2

Behind the Bledsoe house a small, immaculately tended garden provided a perfect setting for two people to enjoy the summer evening. A big yellow moon hung suspended in a brilliant field of stars, and a cooling breeze sighed in the tops of the sycamore trees, carrying the sweetly mingled aromas of rambling rose and climbing jasmine. Curving walkways of crushed rock lined with bricks led to whitewashed benches nestled beneath vine-laden trellises. Delgado thought this a most romantic spot, and he was in a romantic mood. How could he be otherwise, in the company of a young woman as beautiful and desirable as Sarah Bledsoe? Unfortunately, she was still fuming about the scene in the dining room.

"Oh, he can be so insufferable at times!" she said.

"Your father? Perhaps you should have forewarned him. I think your rather novel ideas came as a real shock to him."

"I don't know why you are trying to defend him. Doesn't their talk about the war offend you?"

"Well, I—"

"Doesn't it bother you that they consider Mexico so backward, so benighted, that they use that very thing as an excuse for their aggression and greed and this ridiculous notion that it is their God-given duty to spread the light of American liberty and justice from Santa Fe to Campeche?"

"I didn't hear—"

"Doesn't it concern you that if men like President Polk have their way, all of Mexico will be absorbed into the United States?"

Delgado stopped walking and turned to her with an amused smile curling the corners of his mouth.

"At the risk of encouraging you to think me a ne'er-do-well," he said, "the outcome is of no concern to me, except as it affects my family."

"I pity you," she replied. "You are a man with no opinions on matters of importance." She walked on without him.

Delgado followed, searching carefully for the right words with which to redeem himself. In the near distance a carriage clattered down Laurel Avenue, the shod hooves of its horses clip-clopping on the paving stones. In the far distance a steamboat's bell rang out.

"I am of the opinion," he said sincerely, "that you are the most beautiful and fascinating woman I have ever had the privilege to meet, Miss Bledsoe."

"Surely, I am not the first woman to whom you have spoken those very words," she replied, but she could not completely disguise her pleasure at the compliment.

"That is my opinion, and to me you are a matter of the utmost importance. Let's talk about you, Sarah, and not about me, or the war."

"For one thing, I am proud of my country. I don't

want you to think otherwise. Which is why I feel so strong about slavery and the rights of women."

"So you are an abolitionist to boot."

"I am," she declared defiantly. "There is a link between the oppression of slaves and the oppression of women. Neither can be reconciled with the founding principles of this republic."

"Common law is against you, I'm afraid. William Blackstone himself wrote that in marriage a husband and wife are as one person under the law. The very being of the woman is suspended *by* the law. She has no rights to marital property, which are held wholly in the husband's name, and without property she cannot participate in the body politic. Civic virtue rests in the independent citizen, and personal independence is linked to individual ownership of property. It has always been so. John Adams said that political rights are tied to property rights. Only property ownership allows the economic and moral independence necessary for virtuous citizens." Delgado shrugged. "So, if a woman owns no property . . . I am not saying I believe this to be true, or just. But those are the facts."

"Oh, really? So women are excluded from the rights of citizenship—along with children, criminals, and the insane? Our government was instituted to derive its just powers from the consent of the governed. Am I not one of those governed? Then it is only right that I be permitted to consent."

Delgado laughed, delighted. "You are a remarkable person, Sarah. Your poor father thought he was sending you to the seminary to learn to be a proper young lady."

Sarah smiled. "The headmistress gave me a

copy of Margaret Fuller's book, *Women in the Nineteenth Century.* She made me promise, if ever I should be asked, not to tell anyone where I had gotten it. I'm not sure why she chose me. But the book changed my life. It proves that women have their own identity and deserve social independence, the ability to grow as an intellect and, as a soul, to live freely."

"That sounds positively transcendental."

She took offense at his lighthearted tone of voice. "Is there anything that you *do* take seriously, Mr. McKinn?"

"My apologies. I did not mean to—"

"You had better learn what it means to be an American since, whether you like it or not, you are about to become one. How can we live up to our promise as a nation, as a land of the free, a haven to the oppressed in a world filled with tyranny, when we keep our own people in chains because of the color of their skin?"

"Tyranny. I seem to recall making a very similar speech to Brent Horan."

"Brent!" She clutched his arm. "You know Brent Horan?"

Horan's name, he was sorry to see, provoked strong passions in Sarah.

"I made his acquaintance aboard the river packet. He was trying to murder an abolitionist."

"An abolitionist? What was this man's name?"

"I don't recall. Wait a minute. Rankin, I believe. Yes, that was it. Rankin was his name. As a matter of fact . . ." He reached into his frock coat's inner pocket and withdrew the pamphlet from which he had read during the confrontation aboard the *Sultana.* "I'd forgotten I had this."

Sarah nearly snatched the pamphlet from his

grasp. "The American Antislavery Society. I have attended many of their meetings in Philadelphia."

"Somehow I am not surprised."

She seemed not to hear him. "I do not know this man Rankin. What became of him? Did they . . . did they kill him?"

"No." Modesty prevented Delgado from mentioning that he had done his part to rescue the abolitionist from the rope. "I believe they turned him over to the authorities here in St. Louis."

"May I have this pamphlet?"

"By all means."

"I think I shall go see Mr. Rankin tomorrow. Will you come with me?"

"Of course." Delgado didn't care where she wanted to go, as long as he could be with her.

She bestowed another smile upon him. "This must be our little secret. Father would not approve."

"I will tell him I have asked you to join me in a carriage ride, and that you accepted."

"You're not afraid to get involved?"

"Involved in what? If I get to spend the day with you, Sarah, I would risk the devil's wrath."

She took his arm again. "Let's go back inside. I really should apologize to the guests. If I don't, Father may forbid me to even leave the house."

As they left the moonlit garden, Delgado ruefully observed that their evening stroll had not turned out at all as he had hoped it would.

3

The following morning Clarisse knocked on Delgado's door to inform him, with that exotic creole patois of hers, that Master Bledsoe requested his presence in the parlor downstairs.

Delgado tried to curb his nervousness as he descended the stairs. Had his host somehow become privy to the conspiracy he and Sarah had hatched last night in the garden?

Hugh Falconer was there, slack in a velvet wing chair, looking a lot more comfortable in rough homespun than he had in a frock coat last night.

"By a stroke of good fortune, General Kearny is here in St. Louis," Bledsoe informed Delgado. "Hugh has spoken to him on my—or rather your—behalf, my boy."

"I don't understand."

"Safest way to get you home to your father is with the army," replied Bledsoe. "No resistance is expected, you see."

"Ah," said Delgado. *I wouldn't be so sure of that,* he thought. But he did not speak his mind.

Bledsoe was pacing, hands clasped behind his back. He was clearly agitated. "The general has no objection to your accompanying the expedition, Del. In fact, he is interested in employing you, unofficially, of course, as a sort of liaison with the Mexicans. I realize that may be placing you in a delicate situation . . ."

"Personally I would do anything in the interest of peace," said Delgado. "But I must also consider my father's position."

"Yes, yes. Perfectly understandable."

"I would prefer to consult with him first."

"Of course, of course." Bledsoe continued to pace. "In a related matter, my son, Jeremy, has enlisted with Doniphan's Volunteers. A reckless act. He is indifferent to his father's feelings in this regard. I have tried to talk him out of going back to war, but without success. He is going, and I am nearly beside myself with worry. I almost lost him once. I could not bear it were something to happen to him."

He stopped dead in his tracks and wheeled to look in anguish at Hugh Falconer.

"Hugh, my friend, I have no right to ask this of you. You have a wife, a son. I know it was a hardship on them when I prevailed upon you to go to Texas, into the thick of the fighting, to watch out for my son's welfare. You very nearly lost your life to save his. I can scarcely bring myself to ask you to once again—"

Falconer held up a hand. "I'll go, and gladly."

"I would offer you a substantial sum of money for the service, if I did not think such an offer would be offensive to you."

"It would be, Jacob, so don't bother."

"What will Lillian say?"

"I'm getting kind of restless, and she can tell."

"She is a splendid woman."

Falconer nodded. "I'm lucky."

"In addition, you will see Delgado home safely."

Falconer rose and went to the window to gaze out at the quiet morning street. "Jacob, Del and Jeremy aren't children anymore. They're grown men, and they're capable of taking care of themselves."

"Don't worry, Mr. Falconer," said Delgado, jovial, trying to lighten the mood. "I'll make sure you get safely to Santa Fe. But you will be on your own coming back."

Falconer turned, grinning. "If we're going to be on the same string, Del, you had better start calling me Hugh. That way, if you ever have to yell at me to duck for cover, it will take half as long."

"Hugh it is, then."

"I won't mind the change of scenery," said Falconer. "Truth is, I've got a few old friends out that way I would like to see again. Heard tell there's going to be a rendezvous of sorts at Turley's Mill."

"Why, that's only a few miles out of Taos," said Delgado.

Falconer nodded. "And I'd like to pay a visit to Charley Bent. There's talk they might appoint him governor of the New Mexico Territory. I knew him when we were both still wet behind the ears, right here in St. Louis. Matter of fact, he and his brother William once saved my life."

"When does General Kearny plan to leave?" asked Delgado.

"A week, maybe ten days."

"I know you are eager to be on your way," said Bledsoe.

His thoughts all of Sarah, Delgado managed a wan smile. "I can wait."

"Splendid! Splendid!" Bledsoe clapped his hands together. A great burden had been lifted from his shoulders. "It is arranged, then. Hugh, you are a godsend."

"My pleasure, Jacob." Falconer nodded at Delgado. "See you in a few days, Del." With that, he was gone.

"Come, my boy," said Bledsoe. "Have breakfast with me. I have suddenly regained my appetite."

"Mr. Bledsoe, your daughter has consented to join me in a buggy ride today. With your permission."

"She has? Oh, well, certainly. Certainly. I just

hope she does not pester you with more of that nonsense from last night. I was shocked. Shocked, I tell you."

Delgado allowed himself a clandestine smile as he followed Bledsoe out of the parlor.

A few hours later, as he steered the Bledsoe surrey down St. Louis streets, Sarah by his side, he said, "Your father still thinks you are going to marry Brent Horan."

It was perhaps a bit forward of him to broach such a personal subject, but he felt he had to know where Sarah stood in this respect.

"He spoke to you about that?" she asked.

"Over breakfast. He said you've changed some, and he did not think Brent Horan would think it was for the better."

"Brent and I would be a very good match," she said.

His heart plummeted.

"For Father," added Sarah dryly.

"And for you?"

She gave him a funny look, but did not call him to account for the liberty he was taking.

"I could never marry a slaveholder."

"Perhaps for you he would emancipate his slaves."

Sarah laughed. "I lack the zeal to be that devoted an abolitionist!" When Delgado made no reply, she glanced slyly at him and asked, "Is this idle curiosity, Mr. McKinn, or something more?"

"I think your father wondered the same thing. But he decided I could not do much damage to his plans in a week's time."

"A week?"

Delgado told her about the arrangements made for his journey home. He watched her carefully, while trying not to appear he was doing so, hoping to see even a glimmer of disappointment on her lovely face. If there was one, he missed it.

"Considering events, you must be quite concerned about your parents," she said.

"I confess that I am. Actually, my father prevailed upon yours to try and keep me here until the war had run its course."

Sarah said nothing to that. Delgado chided himself for even cherishing a slender hope that she might encourage him to stay. After all, they had met only yesterday. What did he expect? A breathless affirmation of undying love from her ruby lips? It was one thing to be an incurable romantic, and something else entirely to be a self-deceiving dunce.

St. Louis had only recently presented itself with a new courthouse, a formidable limestone structure set dead center in the square off Market Street, and within sight of the levee. Here, in a basement cell, languished the abolitionist Jeremiah Rankin. As the town constable escorted them down a flight of steps beneath the courthouse entrance, they noticed a group of twenty or thirty men loitering in grim silence on the grounds.

"You see those men?" asked the constable as he used one of his many keys to unlock the basement door. "They're here for the same reason as you folks, Miss Bledsoe."

"You mean Rankin?"

Looking worried, the constable nodded. "The judge holds court on Monday. I just hope I can hold onto Rankin till then. I don't think those men up there are inclined to wait too long for justice."

"What do you think they want to do?" asked Delgado. He wondered if these were some of the men Jeremy had told him were so beholden to the Horans.

"It can go one of two ways. If Rankin's lucky, they'll just tar and feather him and ride him out of town on a rail. If he's not so lucky, they'll lynch him."

"Of course you will see to it that he stands before the magistrate come Monday," said Sarah.

The constable gave her a sour look. "I've got three deputies, ma'am. Two of them just took ill, all of a sudden like. Does that answer your question?"

He threw the creaking door open. Across a barren anteroom and through an iron-plated inner door they passed, to find themselves in a long passageway flanked on both sides by cells of strap iron.

"First cell on your left," said the constable.

Rankin was sitting on a narrow bunk, hunched over, head in hands. When he looked up and saw Delgado, he shot to his feet.

"You!"

Sarah glanced curiously at Delgado as she addressed Rankin. "You know Mr. McKinn, sir?"

Rankin came to the cell door and gripped the strap iron so tightly his knuckles whitened. "I should say I do. He saved my life aboard the *Sultana.*"

"Don't take it personally," said Delgado. "I only intervened because I happen to believe that every man deserves a fair hearing in a court of law."

Rankin's smile was taut. "Which distinguishes you from many others in this part of the country. But, in spite of your efforts, sir, I may not get that day in court."

Sarah turned to the constable. "May I have a few words in private with the prisoner?"

"I don't think that's too good an idea, miss," said the lawman, dubious.

"You know me. I am Sarah Bledsoe. Do you imagine I might be concealing a pocket pistol or steel file in my petticoats? If so, you have my permission to search for them."

The constable turned beet red. "I'll wait outside."

As soon as he was gone, Sarah told Rankin that she was a member of the American Antislavery Society. Rankin was surprised.

"If I can be of any service to you," said Sarah. "Do you have an attorney?"

"In the first place, I think you would be hard pressed to find a lawyer willing to jeopardize his career—not to mention his life—by representing me," replied Rankin, sardonic. "In addition, the *gentlemen* who accosted me on the riverboat cleaned out my pockets. I am as poor as Job's turkey."

"I can provide you with the necessary funds, Mr. Rankin."

"I am grateful, miss. But, again, I doubt I will be in court come Monday. So your money would be wasted."

"You seem resigned to your fate," remarked Delgado.

"I am a soldier in an undeclared war. My cause is just. I have no regrets."

"You may believe your cause is just. That is your right. I only hope innocent people aren't hurt in the process."

"There are no innocent people, sir, where slavery is concerned. Slavery is the greatest evil. You are either for it or against it. To ignore it, to pretend it does not exist, or is of no concern to you, is no defense."

"You deal with morals as you would mathematics," observed Delgado. "Slavery was a fact in the ancient world, and it has only recently been condemned by the Christian world. In this country slavery was a fact when the Constitution was framed. The founders agreed the institution should be protected where it already existed. They abolished the slave trade, though, and prohibited slavery in the Northwest Territory. That demonstrates they did not wish slavery to expand. The general expectation has always been that it would gradually be extinguished. Social change comes slowly. But you abolitionists lack the patience to wait for it."

"The South will never dispense with slavery, sir," said Rankin. "Cotton is king, and as long as that is the case, they must have their slaves."

"So you would destroy the economy of an entire region to right this wrong?"

"I would! And not lose a moment's sleep. As a nation we must hang our heads in shame as long as a single slave remains in bondage within our borders."

"Easy enough to say. We're not talking about the ruin of your part of the country, are we?"

Rankin's eyes narrowed. "You don't like me or what I stand for. So why did you save my life?"

"I told you why. And you are wrong in one respect. I admire your motives, sir, but abhor your methods. You would instigate a slave insurrection to have your way. I think it was the Apostle Paul who said that we are not to do evil that good may come." Delgado turned to Sarah. "My apologies. I know you would like to have your own private discussion with Mr. Rankin. I will wait outside with the constable."

A few minutes later, she rejoined him beneath the courthouse steps. This gave Delgado ample time to realize that, once again, his impulsive nature had gotten him into hot water. He disliked the abolitionist, not because the man's actions were illegal, but rather because they put others in jeopardy. Not least Delgado himself, and Sarah Bledsoe. But this dislike for Rankin had loosened his tongue, and he had promptly trampled on it—and Sarah Bledsoe's convictions in the process. His words would not endear him to her. Of this he was certain.

Thanking the constable, Sarah swept past Delgado and headed for the surrey. Catching up to her, Delgado said, "Miss Bledsoe, I hope you understand, in a sense I was playing the devil's advocate . . ."

She turned on him. To his surprise there was a smile rather than anger on her face. "You have no reason to explain yourself. Your heart is in the right place. I know it must be. That is why I must ask you to help me save Rankin's life. Save him from *them*." She looked beyond the surrey at the grim-faced men lingering like a bad dream in the square.

"I do not have it within my power to say no to you."

"I was counting on that. Wait here for me."

She caught the constable wearily ascending the courthouse steps. There in the bright hot summer sunshine they spoke earnestly for a few moments. The constable glanced several times at the men who hovered menacingly about the courthouse like vultures waiting for a suffering creature's last breath. Then, reluctantly, he nodded, and Sarah rejoined Delgado.

"He'll help us," she said, triumphant. "Like Pontius Pilate, he wants to wash his hands of this business."

"Help us do what? What are you up to?"

"I'll tell you on the way home."

4

That evening, after dinner, Delgado slipped undetected out of the Bledsoe house. At a nearby livery he rented a buggy with a calabash cover and drove back to the corner of Laurel Avenue and the Rue St. Eglise. As he waited, he asked himself for at least the hundredth time why he was being such an utter fool by getting involved in something that was none of his business. For the hundredth time the answer was obvious. He was bewitched by the beautiful Sarah Bledsoe. He had never known such a remarkable woman—and he had made the acquaintance of quite a few fair ladies. Still, the consequences of what they were conspiring to do were too horrible to contemplate.

A short while later, a breathless Sarah joined him, encased in a hooded cloak of black pilotcloth.

"All clear?" asked Delgado.

She nodded. "I told Clarisse everything. She will see to it that our absence is not discovered."

"Hmm," said Delgado, skeptical, as he stirred the horse into motion.

At the courthouse he waited outside in the buggy while Sarah went in to find the constable. She made certain that any who might have reason to be watching saw by the light of the storm lanterns flanking the courthouse door that she was, indeed, a woman, and as she emerged a moment later to accompany the constable down to the basement jail, she was illuminated again.

Humming a tune—it helped him to keep his nerves on an even keel—Delgado waited. A man materialized out of the evening shadows to approach the buggy, a flinty-eyed man wearing a linsey-woolsey shirt and stroud pants, a cold pipe clenched between his crooked teeth.

"Wouldn't have any tobacco to spare, now would you, friend?" he asked, peering at Delgado.

"Sorry. I don't indulge. So many vices—you just have to pick and choose, don't you?"

The man stared at him a moment as though determined to imprint Delgado's features indelibly upon his memory, and then walked away.

A few minutes later, Sarah emerged from the basement, the cloak wrapped tightly about her, the hood concealing her face, and got into the buggy. Delgado whipped up the horse. He didn't remember to breathe until the buggy had quit the square. At one point they passed within a few feet of a clot of dark and silent men. But the men made no effort to interfere with their departure.

"Are we being followed?" asked Rankin, his voice raspy with nervousness.

Of course it came as no surprise to Delgado that it was Rankin and not Sarah Bledsoe cocooned in the black cloak.

"I don't think so. Do you have the money?"

"Yes, she gave it to me. How much is in the envelope, do you know? I didn't waste time counting it."

"Enough for passage north. I suggest you go

home, Mr. Rankin, and stay there. Helping you escape will cost Miss Bledsoe dearly."

"You are in love with her, aren't you? That's why you're doing this."

"Is there a better reason?"

"Yes," said Rankin grimly.

Delgado drove to a secluded spot on the dirt lane behind the levee. The smokestacks of dozens of steamboats stood like a forest of naked tree trunks against the indigo sky. As he stopped the buggy, Rankin jumped out, shed the cloak, and left it on the seat. Even now there was considerable activity along the riverfront, and the silhouettes of men on the levee moved against a backdrop of the riverboat lights. But no one was within a stone's throw of the buggy, and Rankin felt secure enough to discard the cloak.

"Whatever your reasons," said the abolitionist, "you have saved my life, and I thank you. You judge my methods too harsh, but it is a great wickedness that I and my colleagues are dedicated to fighting. I pray that one day the light of truth will dawn on you, sir. A man must stand for something, or the precious life God gave him is wasted."

"You should have been a preacher, Mr. Rankin."

Rankin smiled tautly. "I *am* a preacher, Mr. McKinn."

"Good luck to you." Delgado stirred the horse and left the man without a backward glance.

He entered the darkened square off Market Street at a good clip, and his return caught the men waiting there by surprise. Halting the buggy at the courthouse steps, he saw several of them start forward, coming from different angles. They smelled a rat now, and they loped like wolves moving in for the kill. Sarah came out of the basement door and reached the buggy only seconds before the nearest man, who launched himself at Delgado. Delgado planted a booted foot in the man's chest and pushed. Cursing, the man sprawled on the ground. Another grabbed the horse's cheek straps. Delgado plucked the whip from its stock and drove him back. A second flick of the wrists and the braided leather snapped across the horse's rump, and they were off, the horse at a quick canter in its traces.

"We did it!" exclaimed Sarah, laughing, as they put the square and its dark dangers behind them. "What a wonderful adventure that was!"

"You might have come to harm. There is no telling what those men might have done. They could have been armed, for all we know." He was cross; he gave little thought to the risks he had taken, but Sarah had been in harm's way, and that had given him a bad moment. He was still shaking, just a little.

"You wouldn't have let anything happen to me," she said, with complete confidence.

And what could he say to that?

They left the buggy at the livery and walked back to the Bledsoe house, entering the grounds by a gate in the rear wall that brought them into the garden. Clarisse would be waiting for them at the back door if everything had gone according to plan. There was no moonlight this evening; clouds blotted out the stars, and a distant drumbeat of thunder warned of a coming storm.

Chapter Four

"That's no way for a gentleman to talk."

1

Blackwood, the Horan mansion house, had been built in the Southern colonial style, a grand brick structure, whitewashed, fronted with six Doric columns, adorned with a spacious veranda and balcony, and wings on either side. It crowned a rise overlooking a green incline of pasture, with the fields on one side and on the other a dark line of pines and water oaks that marked the course of a nearby creek. A lane flanked by cedars provided access from the main road. Behind the mansion stood the smokehouse, kitchen, carriage house, stables, spring house, and the ruins of the old log blockhouse where Daniel Horan and his family had lived in the early years. A fire had partially destroyed the blockhouse. Relentless weeds and vines were claiming the neglected remains. When he first laid eyes on Blackwood, Delgado McKinn decided that Daniel Horan had done a more than fair job of bringing the Old South to the raw Missouri frontier.

The curving drive was filled with carriages and saddle horses. Poor weather—slashing rain this morning, now reduced to a steady drizzle—had deterred no one from attending one of the events of the season. The guests spilled out onto the veranda, the gentlemen in fawn- and mustard-colored trousers, lace-fronted shirts, fitted coats of blue and dark green and black, the older women in their dark, staid silks, the young women in brightly colored crinolines and taffetas.

None of the young belles could hold a candle to Sarah Bledsoe—of this Delgado was convinced even before he arrived. Sarah wore a pink crepe de chine dress enhanced with emerald green Chantilly lace. Green moroccan slippers adorned her tiny feet. Her pale round shoulders were enticingly bare. A lace shawl draped with deliberate carelessness over an arm, a painted fan dangling from one wrist by a dainty green ribbon, her gleaming chestnut hair pulled sleekly back in a chignon, with little side curls left free to caress her neck. Tea rose blossoms were tucked into a satin sash that showed off her waspishly narrow waist. She was, without doubt, the most beautiful belle of the ball.

And, mused Delgado as he rode in the carriage which conveyed him along with Jeremy, Sarah, and Jacob Bledsoe up the drive, *she and I are fortunate to even be here.*

Last night's secret undertaking was today's common knowledge. St. Louis was buzzing with talk. Discovered locked in the cell previously occupied by Jeremiah Rankin, the constable had identified Sarah as the one who had passed a hideout pistol to the desperate abolitionist, the very pistol which the prisoner had threatened to use if he was not released. And it was Sarah's cloak that had disguised the fugitive in his flight.

There had, of course, been no pistol, or even the need for one; the constable had been a willing accomplice, and the fiction was necessary only to protect him from retribution at the hands of the clique of angry, frustrated men who had been plotting Rankin's death. Sarah had insisted he identify her as the culprit, to deflect any suspicion away from him. There would be no charges leveled against her. She was a woman, and a Bledsoe, besides. All that remained was for Delgado to confess to being the man in the carriage, although Sarah had wanted him to lie with the story that he had had no inkling as to her motives for the nocturnal visit to the jail, and that Rankin had held a pistol on him and forced him to drive to the levee. Delgado would have none of it.

Jacob Bledsoe's outrage had verged on apoplexy. But for the fact that the ball at Blackwood was in honor of Sarah's return from Philadelphia, he declared, his inclination would have been to confine her to her room indefinitely. As for Delgado, while his honesty did him credit, that could not excuse him for having abused the hospitality extended to him. Delgado could only concur and apologize. But Jacob was still fuming. His daughter and his guest had humiliated him before the entire community.

Their arrival at Blackwood caused quite a stir. Jacob fairly cringed as the women whispered behind their hands, and some of the men looked with stern disapproval. For her part, Sarah seemed blissfully unaware that anything was amiss. Delgado did his best to ignore the keen curiosity turned upon him by all present.

Black boys with umbrellas sheltered them from the elements as they quit the carriage and gained the veranda, where Brent Horan was waiting for them. He greeted Jeremy and Jacob Bledsoe with unfeigned courtesy before turning his attention to Sarah.

"My dear Sarah, you look ravishing."

"Thank you, Brent."

"I am delighted that you are home at last. I missed you more than words can express. Come and say hello to Father."

It escaped no one's attention that Brent Horan acted as though Delgado did not even exist. A calculated insult.

Daniel Horan was enthroned in a high-backed wing chair in the great hall, where he could greet his guests as they entered. Delgado was shocked by the patriarch's appearance. He had never seen a living man so nearly consumed by death. The chair seemed to swallow up his emaciated form. Eyes haunted by pain were sunk deep in black-rimmed sockets. His breathing was labored, his face gaunt and skull-like. He could scarcely raise a gnarled hand, or mumble incoherently in response to the salutations of the new arrivals as they filed respectfully past.

"What's become of him?" Delgado asked Jeremy once they had performed the amenities and moved on.

"Shocking, isn't it? The man's not yet sixty years old and looks a hundred. A few short years ago he was full of vim and vigor. Now he can't walk, and most days cannot speak. A dozen eminent physicians have been consulted. None can make a firm diagnosis, much less propose a cure." Jeremy leaned closer and pitched his voice in such a low whisper that Delgado could barely hear his next words. "Some say God is punishing Daniel Horan for the cruelty with which he has treated his slaves all these years. And then there is the rumor that he is being slowly poisoned."

"Poisoned? By whom?"

Jeremy shrugged. "Who stands to gain if his father is dead, and his brother disappeared these many years?"

"You haven't told me why you so strongly dislike Brent Horan."

Before Jeremy could reply, Sarah approached, having detached herself from Horan. She extended a hand to Delgado.

"You promised me this dance, Mr. McKinn. Or have you forgotten?"

On a raised platform draped with red, white, and blue bunting, the black musicians with their fiddles, bull fiddles, accordions, and banjo had launched into a spry rendition of "Lorena." As Delgado swept Sarah away into the swirling current of waltzing couples, he caught a glimpse of the malignant expression on Brent Horan's patrician features.

"Your old beau is put out with you, Miss Bledsoe."

"Oh my," she said, feigning dismay, with wicked mischief glittering in her eyes. "Could it be because I informed him that I had promised you every single dance?"

It was the first Delgado had heard of this, but he didn't mind. "I guess I don't have to worry about Brent Horan, after all."

"Why on earth *would* you worry?"

"As a rival, I mean."

The trace of coquetry vanished; she gazed very seriously into his eyes. "No, I don't think you need to worry on that score."

The great hall was packed; Delgado estimated that more than a hundred people were present. Brent Horan had gone to great expense to make the soiree as elegant as possible. What seemed like a thousand candles burned with the fragrance of bayberries. They burned in china figurines, in brass stands, in silver and crystal holders, in the wall sconces and the chandelier entwined with ivy. In the corners, beneath bowers of artfully arranged pine branches, sat the old ladies and the chaperones. Along the wall in front of French windows open to the veranda, men clustered in conversation around refreshment tables manned by slaves in handsome livery.

Delgado tried to convince himself that they weren't all staring at him and Sarah, that they weren't all talking about the dark stranger and the brash girl who had come from the East with her head full of silly—some might go so far as to say dangerous—notions. Some were bound to be wondering why Sarah Bledsoe wasn't dancing with their host. Horan's designs where she was concerned were no secret. First the incident on the *Sultana,* then the freeing of the abolitionist, Rankin, and now this—Delgado felt like a man sitting on a powder keg and playing with matches. But with Sarah in his arms he didn't really care. Only one thought troubled him.

Suddenly, he had no desire to go home. The war and all its attendant woes seemed far, far removed and singularly unimportant.

After the waltz came a quadrille, and then one of the new polkas, and Sarah was as light as a feather in his arms, as graceful as a gazelle. She complimented him on his skill.

"I suppose you have danced with many women," she said, fishing for a compliment.

"None as beautiful as you."

She laughed. "How gallant, Mr. McKinn! You

have broken many a young girl's heart, as well, I'd wager."

"Proper young ladies do not make wagers," he replied, a mock rebuke.

"I am hardly that. You should know by now."

"One thing I do know," he said gravely. "I will discover what it is like to have my heart broken when I leave for Taos."

The smile left her lips. His heart raced. Could it be that she dreaded that moment as much as he?

The music stopped. The dance was over, and Sarah expressed an interest in a refreshment. They moved to the most convenient table. With haughty disapproval on their faces, two matronly women took themselves elsewhere. A gentleman performed a stiff bow and also departed.

"You'd think we were typhoid carriers," said Delgado, annoyed.

"If you care what they think, then I am sorry I involved you in last night's affair."

"I have no regrets."

"Oh, dear," she said, surveying the lavish offerings on the table. "I would prefer a cup of switchel. I think there might be some at that table over there. Would you mind terribly?"

"My privilege." Delgado left her and found the switchel—a chilled drink made of molasses, water, and a dash of vinegar—precisely where she had suggested he look. As he waited for the servant to pour, he overheard the conversation of two men who stood nearby.

"No American force will ever be defeated by any amount of Mexican troops, sir," declared one. "Our boys are of superior stock and will give the Mexican's 'a hard lesson' at every turn. They will never acknowledge the corn, as we say, to a mongrel cross between the Negro and the Indian. The war will be of short duration, you can be sure."

The second man wholeheartedly concurred. "Everyone knows the enemy lacks both courage and discipline. But then, what can you expect? The nature of a society reflects the kind of army it is capable of putting into the field. The Mexican people have been oppressed for centuries by military and religious despots. Naturally their character is inferior to ours."

"I think it unlikely," said the first, "that Mexico will long continue her existence as a nation. Already she has lost Texas. Now Yucatan is seeking independence, and California has been semi-independent for years. Mexico's best fate would be to become a protectorate of these United States, sir. By reason of our situation, the genius of our people, and the form of our institutions, we can confer upon the people of Mexico the industry and government that will cure their impoverished state."

"Yo' drink, suh."

Delgado thanked the old Negro and was just turning to look for Sarah when a shout and a crash caused the musicians to cut short the tune they had just begun and made everyone in the hall stop what they were doing. The servant at the table where Sarah stood lay on the floor. Over him loomed a man Delgado did not recognize. Flush with excitement, the man had a piece of paper clutched in his hand, which he shook furiously in Sarah's face.

"You gave this to him. Do not try to deny it. I saw you with my own eyes."

"I don't deny it," was Sarah's calm, defiant reply.

With a knot in his stomach Delgado started forward, but Brent Horan reached Sarah's side before him.

"What is the meaning of this, Taylor?" he asked Sarah's accuser.

"This! This is the meaning." The man gave the paper to Horan.

As the evidence passed into Horan's possession, Delgado recognized it, and the blood ran cold in his veins.

The pamphlet!

The abolitionist manifesto that Horan had taken from Jeremiah Rankin aboard the *Sultana,* which had passed from him to Sterling and then to Delgado, and which in turn Delgado had given to Sarah in the garden two nights ago—and promptly forgotten all about.

Horan took one look at the pamphlet and all color drained from his face. He glared at Sarah.

"Where did you get this?"

"What does it matter? I am a member of the society, and I gave it to your slave, Brent, so that he might share it with the others, in the hopes that at least one might be able to read what it contains, and share the message of freedom with the rest."

"My God," rasped Horan. He seemed to rock back on his heels, as though Sarah had slapped his face. "I welcome you into my home in spite of what you did last night, and this . . . this is how you repay my kindness? My . . . my love for you?" A cloud of untempered fury darkened his features. Trembling with rage, he forgot himself and grabbed Sarah so roughly by the arm that she winced.

A throng of people was gathering; Delgado pushed through them.

"Take your hands off her," he snapped, his black eyes flashing.

"Ah, here he is again," sneered Horan. "The defender of abolitionists." He let go of Sarah.

"Come on, Sarah," said Delgado. "We had better go."

"Yes, take this nigger-loving vixen out of my house," said Horan bitterly.

Delgado whirled. The words, though meant for Sarah, stung him like a whip and ignited his temper. He still had the cup of switchel in his hand; he flung its contents into Horan's face. The crowd uttered a collective gasp.

"That's no way for a gentleman to talk," said Delgado coldly.

He thought for an instant that Horan was going to lunge at him. But Horan, though consumed by a towering rage, stood rigidly in place.

"You will pay for that," he whispered. "My representative will call on you."

Jeremy appeared at Sarah's side, his features taut and pale. "You have insulted my sister, sir," he told Horan. "I, too, will expect satisfaction."

Brent Horan's smile was wintery. He bowed stiffly at the waist. "I am at your service, Mr. Bledsoe."

Delgado escorted Sarah through the ring of spectators, who parted to let them pass. All eyes were on them as they crossed the great hall, a seething Jeremy limping along behind them. Jacob Bledsoe met them at the door, wringing his hands in distress.

"Dear God, child," he gasped at Sarah, "what have you done? What have you done?"

2

"Outrageous! Outrageous conduct!" Jacob Bledsoe paced the rose-patterned rug in the front parlor of his house, so agitated that he could not stand still for a moment. "I rue the day I sent you East, daughter. I should have known better. You are too impressionable. Too impressionable by far! You don't have the good sense to ignore the rantings of abolitionists and other reformist crackpots. Shame, shame on you."

"Shame on *you*, Father!" retorted Sarah. "Aren't you an American? Don't you love freedom? Slavery makes a mockery of our nation's principles."

Bledsoe actually covered his ears with his hands. He looked silly, mused Delgado, but there was nothing really amusing about the situation. He still could scarcely believe that Sarah had been so rash as to smuggle the abolitionist pamphlet into Blackwood and hand it, in front of God and everybody, to the old Negro working the refreshment table. Surely, she had not expected to get away with that. Obviously she had intended to cause a scene. As a result, if Brent Horan had his way, blood would be spilled.

And yet Delgado could not muster one iota of resentment, though his was the blood most likely to be shed. Sarah was headstrong, but that was part of what made her so irresistibly attractive to him. At least she had the courage of her convictions.

"I won't listen to that kind of talk," declared Bledsoe. "No, I won't listen. The circulation of material such as you had in your possession is not only wicked, it is unlawful."

Sarah shook her head. "You don't realize what

you're saying, Father. You support the censorship of ideas? Is that not a conspiracy against the rights of free men and women? Does that not make us the *white* slaves of the masters of black slaves? I suppose the next step will be that we must all get down on our knees when a man like Brent Horan enters the room."

"Oh, what has become of my little girl?" bemoaned Bledsoe.

"Your little girl has discovered that she has a mind of her own," replied Sarah hotly. "And she intends to speak her mind whenever the mood strikes her."

"And you have put at risk your brother's life in the process, and the life of my friend's son."

She glanced at Delgado, and his pulse quickened; undeniably she cared for him and was afraid for his life.

"Don't fear for me," he said. "I have no intention of fighting a duel."

Until that moment Jeremy had been brooding silently, slumped in a chair. Now he shot to his feet.

"I have every intention of doing so! I will not allow any person, least of all Brent Horan, to insult my sister."

"He called me a nigger lover," said Sarah. "I do not consider that an insult. It is the truth."

"Sarah!" exclaimed Jacob Bledsoe.

"I love them as I love all people. What's wrong with that?"

"Horan's intentions are what matter, not his words," said Jeremy stiffly. "From his point of view it was the worst possible insult. And he called you a vixen, besides."

Sarah shrugged a fetching shoulder. "Who knows? Perhaps I am that, as well."

"You have certainly been acting the part since you came home," lamented Jacob Bledsoe.

"Have a care, Father. Jeremy might challenge *you* to a duel."

"There will be no dueling," Bledsoe told his son. "I will not permit it."

"You cannot prevent it," Jeremy said.

"Brent Horan would surely kill you. He has slain two men in previous duels."

"That has absolutely no bearing on my decision."

"Honor," said Delgado, "means doing the right thing regardless of the consequences."

Jeremy stared blankly at him.

"Those were your own words, I believe," continued Delgado. "You went on to define 'right thing' as abiding by the laws of God and man. If you believe in what you say, you must turn the other cheek or take Horan to court. But a duel is no recourse for an honorable man."

Wordless, Jeremy sank back into his chair. He could not argue with himself.

"No one will fight a duel on my account," said Sarah. "I will not stand for it. I was not insulted by Brent Horan's words, so no one else should be."

"Enough," said Jacob Bledsoe. "Quite enough. I will countenance no further discussion on the subject. Sarah, go to your room and stay there until I summon you. Jeremy, Delgado, go pack your belongings. You are both leaving St. Louis tonight."

"I will not run away," said Jeremy.

"I am your father, and you will obey me. I have

sent for Hugh Falconer. He will get you both safely away. I only hope and pray that he arrives in time."

There was nothing more to be said. Delgado and Jeremy followed Sarah upstairs. She did not turn around, or give Delgado so much as a glance. Delgado was in perfect anguish.

The time had come for him to go, and yet he did not want to leave. Before two days ago he had not given Sarah Bledsoe a thought; today the future looked gray and cheerless and futile without her in it.

In his room Delgado packed his bags and then stretched out on the bed, hands behind his head, to stare bleakly at the ceiling. He felt like a condemned man languishing in his cell as he awaited the long walk to the gallows, for leaving Sarah was like death. No, worse than death. She was as much an essential part of his life as breathing. How had this come about so swiftly?

He had known many women in his life; his looks and bearing had always attracted them. In Taos, in England, during his tour of the United States, beautiful women had always been there for the asking. He had admired their beauty and enjoyed their company when it suited him and then gone his way without a backward glance or so much as a twinge of remorse. Perhaps he had broken a few hearts, but he had never given his own.

Sarah, though—Sarah was different. She made him feel so alive. Other women paled into insignificance, seemed such dull and lifeless creatures, by comparison to her. He was miserable just being across the hall from her—to be half a continent apart was an unbearable prospect.

Yet what was there to do? He could not remain

in St. Louis, regardless of Brent Horan. Of course, even if he stayed, he would have to leave this house, and Jacob Bledsoe would probably forbid him to see his daughter again. In that event Sarah would have to choose—her father or him. Delgado could not put her in that predicament. He loved her too much.

A couple of hours later, shortly after the clock in the hall chimed midnight, he heard someone at the door downstairs. Falconer? Or Horan's representative? Perhaps Horan himself, come to have his vengeance, and to blazes with protocol. For Delgado, Horan was of little consequence, compared to the pure torment he suffered over Sarah.

Leaving the room, he went to the head of the stairs and saw Bledsoe and Hugh Falconer in the hall below.

". . . so you can understand why I summoned you at this hour," Bledsoe was saying "Lives hang in the balance."

Falconer nodded. Some sharply honed instinct alerted him to Delgado's presence; he turned and looked up the staircase and smiled at Delgado. That smile, calm and confident, seemed somehow a comfort to Delgado. It reassured him that, as dark as things now appeared, all would be well in the end.

"So, Del," drawled the frontiersman, "you've stirred up a lot of dust."

"I have, though I am not quite sure how it all come about . . ."

"That's the way it happens sometimes. Get your plunder and fetch Jeremy. We'll be off." Falconer turned back to Jacob Bledsoe. "I'll take them to my place tonight, and by daybreak we'll be on the road to Fort Leavenworth."

"I don't know how I will ever be able to repay you."

"Just look out for Lillian and Johnny if they have a need. Lillian doesn't take much looking after, but you never know what might happen."

"You can rely on me in that regard," promised Bledsoe.

With a dejected sigh Delgado went to his room and retrieved his pair of valises. When he returned to the upstairs hall, Sarah was standing in the doorway to her bedroom. His heart soared at the sight of her and promptly plunged at the thought of his imminent departure. She looked as though she had been crying, though he could not be sure.

"Sarah . . ."

"Yes, Del?"

"Sarah, I . . . I have to go now."

"I know."

"I have to leave, but I will return. Will you . . . ? Could you . . . ?"

She gave him a brave, sweet smile. "Of course I will. I will wait forever if need be."

They were the most wonderful words he had ever heard. They gave him all the strength he needed to face the time they would be separated. They told him that she knew as well as he that the two of them were meant for each other, and that no matter what happened or how long it took, they would be together again.

Jeremy came out of his room down the hall, lugging a single bag. He gave Sarah a peck on the cheek. "Good-bye, Sis," he said gruffly, trying to mask his feelings. "Come on, Del. You've got to get home, and I have a war to fight." He moved on and went down the stairs.

Delgado turned to follow him.

"Del?"

She stepped closer and handed him one of the tiny tea roses from her pink sash. He held it as though it were a holy relic. Then, moving closer still, with her small, soft, warm hands on his cheeks, she kissed him ever so lightly on the lips.

Then she fled into her room so that he would not bear witness to her tears.

3

Falconer had come well prepared, bringing along a pair of saddle horses for Delgado and Jeremy. The rain had finally stopped, and the moon played hide-and-seek behind the scudding remnants of clouds as a restless wind stirred dead leaves in the streets. Jacob Bledsoe walked out to see them off. His parting with Delgado was perfunctory at best; Delgado wanted to apologize for having taken advantage of the man's hospitality. He even entertained, briefly, the foolish notion to tell Bledsoe that he was in love with Sarah, and that he would be coming back one day to make her his own. But he did neither.

Bledsoe's parting with his son was a more affectionate scene, at least on his part, but Jeremy was almost curt with his good-bye, and Delgado felt sorry for the old man, so afraid he would never see his only son alive again.

Their passage down the wet and sleeping streets took them past the livery where Delgado had rented the stockinged bay. He prevailed upon Falconer to stop, awakened the livery's proprietor, and struck a hasty bargain, offering a hundred dixies for the horse—he had never gotten around to exchanging the Louisiana paper for gold. It was an offer the owner could not refuse. The man was so happy to have the dixies rather than some less valuable currency that he threw in a saddle besides. In minutes Delgado was astride the bay, leading the horse Falconer had brought into town for him. He knew horses and had a good feeling about the bay.

Departing St. Louis, they took the road for Jefferson City. With the weather and the lateness of the hour they had it all to themselves. No one spoke, which suited Delgado just fine. He was occupied with thoughts of Sarah. She loved him, and he was on top of the world. He had no doubts that she would wait for him, and that made leaving bearable.

Great changes were in store for Taos, and he had to be there for his mother and father in case they needed him. But once things were settled at home he would return to St. Louis, regardless of Jacob Bledsoe and Brent Horan, and claim for his bride the woman he knew with absolute certitude was meant for him.

Falconer lived a dozen miles west of St. Louis, and the road conditions slowed them down, so that it took them the better part of three hours to reach their destination. By that time Delgado was bone-tired.

Despite the hour they were greeted by Falconer's wife, Lillian, a slender and very pretty woman. After they had seen to their horses, they went inside to discover a pot of fresh coffee and bowls of hot burgoo waiting for them. Delgado and Jeremy fell upon the latter—a highly seasoned pot pie made with vegetables and venison—with gusto. Falconer sipped a cup of coffee, but did not eat. Again little was said; they were trying to be quiet as Falconer's stepson, Johnny, was asleep in the cabin's loft. After eating their fill, Delgado and Jeremy lay down to sleep upon pallets of blankets and buffalo robes on the floor.

It seemed to Delgado that he had just closed his eyes before Falconer was shaking him awake. Pearl gray morning light poured through the windows.

Over breakfast Delgado asked Falconer how it was that he had come to work for Jacob Bledsoe.

"I met Lillian three years ago," replied the frontiersman. "She and her boy were part of an emigrant train bound for Oregon. At first we aimed to stay up in the mountains, but there was some Indian trouble, and I decided to bring them back here where you don't have to worry about your scalp every time you step out the door. Figured I would find something to do, though I didn't know exactly what. One day I was in the Hawken brothers' shop on Laurel Street—that's where a lot of us old buckskinners hang around and swap tall tales—when Jacob walked in. He was looking for someone to guide a mule train down the trail to Santa Fe, and decided I was the right man for the job." Falconer shrugged. "Suits me well enough. Pays good, and I'm home half the year. Not much trouble to be found on the trail these days. Every now and again somebody gets into a scrape with Indians, but I've never had a problem yet. Good thing. I'm getting too old for that kind of excitement."

"Too old?" scoffed Jeremy. "Don't let him fool you, Del. Hugh is like tough leather well put together, as they say."

"I regret that you must undertake such a journey on my account," said Delgado. He turned to Lillian. "Your husband has given his word to Jacob Bledsoe that he will see me safely home to Taos. If it were within my power to do so, I would release him from that obligation rather than be the cause of your separation from your husband."

Lillian smiled. "Of course I miss him when he is gone." She put her hand on top of Falconer's. "But it does him good to get away. In fact, he would be impossible to live with if he didn't yonder every now and then. You may as well get used to it, Mr. McKinn. You look to be quite capable of taking care of yourself, but if my husband gave his word, he will keep it, come hell or high water."

After breakfast Delgado and Jeremy went out to saddle the horses. Falconer was brief with his good-byes. He enjoined the ten-year-old Johnny to take over as man of the house while he was away, and told Lillian he would bring her something back from Santa Fe. A pair of hounds roused themselves from the front porch as they started off; Falconer's curt command send the downcast dogs loping back to the cabin. He waved once and never looked back again as they rode west.

Their destination was Fort Leavenworth, regimental headquarters of the First Dragoon Regiment, commanded by Colonel Stephen Watts Kearny. The journey there would take them five days, Falconer said, and their route would follow the Missouri River, past the new German settlement of Hermann, then New Franklin and Independence. The fort lay on the western bank of the Big Muddy between Independence and the newer community of St. Joseph, recently plotted on the site of an old trading post established years ago by Joe Robidoux of the American Fur Company.

The fort, explained Falconer, had been erected twenty years back, along with Fort Gibson where the Verdigris and the Neosho rivers joined the Arkansas, and Fort Towson down near the Texas border, to protect the relocated eastern tribes from the Plains Indians. The land south of the Platte to the Red River had been set aside for the Cherokees, Choctaws, Chickasaws, Creeks, and Seminoles, whose title to their homelands east of the Mississippi had been gradually extinguished by the federal government. The United States had promised to do this when the individual states ceded their western public lands to the new nation and, right or wrong, a promise was a promise.

In 1830, prodded by President Andrew Jackson, Congress had passed the Indian Removal Act, and the deed was good and done. The Five Civilized Tribes had needed protection, too, from the likes of the Pawnees and the Comanches. Nowadays, the Pawnees, once a powerful nation, were a mere shadow of their former glory. Disease had decimated the tribe. That fact, though tragic, made the upper portion of the Santa Fe Trail much safer traveling. The Comanches, however, still posed a threat, even though the Texans had been doing their level best for more than ten years to cut that warlike tribe down to size.

Doniphan's Volunteers were using Fort Leavenworth as a rendezvous. The Missouri governor had authorized eight companies of mounted troops and two of light artillery. It seemed, remarked Falconer, that every farmboy in the state had abandoned his plow, grabbed his old squirrel gun, and set off for Leavenworth and glory.

With the outbreak of war it was the same story in every part of the country, said Jeremy. Secretary of War William L. Marcy had issued a call for fifty thousand volunteers to bolster the small regular army. Taylor's victories at Palo Alto and Resaca de la Palma served to trigger an enthusiastic response. Recruits flocked to the banner, anxious to get involved before it was too late, as it was obvious to just about everyone that the war would be of short duration. Thirty thousand Tennesseans responded, when only three thousand could be taken from that state. Ohio's quota was filled in less than two weeks. Illinois was authorized to raise four regiments; it soon had enough volunteers to fill fourteen.

Jeremy had heard of an incident in Paris, Kentucky, where, while the local volunteers were organizing themselves into an infantry company, word arrived that the state's quota for infantry had already been filled. Only one vacancy remained open for a cavalry unit. The Paris men collected enough plow mares to qualify themselves as cavalry, elected a captain and a lieutenant, and dispatched these officers on the forty-mile trip to the state capital at Frankfort to report to the governor. Upon reaching Lexington, these men learned that a cavalry company had been formed there as well, and its officers had earlier started off for Frankfort. Getting a fresh horse for their buggy, the Paris men pressed on. They overtook their Lexington counterparts and were well ahead in the race when one of the buggy's splintered. The captain mounted the horse and raced on. He reached Frankfort at midnight, minutes ahead of the Lexington men, and roused the governor out of his bed—only to learn that a local company had filled the last cavalry vacancy a few hours earlier.

With a grim smile Falconer shook his head. "The poor fools think there is glory in war. I hope they don't have to die to find out otherwise."

Delgado told them that he had heard people say that the Mexicans were an inferior race who would be easily conquered.

"I know better," said Jeremy. "Remember the Rancheros, Hugh?"

Falconer nodded, and it was apparent that the memory was not a pleasant one.

"They were Mexican irregular cavalry," Jeremy told Delgado. "Fought at Palo Alto and Resaca de la Palma. It was a Ranchero who shot me and then Hugh. I would liken them to the Russian cossacks. The Mexican people call them the 'hawks of the chaparral.' They are fearless, and they give no quarter. I've heard others say that they are cowards, who fight only from ambush, but I know that is not the case. I've not seen better shots, more superb horsemen, or braver men."

"I will tell you this much," responded Delgado. "Military discipline does not sit well with a Mexican, but he will fight like a tiger to protect his land and his family, and because he is afraid the American will make him a slave."

"As to that," said Jeremy, "isn't it true that the peon is a slave in all but name? Indebted for life to a big landowner, is he not forced to work like a slave?"

"In some cases that is true. But do not call him a slave to his face. The Constitution of 1824 prohibits slavery in the Republic of Mexico. The peon will prefer that constitution to your own, Jeremy, which permits slavery to exist."

"I haven't asked you where you stand in this affair, Del," said Jeremy gravely. "But I'll wager Colonel Kearny will."

"My family is my chief concern, to my mother and father my only allegiance."

Delgado had a feeling that Jeremy Bledsoe did not believe him. Jeremy could not conceive of a man without patriotism. Delgado thought this was an odd kind of myopia, since Jeremy lived in a country where some men—call them nullifiers or secessionists or what you will—were ready to sacrifice their country for the sake of their own selfish pursuits.

On their third day out of St. Louis a lone rider on a lathered horse caught up with them. It was Sterling, of the *St. Louis Enquirer*.

"Hope you boys don't object to some company," said the newspaperman. "I too am bound for the fields of glory, you see."

"You volunteered?" asked Jeremy.

"Oh, no." Sterling laughed. "I leave the heroics to younger men. But there is an intense competition for war news. Newspapers all over the country are sending out their special correspondents. My friend George Wilkins Kendall of the New Orleans *Picayune* has gone to war. Of course this isn't the first time for George; he was part of the Santa Fe Expedition in 1842 and spent some months languishing in a Mexican jail for his trouble. Thomas Thorpe of the *Tropic* is somewhere down along the Rio Grande with Taylor. And I have it on good authority that James Gordon Bennett has dispatched no less than four correspondents to represent the *New York Herald*. They say Bennett is establishing an express to carry the news north from Mobile, and the Philadelphia and Baltimore penny presses have thrown in together to purchase sixty blooded horses for a pony express from New Orleans. The New York papers are discussing the idea of organizing into something called the Associated Press. The idea is that they will share the cost as well as the news. The *Enquirer* is not to be outdone, naturally."

"Come along, then," said Falconer, "and welcome."

"My thanks." Sterling peered curiously at Delgado. "I have heard tell of your clash with our mutual acquaintance, Mr. Horan. He has declared you a rank coward for running away."

Delgado bristled, then calmed himself. "Let him say what he will."

He could see that his response was, for Jeremy at least, most unsatisfactory.

Chapter Five

"Old scores remain to be settled."

1

Thanks to Stephen Watts Kearny, Fort Leavenworth was a true American fortress on the frontier. It had not always been so. Upon taking command of the First Dragoons, the legendary Indian fighter's first priority had been to strengthen the fort's defenses, which were deplorable. Two blockhouses were constructed. A hospital and guardhouse followed. The condition of the barracks and officers' quarters was substantially improved. Before Kearny, assignment to the garrison at Fort Leavenworth was, as one subaltern put it in a letter to his sweetheart, "worse than being posted to the lowest level of Satan's kingdom." Now, though, life at the fort was far from a dull ordeal. Frequent dinner parties and dances, or "hops" as the soldiers called them, enlivened the post. Sometimes theatrical companies disembarked from river steamers, which regularly plied the tumultuous waters of the Missouri River.

This was not to say that Kearny did not work his men hard. When not drilling the dragoons, he had them deployed on far-ranging patrols. His duty was to protect a thousand miles of frontier with a force that never exceeded six hundred men. He was to preserve the peace among the various Indian tribes, escorting the eastern Indians—some ninety thousand in number—to their new homeland, and making sure the indigenous Indians—estimated to number a quarter of a million—did not prey upon the newcomers. Then, too, an increasing number of emigrants were embarking on the Oregon Trail for points west, and their presence was a source of never-ending concern to the redman.

Fortunately, most of the Indians in the region knew and respected Kearny. They called him *Shonga Kahega Mahetonga*—Horse Chief of the Long Knives. They knew his word was good, and they usually thought twice about incurring his wrath.

Kearny was respected by the men under his command, too. At the age of nineteen he had been commissioned a captain during the War of 1812. He had served with distinction in the Winnebago War and been involved in a highly successful military expedition to the Yellowstone country. Few soldiers knew the frontier as well as he.

A strict disciplinarian, Kearny had molded the First Dragoons into what all agreed was the finest fighting force in the United States Army. They were drilled to perfection. Kearny himself had written the *Carbine Manual of Rules for the Exercise and Maneuvering of U.S. Dragoons*, the Army's standard text on cavalry training and tactics. Every soldier in Kearny's command was steady, industrious, healthy, and vigilant, reported General Edmund P. Gaines, commander of the Western Department, and no regiment presented a finer appearance on parade—an appearance enhanced by the fact that Kearny had assigned the regimental mounts to the various companies according to color. In summing up his inspection of the First

Dragoons, Gaines concluded that Kearny's command were "the best troops I have ever seen."

Hugh Falconer thought well of Kearny. "He is one of the few officers I have met who is worth his salt," declared the frontiersman, and during the journey from St. Louis to Fort Leavenworth he related to Delgado some of Kearny's accomplishments.

There had been a problem with the Seminoles. Of the Five Civilized Tribes, the Seminoles had contested removal most vigorously, to which any veteran of the First or Second Seminole Wars in Florida could attest. Even after being transferred to their reservation on the Canadian River in the Indian Territory, the Seminoles continued to be recalcitrant troublemakers, especially among the neighboring Cherokees. With five companies, Kearny marched through rough country to settle accounts once and for all with the Seminoles.

When Nacklemaha, the Seminole chief, responded to Kearny's request for a parlay, he arrogantly proceeded to inform the colonel that his people did not like the land to which they had been assigned. They preferred the land given to the Cherokees. That, replied Kearny, was just too damned bad. He ordered the Seminoles to depart at once for the Canadian. Instead, they made a break for open country. Kearny pursued, executing a perilous crossing of a rain-swollen river, and captured the Seminoles without the loss of a single life on either side. Nacklemaha realized then that he had met his match in Kearny, a man of iron will and steel nerves who would have his way regardless of the obstacles in his path. Thereafter, the Seminoles made relatively little trouble.

On another occasion the caravan of an Albuquerque trader, laden with furs and gold bullion, was ambushed by a gang of Texas plunderers led by one "Captain" McDaniel. Border desperados like McDaniel claimed to have commissions issued by the Republic of Texas to prey on the New Mexican caravans, in the same way that privateers used letters of marque to prowl the seven seas in search of booty. Falconer believed such Texas commissions had in fact been issued. But, commission or not, Kearny considered McDaniel and his gang nothing more than common road agents and ordered a vigorous manhunt, which finally led to the apprehension of the Texans. McDaniel and one of his cohorts were tried and hanged, and the rest imprisoned, prompt justice which, Falconer testified, had gone a long way toward making the Santa Fe Trail a safer route to travel, since other Texas raiders thought twice about tangling with Colonel Kearny and the First Dragoons.

By the time he reached Fort Leavenworth, Delgado was eager to meet this man Kearny, who had only recently been promoted to the rank of Brevet Brigadier General. His wish was immediately granted. Upon being informed of the arrival of Falconer's party, the general requested their presence in his office, forthwith. While he and the frontiersman greeted one another like old friends—and Kearny elicited Falconer's agreement to serve as the expedition's chief scout—Delgado had a moment to take Kearny's measure. He saw a man in his early fifties, yet fit and trim, without an ounce of fat on his athletic frame, impeccable in his dark blue uniform, with a firm, determined mouth and a direct, almost piercing gaze.

Delgado had wondered how he would be received by Kearny, who was, after all, the man who prepared to lead an expedition against the Republic of Mexico, but if Kearny had any doubts regarding Delgado's loyalties, he did not reveal them.

"I am glad to meet you, sir," said Kearny, proffering a hand, which Delgado took in his own firm grasp. "I am sorry I did not have the time to do so in St. Louis. As you are a resident of Taos, I wonder if you are acquainted with Governor Armijo?"

Delgado smiled. The pleasantries attended to, it was right down to business with Kearny.

"Yes, I know Manuel Armijo fairly well."

"The Santa Fe traders have brought me rather uncomplimentary reports of the governor. They say he is an avaricious, unscrupulous rogue. That he wears flashy uniforms to impress the Indians and mestizos. And that, like the coyote, he is cunning and cowardly. What do you say?"

Delgado paused, crafting his response judiciously. "Manuel Armijo once told my father that it is better to be thought brave than to be so."

"The president's advisers tell him my force will encounter only slight resistance from such a man. On the other hand, I've heard a rumor that Armijo has called for five thousand volunteers to meet us on the field of battle. They are to be commanded by a militia officer named Diego Archuleta."

"It is hard to say about Armijo, General. He may be greedy and tyrannical, and he may even be a coward, but he is no fool. No, sir, on the contrary. He is a very clever fellow, who is able to use both the Indians and the local priests as he pursues his schemes. If he believes he can somehow profit by war, he is capable of stirring the people into resistance. But if he thinks he can profit more by cooperating with you, then he will present you with the keys to the city."

"I see." Kearny was clearly pleased by the tenor and quality of Delgado's reply. "Then perhaps I should extend the olive leaf to Armijo with one hand, while I draw my sword with the other."

"General, the Mexican government has virtually abandoned New Mexico. It has never been able to protect the people there from Indian raids. Its soldiers more often prey on the people rather than protect them. Extremely high taxes have been levied, and the merchants must pay duties so high they amount to extortion on the goods that come into the province from the United States. Ever since the province of Texas successfully revolted, New Mexico has been contemplating rebellion."

"So you are saying that the province is ripe for conquest?"

Delgado shrugged. "That depends in large measure on how you handle the situation, sir."

Kearny nodded. "Understood. I am a soldier. Diplomacy is not one of my virtues. But I suspect I shall have to make it so, somehow. Mr. McKinn, would you consider acting as my envoy in this matter? Or, at the very least, my adviser? You know the people we will have to deal with far better than do I or anyone else in my command."

Delgado was taken aback. This was a grave responsibility Kearny was offering him, and his first instinct was to refuse it. But he did not want to antagonize the general.

"I will do what I can to prevent bloodshed," he replied. "As long as whatever I do does not have an adverse effect upon my family or my father's business."

"Very diplomatic," said Kearny wryly. "I see

you have the requisite skills for the task at hand. Very well, then, we will leave it at that for the time being."

"Let me say one more thing, General. I have heard some Americans express the opinion that the Mexican people are an inferior race who will not stand or fight, or who, if they do fight, will be easily beaten. I hope you do not share that opinion, sir. I know these people. They are proud and prone to be fiercely independent. Armijo may be tyrannical in his habits, but even he is wise enough not to push the people too far, or to try and fool them into thinking he is not robbing them of their freedoms."

"Thank you, Mr. McKinn. I will take your advice to heart."

"I hope I have not offended you by anything I have said."

"On the contrary. I appreciate a forthright man." Kearny turned to Jeremy. "So, Lieutenant Bledsoe. I understand you have resigned your commission in the Army and joined the volunteers."

"I had no choice, sir," replied Jeremy. "After being wounded at Resaca de la Palma, the Army placed me on the inactive list. To be removed from that list requires an assault on the War Department bureaucracy, and you must know yourself how long and frustrating such an endeavor can be."

"So you were afraid the war might be over before you could get back into the thick of the action, is that it?"

"In a nutshell, sir."

"Well, personally, I believe the war will drag on for years. The Army will miss a man of your obvious qualities, Mr. Bledsoe. But God knows the volunteers can use all the help they can get." Kearny moved to the window from which he could see Fort Leavenworth's parade ground. A company of the First Missouri in their sky-blue roundabouts was at this very moment drilling, much to the amusement of a handful of off-duty Regulars who had gathered to watch the show. Kearny pursed his lips and shook his head. "They are full of enthusiasm. The *rage militaire* has swept the land. But they are blissfully unaware of the awful price in human suffering which men must pay in war."

"There's revenge, too," said Falconer. "It isn't just the Texans who still resent what Santa Anna did during the revolution down there. Men from nearly every state in the Union died at the Alamo and at Goliad. There were fifty Pennsylvanians, five companies of Georgians, and more than one hundred Alabamians among those who were massacred alongside Fannin. Old scores remain to be settled."

"That is precisely what worries me," confessed Kearny. "I must keep a short rein on Doniphan's Volunteers once we reach New Mexico, or we may find ourselves ankle-deep in blood."

2

Missouri's Governor Edwards had called for one thousand volunteers, and though Doniphan's command was known as the First Missouri Mounted Volunteers, Kearny had received authorization from the War Department to turn eight hundred of them into infantry. He gave as his reason for making the request the scarcity of forage around Santa Fe, the wisdom of which was swiftly confirmed by Washington. That suited Doniphan, since many of his raw recruits had arrived on foot, and he would have had a difficult time trying to find enough mounts for a thousand men.

Part of the problem was that in addition to four thousand pack and draft mules, Kearny had combed the countryside and requisitioned nearly five hundred horses for transport and supply. The general had also commandeered every wagon and teamster in the region. Thousands of head of cattle were rounded up, beef on the hoof.

Doniphan's Volunteers were mustered into service and assigned to their companies as they arrived at Fort Leavenworth. Already, enough recruits had answered the call to arms to fill thirteen companies.

"These men live on the frontier," Doniphan told Jeremy Bledsoe when the latter reported for duty. "They can ride and shoot. No one needs to teach them about guns and horses. It's the rudiments of tactics we must instill in them, and that is where your experience in the Regulars will pay dividends. But I warn you, sir, this will be no easy task. For three weeks they have been drilled morning and afternoon, and believe you me, they do not relish military discipline. The novelty of army life has worn off. These boys can't figure out how strict discipline and monotonous drill and prompt obedience to orders can have much of anything to do with the destruction of Mexicans, for which they seem to have a raging thirst."

Doniphan went on to inform Jeremy that, since it was time-honored tradition for the volunteers to elect their own officers, he was assigning Jeremy to his own staff. "I will encourage all company commanders to consult with you regarding drill. Most of them are as unacquainted as their men with the manuals." The lawyer turned soldier smiled. "In fact, if the truth be known, so am I. Ask me anything about Kent's *Commentaries* or Rawles's *On the Constitution* and you will have your answer. But I must confess I am struggling with the *Carbine Manual.*"

The post surgeon, John Strother Griffin, a veteran army doctor whose better than average medical skills were matched by his talent for profanity, was still conducting physical examinations on the hundreds of volunteers. Because of the rush to put men into the field, the physical exams of volunteers did not often meet War Department requirements. But Kearny insisted that the men who followed him to Santa Fe were to be subjected to physicals in strict accordance with the Army's regulations. The expedition would be an arduous one, and Kearny did not care to be hampered by a long sick train.

Regulations required that the recruit disrobe completely. This was so the inspector could search for brands authorities might have previously applied to the man's flesh. D for deserter, or HD for habitual drunkard, were often tattooed on a hip or under an arm of any man who had already proven himself unfit for military life.

In addition, the doctor looked for obvious abnormalities that might have been successfully concealed by a fully clothed enlistee. Any man with a deformed or missing limb, or flat feet, was immediately rejected, as was any person who happened to be blind, or nearly so, in one eye. The recruit also had to have his own front teeth, and they were to be strong enough to tear open a musket cartridge. A man was asked to stand on one foot and then the other to demonstrate a sense of balance.

These examinations of Doniphan's Volunteers exposed an extraordinary situation on the very day that Delgado and Jeremy arrived at Fort Leavenworth. A man had previously asked for and received permission to bring his younger brother along on the expedition, explaining that otherwise the boy would be left completely on his own and destitute, as their parents had recently drowned during a river crossing. Rumors had begun to circulate regarding the true relationship of the two, so that Doniphan had asked Dr. Griffin to examine the boy, who in the normal course of events would not have been given a physical. The boy turned out to be a young lady, one of dubious virtue, an abandoned female who had served as a camp helper during the day and satisfied the recruit's sexual cravings at night. The woman was sent on her way, and the recruit was tossed into the guardhouse.

After passing the physical examination, the recruit was given a thorough washing. His hair was cut close to his head. He then received his uniform. These were to conform as closely as possible to that worn by a Regular. The U.S. Army infantryman wore sky-blue trousers and a close-fitting wool jacket called a roundabout, a single-breasted garment with pewter buttons and a stiff collar. Most of the volunteers had uniforms that closely approximated this garb.

The law calling the volunteers to service also required the government to provide the recruits with weapons. Many of the men had brought along their own guns, but trying to supply an army with ammunition to fit every variety and caliber of rifle and musket was impossible. As a consequence, Doniphan's men were armed with the standard, government-issue, .69-caliber smoothbore flintlock musket, delivered from a federal armory, in addition to bayonets and cartridge boxes. The cartridge, known as the "buck and ball," contained a round lead ball weighing about one ounce, and three smaller balls, or buckshot, contained in a paper cartridge along with a measure of gunpowder, the whole held together with a combination of glue and string. The shooter tore the end of the cartridge open with his teeth, poured a little powder in the pan, closed the frizzen over the pan, then poured the rest of the powder in the barrel, along with the "buck and ball" and the cartridge paper itself. This was tamped down firmly into the barrel with a ramrod. The musket was then cocked and fired. The flint secured in the cocking piece struck the steel frizzen, which flipped forward, allowing sparks to fall into the gunpowder contained in the pan. The powder, in burning, dropped a spark through a small hole in the barrel, which in turn ignited the main powder charge, discharging the "buck and ball."

Doniphan assured Jeremy that most of the volunteers could shoot, and Jeremy found this to be true, which was fortunate, since the musket was notoriously inaccurate and had a range of approximately one hundred yards. "Test firings," he told Delgado, "have demonstrated that if ten men fire by volley five times at a target two-foot-square at a range of one hundred yards, only five of the fifty balls will hit the target. At a range of two or three hundred yards a man could shoot at you all day and you might never know it."

The problem was not in teaching the volunteers how to shoot, but rather how to handle their weapons according to the manual of arms. Winfield Scott's drill manual was the one currently in vogue. Jeremy discovered to his dismay that quite a few of the volunteers were recent German immigrants who had a less than adequate grasp of the English language. "They don't understand the difference," he complained to Delgado, "between the commands to charge their muskets, charge the enemy, and charge the United States for services rendered!" From what he saw, Delgado could sympathize with his friend. These raw recruits were very raw indeed.

For a week Delgado idled about Fort Leavenworth, trying to stay out of the way. He was anxious to get started on the trek. So was Kearny. But the general had many logistical problems to deal with first. Tent and camp kettles were in very short supply. With so many of his Regulars needed for patrols, he could spare only three hundred dragoons for the expedition. This number was augmented by the one hundred men in an irregular but well-trained unit called Laclede's Rangers, an experienced bunch of mercenaries from St. Louis. As a result, Kearny realized that Doniphan's one thousand men, forming the bulk of what was being called the Army of the West, needed to be as well-drilled as possible. On the other hand, Kearny did not want to linger too long at Fort Leavenworth, for fear that the unruly recruits would be more easily controlled once they were on the march. While here, they had demonstrated a tendency to go over the wall. Some indulged in a little innocent hunting or fishing, while others engaged in pursuits far less innocuous. Peddlers were enjoying a brisk trade selling the volunteers overpriced "Canal Water"—cheap whiskey—and nearby settlements complained about visitations by these frolicksome and usually drunken hell-raisers.

Meanwhile, Hugh Falconer was getting acquainted with the Shawnees and Delawares, some fifty in number, whom Kearny had wisely employed as scouts. These Indians, once members of powerful Eastern tribes, had ventured west to make their living in the fur trade. Falconer knew some of them; they were invariably friendly to the whites, were generally trusted by the mountain men, and had been fixtures at the annual fur trade rendezvous held in the high country for the past twenty years. As a whole they knew and respected Falconer who, among the mountain men, held an exalted position equaled only by the likes of "Broken Hand" Fitzpatrick, Jedediah Smith, William Sublette, and Jim Bridger.

During this time Delgado's thoughts were on Sarah Bledsoe nearly every waking moment. He chafed at the bit, knowing that the sooner he got home the sooner he would get back to St. Louis. At last he confided in Sterling; their acquaintance had matured into friendship, and they spent a lot of time together since both of them had a lot of idle time. They challenged, and in almost every instance defeated, Kearny's officers at whist.

"I would like to write to her," Delgado told the newspaperman. "But I am fairly certain her father will intercept any communication bearing my name."

"I heard about what you and Miss Bledsoe

did," said Sterling, amused. "The two of you brewed up quite a storm in a very short time."

"You don't approve?"

"Oh, no, I didn't say that, my friend. But I can understand Jacob Bledsoe's point of view. He wants to keep you and his daughter apart for the same reason a man would want to keep fire and gunpowder separated. You and Miss Bledsoe are an explosive combination."

"From wanting to keep me in St. Louis for my father's sake, Mr. Bledsoe made a quick turnabout. He couldn't wait to be rid of me. But he will not be able to keep Sarah and me apart. I love her, and she has promised to wait for me. I will return one day soon."

"By that time, Del, I suspect Jacob will have come to his senses. He had his heart set on pairing his daughter with Brent Horan, with his eye firmly fixed on the Horan fortune. But he will not press the issue once he realizes that to Sarah you are more than a passing fancy. He loves his daughter, when all is said and done, and wants her to be happy. And sooner or later it will occur to him that you are not exactly a pauper. You stand to inherit your father's business, I presume."

"Well, yes . . ."

"There you are, then. Don't worry about Jacob Bledsoe. Now, Brent Horan is another matter entirely. You have put a gun to his ribs, and then you stole his girl. I warrant he won't soon forget you."

"I'll worry about that when the time comes."

"Good idea. You can't very well cross a bridge before you come to it, now can you? As for your communicating with the future Mrs. McKinn, the solution is simple. We will attach your letters to my correspondence with the *Enquirer*. There is an individual there upon whom we can rely. He is not only discreet, but resourceful. He is also very loyal to me, as I am responsible for his present position. He will make certain that Miss Bledsoe receives your letters, and her father will be none the wiser."

"But how?"

"Clarisse will serve as go-between. She is devoted to Miss Bledsoe. And my associate, in turn, is devoted to Clarisse. So you see, for every problem there is a solution."

That evening Delgado wrote his letter, pouring out his heart to Sarah, telling her how much he loved her, how terribly he ached being apart from her, and how determined he was to return as soon as possible so that they could begin their life together. The following morning this letter, among Sterling's dispatches, headed for St. Louis aboard the downriver steamer.

3

With no enemy within hundreds of miles, Kearny had seen no risk involved in dispersing his force. Within a few days of Delgado's arrival, he had sent three companies of dragoons down the trail to Santa Fe, and now, a week later, he dispatched several companies of the First Missouri Volunteers.

"Forage and firewood will be a problem, especially as the summer progresses," he explained to Sterling, who assured the general that his readers would want to know why the Army of the West was being conveyed westward in a piecemeal fashion. "Tomorrow, Colonel Doniphan will depart with the remainder of his regiment. I shall follow the day after with the rest of my dragoons. Doniphan will be in charge of the wagon train and the cattle herd. In all, we shall field sixteen hundred men. You will see, Mr. Sterling, that our advance will be more timely, and more comfortable for all concerned, if we are not all bunched together in a single column."

On the evening prior to their departure from Fort Leavenworth, Kearny invited Delgado, Falconer, and Sterling to dine with him and his staff officers, which included Surgeon John Griffin and Lieutenant William Emory. The latter headed a detachment of Topographical Engineers recently sent from Washington to accompany the army. It was a hearty meal consisting of beef steaks, glazed duck, fresh vegetables culled from the fort's prospering gardens, cherry cobbler, and plenty of hot coffee and brandy.

"Gentlemen," said Kearny after everyone had eaten their fill, "I have just today received two communiques which I am confident will be of interest to you. One is from Charles Bent, who only recently left the Taos and Santa Fe area. He has met with Governor Armijo, and the governor told him that he was expecting from three to five thousand troops from Mexico, under the command of General Urrea."

"Urrea!" exclaimed Emory. "Is he not the Mexican commander responsible for the Goliad massacre?"

"The very same," replied Kearny, "although I have heard he was merely following the orders of Santa Anna, and actually lodged a formal protest."

"Regardless, he had five hundred Texas prisoners shot down in cold blood," said Emory. "Our volunteers will certainly like to know this."

"I believe we shall have a fight on our hands," remarked Sterling.

"Don't be too sure," said Delgado. "For one thing, I will be very much surprised if Mexico can spare so many troops. For another, perhaps Mr. Bent did not know to inform you that Armijo and General Urrea have a strong dislike for one another."

"I was unaware of that," confessed Kearny. "Mr. McKinn, you have already proven yourself a valuable asset to this endeavor."

"I am only glad to be of service, General."

"I have also been informed, by confidential and reliable sources, that a group of American settlers in California, with the blessings of Captain John C. Frémont, have created the Bear Flag Republic. As you all know, the president has vowed to assist Californians in their bid for independence."

"Don't you think that is rather contrived, General?" asked Sterling wryly. "There are perhaps nine hundred Americans residing in California, less than one tenth of the province's total population. I don't think anyone can honestly say that California as a whole seeks independence from the Republic of Mexico. We all know California is what President Polk is really after. He simply doesn't want it to appear as though we have taken it by conquest."

"Sir," said Emory, "it is well known that British investors hold Mexican bonds in great quantity—bonds which are about to mature, and which Mexico cannot redeem. Britain also holds a mortgage on the province of California as security for the payment of that debt. I have been told, and believe it to be true, that the British will take possession in six months."

Sterling shook his head. "Really, Lieutenant. Your facts are slightly skewed in favor of your politics. The Mexican minister in London offered options on vacant lands in a number of provinces to the bondholders in lieu of cash payment. None of the options have been exercised, nor are they likely to be."

"I take it you are a Whig, sir," said Emory, with distaste.

"I am. And a Clay man, besides. I would have mentioned it before now, but I did not want to ruin anyone's appetite."

Emory chuckled at that. "The Hotspur of Kentucky opposed annexation, and it kept him out of the White House in '44. A majority of the people are on Polk's side in this."

"You may not share with your readers what I am about to say next, Mr. Sterling," said Kearny.

"You may always rely on my discretion, General."

"I know I can. Events in California require us to settle affairs in Santa Fe as quickly as possible, for my orders are to press on to the westward and reach the Pacific coast as rapidly as events allow."

"I may be a Whig," said Sterling, "but I cannot deny that I have always wanted to see California."

"You will get your chance," replied Kearny. "I will leave a contingent behind in Santa Fe in order to secure the authority of Charles Bent, who will replace Manuel Armijo as governor."

"Charley Bent is good choice," said Falconer. "I think Del will confirm that he is greatly respected in Santa Fe. But, General, in light of this information, I must tell you I think I will go no farther than New Mexico with you. Ten years ago I visited California, and saw all I care to see of the place—including the inside of a jail cell."

Kearny nodded. "As you wish. One more thing, gentlemen. As you may all know, the president has been in contact with Santa Anna, who is living in exile in Havana. Santa Anna has promised that if he is returned to power in Mexico, he will guarantee a friendly arrangement with the United States. The Paredes government is on the verge of collapse, and I predict that Santa Anna will have little difficulty taking over. I believe that even as we speak he is on his way to his homeland."

"This is a grave error in judgment on the president's part," said Delgado. "Santa Anna is not to be trusted. The people will rally to him only if he promises to drive the Americans out of Mexico."

"You're saying he will break his promise as soon as he is back in power?"

"I'd be willing to bet on it, General."

"If he does, then we will have to take all of Mexico and be done with it," said Emory. "We won't have much trouble defeating the Mexican army. I mean, my God, Sam Houston and a handful of untrained Texas farmers did it at San Jacinto, and it only took them eighteen minutes."

Surgeon Griffin spoke up. "Did you know that a Cincinnati phrenologist examined the skulls of several Mexican soldiers who fell at the Battle of Palo Alto? He claims that the thickness and measurements of the skull reveal that the Mexican is an ignorant, brutish individual. Personally, I do not hold much with phrenology, but there you are."

"I've heard the wolves who scavenged the battlefield there at Palo Alto preferred the bodies of the Americans to those of the Mexicans," remarked Emory.

"A dubious distinction," said Sterling. "Americans make better carrion."

With a glance at Delgado, Kearny said, "I would not underestimate the Mexican soldier, Lieutenant, if I were you."

"The fact remains," said Emory, "that Mexico is ours for the taking. The people will support us if we make it clear to them that we are their republican brethren, come to fight tyranny, to bestow the blessings of democracy, to free them from oppressive tariff duties and Church levees on the poor."

"And don't forget also to spread the institution of slavery," said Sterling, sardonic.

"This discord over slavery disturbs me deeply," said Emory. "I believe the acquisition of Mexico is necessary to save the Union, sir. The use of slaves is required for the production of money crops such as cotton, which eventually destroy the soil. The system, therefore, only survives by constant relocation, out of the areas where the soil is rendered lifeless. I am from Maryland, and I can vouch that slavery has been in retreat from the border and seaboard states to the south and southwest. It has flowed quite naturally into Texas and Louisiana. Before too very long, slavery will be concentrated in Texas. But, inevitably, the soil there will also be exhausted. The slaveholder will look to Mexico. And yet the soil in Mexico is not suited to his money crops. He will face ruin if he does not then emancipate his slaves.

"The freed slaves will turn southward into Mexico and Latin America," continued Emory, "where prejudice does not exist, and where they have the hope of social equality, a prospect they will never enjoy in this country. So you see, gentlemen, that the annexation of Texas and Mexico will have an effect opposite to that predicted by the abolitionists and other Whig doomsayers. Ultimately, it will cause slavery to disappear from the United States, and with it will go the issue which has proven so divisive."

"I see you are well acquainted with Robert Walker's thesis," said Sterling dryly.

Delgado had heard of Walker, who was currently Polk's Secretary of the Treasury—a Northerner by birth, a Mississippian by adoption, a planter and expansionist who believed slavery to be a transient evil, and who had written a thesis designed to recruit Northern support for Texas annexation, the gist of which Emory had just espoused. The Walker Letter, as it was called, had achieved a circulation of millions.

"Well," said Kearny, "unlike Generals Taylor and Scott, I have no interest in politics. I am a soldier, and as such I advise you gentlemen to be early to bed tonight. Tomorrow will be here sooner than you think."

With that they broke up. Outside, Delgado pulled Hugh Falconer aside. "General Kearny has only a passing interest in what happens in Santa Fe or Taos," he told the frontiersman. "His eyes are fixed on California. When Armijo finds this out, he will be wise enough to wait until Kearny and most of the soldiers are gone before he stirs up trouble. He can no more be trusted than Santa Anna. Both men will smile and shake your hand and earnestly profess eternal friendship—before they stab you in the back."

Falconer nodded. "I'm with you, Del. Which is

why I told the general I was planning to stay behind when he marched on to California. Charley Bent once saved my life, long ago. I think I may get the chance to return the favor." Packing a clay pipe with honeydew tobacco, he shot Delgado a curious glance. "You've heard a lot of poor-talking about the Mexican people. Are you insulted?"

Delgado smiled. "I can tolerate it. I've heard the same kind of talk at home—about Americans. Some of them believe you are barbarians who eat little children for breakfast. As they get better acquainted, each side will discover they have more in common than they have differences."

"I only hope," said Falconer, "that the acquaintance is not made over the barrel of a gun."

Chapter Six

"We'll start with this traitor!"

1

It was the bright, warm morning of the last day in June when Delgado left Fort Leavenworth on the final leg of his long journey home. It was a journey that had begun halfway around the world, that had taken him from London to New York to New Orleans to St. Louis and finally to the eastern terminus of the fabled Santa Fe Trail, a journey that had delivered him from the cloistered halls of Oxford University, steeped in tradition, to the raw frontier among the ranks of stern-faced dragoons marching off to war for the glory and aggrandizement of the young republic called the United States of America. Along the way he found the woman of his dreams. He wondered what he would find at the conclusion of the journey.

Brigadier General Stephen Watts Kearny, astride a sturdy bay horse, waved good-bye to his wife and children and led the way; tall, straight, and lean, he looked to Delgado the perfect soldier. Delgado was glad that the fate of Taos and Santa Fe rested in this man's hands, for he believed that Kearny was an honest, capable, and fair-minded man. Best of all, like most professional soldiers, Kearny was deeply committed to peace. Perhaps more so that the average citizen.

With Kearny rode his staff officers, Emory and

the topographical engineers, a battery of light artillery—mountain howitzers with their brass neatly polished—and the final detachment of the First Dragoons. The latter wore broad-brimmed black hats, blue flannel shirts and trousers, and every one was armed with carbine, two pistols, and a Bowie knife. Delgado and Sterling rode with Kearny's staff. Hugh Falconer had departed at first light to go ahead with a handful of his Delaware and Shawnee scouts.

The first part of their journey was pleasant enough. Crossing the Kansas River, they camped on the west bank among friendly Shawnees. This tribe, which under the leadership of men of genius like Tecumseh and Blue Jacket had wrought havoc for more than a quarter of a century among settlers in Kentucky and the Old Northwest, was now one of prosperous farmers, whose corn fields were as fine as any Delgado had ever seen. The Shawnees supplied the troops with vegetables, milk, butter, and eggs. It would be the last time Kearny's Army of the West enjoyed such luxuries until they reached their destination.

The country here was fertile, with fine rolling prairie and abundant stands of timber. But in the days to come the timber, water and graze grew ever more sparse. Midday temperatures soared to a hundred degrees Fahrenheit and beyond. Men and livestock suffered immensely. In the evenings swarms of mosquitoes plagued them. The water, when it was available, was often rancid or alkaline, and the sick rolls increased at an alarming rate.

One thing the expedition never lacked was fresh meat. Vast herds of buffalo were a frequent occurrence, and often the men could supplement their standard ration of bacon, biscuits, and coffee with a succulent slab of hump meat. When buffalo weren't readily available, there was always the herd of cattle that had been brought along. On the treeless plains the soldiers used buffalo chips in lieu of firewood. Every day men would venture out and skewer the dung patties on their ramrods until they had enough to build their fires.

They saw numerous Indians of various tribes, for this was the season of the buffalo hunt. Hugh Falconer proved his worth a hundred times over, because the Indians invariably knew him or knew about him, and as a consequence there was never any trouble, not so much as a horse turned up missing. Kearny thought this was remarkable, since the Plains Indians had made an art form of horse stealing.

Kearny kept the column moving at a brisk pace. It was not uncommon for the Army of the West to make twenty-five miles in a day. The general seemed to be everywhere, in the saddle from before dawn until after dark, one day with the vanguard, the next day at the rear of the column. Tireless, he kept an eye on every detail. The sore-footed infantry often cursed Kearny for pushing them so hard, and President Polk for issuing a call to glory that had lured them into the rash folly of enlisting. But though they moaned and groaned, the men had complete confidence in their leader.

One day Delgado rode out with Falconer and his scouts. In buffalo country it was Falconer's habit to leave camp about midnight, reaching the site of the vanguard's next camp by first light, so that by the time the weary soldiers dragged in, they would, if all went well, find plenty of fresh-killed game waiting on them. On that day Falconer took Delgado to the top of a rock outcropping to gaze out upon the largest herd of buffalo Delgado had ever seen. The beasts resembled a shaggy brown carpet reaching into infinity. The dust that rose from beneath their hooves turned the sky dun colored. Falconer estimated the herd to number three or four hundred thousand head. "Enough meat for all the armies in the world," said Delgado, awestruck. Falconer nodded. But Kearny had given strict orders against the wholesale slaughter of the buffalo. It had proven difficult to restrain the volunteers in this respect. They were inclined to shoot at anything that moved, just for sport. Falconer and his Indian scouts, though, were a highly efficient team of hunters. Delgado watched them kill the requisite number of shaggies, then swiftly butcher them out. The hides, bones, sinews, and sometimes choice cuts of meat were always given as gifts to the ubiquitous Plains Indians, who always seemed to be hovering nearby; Delgado became accustomed to seeing twenty or thirty of them a day.

Despite the plentiful game, and the peace so meticulously kept with the Indians, the Army of the West suffered casualties. A few men perished by drowning when sudden thunderstorms transformed dry gulches into raging cataracts. Several more were lost to sudden illnesses. A couple were snakebit. One was trampled to death by his own horse. Burial with full honors always followed. Wrapped in a blanket, the deceased was promptly interred. After a brief passage from the Bible was read by an officer, three volleys were fired into the air by an honor guard. Then horses were ridden over the grave until it was indistinguishable from the rest of the prairie—this to thwart scavenging wolves, or Indians who would think nothing of desecrating the grave in search of valuables. Indian dead were buried with all their weapons and finery, and they assumed the white man did the same.

Two weeks out of Fort Leavenworth they saw the white mountains which, according to Falconer, the Indians called Wah-to-yah, the "Breasts of the World." They rose from the plain in sharp contrast against a line of ominous black thunderheads. These were the first real mountains some of the Missouri volunteers had ever seen, and they raised a shout of elation at the sight. The twin peaks were visible proof that they had accomplished a truly remarkable feat—in three weeks' time they had marched nearly five hundred miles!

A few days later, Falconer came riding in to find General Kearny. With him was another legendary mountain man—Tom Fitzpatrick. The buckskinner the Indians called Broken Hand had come from nearby Bent's Fort with news of events in Santa Fe. While the common people of New Mexico were inclined to accept the imminent American occupation without resistance, Manuel Armijo had summoned a council of the province's leading men and convinced them that they would face ruination or worse if they did not try to turn back the Americans. There was, reported Fitzpatrick, no reliable word regarding Urrea and the army of three thousand battle-hardened Mexican Regulars rumored to be on the march from the South.

The following morning Falconer rode into Bent's Fort, only a few miles in advance of the Army of the West.

2

Bent's Fort had been built in 1833 by Charles and William Bent and their business associate, the French-American, Ceran St. Vrain. The oldest of four brothers destined to leave their mark on the American frontier, Charles had been six years old when his parents moved to St. Louis. There he had grown up rubbing elbows with trappers and traders. Thrilled by their tales of life in the untamed wilderness, Charles joined the Missouri Fur Company at a tender age, and then became involved in the lucrative Santa Fe trade. In 1830 he organized the Bent & St. Vrain Company. His partner, though born in Missouri, lived in the Taos area. The partnership prospered, and soon Bent and St. Vrain ruled a commercial empire.

Where Charles was the entrepreneur, his younger brother William was by nature the true frontiersman of the family. It was William, therefore, who saw to the day-to-day operations of the trading post and wilderness stronghold that came to be known as Bent's Fort. Married to a Cheyenne princess named Owl Woman, William had tremendous influence among the Indians, and not only did he cement strong trading relations with the various tribes, to the immense benefit of the Bent & St. Vrain Company, but he also proved instrumental in keeping the peace between the Indians and the pioneers.

Charles Bent spent a lot of time in St. Louis and New Mexico. He was married to an affluent Mexican widow and had established a permanent residence in Taos, becoming one of that community's leading citizens. Bent's Fort was only two weeks' journey from Santa Fe.

Bent's Fort was located on the northern bank of the Arkansas River, a hundred miles east of the Rockies. The walls, fifteen feet high and four feet thick, were built of adobe in the form of a hollow square, and the compound contained twenty-six rooms surrounding a courtyard. There were bastions at two corners, and parapets on all sides, and a small cannon on the wall above the gate, where the Stars and Stripes proudly flew. In the center of the courtyard were three large rooms. One was a storehouse and magazine, another a dining hall, and a third a council room. The fort could accommodate more than one hundred souls comfortably, and on any given day one could find Santa Fe traders, mountain men, Indians, emigrants, and soldiers there. One of the fort's most notable assets was Charlotte, a black woman who served as cook, and who was justly famous for her pancakes and pumpkin pies.

Falconer and Charles Bent were old friends, having met in St. Louis as youths more than twenty-five years earlier. When he heard that the Army of the West was only a few miles away, Bent was overjoyed.

"As you can see," said Bent, "trade with Santa Fe has come to a complete standstill. If something isn't done, and soon, many of our friends will be ruined, Hugh."

Falconer had counted more than a hundred wagons, all filled with merchandise, in a sprawling encampment of idle and disgruntled traders on the other side of the Arkansas River.

"General Kearny is authorized to offer you the position of provisional governor of New Mexico," Falconer informed his friend. "Will you take the job?"

Bent nodded grimly. "It is a task I do not relish, but I will not decline. I have many friends in New Mexico, and I want only the best for them."

"I know, and most of them know that, too. They're bound to prefer you over Manuel Armijo. With any luck we'll pull this off without a shot being fired."

"You've become an optimist in your old age," said Bent, grinning.

When Kearny and his troops arrived, they bivouacked across the river from the fort, near the trader's camp. Kearny dispatched Captain Moore and his company of dragoons on a reconnaissance in the direction of Raton Pass. Moore promptly returned with three Mexican prisoners, whom he declared were spies. These men were incarcerated at Bent's Fort and Kearny turned to Delgado for a favor.

"Go and talk to the prisoners, Mr. McKinn. Find out what they were up to, and what the situation is on the other side of those mountains."

In a few hours Delgado reported back to the general.

"They admit to being spies, General. Armijo sent them. They expect to be lined up against a wall and executed by firing squad. What they have seen of your army has made them despair. They are especially impressed with your artillery. In fact, one of them wept. He asked me what would become of New Mexico. Armijo's got them believing your army has come to rape and pillage."

"I have no intention of executing them," replied Kearny. "I want them to see everything there is to see, and then I will set them free, so that they can report back to Armijo. What do you think of that, Mr. McKinn?"

Delgado smiled. "I think that's a very wise decision, General."

"Tell them we have not come to make war upon the people. I enjoin the citizens of New Mexico to remain quietly in their homes, and not to take up arms against us, as we mean them no harm. If they will do this, I guarantee that their rights, both civil and religious, will be scrupulously respected, and they will not be interfered with in their daily pursuits."

"I'll tell them, sir, and gladly."

Kearny remained at Bent's Fort for a week, making arrangements for the final push across Raton Pass to Santa Fe, and for leaving the sick behind at the frontier outpost. This gave Delgado plenty of time to visit with Charles Bent, whom he knew well; he had been a guest at the wedding of Bent and Maria Ignacia Jaramillo, and the Bents had accepted invitations to the McKinn house on numerous occasions.

"You know, Del," said Bent as he and Delgado and Falconer visited over drinks in Bent's quarters one evening, "in all this talk about the possibility of a clash between the Americans and the Mexicans in Santa Fe, we have overlooked one very important and volatile ingredient. The Pueblo Indians."

"What do you think they will do?" asked Delgado.

Bent shook his head, and Falconer said, "With the Pueblos, there is no way of knowing."

"Well," said Bent, "they were here long before anyone else. They are, after all, direct descendents of the Anasazi, the Ancient Ones. And, though they've been at peace for a long time, they know how to fight. Long before the first conquistador arrived, the Pueblos were defending their homes against the Comanches and the Apaches. Remember, when Coronado came searching for the golden cities of Cibola, the Pueblos resisted and nearly killed Coronado himself."

"Then the missionaries came," said Falconer, "and tried to make good Christians of them, which they didn't appreciate, either."

"Yes," said Delgado, "the Pueblos revolted, led by a chief named Pope. Several of my mother's ancestors lost their lives in that revolt. They drove the Spanish away, and it took my mother's people twelve years to regain control of the province."

Bent sighed. "If Armijo is smart, and he is that, he will try to stir up the Pueblos, too. And if that happens . . ."

He didn't finish. Didn't need to. Both Falconer and Delgado knew what would transpire if the Pueblos Indians revolted. It was not a pleasant thought.

3

The following day, Falconer and a handful of his Shawnees and Delawares, joined by a few of the mountain men who were idling away their time at Bent's Fort, reconnoitered the mountain passes to the south. They returned to Kearny with word that the passes were clear. On August 1st Kearny put Doniphan's Missouri Volunteers on the trail. The day after, Kearny and his staff accompanied the dragoons and Laclede's Rangers as they embarked on the final leg of their journey.

By the fourth day of August they were deep in the Raton Mountains. The snowy peaks of the Sangre de Cristo range seemed to float in the far distance, disembodied above the desert plain. The climb to the divide was an arduous one, and Kearny let his troops recuperate for a day while Falconer and the scouts ventured on ahead into enemy territory. The men enjoyed the scenery, and the cool, wildflower-scented air at seventy-five hundred feet above sea level was refreshing after the stifling heat of the plains below. The pine forests provided them with shade from the summer sun.

Again Falconer came back with news that no sign of a hostile enemy force could be found, and the Army of the West began to descend from the Ratons onto the desert plains, red earth cut through by purple arroyos beneath a dazzling blue Mexican sky.

Delgado felt a stir of excitement. Taos was only a couple of days ride. This was his homeland. He had been away for three long years, and he realized just how much he had missed this country now that he was back.

A man from Taos, a trader, came to sell a quantity of flour to the army, which Kearny was quick to purchase. Delgado knew the man and asked about his mother and father. The trader assured him that, as far as he knew, they were both well. But all was not well in Taos. In these turbulent times the situation could change in a heartbeat . . .

"Governor Armijo has issued a proclamation placing the entire province under martial law," said the trader. "He has called upon all able-bodied citizens to take up arms. He is using the priests to tell the people of the many horrors that the Americans will visit upon them. Many of the people believe these lies, and there are at least two thousand who have answered the governor's call. That includes many Pueblo Indians."

"You take a grave risk, then," said Delgado, "by coming here to trade with the army."

"I have been doing business with Americans for many years. Armijo is a liar. He is only concerned with himself. He knows the Americans will strip him of his authority, and power is life itself to Armijo."

"What does my father think about all this?"

The trader grimaced. "I regret to say this, Delgado, but your father refuses to take a firm stand either way. I, and others, have pleaded with him to speak out publicly for peace. He has great influence, and a lot of people would listen carefully to what he has to say. Excuse me for saying so, but your father has taken the coward's way. He waits to see in which direction the wind will blow the grass."

Delgado did not take offense. After all, this man had risked everything by coming here. In trading with the Americans he was making a very strong statement regarding where he stood on the issue. It was a courageous thing to do, and Delgado respected him immensely for it. And he had to admit that the news of his father's fence straddling did not really surprise him.

"A man must stand up for what he believes is right, my friend," said the trader. "I hope you will be able to persuade your father to do what he knows in his heart he should do. The future of our people must be our foremost concern. I am sure we will fare better under the American flag than we have as part of the Republic of Mexico.

The people have no say in their own government. They remain poor because what they do not pay in taxes to the government they are required to give to the Church. Your father knows all these things. But still he will not act."

"My father has always believed that his first duty is to his family," said Delgado, but he spoke with a noticeable lack of conviction. It was the same tired old refrain, and it did not hold up particularly well against this man's intrepid loyalty to his principles and his people.

That evening Kearny called Delgado to his tent. Falconer was present, along with Lieutenant Emory, and members of the general staff.

"While we were at Bent's Fort," Kearny told Delgado, "I sent Captain Cooke on a confidential mission of the most crucial nature—and one, I might add, that was not without its risks. Do you know Captain Cooke, Mr. McKinn?"

"Certainly," replied Delgado, "and I do not wonder that you have the utmost confidence in him."

Philip St. George Cooke was a bold and resourceful army officer who was much admired in New Mexico. He had been responsible for the capture of a band of Texas freebooters known as Snively's Invincibles a few years ago. In the process he had saved a Santa Fe caravan. Texas, then an independent republic, had lodged a stiff protest with Washington. The United States government had sought to placate Texas by bringing Cooke before a court of inquiry. Kearny had given Cooke strong support during the proceedings. The court ruled that Cooke had acted properly. Now Cooke was devoted to Kearny, and in turn he was the subordinate most trusted by the general.

"Cooke volunteered to deliver a message to Governor Armijo," continued Kearny, "which expressed my earnest desire for peace, along with certain guarantees. I have today received a reply from the governor. He has agreed to meet with me in Las Vegas for negotiations."

"Negotiations!" exploded Emory. Impaled on Kearny's flinty gaze, he cleared his throat and shifted his weight from one foot to the other. "Pardon me, sir, but may I speak freely?"

"By all means."

"By all accounts Governor Armijo is a treacherous individual. We cannot trust him. Besides, we have no need to negotiate. The Mexicans cannot stand against us. They were reptiles in the path of democracy. It is our destiny to have this land, and it is the fervent desire of every soldier in this army to meet the enemy upon the field of battle and prove the superiority of American arms. That is why they have come so far and suffered so much."

"I presume you are referring to the Missourians," said Kearny. "My dragoons came so far and suffered so much because they were under orders to do so. It is my wish to avoid a confrontation. I believe I can reason with Manuel Armijo, and I am bound to try."

"Not to forget," remarked Falconer, "that Captain Cooke's life may depend on it."

"They are holding him as a hostage?" guessed Delgado.

"Yes," replied Kearny. "Mr. McKinn, I know you want to get home to Taos. But I am turning south for Las Vegas in the morning. I want you to come along with me. Your name is known and respected in these parts. In Las Vegas we may face the moment of truth. There, our actions may dictate whether we have peace or war. I want your help, I need it, but I will not force you to go."

Delgado sighed. "I cannot refuse, General, since you put it like that."

"God bless you, sir."

God help me, thought Delgado. He had a distinct feeling that he was getting in way over his head.

4

They marched in a very orderly and impressive array through the green corn fields surrounding the village of Las Vegas. After a long, dry march across the desert from the Raton Mountains, these corn fields, even the chocolate brown water in the irrigation ditches, looked appealing to both men and livestock. But Kearny had issued strict orders that not so much as an ear of corn was to be touched. The private property of the citizens of the town was to be respected. A good impression here was essential to the general's hopes for the peaceful occupation of the province.

Worrisome was Falconer's report that at least six hundred armed men—militia, not Regulars—held the Vegas Pass, a few miles past the village, down the road to Santa Fe.

Kearny halted the column at the edge of town. Las Vegas appeared deserted. The dusty streets were empty and eerily silent. The doors and windows of the low, flat-roofed adobe homes were shut tight. The general summoned Delgado to his side.

"Will you ride in with me under a flag of truce,

Mr. McKinn?" asked Kearny—as always, blunt and to the point.

"Not with you, sir, surely!" exclaimed Lieutenant Emory, who had overheard. "This smells like a trap to me, General. I beg you to reconsider."

Kearny scanned the empty street before him, then glanced at Delgado. "What do you think?"

Delgado was slow to answer. His feeling was that the residents of Las Vegas were merely scared out of their wits. If Governor Armijo and the priests had done their jobs, many of the people honestly believed that the Yankee barbarians would impale their children on bayonets and roast them over their campfires. But what if he was wrong and Emory right? Delgado liked and admired Kearny. If the general was killed, full-scale war would undoubtedly erupt. The Army of the West was fiercely loyal to its commander, there would be no restraining or reasoning with them if Kearny was shot down—especially if the deed was done from ambush.

"I will go in, and gladly," said Delgado. "But not with you, General. You would be taking too great a chance."

"I am a soldier, Mr. McKinn. That's my job, and it's for me to worry about."

"No, sir, I respectfully disagree. Without you there will be no peace."

"Well," said Kearny, mollified. "I hadn't looked at it from that point of view. Are you acquainted with the alcalde of this town?"

"I know of him. And I think he will recognize my name."

"You know what to say to him?"

Delgado nodded. "I think so, General."

"Then I will trust you to speak for me."

Falconer was sitting his tall coyote dun nearby, listening. Now he spoke up. "I'm riding with you, Del."

"That isn't necessary." Delgado didn't want Hugh Falconer to ride into an ambush either.

"Part of the reason I'm here is to get you home in one piece. I intend to do just that."

Delgado knew nothing would be gained by debating the point. The mountain man's mind was made up—and that was the end of that.

They rode in stirrup to stirrup, Delgado holding the truce flag, a piece of white cloth tied to a musket's ramrod. Falconer kept his Hawken mountain rifle in its fringed buckskin sheath, but it rode across the saddle, and Delgado figured the frontiersman could bring the long gun into play in the blink of an eye. Maybe quicker. Delgado prayed it would not come to that.

Entering the square, they saw several men emerge from an adobe into the bright summer sunshine. One was an older man, gaudily garbed in a maroon claw-hammer coat, with a gold vest straining to stretch over his paunch. White hair beneath a broad-brimmed hat framed a walnut brown face creased by the passage of many years. He was flanked by two younger men, both of whom were armed.

Delgado rode straight up to the men. Dismounting, he identified himself to the elder, who, as he had surmised, was the alcalde of Las Vegas. His name was Herrera, and Delgado could tell he was striving to conceal his anxiety with a gruff exterior. While scanning the rooftops, Falconer tried to keep one eye on the two scowling men with Herrera—they both had a pistol and a knife in their belts. His instincts warned him that the pair with Herrera weren't the only threat—instincts finely honed by playing cat and mouse with often hostile Indians in the deep woods of the high country. You often did not see an Indian until he was in the process of taking your topknot.

"I know your father," the alcalde told Delgado. "Is he aware that his son is a traitor?"

That struck the flint of Delgado's temper, but he endeavored to keep his anger in check. "Am I a traitor because I want to keep the peace?"

His earnestness appeared to give the alcalde second thoughts. But one of the younger men spoke up. His tone and demeanor was so truculent that, for the moment, Falconer gave him his undivided attention.

"You are the lackey of the Americans," sneered the man, laying a hand on the butt of his pistol. "They have come to plunder and rape."

"You don't know what you're talking about," replied Delgado sternly. He turned back to the alcalde. "You are a wise and reasonable man, Senor Herrera. You must realize that this is inevitable."

The alcalde knew exactly what he meant, but he wasn't quite ready to admit it.

"If they come in peace, why so many soldiers?" he asked.

"Because Armijo and men like him are willing to sacrifice your lives to hold onto their power."

"Armijo has run away," said the alcalde bitterly. "He lost his nerve and fled into Mexico when he heard that the government would not send troops to support him."

Startled by this news, Delgado glanced at Falconer. He was relieved to know that Armijo was gone. This greatly reduced the chance of war. Obviously, the wily governor had never intended to keep his appointment with General Kearny. He had been buying time.

"Are you certain of this?" asked Delgado. There had been so many rumors. Perhaps this was just one more.

The alcalde nodded gravely. "We were prepared to fight to protect our families and our homes. But the governor deserted us."

"Your homes and families will be protected. General Kearny swears it, and he is a man of his word. Unlike Manuel Armijo, I might add. All I ask is that you hear him out, Senor Herrera. Then you can make up your mind."

Seeing that the alcalde wavered, the man who had previously spoken stepped forward.

"Don't listen to him! The Americans will rob us. They will violate our women. Murder our children. They will turn us into slaves."

The alcalde frowned. "You know the Americans," he said to Delgado. "Is it not true that they believe all people whose skin is darker than their own are inferior to them? Do they not force such people to live in bondage?"

Delgado was taken aback by the question. Images flashed through his mind—of Brent Horan buying the mulatto girl, Naomi, on the lane behind the levee in St. Louis; of the slavecatcher, Talbott, bringing the dead field hand out of the woods, surrounded by his hounds; of the abolitionist, Jeremiah Rankin, on the verge of hanging for his sins aboard the side-wheeler *Sultana*. Snippets of conversations came to him, too—"reptiles in the path of democracy," "a mongrel cross between the Negro and the Indian," "the Mexican is a rather ignorant, brutish individual."

How can I defend men who do and say such things? wondered Delgado. *Why would I even want to?* On the face of it, the alcalde's concern was a valid one. The history of the Americans made it so. On the subject of liberty and equality of opportunity, they talked a good game, but their actions left a lot to be desired.

His hesitation birthed a light of grim exultation in the eyes of the alcalde's young hotspur. "You see?" exclaimed the man. "He knows what I say is true. We have no choice, Alcalde. We must fight! We must drive the invaders from our land, or let our soil drink their blood. And we will start with this traitor!"

With these words the man sprang forward, drawing the pistol from his belt, planting it in Delgado's chest before the startled Delgado could react.

Falconer struck the pistol down with the sheathed barrel of his rifle. The pistol discharged. The bullet plowed into the red dust inches from Delgado's foot. Then the mountain man struck Delgado's would-be-assassin in the face with the butt of the Hawken. The man fell like an axed tree, out cold. His cohort moved as though to bring his own pistol into play, but Falconer swung the rifle in his direction. The glimmer in the frontiersman's eyes froze the young New Mexican. In that same instant a dozen men seemed to materialize out of thin air on the rooftops ringing the square. They all had muskets or rifles, and they were aiming their weapons at Delgado and Falconer. Delgado felt a curious tingle start at the base of his spine and spread quickly through his body. At that moment, on the brink of death, he never felt more alive.

"*Espere!*" cried the alcalde. "Wait! Manolo, put down your weapon."

"But, Father—"

"Do as I tell you!"

With a glower at Falconer Manolo laid his pistol on the ground.

"Now look to your brother," said the alcalde sternly.

"Your son?" asked Falconer, who knew enough Spanish to get by. He glanced at the unconscious man sprawled at his feet.

"Yes," said the alcalde gravely.

"I'm sorry, but I had to do it."

"I am glad you did not kill him. You could have. And," added the alcalde, looking apologetically at Delgado, "I am glad my son did not kill you, Senor McKinn."

"Will you at least listen to what General Kearny has to say, Alcalde?" pleaded Delgado, trying to appear unrattled.

"Yes. I will hear him out."

5

As it happened, all the people of the village of Las Vegas listened to General Kearny. Accompanied by the alcalde, he addressed nearly two hundred locals gathered in the square, who had been coaxed out of hiding by Herrera's assurances that no harm would come to them. Delgado admired the old man; it had required of him a great leap of faith, but he yearned to avoid bloodshed, too. Kearny stood on the flat roof of one of the buildings facing the square, with Herrera and the captain of the local militia.

"People of New Mexico, I have come here on the orders of my government, to take possession of this country and extend over it the laws of the United States. We come as friends, not as enemies, as protectors, not plunderers. We come among you for your benefit, not for your injury. Henceforth I absolve you from all allegiance to the government of the Republic of Mexico, and from all obedience to Governor Armijo. He is no longer your governor."

This caused quite a sensation among the civilian listeners.

"For the time being, I am your governor," continued Kearny. "I shall not expect you to take up arms against those of your own people who may oppose me. But I tell you that those who remain peaceably at home, tending to their crops and their herds, shall be protected by me and by my soldiers, in their property, their persons, and their religion, and nothing they possess shall be disturbed or taken by the men under my command without payment or the consent of the owner. But if any person promises to live in peace and *then* takes up arms against me, he will hang.

"You have never received protection from the Mexican government. The Apaches and the Navajos come down from the mountains and carry off your sheep, and sometimes even your women and children. My government will correct this. We will protect you.

"I know you are all good Catholics. Your priests have told you all sorts of stories about the Americans. These stories are false. My government respects your religion and allows every person to worship his Creator as he sees fit. Our laws protect the Catholic as well as the Protestant, the weak as well as the strong, the poor as well as the rich."

Kearny turned to the alcalde and the militia captain. "The laws of my country require that all men who hold office must take an oath of allegiance. I do not wish to disturb your form of government, and if you are prepared to take such an oath, I shall continue you in office and support your authority."

Both men wavered, but finally relented under Kearny's steely gaze. Once the formality had been observed, the American soldiers gave three rousing cheers. The civilians responded in a more lackluster manner.

That same day the Army of the West resumed its march on Santa Fe. As they drew near Apache Pass, Kearny sent the dragoons ahead, sabers drawn, even though Falconer had earlier seen no sign of resistance. The pass was still clear. Just beyond they were joined by Captain Cooke. Kearny learned that his favorite officer had been present at a meeting between Manuel Armijo and Colonel Diego Archuleta, commander of the provincial militia, in the Palace of the Governors. It was there that Armijo had suddenly decided not to defend Santa Fe, after all. Archuleta had vigorously protested against capitulation, but Armijo stood firm. No longer a hostage, Cooke was released.

"Armijo told Archuleta that they would cede only the northern part of the province," Cooke informed Kearny. "Then he headed for points south in all haste, and left Archuleta as acting governor."

"To reach California I must cross the lower, or Rio Abajo, portion of New Mexico," said Kearny, frowning. "Do you think Archuleta will resist us?"

"He probably won't as long as he believes only the north will be given up. But if he does resist us, we'll be in for one bloody scrape, General. He's that kind of a man."

Kearny grimaced. "So I must mislead him to keep the peace."

"I would heartily recommend that course of action, sir. At least until we are in possession of Santa Fe."

"Thank God Armijo let you go."

"He's no fool, sir. He's hedging his bets, just in case he gets captured, hoping he'll be as well treated as I was. And I was—no thanks to Archuleta. I think he would have preferred to see me shot."

The following day, before the army marched the last twenty miles through pine-covered hills to Santa Fe, Kearny had General Order Thirteen read to all his troops. In it he demanded that every soldier respect the persons and property of the inhabitants of New Mexico. Failure to do so would result in the most severe punishment.

They entered the New Mexican capital in the afternoon. All day it had been raining; now, suddenly, the rain stopped, and the sun broke through the dispersing clouds. Kearny rode at the head of the column, followed by his dragoons. In spite of having just made an arduous nine-hundred-mile journey, Delgado thought the Regulars looked impressive, the first company mounted on black horses, the second on white, and the third on sorrels. Then came Doniphan's Volunteers, looking hardly less gallant and martial than the dragoons.

They were met by several functionaries at the Palace of the Governors. These men seemed to capitulate with as much grace as one could be expected to muster. At Kearny's order, dragoons rigged a flagpole on the roof of the palace so that the Stars and Stripes could be run up atop the seat of provincial—now territorial—government. Drums rolled as the soldiers presented arms in the square. From a ridge outside the city, Kearny's thirteen artillery pieces made their thunder. As a magnificent sunset painted the western sky in bold strokes of gold and crimson, Kearny appeared to make a statement to the hundreds of civilians who stood, quiet and somber, in the square. It was essentially the same speech the general had given at Las Vegas, and the response was just as subdued. Most of the town's populace, judged Delgado, remained in their homes, fearing the Americans would be set loose upon them like a pack of wild, ravening dogs.

That evening Delgado slipped away and took a stroll. The clouds were gone, and millions of stars glittered in the night sky. At this elevation over a mile above sea level, even in summer the nights were refreshingly cool. The crooked narrow streets of Santa Fe were dark and silent. The dragoons had bivouacked in or near the square, as their commander and his staff were quartered in the Palace of the Governors.

Delgado knew this town well. He had often come here from Taos, which lay only seventy miles to the north. The population of Santa Fe numbered no more than three thousand. The square, which was fronted on the north side by the palace and on the other three sides by the shops of merchants and traders, was the commercial heart of the province. Delgado was accustomed to seeing it filled with Mexican farmers and Indians from the nearby pueblos, selling their wares, with mule trains constantly entering the town laden with the manufactured goods that were always in such great demand. There was no sign of such commerce now. The shops, like the houses, were closed up tight. The people lurked behind closed doors, some afraid, some sullen, a few perhaps pleased with the change. But only a few, mused Delgado. The change had come so suddenly. Perhaps in time the people would come to accept it.

Returning to the vicinity of the palace, he found Sterling in the shadows of the long front gallery, the tip of the long, thin cigar he was smoking a pinpoint of orange heat in the gloom.

"Well, McKinn," said the newspaperman, "the deed is done. And with considerably less violence than I expected—or the Missouri volunteers hoped for."

"Listen," said Delgado. "Do you hear that?"

"What? I don't hear anything. All is quiet."

"Too quiet. The dragoons are silent. Usually someone is playing a fiddle, or singing a song, or there is loud talking around the campfires."

"Come to think of it, you're right. What do you make of it, my friend?"

"They're worried. This has been too easy."

"Well, General Kearny is bound for California, and he'll waste precious little time getting started. As I understand it, Doniphan and his regiment will wait here until Charles Bent is secure in his new role as governor, and then they are bound for Mexico to join Old Rough and Ready Taylor's army."

"And you? Where are you bound?"

"I would very much like to see California. You?"

"I suppose I will be going home tomorrow."

Sterling extended a hand. "I shall expect to see you back in St. Louis before too very long. I also anticipate, with relish, an invitation to your wedding."

Delgado grinned as he shook the newspaperman's hand. "You can count on that."

He met Falconer inside the Palace of the Governors. The mountain man was on his way out, a wry smile on his weathered face.

"The general visited Armijo's office a while ago," said Falconer. "Found a pair of human ears nailed to the wall."

Delgado nodded grimly. "That sounds like the Armijo I know. What did the general say?"

"Not much. You're bound for Taos, I guess."

"In the morning."

"I'll be going along."

Delgado sighed. "I'll make it the rest of the way safely, Hugh."

"I know that. But there are some old friends up that way that I want to see. Simeon Turley lives at the Arroyo Hondo, and you can always find a few of my kind lingering there, drinking up his liquor."

"You're not going to Mexico with Jeremy?"

"Don't know. I'll make a decision about that when the time comes."

"There is something else," said Delgado. "You know it's not over here, don't you?"

"No, it's not over," said Falconer, his smile fading. "Kearny thinks so, but he's dead wrong. There's big trouble brewing. I can almost smell it."

Chapter Seven

"Keep your eyes open and your guns loaded."

1

The return of his only son after a three-year absence should have been cause for great rejoicing for Angus McKinn. Yet Delgado found his father troubled and strangely aloof. He would not speak of the cataclysmic changes that were occurring in the province. Delgado had the impression his father was hoping that if he ignored all the turmoil it would just go away. Since the American conquest seemed an accomplished fact, Delgado did not mention the Taos trader he had met a fortnight ago in the army encampment, the man who had been making a statement by selling flour to General Kearny's quartermaster, and who had enjoined Delgado to persuade his father to take a firm stand on the issue of the American occupation.

All that Angus McKinn would say was that he had hoped his son would have demonstrated the good sense to stay in St. Louis for a while, as he had wanted him to.

"I could not stay, for two reasons," replied Delgado. "One is that I wanted to be with my family during these troubling times. For another, I abused Jacob Bledsoe's hospitality, and a man wanted to challenge me to a duel."

Over a homecoming dinner of wild duck, boiled

custard, and Madeira, he told his parents about Sarah, and Brent Horan, and the rescue of the abolitionist, Jeremiah Rankin. He told them the whole story, the unvarnished truth, omitting nothing, and saving for the end the revelation that he was in love with Jacob Bledsoe's daughter, and she with him, and that he would return one day soon to St. Louis to claim his bride, regardless of the risks.

Recovering from his surprise, Angus looked pleased. "Well, my boy, I didna think you would ever settle down into marriage. This is good news. I suppose she is a bonny lass?"

"Angus!" scolded Juanita McKinn.

"What? What did I say?" Angus feigned innocence.

"Yes," said Delgado, smiling. "She is the second most beautiful woman in the world."

"The second?" queried his mother, mystified.

"Next to you, Mother."

Angus chuckled. "You're a sly devil, Del. I'll give you that. This is grand news. By this match, why, you and your bride will one day rule a vast commercial empire."

"Really, Angus," sighed Juanita. "Is that all you ever think about?"

"What's wrong with thinking about it? For Christ's sake, woman!"

Juanita winced. A devout Catholic, she had not grown accustomed, even after twenty-five years of marriage, to the casual profanity of her husband.

"I wish Jacob Bledsoe was as keen on the idea as you are, father," said Delgado.

"Don't worry your head about old Jacob, lad. He'll come around to seeing the good of it. You and I will go to St. Louis with the spring caravan, and I'll talk some sense into him."

"The spring! I'm not sure I can wait that long, Father."

"There are plenty of young and available senoritas right here in Taos to amuse you until then."

"Angus McKinn," said Juanita curtly. "That is a horrible thing to say. If Delgado is in love with this girl, as he appears to be, he will have absolutely no interest in other women. Nor should he."

"I was merely suggesting that he enjoy his freedom while he may."

"His freedom!" Juanita's dark Spanish eyes flashed fire. "So you think of marriage, perhaps, as a life sentence in prison?"

Realizing he had well and truly put his foot in his mouth, Angus grimaced. "I didna mean to imply any such thing, woman," he growled.

Suppressing a smile, Delgado excused himself and rose from the table. His parents were both willful and outspoken people, and they often clashed in this way, only to mend their fences later. It was good to know that some things never changed.

He was glad, in a way, that his father had refused to discuss the coming of the Americans, for that exonerated Delgado from having to defend his own actions as General Kearny's unofficial envoy. He did not regret having done his part to prevent bloodshed, but he had to wonder how Angus McKinn felt about his activities on behalf of the Americans.

The days that followed were uneventful. Like Angus, all of Taos seemed to be living in a state of denial. Delgado could find no one who was inclined to discuss the current state of affairs. The people went about their business with a grim determination to pretend that nothing unusual had occurred, and that their lives would go on just as before.

Two weeks after Delgado's homecoming, Jeremy Bledsoe showed up in Taos, bringing with him a lot of important news.

Kearny had gone out of his way to allay the fears of the New Mexicans and win their trust. He had immediately abolished a stamp act and other burdensome levies under which the New Mexicans had been laboring for many years. Though himself an Episcopalian, the general was regularly attending mass at St. Francis Church. He had given a ball at the Palace of the Governors to which the "common people" had been invited. At least five hundred Santa Feans had accepted the invitation. The ballroom had been festooned with the flags and banners of the Army of the West. A good time had been had by all, said Jeremy, who remarked on the numerous attractive senoritas who had graced the affair with their presence.

The general had issued a bill of rights for the new territory of New Mexico, consisting of thirteen sections and obviously derived from the Declaration of Independence and the first ten amendments to the Constitution of the United States. Called the Kearny Code, it had been written in large part by Alexander Doniphan, an accomplished lawyer in civilian life.

"Confidentially," said Jeremy, "Colonel Doniphan has informed me that in his professional opinion the code is completely unconstitutional. Only Congress can confer civil rights upon the people of New Mexico. Still, it is a smart move on the general's part, and should go a long way toward allaying the fears of the populace."

Delgado agreed, then learned that Jeremy's visit was not entirely a social call; he had brought along a stack of handbills that included the Kearny Code in both Spanish and English, and which he was charged with distributing in Taos.

"We've had more rumors concerning Manuel Armijo," said Jeremy. "They say he has joined forces with five hundred Mexican Regulars somewhere to the south. So General Kearny has taken his dragoons and Laclede's Rangers to investigate." Jeremy grimaced. "Leaving us Missouri volunteers to look after Santa Fe—where absolutely nothing is going to happen."

Delgado smiled. "Glory is an elusive creature, isn't it? I wouldn't worry about Armijo. By running away he lost the support of the people. The dragoons will have a long, hard march and nothing to show for their efforts at the end."

"Where's Hugh Falconer?"

"He left as soon as we arrived here, and I assume he is still at Turley's Mill."

"Let's pay him a visit, Del. What do you say?"

Bored and restless, Delgado was quick to agree. "We will leave first thing in the morning," he said.

But he came very close to never seeing the morning.

2

For some reason he could not sleep, tossing and turning well into the night. The house was silent. Everyone else had turned in long ago, including Jeremy, who had been given the guest room next door to Delgado's room. Finally, disgusted, Delgado threw aside the covers and went to the narrow louvered doors that provided access to the courtyard and pushed them open. Perhaps some cool night air would help him sleep. The McKinn house was shaped like a U with squared-off corners, and every room opened onto the courtyard, from which one had a fine view of the snow-clad peaks. Delgado could tell at a glance that there were no lights on in any of the other rooms. Apparently, no one else in the household was afflicted with insomnia.

He went back to bed—and still he could not sleep. He got up again, angry now, and lighted a candle, and sat down in his nightshirt at the old walnut secretary, intent on writing another letter to Sarah. He had written one yesterday, and another the day before. At least part of what bothered him was that she had not written back. Or, at least, he had not received a letter from her. He told himself that this was probably because the war had disrupted travel on the Santa Fe Trail. But, now that by all appearances the American occupation of New Mexico had been peacefully accomplished, that was beginning to change; some of the traders he had seen whiling away the days and weeks at Bent's Fort had started to show up in Taos and Santa Fe. The trail was opening up again. The great artery of trade was once more flowing freely.

So why had he not heard from Sarah? As Sterling had suggested, he was still sending his letters to the offices of the St. Louis *Enquirer,* care of a Mr. Stephen Maitland, the fellow Sterling had said was in love with Clarisse. But perhaps the arrangement wasn't working as Sterling expected it to. Perhaps, for some reason, Sarah wasn't getting his letters after all. He had decided to ask Falconer if he could send his next missive by way of Lillian; he hated to involve the Falconers, but he was getting desperate. Of course, Hugh Falconer was an employee of Jacob Bledsoe, and he might not want to risk incurring Bledsoe's wrath by aiding and abetting a relationship between Delgado and Sarah—a relationship which, as far as Delgado knew, Bledsoe still strongly opposed. But Delgado was resolved to risk it and ask Falconer for help. The mountain man would tell him straight out if he didn't want to get involved.

Then there was the other possibility—the one Delgado feared most of all: that Sarah Bledsoe *had* received his letters and just did not *want* to respond. Delgado didn't care to believe this could be the case; he *refused* to believe it. Yet the doubts tortured him just the same. In his case, absence did indeed make the heart grow fonder. But what if such was not the case with Sarah?

In this state of pure mental torment he wrote . . .

Sarah, my dearest love,

I have yet to receive a letter from you, though I have written at least a dozen times since my departure. If you had a change of heart please let me know and release me from this anguish . . .

Pausing, he stared with dissatisfaction at the lines he had written.

It was then that the sound behind him made him turn.

A man was crouched in the open doorway to the courtyard. He was wearing a dark cloak, and the brim of his hat was pulled low over a face partially concealed by a bandanna. His eyes glittered in the candlelight, and the blade of the dagger in his grasp gleamed. Seeing that he had been discovered, the man leaped forward, raising the dagger.

Delgado whirled to face his attacker, overturning the chair in which he had been seated. As the would-be assassin crashed into him, he tried frantically to deflect the blade. He was only partially successful. The steel bit deep into his shoulder. A guttural cry escaped Delgado's lips—a sound that blended fear with pain and rage. He struck back with the only weapon at his disposal—he still had the quill pen in his hand. The sharp steel point tore at his assailant's throat. The man's hot blood spewed onto Delgado's arm. They fell, grappling, over the fallen chair, and then the man broke away, scrambling to his feet, the knife in his hand red with Delgado's blood. He clutched at his throat, though he still had not uttered a sound. Delgado tried to get to his feet, feeling suddenly weak and light-headed. The man turned on him, pure hate blazing in his eyes.

"Traitor!" he snarled and raised the dagger again.

"Del! Del, are you all right?"

This was Jeremy, pounding on the door to the hall so hard that it rattled on its hinges.

The assassin glanced at the door, at Delgado, and then fled into the shadows of the courtyard, an instant before Jeremy burst into the room. Jeremy paled as he saw Delgado's blood-soaked nightshirt.

"My God! What's happened?"

Delgado could not trust himself to speak. He

gestured at the door open to the courtyard. Undaunted by the fact that he was without a weapon, Jeremy rushed out into the night.

Angus appeared just as Delgado, leaning against the secretary, began to lose his balance. Catching his son, Angus laid him gently down on the floor. Jeremy returned from the courtyard.

"Whoever it was, he's gone now. But there's blood on the wall where he went over. You hurt him, Del. Hurt him badly." Kneeling with Angus at Delgado's side, he added, "Don't worry, Mr. McKinn. It isn't a fatal wound."

"Praise God," breathed Angus. "Watch over him. I will go myself for the doctor."

Jeremy nodded. "Who was it, Del? Who did this?"

Delgado shook his head. He had not known the man.

Standing, Angus McKinn trembled with rage. "In my own house," he muttered. "In my own house!"

As he turned to leave the room, Juanita McKinn appeared in the doorway and gasped through the hands that flew to her face as she saw her son on the floor. "Remain calm, woman," said Angus gruffly. "Boil water, and we'll need bandages. Our son will live—which is more than I can say for the bastard who tried to kill him."

3

The next day Hugh Falconer rode into Taos. He found Delgado in his bed, attended by his concerned mother, who had not left his side. Jeremy was there, too. But Angus was conspicuously absent, and when the frontiersman asked his whereabouts, Jeremy announced that the elder McKinn was in the process of turning the town upside down, looking for the man who had tried to kill his son.

"So it has begun," said Falconer.

"What?" asked Juanita. "What has begun?"

"Never mind, Mother," said Delgado. "How did you hear of this so quickly, Hugh?"

"That kind of news travels fast. Simeon Turley tells me he's heard rumors of a conspiracy brewing right here in Taos. A conspiracy by those opposed to New Mexico becoming a territory of the United States."

Juanita McKinn looked up at Falconer, but she said nothing, and there was no surprise in her eyes. The frontiersman realized that this woman, who had lived here all her adult life and knew the people well, was aware of the undercurrent of violence rushing just beneath the placid surface of the province. She wasn't as naive as Delgado assumed. She was just acting as though she were.

"You were to be an example, Del," continued Falconer. "An example to anyone who might contemplate betraying this conspiracy. Since you've collaborated with us Americans, you're a perfect target."

"I think you ought to get out of here," Jeremy told Delgado. "Maybe you could go back to St. Louis. I know one person in particular who would be happy to see you."

"If you'll recall," said Delgado wryly, "there is also a person in St. Louis who wants me dead."

Jeremy shrugged. "That has probably blown over by now." But Delgado thought he was saying that for Juanita McKinn's benefit.

"I won't go," said Delgado. "And that isn't foolish pride talking, either. I can't leave just yet. These people you're talking about, Hugh, have no honor. If they'll send an assassin to murder me in the dark of night, they could try to harm my father or mother."

"I don't care about that," said Juanita. "Your safety comes first."

"But your safety comes first with me. I am staying until this matter is resolved, and that's my final word."

Juanita turned to Falconer. "What can we do?"

"Not much. Wait. Keep your eyes open and your guns loaded. It won't be long."

"I'll ride back to Santa Fe immediately," said Jeremy, "and report everything to Colonel Doniphan. I must convince him—and he must convince General Kearny—to stay until whatever is going to happen happens."

A half hour later, Angus McKinn returned, cold fury on his craggy face.

"No one can tell me anything. Bloody amazing, isn't it, that nary a soul in Taos heard a single word about a plot to murder my son? Or about a man with a peculiar wound to the neck. I thought I had friends here. After all these years I see I was mistaken on that score."

"Now Angus," said Juanita, "perhaps they are too afraid to talk."

McKinn uttered a skeptical grunt in response. He looked sternly at Delgado. "I do not approve of what you've done, lad. You shouldna have been involved."

"I disagree, Father. In something like this a man cannot straddle the fence. He can't, and he shouldn't. Jeremy's sister taught me that."

"I don't object to the Americans taking over," said Angus. "I have no love for the tyrants who reside in the presidential palace at Mexico City. The events of 1824 gave me high hopes, but men like Pareda and Santa Anna have dashed those hopes. I left Scotland to get out from under the English heel, you know. Still, I didna want to jeopardize my business concerns—that is to say, your future, son."

"Well, I've done that for you," replied Delgado. "In the eyes of those who oppose the Americans, I am a traitor. And you, Father, are guilty by association."

Angus sighed and nodded, his expression one of grim resolve. " 'Tis true, and I canna deny it. You know I'll stand by you, Del, and the devil take the hindmost."

4

Delgado spent more than a fortnight recuperating. He was weak as a kitten, having lost a lot of blood, and the doctor admonished him to stay in bed until the wound had completely closed, lest he retard the healing process. For the first week he slept a lot—so much that he began to wonder if something was really wrong with him, something mental rather than physical. He could scarcely keep his eyes open for more than an hour or two. Jeremy told him not to worry. The same thing had happened to him after he'd been wounded at Resaca de la Palma.

After that first week, feeling stronger every day, Delgado began to rebel against his confinement, a rebellion that finally won him the right to spend some time in the courtyard, sitting in the warm sun of late morning, or in the cool afternoon shade.

He parents were afraid that another attempt might be made on his life; Delgado gave that prospect very little thought. Apart from being bored and feeling isolated, his main concern was Sarah Bledsoe. Impatient, he prayed that something—anything—might happen so that the situation here resolved itself. The waiting, the not knowing, was the worst part. Then he could return to St. Louis and resolve *that* situation.

Angus hired several men to guard the house. Falconer told him that these hired hands were practically worthless if their loyalty was to money and not the McKinn family. Delgado thought Falconer was right about that, but Angus kept the men on. He didn't agree with the mountain man. In his book loyalty to money was the kind one could really rely on. For his part, Delgado made certain his derringer was always within easy reach. He would not be caught by surprise a second time.

Jeremy rode to Santa Fe to report the assassination attempt to Colonel Doniphan, and returned a few days later. "The Colonel has assigned me the task of keeping an eye on developments here in Taos," he announced. But it seemed to Delgado that Jeremy's true purpose was to keep an eye on him. Every time Delgado looked up, Jeremy was there. When confronted, Jeremy just smiled and said, "Well, I can't very well let my future brother-in-law get killed, now can I?"

"I don't know that Sarah even thinks of me anymore," admitted Delgado, despondent and feeling sorry for himself. "It all happened so quickly between us. It could be possible that I misconstrued her feelings for me."

"You're selling my sister short."

"Are you sure you want me for a brother-in-law? After all, you were angry that I did not choose to defend her honor against Brent Horan's insults."

Jeremy became very serious then. "You'll have no choice, Del. Mark my words, if you go back to St. Louis, you will have to kill Horan, or he will kill you. Is your love for Sarah strong enough that you are willing to take that risk?"

"It is," said Delgado without hesitation. He did not think it would come to that.

"Then the answer is yes. I would be honored to have Delgado McKinn as my brother-in-law."

The next day Jeremy was in a grim mood.

"I have just received word from Colonel Doniphan that General Kearny is leaving tomorrow, or the next day at the latest. He is going on to California, Del, and taking the dragoons with him. Doniphan says Kearny is convinced that the people of New Mexico are content with the change in government, that there is not and never will be any organized resistance. In a couple of months Doniphan will be on the march, too, south into Mexico." He glanced bleakly at Delgado.

"Leaving Governor Bent and the rest of us to fend for ourselves if Kearny is wrong," remarked Delgado.

Jeremy nodded. "I'm afraid that's the case. Supposedly, another regiment of Missouri volunteers is being formed, and will be on the Santa Fe Trail in a few weeks' time. But I personally don't expect them until early next year."

"Well," said Delgado, philosophically, "that's

where the glory is, Jeremy—California and Mexico. You must admit your volunteers have been spoiling for a fight since they left Fort Leavenworth."

"But the fight will be right here, I'm certain of it. I just can't seem to convince anyone else."

"I'll be sorry to see you go."

"Who says I'm going anywhere?"

"I just assumed that when the First Missouri marched, you'd be going with them . . ."

"I have a few cards up my sleeve," said Jeremy, with a sly wink. "Oh, and something else." He drew a letter from beneath his roundabout and handed it to Delgado. "This is addressed to you. It smells like my sister's perfume."

Delgado's heart lurched in his chest as he took the letter. Jeremy was grinning at him, and only after Delgado had paused, the letter half open, to look pointedly at him did Jeremy remember his manners.

"Oh, I suppose you would like some privacy."

"That would be nice, thank you."

Chuckling, Jeremy left the courtyard. His hands shaking, Delgado finished opening the letter. Would his worst fears be realized? Or his wildest dreams?

My dearest Del,

I have missed you terribly, and I tell you now what I should have told you before you left St. Louis—that I love you with all my heart and soul and I will wait forever, if I must. Only I hope that very soon I can hold you in my arms and smother you with kisses. . . .

Delgado heaved a sigh of relief. All was well. Then he laughed, thinking about Jacob Bledsoe. If Sarah's poor father ever read this letter, he would despair of his daughter ever becoming a proper young lady.

5

A few weeks later, Charles Bent, the newly appointed governor of New Mexico Territory, left Santa Fe and returned to his home in Taos and his wife, Maria Jaramillo. The Bents lived in a modest adobe house on the north side of the plaza, only a few hundred yards away from the McKinn residence. On the morning after his arrival, Bent strolled across the plaza and paid a call.

"I was informed of the attempt on your life," Bent told Delgado. "I feel confident that you are no longer in any real danger."

"I don't know how you can be so sure," protested Angus McKinn.

"There was a conspiracy, true enough," replied Bent. "But we have nipped it in the bud. They were waiting for General Kearny's departure for California. Before they could carry out their plans, an informer came forward. All the ringleaders save two have been arrested. Those two are Diego Archuleta and a man called Tomas Ortiz."

"Archuleta!" exclaimed Angus.

Bent nodded. "The man in charge of Manuel Armijo's provincial militia, and his lieutenant governor. If you recall, he was not happy with Armijo for capitulating without a fight. When he learned that Armijo had lied to him—that more than just the northern portion of the province had been given up—he began to scheme."

"What was the plan?" asked Delgado.

"They were fanning the flames of discontent among the peons and the Pueblos. In the dead of night they were going to take me as a hostage and storm the arsenal at Santa Fe. Every American soldier was to be killed on sight. No quarter would be given. It was a devilish plot. But the danger has passed. My only regret is that we failed to capture those two, Archuleta and Ortiz. Colonel Doniphan has several patrols out searching for them, but I fear the fugitives will make good their escape into Chihuahua.

"Sadly," continued Bent, "it has come to light that a number of Santa Fe's leading citizens were actively involved in the planned uprising. Manuel Chaves, Miguel Pino, and his brother Nicholas, to name a few. Furthermore, we suspect Father Antonio Martinez of playing a key role in inciting the people to revolt. We don't yet have enough evidence against the padre to arrest him."

"What do you intend to do with these men?" asked Angus.

"I will show them more mercy than they intended to show us," replied Bent. "If they agree to take an oath of allegiance to the United States, I will set them free."

"Set them free?" roared Angus. "You canna do that, Charley. They'll have another chance to slit our throats while we sleep."

"It's absolutely the right thing to do, Father," said Delgado.

"I think so, too," said Bent solemnly. "I want to prove to the people that they will be fairly treated as long as I occupy the Palace of the Governors. My predecessor no doubt would have already executed the conspirators."

"It will be seen as a sign of weakness on your part," insisted Angus.

"You've become quite bloodthirsty, Angus."

"Aye, that I have—ever since my son was nearly murdered by one of these rascals."

"Thank heavens you were forewarned, Charles," said Juanita.

"Yes, but it's all over now. To celebrate, I would like to invite all of you to dinner tomorrow evening."

"We'll be there," promised Angus.

"We'd be delighted to accept," said Juanita.

"That's settled, then. If you will excuse me, I have a few more calls to make this morning. Until tomorrow."

That evening, at the dinner table, Delgado announced his intention to return immediately to St. Louis. "If I leave in the next few days," he said, "I should reach my destination before the worst of winter sets in."

"I think you should definitely wait until spring," said Angus. "I'll be sending a caravan up the trail in April. It would be safer for you—"

"I won't be traveling alone, Father," said Delgado. "Hugh Falconer is eager to see his family again. He will jump at the chance to go with me."

"Still," said Angus grimly, "I don't see why—"

"Dear," said Juanita with a smile, "our son has made up his mind. He is in love, and you will not persuade him to stay. I remember how determined you were thirty years ago, even though my family counseled patience."

"Because they hoped you would come to your senses and turn me away," said Angus, chuckling.

"Oh, very well then. But what about Jacob? And this fellow you told us about—Horan?"

"Sarah has written that her father is beginning to come around," replied Delgado happily. "As for Brent Horan, she says he is seldom seen outside of Blackwood these days. His father died a few months ago. They still aren't sure what killed him. Ever since then Horan has kept to himself. It sounds to me as though Horan wants nothing more to do with Sarah. And why should he? She's become what he despises most—an abolitionist."

Angus rose and came around the table. Delgado also got to his feet, not knowing exactly what to expect. His father extended a hand, and when Delgado took it, Angus embraced his son.

"My prayers and good wishes go with you, boy."

"I would not leave," said Delgado, his voice thick with emotion, "except that matters here seem finally resolved."

That very night, when the streets of Taos ran red with blood, he found out how wrong he was.

6

In the early morning hours angry voices in the plaza and an insistent hammering at his front door roused Charles Bent from deep slumber. As he got up to don a heavy cloak over his nightshirt—the night was cold and the fire in the hearth had burned down to embers glowing in a gray mound of ash—his wife, Maria, awoke startled and fearful from bad dreams and asked him what the matter was.

"I don't know, my dear," he replied. "I have

no idea who could be at our door at this ungodly hour."

"Don't go, Charles. Don't open the door."

Bent smiled and gave her a reassuring pat on the shoulder. "Now, now, my dear. There is no cause for alarm."

"I fear for your safety, my husband," she confessed, suffering a strong premonition of disaster.

"Who would wish to harm me? I refuse to believe that these people, whom we know so well, and who know me as a man who has always had their best interests at heart, would threaten me or my family over, of all things, a political issue. My own children have Mexican blood in their veins! And in the early days, before Taos had a doctor in residence, was it not I who nursed so many men, women, and children back to health? No, my dearest Maria, we have nothing to fear from these people."

A moment later, he opened the door to confront a mob of about twenty individuals. Some of them were Mexicans, while the majority were Indians from the Taos Pueblo.

"Two of our people are in jail," said one of the Pueblo Indians. "We want you to release them."

Bent smiled grimly. He felt sure they were just testing him. Would his responsibilities as governor prevent him from doing a favor for his neighbors?

"I cannot interfere with the process of law," he replied, affable. "I could not, even were I so inclined. But I assure you that if it is within my power to show clemency to these individuals of whom you speak, I will do so. What are their names and what are the charges against them?"

A man in the rear of the crowd, whose features

were concealed from Bent by the hood of his cloak, spoke up.

"They are charged with being patriots to their country. For trying to defend their homeland against the American plunderers. From people just like you, Bent."

Bent caught a glimpse of the knife's blade just before it was plunged into his belly. He gasped as the cold steel ripped through him. The man who had attacked him, a swarthy Pueblo, stepped back. Bent clutched at the wound, felt his own hot blood sticky on his hands, and gaped in disbelief at the man.

"In the name of God, what have you done?"

The man in the hooded cloak brandished a pistol and fired. Bent was blinded by the muzzle flash. The bullet struck him in the chin. He reeled backward and fell, then tried to crawl away, tried to shout a warning to his wife and children and the old Indian woman who had been Maria's devoted servant for more than thirty years. As he crawled, the men surrounded him. Grim and silent men, they stood and watched him in his agony. One of them slashed at him with a cane knife, inflicting wounds upon the arms that Bent threw up in a feeble attempt to protect himself. His mouth was full of blood, and he could make only incoherent sounds.

Somehow he reached the courtyard around which his house was built, in the Mexican style. Here the man in the cloak said, "Finish it."

By a supreme effort of will, Charles Bent grabbed the man's cloak and pulled himself upright. He threw the hood back so that he could identify the man who had ordered his execution.

Diego Archuleta's stern, hawkish face was

creased by a faint, chilling smile. "Yes, Governor. It is I, Colonel Archuleta. Did you think I would forsake my country without putting up a fight?"

He shoved Bent away, and the American fell to the cold stones of the courtyard. Archuleta nodded to one of the Pueblo Indians. A cane knife rose and fell. The stroke completely severed Bent's head from his body.

In the shadowed corner of the courtyard, Maria Jaramillo Bent watched her husband die and screamed. Several of Archuleta's assassins started toward her with murder in their hearts, but the colonel stopped them with a sharp command.

"We do not war on women and children," he said. "Come, we have much more work to do this night."

7

It was a gunshot that woke Delgado from a sound sleep, but at first he did not realize it, and lay in his bed, listening, a vague disquiet dwelling within him. He gave some thought to getting out of bed and taking a look around, but the night had turned bitterly cold, and he was pleasantly warm beneath the covers. The coldness of the night was a warning; soon the first snows would fall. He could not delay his departure for St. Louis.

Then he heard the men in the street—voices raised in anger, a horse galloping past the front of the house, another gunshot, this one quite near, and he sat bolt upright as Jeremy entered the room without wasting time with the formality of knocking. Jeremy had his shirt and trousers on, but was barefoot and coatless. He had a pistol in one hand, a saber, still sheathed, in the other, and his shot pouch slung over a shoulder.

"Get dressed, Del," he said, with a fierce calm. "I'll wake your parents."

He was gone before Delgado could form any questions.

Dressing swiftly, Delgado stepped out into the hall, derringer in hand. His mother and father were emerging from their room to join Jeremy, and at that instant all heard a heavy hammering on the front door. Delgado led the way to the front of the house. As they reached the front hall, the door burst open with a splintering of wood, cracking back on its hinges.

The first man through was a Pueblo Indian. Delgado saw the cane knife in the man's grasp and without hesitation raised the derringer and discharged one barrel. The Pueblo was coming at him, and there were others pouring in behind him, but Delgado's attention was fixed on the first man through, and he saw the Indian's features, twisted in a rictus of hate, seem to melt in a black mist as the bullet stuck him in the forehead. His legs ran out from under him, and he hit the floor hard and went into convulsions. The cane knife skittered across the tiles and came to rest at Delgado's feet.

"Out through the courtyard!" yelled Jeremy.

The other end of the hall was filled with men now; they jostled one another as they surged forward. Delgado saw a muzzle flash, then heard the deafening report of a pistol, and his body tensed involuntarily, but he wasn't hit, and he triggered the second barrel of the derringer, firing into the press of men. At the same instant Jeremy's pistol discharged behind him and to his right, so close to his face that Delgado felt the pinprick burn of fleck's of powder on his cheek. Two more of the intruders fell, one sprawling on his face, the other sinking to his knees in agony, and the forward surge of the men faltered. Delgado bent to retrieve the cane knife; he couldn't be certain in the semi-darkness, but the broad blade seemed to have black stains on it—blood.

Then his father lunged forward. "You bloody bastards!" yelled Angus, infuriated. "Get out of my house!"

"Father!" cried Delgado. "Get back!"

A pistol spoke, and Angus McKinn, with a shuddering groan, fell. Delgado dropped to his knees beside him and stared in disbelief at the bullethole in his father's forehead. His lifeless eyes looked right through Delgado.

Jeremy yanked him to his feet. "Come on, Del! For God's sake, come on!"

Delgado had given no thought to retreat. In cold fury he had resolved to stand his ground, to avenge the cold-blooded murder of his father. But of course Jeremy was right. To stand meant to die. And he had to make sure his mother got safely away. They had purchased a few precious seconds by their stern resistance in the hallway. Now was the time to withdraw. He could grieve later.

They turned and ran, following Juanita out into the courtyard, and Delgado realized that in the confusion Juanita had not seen her husband fall. When their prey bolted, the band of assassins gave chase, their bloodthirsty shouts not unlike the baying of hounds.

Reaching the courtyard, Delgado saw that his mother was at the back gate. Juanita was struggling at the stubborn iron latch on the heavy timbered door. Delgado turned, once more to confront the killers. The nearest man raised his cane knife, running full tilt at Delgado, a snarling shout on his lips. Delgado parried the man's downward stroke with almost contemptuous ease, forcing the man off balance. He had mastered the art of fencing at Oxford—had in fact relished the lessons as a break from the seemingly endless hours spent at his studies. The cane knife was a clumsy weapon compared to a rapier, but some of the technique he had learned still applied. With a deft twist and slash—and a twinge of pain from his just-healed shoulder—he opened the man from hip to armpit. The man screamed in agony and fell.

Jeremy had unsheathed his saber and closed with another of the assassins. This one was armed with a club and a dagger, and Jeremy made short work of him. The saber cleaved the man's shoulder, cracking the collarbone, driving him down to his knees and wrenching a guttural cry of pain from his lips. Then a pistol was fired, and Jeremy was spun around, falling to one knee. Delgado helped him up and they ran for the gate which Juanita had forced open. Only now did she realize that her husband was not behind her. She stood with her back to the gate, horror dawning in her eyes, and Delgado pushed her on ahead of him before she could ask the question she did not want to ask and he did not want to answer.

Beyond the gate was a narrow passageway between high adobe walls. Delgado was relieved to see that his mother remained calm; she knew now that Angus was dead, but she had been bred to remain dignified no matter what the situation. Jeremy sagged against Delgado, and Delgado kept him on his feet. "Are you badly hurt?"

"Just a flesh wound," said Jeremy through clenched teeth. "Where now?"

"To the church. It is our only refuge. Hurry!"

They had gone only a few yards when the gate swung open and several of the assassins ventured into the alley. Delgado and Jeremy turned, wielding cane knife and saber, ready to stand and fight right here in order to let Juanita escape. At that moment Delgado felt admiration and gratitude beyond measure; here stood Jeremy Bledsoe, no less willing than he to fight, and die if necessary, so that his mother might survive.

But the assassins did not press the attack. They looked warily at Delgado and Jeremy and, with a muttered exchange, returned to the courtyard. The last one expressed himself in a parting shot by spitting contemptuously at the ground. Then he, too, was gone.

Delgado and Jeremy looked at each other in disbelief.

"I suppose," said Jeremy, "we charged too high a price for our lives."

"Let's go."

Leaving his mother in the sanctuary of the church, Delgado and Jeremy crossed the plaza at a run to the Bent house, drawn there by a commotion. Seeing what had happened to the governor, Delgado's blood ran cold.

"I must warn Falconer," he said. "I will ride to Turley's Mill tonight."

"I'll go with you," said Jeremy.

Delgado shook his head. His friend had suffered more than a mere flesh wound. The sleeve of his shirt was soaked with blood. It dropped from his fingers. He was pale and trembling. But Delgado instinctively knew better than to try to convince

Jeremy that he was in no condition to ride, that he would not even make it halfway to Turley's Mill.

"Stay with my mother, Jeremy. I can trust only you to see to her safety."

"She is safe enough in the church, surely. Not even those bastards would commit murder on holy ground."

Delgado glanced briefly at the decapitated body of Charles Bent. The governor's wife was on her knees on the blood-slick stones, rocking slightly, hands clasped in prayer as silent tears coursed her cheeks. Several men—neighbors who had come running when they heard her screams—stood about in grim, stunned silence.

"There is no way of knowing what they are capable of doing," replied Delgado. "Please, my friend. Do this for me."

Jeremy nodded. He knew in his heart he could not ride with Delgado. "She will be safe. I swear it, on my life." He wanted to tell his friend how sorry he was that Angus McKinn had fallen. One look at Delgado's face, and he decided not to. "But you," he said, "I'm not so sure."

"Hugh Falconer saved my life," said Delgado. "I owe him this, at least."

He made it to the stables without mishap, and there learned that the killers had preceded him. The old man who worked in the stables and slept at night in the hayloft was cowering in the shadows. Two men lay dead in one of the empty stalls. They had been hacked to bloody pieces.

"Who were they?" asked Delgado. The old man stammered an incoherent reply; he was so terrified he could barely stand. "Calm down and tell me who they were."

"Pablo Jaramillo," said the old man. "Brother

to the governer's wife. I think the other was . . . was Narciso, Judge Beaubien's son. They ran in here to hide, senor. But there was no escape for them. Madre de Dios, what is happening?"

"Revolution," replied Delgado, tasting bile. "Go to the church, old man. You will be safe there."

He quickly saddled the bay and rode full tilt through the streets of Taos, expecting at every turn to be waylaid by the men who had murdered his father and Charles Bent. But the streets were silent and empty, abandoned by the living, walked only by the ghosts of those recently slain.

Chapter Eight

"He believes himself to be a patriot."

1

Delgado felt certain that the Americans at Turley's Mill would be a target of the revolutionaries. He just hoped he could get there in time to warn them.

His destination was only a few miles from Taos. He knew the way—knew his country like the back of his hand. In his younger, more carefree days he had ridden over every foot of it. But this night's ride seemed to go on forever. At any moment he expected to be attacked from the shadows. He was weaponless now, having left the bloody cane knife at the stables. He wasn't sure why, really. Wasn't sure of a lot of things. The whole affair was like a nightmare from which he had yet to awaken. Worst of all was his father. Tears of grief streaked his cheeks as he rode on through the night.

He was calm, though. Not unafraid, but he had the fear under control, and the fear served to sharpen his senses. In a way he was relieved that this business, however bad, however bloody and tragic, had finally begun. The waiting, the wondering, was over. Thank God it hadn't started a few days later, for then he would have been on the trail for St. Louis, and in all likelihood his mother would have been murdered, too, by the killers who roamed the streets of Taos.

It was madness, but there was method to it, and he was not so grief-stricken that he could not think it through. Foreigners and those native-born New Mexicans who were viewed as collaborators with the Americans were the targets. And the revolutionaries were a mix of Mexicans and Pueblo Indians. They had been biding their time until Kearny and his dragoons had marched away. How many of them were up in arms? Probably not many. Yet. They would be hoping that the murder of Governor Bent and other prominent figures would trigger a massive uprising.

When he saw his destination, a collection of structures that included Simeon Turley's home, a trading post, and a mill, Delgado's spirits soared. All seemed peaceful enough. Turley's Mill straddled a rocky creek, the Arroyo Hondo, lined with willows and cottonwoods. The other buildings were back up on the sloping foot of a steep butte. Water, timber, shelter from the bitter cold north wind of winter—these were the attributes Turley had been looking for in a piece of land, and he had found all of them here.

The house, trading post, and still—Turley was justly famous for his home-brewed whiskey, Taos Lightning—were connected by low adobe walls or brush fences, forming a compound. Beyond the still house was a fenced vegetable garden, adjacent to a corral, which was full of horses; Delgado estimated about twenty head. He could see it all quite clearly as he neared the Arroyo Hondo, the bay resolutely picking its way across broken ground; the moon, about to set, provided plenty of illumination on this crystal clear night. Beyond the butte the snowy peaks of nearby mountains seemed to float in the star-spangled sky, detached from the earth. All in all, a peaceful and picturesque scene.

Delgado saw someone rise up from the concealment of rocks and cedar brush to his right, perhaps a hundred yards away. A blossom of yellow flame appeared in front of the dark, sinister shape; Delgado felt the bullet strike the bay just forward of the saddle, felt it even before the gunshot reached his ears. With a shrill whinny the bay went down, mortally wounded. Delgado landed like a cat, on his feet and running.

Shouts pursued him as he plunged into the icy cold water of the creek. The bank of the Arroyo Hondo opposite Turley's Mill was suddenly swarming with men. More gunshots. Delgado flinched at the *crack!* of a bullet passing very close to his head. Instinctively, he hurled himself down into the shadows. Sharp rocks just beneath the surface knocked the wind out of him. Though shallow, the creek was fast-running. The current rolled him over on his side as he thrashed painfully about, wheezing to get air into his lungs and choking on a mouthful of water instead.

Several men were leaping into the creek after him. They were bent on killing him; Delgado doubted if they knew who he was, or that they even cared. They had obviously been waiting for moonset to attack Turley's Mill, and he had blundered into the trap and now he was fair game. A part of his mind remained very lucid and analytical while the rest screamed in panic; they would have done better to let him pass through their lines unhampered. Now Falconer and Turley and whoever else happened to have the great misfortune to be in the compound were alerted. This was small comfort to Delgado; he had come here to warn them, and now they were warned, but he was going to die for his trouble.

Confronted with certain death, Delgado managed to move his pain-racked body. Stumbling over rocks, slipping, getting back up, lurching forward, he dared not look back. He knew they were hot on his heels. If he could only make it to the other side. If he could just reach solid ground, then he might have a chance. Perhaps then he could outrun them and reach the compound. But down deep he knew this was a forlorn hope. He wasn't going to make it out of the Arroyo Hondo alive. The swift waters of the creek would carry his blood away. A sudden image came to his mind's eye—of Sarah Bledsoe standing in the upstairs hallway of the house in St. Louis, so becoming in her pink *crepe de chine* dress, with that brave sweet smile and those words, those wonderful words, *I will wait forever.* She would indeed, thought Delgado, despairing. She would wait until eternity before she ever saw him again . . .

His feet were like blocks of ice. He couldn't feel anything from the calves of his legs down. So he wasn't surprised when he slipped on the smooth stones below the surface, wrenching his ankle, falling clumsily, hurting his arms and hands in an attempt to break his fall. He caught a glimpse of a man only a few feet behind him. Immediately, the man was on him, raising a hand axe. *My God, he is going to hack me to pieces,* thought Delgado, curiously detached from the scene of his own destruction. I'd rather a bullet in the brain.

He closed his eyes.

Then he heard the rifle, and his eyes snapped open, and he saw the man looming over him suddenly jackknife, saw the hatchet fly from a dead man. Delgado was stunned. He was still alive. He couldn't believe it.

"Run, Del! Get up and run!"

It was Falconer!

Delgado got up and ran.

There were five or six men right behind him, some of them yelling bloody murder. Delgado forgot all about his twisted ankle and sprinted like a man pursued by the devil himself. He saw a few dark shapes separate from the trees on the Turley side of the Arroyo Hondo. One of them was in the creek now, running toward him. Falconer, the moonlight in his long yellow hair. More gunshots; he heard a yelp of pain behind him. He kept his legs churning. Falconer went right by him, going the other way, closing with the men pursuing him. There was a savage expression on the mountain man's bearded face. He had a pistol in one hand, a Green River knife in the other. Delgado slowed and turned, saw Falconer drop one man with a point-blank shot from the pistol, duck under a machete, and gut the man swinging the blade with the Green River. A third man fell, shot from the bank—one of the men on Turley's side had hit his mark. That left only two survivors of the six who had chased Delgado into the creek. They stopped dead in their tracks, confronted by a vision of death in buckskins called Hugh Falconer.

"Come on, boys," said Falconer, a fierce shout. "Come and meet your Maker."

Delgado wasn't sure if they understood the words, but they understood the meaning well enough—and they turned tail.

Guns were popping on the far bank, yellow blossoms of muzzle flash in the rocks and scrub cedar. Falconer spun, saw Delgado standing there, grabbed him by the arm in passing. "Head for the timber, Del. They're slinging lead our way." Delgado didn't need to be told twice. Bullets slapped at the water, whanged off a rock, and buzzed in the air like angry hornets.

They reached the trees on the Turley side, by some miracle unscathed. Sheltered by the trunk of a split willow, Delgado sank to the ground, wheezing like a blacksmith's bellows.

"Are you hurt?" asked Falconer, standing over him.

"Twisted my ankle," gasped Delgado.

"Well, that's not so bad."

Delgado laughed—a mildly hysterical laugh. "No, it could have been much worse."

Someone was running toward them, running the gauntlet of hot lead still being slung by the ambushers on the other side of the Arroyo Hondo.

"Delgado McKinn!" exclaimed Simeon Turley, dropping down onto his haunches in front of Delgado as he tossed Falconer's rifle to its rightful owner. "Careful, Hugh. That there buffalo gun is loaded."

"Obliged, Sime."

"Don't mention it. Del, what the infernal blazes are you doing out here?"

"I came to warn you."

Turley glanced up at Falconer. He was a wiry, leather-skinned character with a full black beard, cut from the same cloth as Falconer, but dark-haired and smaller in build.

"That was a mighty Christian thing for you to do, Del," he drawled. "I take it there's been some blood shed in Taos."

"Governor Bent's been murdered. Along with some others."

"Charley Bent—dead?"

"Yes. They broke into his home tonight and cut off his head."

"They?"

Delgado shook his head. "Some Pueblo Indians, along with some New Mexicans. I don't know who they were."

"Well, whoever they were, God damn their mangy hides," muttered Turley.

A bullet smacked into the willow tree that provided all three of them with partial cover.

"We'd better pull back," advised Falconer.

"I second that motion," said Turley. He put two fingers in his mouth and cut loose with a piercing whistle. Several men began to fade back through the trees, away from the creek and toward the compound.

"Can you walk, Del?" asked Turley.

"I can do better than walk. I can run."

And he did, although now he could feel shooting pains in his ankle. Falconer stuck close by him, in case he stumbled and fell, but Delgado made it to the compound, and took cover behind the four-foot adobe wall that ran from Turley's home to the trading post. Falconer and the other man vaulted the wall and spread out, rifles loaded and ready, but suddenly the gunfire died down. Their adversaries had pursued them through the trees, only to fall back to the Arroyo Hondo.

"Well I'll be," muttered Turley, amazed. "Why'd they quit, you reckon? Must be fifty, a hunnerd of 'em."

"More," said Falconer, and he didn't sound like he was making a wild guess.

"They could have run right over us," said Turley, mystified. "You figure they gone and lost their nerve, Hugh?"

The moon had just set, and the night had become suddenly much darker. Falconer searched the blackness, but even his keen eyes could not see much.

"I think they're mostly Pueblo Indians," he said. "Maybe a few Mexicans thrown in for good measure."

"Meaning?"

"Meaning a lot of them probably don't have guns. We gave them a bloody nose down at the creek, and my guess is they're thinking things over. They can't be too sure of our numbers."

"How many are here?" asked Delgado.

"Well, let's see," drawled Turley. "There's Tom Tobin, Ike Claymore, Billy Russell, and that breed partner of his. Stump Willis, and Amos Marsh, too. Then there's me and Hugh, of course. You're the ninth man, Del. Two women—my wife and Ike's squaw. I'd sure like to get them clear of this. Problem is, I know for a gold-plated fact that my woman wouldn't leave. And I reckon Ike's little Cheyenne gal's made of the same stuff."

"Nine men," mused Delgado. "Against a hundred? Maybe we'd all better try to make a run for it."

Neither Turley nor Falconer made a quick response to this suggestion. Delgado assumed they were giving it careful consideration.

"If we do," said Falconer, "we'd better go tonight."

"I dunno," replied Turley, dubious. "I don't cotton to being run off my own place. But then again, I'd like to keep the little hair I got left."

His back to the wall, Delgado closed his eyes,

wincing at the pain. His ankle was swelling up nicely.

A shot rang out on the other side of the compound, followed by a shout and a short but fierce flurry of gunfire. A moment later, when all was quiet once more, another buckskinner came loping across the hardpack in a running crouch.

"I've got good news and bad news, gents," he said, dropping to one knee. "Amos and me dispatched a couple more of them scoundrels. That's the good news. The bad news is, we're plumb surrounded." He gestured at the steep slope of the high ground looming above the compound. "That butte yonder is fairly crawling with Injuns and such."

Turley drew a long breath. "So much for escaping."

Falconer introduced Delgado to the buckskinner, who turned out to be Tom Tobin. Tobin crushed Delgado's proffered hand in his big paw.

"If you've got any notions," said Tobin amiably, "as to why these Injuns are all of a sudden so riled up, I would purely love to hear them."

"Revolution," replied Delgado.

"Charley Bent's been kilt," Turley told Tobin.

"Charley's dead? That sure burns my bacon."

"How many others, Del?" asked Falconer. "Was your family spared?"

"My father is dead. But my mother is safe. Jeremy is with her now. I think it's all over in Taos. For the time being, at least."

Falconer didn't offer any sympathy, and that suited Delgado just fine. Once again Delgado found himself trying to set aside his grief. Time enough for grieving later—if he survived.

"How's that ankle?" asked Falconer.

"Not too bad."

"Better take him on up to the house," suggested Turley. "I'm going to bring the horses in here and then I'll join you."

Falconer helped Delgado across the hardpack to the adobe house. Now that the swelling had increased, Delgado could not support any weight on the damaged ankle and had to lean heavily on the mountain man. He was no burden to Falconer; Delgado remembered how Falconer had handled his heavy valise on the St. Louis levee. Though in his forties, and some would say past his prime, Hugh Falconer had the strength and stamina of two or three ordinary men, which was no surprise to Delgado when he remembered the kind of life Falconer had led.

Though furnished in a simple, rustic fashion, the Turley home was a comfortable one. The fire on the stone hearth made Delgado feel warm for the first time that night since leaving his bed. Falconer put him in a chair close by the fireplace and propped his injured leg on a three-legged stool and had to cut Delgado's boot with his Green River knife in order to get to the ankle. When the frontiersman touched the ankle, Delgado hissed at the pain through his teeth. His body went rigid. Mrs. Turley, a plump and pleasant Mexican woman who was trying very hard to act as though nothing was amiss, looked on with genuine solicitude.

"Doesn't seem to be anything broken," said Falconer after moving Delgado's foot this way and that—much to Delgado's detriment. "But it's as severe a sprain as I've ever seen." He turned to Turley's wife. "If you have some lard and turpentine, we'll make a poultice that should take the swelling down some."

She nodded and left them to fetch the makings.

Another shot rang out from the far side of the compound. Delgado listened with bated breath, then sighed with relief when all was quiet again. Falconer was watching him with an unfathomable expression.

"I wish you hadn't come, Del," said the mountain man. "I appreciate what you've done, why you came out here. We all do."

"But you already knew they were out there, didn't you?" That was why Turley and Falconer and some of the others had been hiding in the trees down at the Arroyo Hondo.

Falconer nodded.

"What happens if they're still around when the sun comes up?"

"They'll know how weak we truly are."

Delgado had guessed as much. "And then we'll have no chance, will we?"

"Anything can happen." As he said it, Falconer looked away.

"No. You're lying. You know we're finished. There is no hope. Aren't you afraid, Hugh? Afraid to die?"

"We all die. We don't usually get to choose the time or place. Guess that's the price we pay for getting to live."

Delgado's thoughts turned to Sarah. He hadn't had a chance to live, not really, because his life had started, in a way, the moment he'd met her. He'd left her letter behind in Taos and wished now that he had it with him, so that he could read the words again, imagine he could hear her say those words, because now he knew he would never actually hear her voice again.

2

As dawn approached, they had done all that could be done to prepare for an attack by overwhelming numbers. The horses had been brought into the compound from the corral. The trading post had been emptied of all powder and shot and the few firearms it contained. All the men had been fed by the industrious and seemingly tireless Senora Turley. The last couple of hours of this, without question, the longest night in Delgado's life, were uneventful. No further gunfire, no more probes by the Pueblos and their Mexican allies to test the defenses of Turley's Mill. Delgado began to entertain the hope that the insurgents had withdrawn. But Falconer and Turley knew better.

"We'd hear 'em go, just like we heard 'em coming," explained Turley.

He and Falconer and Delgado were in the house, busily using molds to make shot. Though exhausted, Delgado had insisted on making himself useful. Falconer had tried to talk him into getting few hours of sleep, but Delgado knew that sleep would be impossible. Soon enough he would sleep for all eternity.

Turley explained that a man he did not know had galloped up to the compound yesterday morning, an old Mexican on a swayback nag, and warned them that they would soon come under attack. Turley had been holding a reunion of sorts, an old-fashioned rendezvous with Falconer and the other mountain men now trapped here. From that moment on every man had kept his eyes peeled and his rifle ready. Not one of them, Turley pointed out, had opted to make for the tall timber. "You can always count on Hugh and the others to stick when the fur starts to fly. I wasn't gonna be run off my own place, and they knew it, so they decided to stand with me."

Falconer smiled. "Or you could say we were just too plain dumb to know any better."

Turley chuckled. "Can't say as I'm surprised by all of this, boys. Figured something was bound to happen, sooner or later. I wonder who's behind it all? You reckon that scoundrel Armijo is back, Hugh?"

"It isn't Armijo," said Delgado. "Mrs. Bent said that Diego Archuleta was leading the men who murdered her husband."

"Archuleta!" Turley grimaced. "He's worse than Armijo, because he's got guts. And he's smarter, too. That's a bonafide piece of bad news, Del."

"And he believes himself to be a patriot," added Delgado.

"That's a good point," acknowledged Falconer. "Armijo was thinking about putting up a fight to hold onto his power. He's a greedy man who cares only for himself. Archuleta, on the other hand, doesn't care about himself, only for his people. He believes his cause is just, and he'll be willing to die for it. Which makes him a very dangerous adversary."

"But a blind man could see that the people in these parts would be better off with American rule than they would under the likes of Manuel Armijo," said Turley.

"All they know is what they've been told," replied Falconer. "Told by men they're accustomed to obeying—men like Armijo and Archuleta and the priests."

Turley glanced with furrowed brow at Delgado.

"You know better, though, don't you, Del? So if you know, how come these other folks don't?"

"What I know is that men like Governor Bent and General Kearny have the best interests of my people at heart. But that isn't true of all Americans. Some Americans just see my people as obstacles to their fulfilling a manifest destiny, as John O'Sullivan so aptly put it."

"O'Sullivan?" asked Turley. "Don't think I know that pilgrim."

"As for the Pueblos," continued Delgado, "they don't want to swear allegiance to the Stars and Stripes or any other flag. In their opinion we are all interlopers, and when given the chance to fight they seize it."

A buckskinner Delgado did not know burst through the door, to find himself staring down the barrel of Turley's percussion rifle.

"Got a bad case of nerves, do you, Sime?" The new arrival grinned.

"Go to hell, Amos."

"Reckon we'll all be going there together, soon enough," said Amos Marsh cheerfully. "And the devil will rue the day. But first there are some people out here who want to palaver with you."

They all moved to the door to look out, Delgado hopping on his one good leg. In the pearly gray half-light of dawn they could make out a group of five men in the cleared ground between the east wall of the compound and the trees that marked the course of the Arroyo Hondo. Two were mounted, the rest afoot. The riders were Mexicans, the others Pueblo Indians; the latter in breechcloths, brightly colored himpers, and wearing red or blue cloths tied around their heads.

"Might as well go see what they want," muttered Turley. "But whatever they're selling, I don't reckon I'll buy any."

"*Cuidado, marido,*" said Senora Turley.

"Don't fret, gal. You ought to know by now that I'm dang near indestructible."

They watched Turley cross the compound and go out through the gate, bold as brass. He conferred with the delegation for about five minutes. One of the mounted Mexicans did most of the talking. At this distance Delgado couldn't hear a word or read their expressions. But he was sure that neither of the mounted men was Diego Archuleta. That made him think that Archuleta wasn't even here. No doubt the man was making mischief elsewhere.

When the parlay was over, the Mexicans and their Pueblo cohorts melted back into the trees. Turley was wearing a grim smile when he returned to the house.

"Don't tell me, Sime," said Amos Marsh. "Let me guess. They want to surrender."

"You got it all backward, hoss, as usual."

"You mean they want us to surrender? Us?" Marsh snorted. "That'll be the day."

"They said they'd let the woman live if we gave up," said Turley. "We all know that's a bald-face lie if ever there was one. They claim to number three hundred."

"Which means maybe half that," mused Falconer.

This was cold comfort to Delgado. Nine against a hundred and fifty was still pretty steep odds.

"Come on," said Turley. "I want to show you folks something."

He pushed a table aside, lifted a rug, and pulled open a hatch cut flush into the floor. A black hole yawned at them.

"I dug this when I first come here," explained Turley. "Dang near kilt me, but I done it. Goes down about five feet, then straight south." He pointed in the proper direction. "Runs about eighty feet, beyond the wall, and empties out into a dry wash. A pile of rocks hides the exit hole. The wash wanders on down into the trees, toward the crik. If this business takes a turn for the worse, we might have a slim chance of gettin' out this way."

A gunshot, then another, and several rifles spoke at once, dimly audible above a chorus of bloodcurdling shouts from beyond the compound. Amos Marsh bolted out the door, with Turley on his heels. Falconer hesitated just long enough to order Delgado to stay put. Then he, too, was gone. Gone, Delgado was sure, to his death.

Delgado glanced at Turley's wife. She was kneeling near the fireplace, hands pressed together, face upturned to heaven, her eyes closed. She murmured a prayer and crossed herself and then opened her eyes to look at Delgado, and he had to look quickly away, because her eyes reflected the hopelessness of their situation. She had resigned herself to her fate. Delgado wasn't quite ready to do the same. Snatching up a rifle, powderhorn, and a bag of shot, he hopped one-legged out onto the adobe's weathered wooden porch.

They were coming in from all sides, down from the high ground to the west, swarming out of the trees to the east. Some had already entered the compound—the perimeter could not be held by so few men. Knots of them formed around the frontiersmen, and one by one the mountain men fell beneath the cane knives and clubs of the Pueblos, fighting to the last breath. They died as they had lived—valiantly.

A quivering arrow sprouted from the post against which Delgado leaned for support. Several Pueblos were rushing the house, and one of the mounted Mexicans was galloping forward, too, aiming a pistol at Delgado. He fired before Delgado could bring his rifle to bear, but the shot went wide. Delgado's didn't, and the man was hurled backward out of the saddle. He was dead when he hit the ground.

Before Delgado could reload, the three Pueblos reached the porch. He knocked one down with the rifle, using it like a club and splintering the stock against the Indian's skull. The Pueblo sprawled and lay still. The second Indian plowed into him, and Delgado fell, grappling with the man, clutching at his arm as the cane knife came sweeping down.

The third Pueblo apparently believed his companion could make short work of Delgado and made for the front door. Turley's wife blocked his path. He snarled an obscenity at her and struck with his club—just as she drove the knife, previously hidden in the folds of her skirt, into his belly. She went down, the bones in her shoulder smashed by the club, but she proved hard to kill, and with her last breath she twisted the knife and opened the Indian up from sternum to groin. The club split her skull open, and she fell in a heap. The Pueblo pitched forward to lay on top of her, writhing a moment before death claimed him, too.

Delgado managed to pitch the Pueblo sideways and rolled clear as the big knife came down where his head had been just an instant before. Grabbing a shaggy cedar post, one of the porch uprights,

Delgado hauled himself to his feet, ducked as the Indian swung the knife again. This time the knife, biting deep into the post, stuck fast. Delgado punched the Pueblo in the face. The Indian staggered back on his heels, spitting blood. Then a bullet drove him sideways and down. Delgado turned to see Falconer running across the hardpack, reloading his Hawken on the move.

"Into the tunnel, Del!" yelled the mountain man.

Glancing past Falconer, Delgado could see that the compound had been completely overrun. He did not see any other buckskinner left standing.

Reaching the porch, Falconer grabbed Delgado and virtually lifted him into the house, vaulting over the bodies of Turley's woman and the Pueblo Indian who had killed her. Falconer slammed the door shut and dropped the bar—a few seconds later, Delgado heard bodies thump against the door. The bar splintered but held. He knew it would not hold for long.

"Go on!" snapped Falconer. As Delgado lowered himself through the trapdoor, the mountain man snatched up a lantern that had been lit last night and was still burning and smashed it against the door. Flames licked hungrily at the timber and spread swiftly across the puncheon floor. Falconer dropped down through the hatch. Delgado was already dragging himself blindly along the pitch-black tunnel. It was barely wide enough for him to squeeze his broad shoulders through. Over the roar of the flames above he heard the door give way. But the fire was already too much for their pursuers, and no one could follow them down through the trapdoor.

Ignoring his pain, Delgado clawed and squirmed

his way through the tunnel as fast as he could. Falconer was right behind him. The mountain man did not urge him to go faster; Delgado knew he was slowing Falconer down, but he was doing the best he could and Falconer was aware of that.

He saw a thread of pale morning light up ahead. Reaching a pile of rocks which concealed the exit, Delgado pushed against them, and the rocks gave way, tumbled and clattered down into the dry wash. Delgado squeezed through the hole and rolled down the rocky slope, gasping as he banged his ankle against stone. Falconer emerged right behind him, and together they crawled up to the rim of the wash.

Black smoke plumed from the windows of Turley's home. The shooting had ceased, but there was a great deal of shouting inside the compound. Delgado grimaced. The insurgents were celebrating. Turley and Amos Marsh and all the others were dead. Delgado could hardly believe he was still alive. He didn't expect to be for very much longer.

"Let's go," said Falconer.

They moved down the wash in a crouch, Falconer draping Delgado's arm around his neck and lending him support. Reaching the trees, they paused again to peek over the rim. It seemed that all the rebels were in the compound—they saw no one in the trees or along the Arroyo Hondo. Now that the killing was done, it was time for the looting to begin, and nobody wanted to miss out on collecting his share of the spoils.

Moving on to the Arroyo Hondo, Falconer and Delgado turned south, in the direction of Taos.

Chapter Nine

"I want to see Diego Archuleta's corpse."

1

Once again Delgado found himself bedridden, a virtual prisoner in his own room.

He and Falconer had made it back to Taos without mishap. Knowing that Delgado could not go all the way on foot, and refusing to even consider Delgado's suggestion that he go on alone and return with help, Falconer had staked out the main road north of Taos. Within the hour an old man driving a *carreta* appeared. Falconer stopped him, questioned him, and was convinced that the man remained blissfully unaware that a revolution was under way. The ancient one was merely transporting his produce to market, and he readily agreed to take them into Taos. Delgado rode the rest of the way home in the back of the two-wheeled cart.

In Taos all was peaceful after the storm. Diego Archuleta and his rebels had struck swiftly and then vanished, leaving the populace stunned and fearful. The streets were empty, the doors and windows closed and latched. It reminded Delgado of the reaction of the people to the arrival of the Army of the West.

His mother was safe. She and Jeremy had returned home, to find the butchered body of Angus McKinn where he had fallen. A doctor was summoned to remove the bullet from Jeremy's shoulder. He, too, was an invalid, and though he kept insisting that his duty was to rejoin Colonel Doniphan and the Missouri Volunteers, he was too weak to get out of bed, much less ride to Santa Fe. He had lost a lot of blood.

The day after Delgado's return, Colonel Doniphan himself came to visit. Only then did Delgado learn the full extent of the rebellion.

In addition to the slaughter in Taos and at Turley's Mill, two more mountain men, Harwood and Markhead, had been waylaid at the Rio Colorado, a few miles north of the Arroyo Hondo. Both men were killed, scalped, mutilated, and left for the wolves and buzzards. The village of Mora had also been attacked. Several Missouri traders, having left Bent's Fort in the belief that the American occupation of New Mexico had gone off without a hitch, were killed. Their names were Romulus Culver, Lewis Cabano, and Ludlow Waldo. Several other Americans also lost their lives in and around Mora.

"Obviously," said Doniphan, "the object of the rebels is to put to death every American in New Mexico, as well as every New Mexican who has aided us."

"What are your plans, Colonel?" asked Delgado.

"I am told the rebels are holed up in the village of Canada. I have five companies of my Missourians and a company of Santa Fe volunteers commanded by Ceran St. Vrain, Charley Bent's business partner. I also have four mountain howitzers. I intend to take Canada and capture or kill every last insurrectionist."

"I know that place," said Falconer. "There is

high ground to the south of town. They'll likely dig in there and make you drive them out."

"Which is precisely what I intend to do," said Doniphan. "These rebels are murderers and cowards, who slaughter innocent, helpless civilians. I doubt they will hold their ground in a stand-up fight against trained soldiers."

"You weren't at Turley's Mill," said Falconer.

"What is that supposed to mean?"

"He means you wouldn't underestimate these people had you seen them in action at Turley's Mill," said Delgado.

"Nonsense," said Doniphan. "There were—what?—two or three hundred of them and nine of you? I hardly think that situation called for heroics on their part."

Delgado didn't feel up to arguing the point. Doniphan was merely exhibiting that same arrogant overconfidence he had seen portrayed by so many other Americans. The lawyer turned soldier and his volunteers were aching for a fight. Now they would get their wish—and learn the hard way that Delgado and Falconer were right. Delgado found himself wishing General Kearny was still in New Mexico, and that Charles Bent was still alive. Those two men would not underestimate Archuleta and his rebels, and many lives would probably be saved as a consequence.

Jeremy, of course, was upset that he would not be able to participate in the big fight. That was a part of the young Bledsoe that Delgado did not understand: his desire to place himself in harm's way.

"I would have thought," Delgado told him, after Doniphan had gone, "that after what happened here a few nights ago you'd have seen enough of the rebels. I know I have."

"Some men are born to be soldiers and others are not," replied Jeremy, sullen.

"Well, I'm certainly no warrior. But Jeremy, twice in the span of one year you've nearly been killed."

"I don't care about that."

"Do you *want* to die?"

Jeremy didn't answer. Delgado was troubled. Jeremy had become more than a friend in the past months; he was almost like a brother. But there was part of him that Delgado could not fathom—a dark, angry, violent part. What was Jeremy trying to prove by flirting with death?

A fortnight later, news arrived of the battle at Canada. As Falconer had predicted, the insurgents occupied the high ground south of the village. The Missouri volunteers charged valiantly up the steep slopes, even though the rebels outnumbered them by a ratio of three to one, their ranks having swelled as a result of the revolution's initial success. But many of the insurgents did not have guns, and they could not take the pounding from Doniphan's mountain howitzers. The Americans dislodged the rebels and sent them running. A few more well-placed rounds from the howitzers and the retreat became a rout. Only the advent of night prevented Doniphan from pursuing. Miraculously, the volunteers had only two men killed, with six more wounded.

After two days of regrouping at Canada, Doniphan pressed on after the rebels. The Missourians ran into eighty guerrillas in a canyon near the village of Embudo, brushed them aside, and then ran into a much stronger force, nearly six hundred insurgents, dug in on the slopes of a mesa. While Ceran St. Vrain led his Santa Feans around one flank of the enemy position, a detachment of Missourians went up and around the other side. Once again the rebels slipped away. Doniphan lost one man. His adversaries left twenty dead behind.

By now the Missourians were beginning to suffer from two weeks of hard marching across snowy, rugged county to come to grips with an elusive foe. Then Doniphan got the break he was hoping for. The rebels sought refuge in the Taos Pueblo. They had finally stopped running. The Missourians encircled the pueblo and prepared for the final confrontation.

The rebels enjoyed a strong defensive position, and Doniphan ordered an artillery barrage. But the cannon shot had little effect on the thick exterior walls of soft adobe brick. The next day Doniphan ordered an assault. The rebel stronghold seemed to be a church on the northern side of the pueblo. Under cover of the artillery, two companies of volunteers hacked through the northern perimeter wall, reached the church and, using ladders to gain the roof, chopped holes in the ceiling large enough to drop artillery shells by hand into the building. Meanwhile, a pair of six-pounders were rushed into the pueblo through the breach in the north wall. Round after round of grapeshot wrought havoc upon the rebels, who tried to drive the Americans out of the pueblo. Finally, they abandoned the attempt. While some took refuge in various parts of the pueblo, sixty tried to escape. All but a few of these were cut down by St. Vrain's men, who had been posted on the other side of the pueblo to prevent any insurgents from fleeing into the mountains.

As a day of hard fighting drew to a close, Doniphan was confronted with the prospect of having to clear the pueblo of rebels house-by-house. The losses on both sides would be extremely high. He was saved from having to give the order to proceed in such costly but necessary work by the arrival early the next morning of several Indian residents of the pueblo, under a flag of truce. They wanted to surrender and save their homes from destruction. Doniphan agreed to spare the pueblo if the leaders of the revolt were handed over. In addition, all firearms would be confiscated. A few hours later, two ringleaders, Pablo Montoya and El Tomacito, were delivered into Doniphan's hands.

A mountain man who called himself "Uncle Dick" Wootton showed up at the McKinn house, looking for Falconer. Since the fight at Turley's Mill, the latter had been a guest of the McKinns, taking upon himself the responsibility of protecting the other occupants. Every night he had maintained a tireless vigil in case the assassins returned to make another attempt on the lives of his friends.

As he polished off a bottle of *aguardiente*, Wootton told Falconer, Delgado, and Jeremy what had happened at the Taos Pueblo.

"I was up north a ways when I heard the news about what happened at Turley's," said the shaggy, fierce-eyed buckskinner. "Some of my best friends got themselves kilt that day. Figured you were gone beaver, too, Hugh. I was happy as a pup with two tails to learn otherwise. I come down to hit a lick agin them what kilt my friends. Got here in time for the big scrape at the pueblo. I was right surprised you warn't there, Hugh."

"Not much interested," said Falconer.

Uncle Dick gave him a funny look. "What about Sime Turley and all them others?"

"What about them?

"An eye for an eye, Hugh. That's the way we've always lived."

Falconer shook his head, "Maybe I'm just getting old, Dick, but live and let live sounds better to my ear."

Wootton grunted in amazement. "Well, you sure as hell must be. The Hugh Falconer I knew twenty years ago would have spilt a river of blood on account of what happened at Turley's place. Hell, ain't you the one who curled Wolf Montooth's toes for takin' your plews and leavin' you to the mercy of the Blackfeet?"

"I was young and foolhardy then, Uncle Dick. I've got more to live for these days."

"Oh, yeah. You got hitched to a white woman, didn't you?" Wootton gulped down some more *aguardiente,* gasped as the liquid fire exploded in his belly, and chuckled. "Gettin' squawed up is bad enough, but marryin' a white woman is downright dangerous. They'll make a gelding out of a man ever' time."

Listening to this exchange, Delgado expected Falconer to take offense, but it didn't happen. Falconer just smiled tolerantly.

"It's not so bad," he replied. "You should try it, Dick. A good woman might even be able to make a halfway decent human being out of you."

Wootton guffawed at that notion.

Jeremy leaned impatiently forward in his chair. "What happened at the Taos Pueblo, Mr. Wootton?"

"*Mister* Wootton? Good God, call me Uncle

Dick, boy! I'll tell you what happened." The mountain man related the events of the battle—the artillery barrage, the assault, the taking of the church, St. Vrain's cutting off the rebels' escape, and the appearance the following morning of the delegation under the white flag.

"I reckon," added Wootton, "that Montoya and El Tomacito chose between the lesser of two evils when they gave themselves up to Colonel Doniphan."

"What do you mean?" asked Jeremy.

"Sounds to me like the Pueblo Indians had had enough," said Delgado. "They probably threatened to kill those two if they didn't surrender."

Wootton nodded. "I reckon that's the long and short of it.'

"What about Diego Archuleta?"

Wootton shook his head. "No sign of him. He's a slippery one. El Tomacito—he was the Indian leader—was placed under guard, and we were going to give him and Montoya a fair trial, except a man named Fitzgerald saved us the trouble. Fitzgerald's a dragoon, one of them that was too sick to go to California with Kearny, but when the shooting started, he joined up with the Missouri Volunteers. Doniphan let his men file past the room in the pueblo where El Tomacito was being held. Fitzgerald got in line, and when his turn came, quick as a flash, he drew a pistol and shot El Tomacito in the head. Killed him right off."

Delgado shook his head. "That won't help matters."

"Well, El Tomacito would have been hanged anyroad," said Wootton. "That's what'll happen to Pablo Montoya, or my name ain't Uncle Dick."

"But you've made a martyr of El Tomacito," said Delgado.

"I think we've knocked all the fight out of them Injuns," said a confident Wootton.

"Del's right," said Falconer. "Archuleta and a few rebels are still loose up in the hills, and when they hear about El Tomacito, they'll wonder if they should surrender, since the same thing might happen to them."

2

Returning to Santa Fe, Colonel Doniphan stopped off briefly in Taos, detaching a company of his Missourians as a garrison there, and handing over the captives taken at the Taos Pueblo to the local authorities for prosecution in the civil court. In addition to Pablo Montoya there were fifteen other men in irons. The court would be presided over by Judge Charles H. Beaubien, whose son was one of the two men Delgado had found murdered and hacked to pieces in the livery. The prosecutor was Frank Blair, son of Francis P. Blair, newspaper editor and politician, whom Delgado had met at Jacob Bledsoe's. Frank Blair had recently been appointed the territorial district attorney. Delgado was sure the jury would be staunchly pro-American. The defendants didn't have a prayer.

"Judge Beaubien will want vengeance," he told Jeremy, "and Frank Blair is desperate to prove that he was the right choice for the job of district attorney."

He and Jeremy had walked the short distance from the McKinn house to the square to join the hundreds of spectators who, in spite of the blustery cold day, were gathered to watch the arrival of the Missourians and their prisoners. For the past few days he and Jeremy had ventured out every afternoon, two of the walking wounded helping each other along. The snow was piled deep in the streets, and the cold wind knifed right through them, but they would not be deterred from escaping the confines of the house.

Delgado noticed that the Missouri volunteers were not the same brash and boisterous men with whom he had journeyed west from Fort Leavenworth. These were grim, haggard veterans of a difficult winter campaign against an elusive and determined foe.

As gaunt and weary as the Missourians looked, their prisoners looked much worse. Burdened by heavy iron shackles and chains, they shuffled single file under heavy guard across the square.

"They might as well have stood them up against a wall and shot them," said Jeremy.

"A trial is supposed to at least give the impression of justice," said Delgado, dryly.

Jeremy gave him a sharp look. "Don't tell me you feel sorry for them! These are the men responsible for your father's death."

"Diego Archuleta is the man I hold responsible."

"He's probably halfway to Mexico by now."

Delgado didn't think so. Archuleta was not the kind of man who would run away. He would fight on, even if his cause was lost.

They stood there, at the corner of the crowded square, their breath white vapor in front of their ruddy, frozen faces, watching as the prisoners were paraded in front of the Bent house. Clad head to toe in black, the governor's widow stood at her front gate. A veil concealed her features. Delgado wondered what she was feeling. Did her soul cry out for revenge? Did she long to see these men hang? Or did she realize, as he did, that their deaths would not atone for the loss that both of them had suffered. Would the grief she felt be blunted the day these sixteen men were laid to rest in their graves? Delgado doubted it.

"Pardon me, Captain."

Jeremy and Delgado turned to see a young man clad in a long buffalo coat, his broadbrimmed hat pulled low over his face, standing behind them. He had addressed Jeremy, who wore his uniform beneath a woolen Regular Army longcoat.

"My name is Langdon Grail," said the stranger. "I am from Missouri, by way of Bent's Fort."

"I'm a Missourian as well," said Jeremy and introduced himself. "This is Mr. Delgado McKinn."

"You're the one whose father was killed, then," said Grail, shaking Delgado's hand. "My sincerest condolences. And you, sir, must be the son of Mr. Jacob Bledsoe of St. Louis."

"You know my father?"

"I know of him. You might say I am in the same business. I came west with a trading caravan out of Westport Landing. I was at Bent's Fort when news arrived of the rebellion. William Bent recruited me to come to Taos and avenge the death of his brother."

Delgado stared at Grail. This amiable youth, who could scarcely be more than twenty years of age, was a hired assassin? He certainly did not seem to fit the part.

"You're a little late, Mr. Grail," said Jeremy.

"The rebellion is over. The leaders are the men you see over there, and they are as good as dead."

"Justice is swift in Taos," said Delgado. "Always has been. There's a saying here that a convicted murderer is hanged before the transcript of his trial is finished."

"I've been asking questions around town," said Grail, "and I understand that the man I am seeking is still at large."

"Diego Archuleta," said Delgado. He noticed that Grail's eyes were so dark blue in color as to appear black. They were cold, piercing eyes, untouched by the warmth of the young man's callow smile.

Grail nodded. "Indeed. I would think, Mr. McKinn, that you and I are after the same thing."

"And that would be what?"

"Archuleta's demise."

"Is William Bent paying you to hunt down Archuleta?"

"No, I volunteered for the job."

"Wouldn't hurt to have a man like William Bent beholden to you," said Jeremy tersely. He did not care for Langdon Grail, and that was evident by his tone of voice.

"Quite so," agreed Grail. "I think questioning those prisoners yonder about Archuleta's whereabouts might be productive. Don't you think so, Mr. McKinn? Perhaps you would consent to help me."

"Help you? In what way?"

"You know the judge, I imagine, and other people in positions of authority and influence here in Taos, do you not? Perhaps you could arrange it?"

"That wouldn't do any good. Those men would not betray Diego Archuleta."

"Not even if their lives were spared in return for information?"

"I could not offer them their lives. It is not within my power to do so. Neither could you."

"Couldn't I? Well, perhaps I will see you gentlemen at the trial. Good day."

They watched Grail melt into the crowd of onlookers.

"I wouldn't want to be Archuleta," muttered Jeremy. "There is something about that fellow—I would hate to have him hunting me."

Delgado could only agree.

3

The trial of the sixteen insurgents began immediately. All were charged with murder. In addition, the charge of treason was leveled against five of them. Thanks to the McKinn name, Delgado was allowed into the packed courtroom, and he took Jeremy along with him. Hugh Falconer had expressed no interest in witnessing the trial. The mountain man seemed perfectly content with waiting out the winter in Taos. He planned to leave for home as soon as the weather allowed. He wanted to get back to Lillian as badly as Delgado wanted to see Sarah Bledsoe again.

The treason charges troubled Delgado. How could a person conquered in war be tried for treason against the conquering country? He doubted that these men had ever sworn allegiance to the United States of America. They were only defending their homeland.

The prosecutor, Frank Blair, produced the Kearny Code as evidence that the defendants had indeed committed treason. These laws, drawn up by Alexander Doniphan and promulgated by General Kearny in his capacity as military governor prior to the arrival of Charles Bent, were, by the admission of the very man who had produced them, of dubious constitutionality. They purported to establish a permanent territorial government in New Mexico and to bestow upon the people all the rights enjoyed by citizens of the United States—actions that properly could only be carried out by the Congress. With the rights of citizenship, argued Blair, came certain responsibilities, one of which was to refrain from taking up arms against your own country. Delgado did not accept his argument. One could not commit treason against a country of which he was not a citizen, and these sixteen defendants were not citizens of the United States just because the Kearny Code said so. He had argued as much with Colonel Doniphan, who, the previous night, had enjoyed the hospitality of the McKinn house.

"For better or worse," said Doniphan, "the Kearny Code remains the only version of American law in New Mexico. It was put in place for the purpose of preserving order and protecting the rights of the inhabitants, and if any excess of power has been exercised, it stems from a patriotic desire to extend to the people here the privileges and immunities cherished by all Americans and which can only improve their condition and promote their prosperity."

"Besides," said Jeremy, who sat with them and drank more than his share of brandy, "what difference does it really make? Those rebels will hang for murder anyway. The charge of treason is of no consequence. You can't kill a man twice."

"In a way you make a valid point," said Delgado. "Why even level a charge of treason in the first place? It will only serve to alienate some of the people. They can understand why a man must be executed for committing murder, and few will argue that the rebels killed innocent civilians. But they will not understand the treason charge. Some would say that I am the real traitor. That I turned against my people when I helped you."

"You are not a traitor according to the Kearny Code," said Doniphan. "You are an American, Mr. McKinn, and you have served your country well."

"My country?" Delgado smiled. "And if Santa Anna marches north and recaptures New Mexico am I a Mexican citizen again at that moment? Do I have any say in this? Or does my citizenship solely depend on which flag happens to be flying above the Cabildo today?"

"I thought you understood," said Doniphan, frowning. "I thought you wanted New Mexico to become part of the United States, that you realized the advantages inherent in that reality."

"I wanted to do what I could to prevent bloodshed. Obviously, I did not do enough. But I must be careful, Colonel, lest I say the wrong thing and find myself charged with treason."

The trail was swift. The witnesses touched their lips to the Bible and then, pointing accusing fingers, condemned the prisoners to certain death. When the testimony was completed, the jury retired to deliberate. They were absent from the courtroom less than fifteen minutes. The verdict: guilty on all counts. Judge Beaubien sentenced each man to be hanged on Friday, traditionally the hangman's day. After uttering the sentence, the judge solemnly concluded with "*Muerto,*

muerto, muerto." The defendants accepted their fate with admirable stoicism. There was a heavy stillness in the chamber—no jubilation, no cheers, no weeping, nothing. The people filed silently out.

That evening, Langdon Grail knocked on Delgado's door.

"Judge Beaubien has consented to see me," said Grail. "Would you like to come along, Mr. McKinn?"

"What for?"

"I wish to persuade the judge to let me interview the prisoners for the purpose of learning the present whereabouts of Diego Archuleta."

Delgado was of half a mind to decline. But in the end his curiosity got the better of him, and he agreed to accompany Grail.

Judge Beaubien was in his study, slumped in a chair by the hearth, brooding in the darkness, when they were ushered in to see him. The servant lighted a lamp and withdrew. Beaubien gestured at a sideboard.

"Help yourselves, gentlemen. Forgive me for not rising. I am an old man, and of late very tired. I confess that I have not slept at all well since the death of my son."

Delgado felt sorry for the judge. A widower, the only joy in his life had been his son, Narciso.

"You must be Senor Grail," said Beaubien as the young Missourian sat in a chair facing him. "Of what service can I be to you?"

Grail told him what he was after. Delgado watched Beaubien, and when Diego Archuleta's name passed Grail's lips, the judge's eyes blazed with a vengeful light. In that instant Delgado knew that Langdon Grail would get his wish.

When Grail finished making his request, Beaubien pondered for a moment in grim silence. Delgado thought he knew what the man was thinking. He wanted all sixteen of the men whom he had today sentenced to die to keep their appointment with the hangman. There was no mercy in Beaubien. It had died the night Narciso was cut to pieces by the insurgents. Now the judge had to weigh letting live one of the men he held responsible for his son's death against the chance to bring Archuleta to task for his role in the uprising. By all accounts, not one of the sixteen men doomed to death this day in Beaubien's courtroom had been among those who, for an hour or two, had wrought such terror and bloodshed in Taos. But that didn't matter. That was a minor point. They were the available targets for the vengeance burning in Beaubien's grief-ridden soul, and he was loath to let even one of them live past Friday.

Finally, he raised his haunted eyes and fastened them on Delgado.

"I assume by your presence here that you support Senor Grail in this scheme."

"I want Archuleta brought to justice. As long as he is free, no one is safe. But while I think he is a murderer, I do not consider him a traitor."

Beaubien dismissed that distinction with a gesture. "It matters not. Archuleta will not be taken alive." He turned back to Grail. "You will see to that, won't you Senor? I will write a letter that will permit you to talk to the prisoners. There is one condition."

"Of course, sir."

"I want to see Diego Archuleta's corpse with my own eyes. I want to be absolutely certain, beyond a shadow of doubt, that he is *muerto*."

But that will not help you sleep, thought Delgado sadly.

Armed with the letter from Judge Beaubien, Grail and Delgado crossed the snow-covered plaza to the jail. The Taos sheriff, an American, had been among those slain by Archuleta's rebels, and since no one, perhaps understandably, had stepped forward to take his place, the safekeeping of the prisoners was the responsibility of Doniphan's Rifles. A half dozen volunteers stood guard. Grail presented the letter to a lieutenant who was the officer in charge. As they were allowed into the cell block, a vivid memory assailed Delgado—of going with Sarah Bledsoe to the St. Louis jail to visit the abolitionist, Jeremiah Rankin, of running the gauntlet of men who prowled the Market Street square with murder in their hearts. Sarah had been determined to save Rankin from a lynching; now here was Langdon Grail with the power to save one of the rebel leaders from the hangman's noose. Odd, thought Delgado, how once again he was being drawn, more or less against his will, into a game of life and death.

"My Spanish is atrocious," Grail told him. "Will you be so kind as to translate?"

"Of course."

"Show each man this letter. It bears Judge Beaubien's signature. In it he promises to suspend the death sentence of the man who tells me where Diego Archuleta can be found. That is all I need to know. Nothing more need be said. We will start with these men."

He indicated the trio of prisoners confined in the first strap iron cell. One sat in a corner of the barren cell, a second leaned against the far wall, beneath the small, barred window, and the third lay on a blanket spread across the cold stone floor. There was no heat in the cell block, and Delgado knew the prisoners must be suffering terribly from the below-freezing temperatures. He had to remind himself that these men had been identified as the instigators of a revolt that had cost many innocent people their lives, including his father. Still, he felt sympathy for them. Perhaps Jeremy was right. It might have been better, more humane, had they been promptly executed by firing squad. That would be a more dignified death. Better for them, anyway, since now they would spend the last days of their lives dreading the long walk to the gallows.

All but one of them, anyway—the one who saved his own life by condemning Diego Archuleta to death.

He held up the letter so that the three cell mates could see it.

"Judge Beaubien will suspend the death sentence of the man who tells us where Diego Archuleta can be found."

None of them moved or spoke. They glared at him with their dark, doomed eyes.

"You will live if you tell us."

No response.

"Next cell," snapped Grail.

Delgado moved to the next cell and repeated the offer. There were four men in this strap iron cage. Grail gave them thirty seconds to think it over. No more, no less. He had no compassion for the condemned. He did not care whether they lived or died, as long as he got what he was after, the location of his prey.

"Next cell."

And so four more men were doomed.

In the third cell was the man Langdon Grail had been looking for.

"I know where he is," said the Mexican even before Delgado could begin his statement. He had heard the deal twice offered. He didn't need a third rendition. "I will tell you."

"Bastard!" snarled one of his cell mates. "Diego will kill you."

"No," said a third man. "Diego will not have the chance."

He hurled himself at the betrayer, bearing him to the floor and throttling him with both hands and banging his head against the cold, smooth stones.

Grail calmly drew a Colt Paterson .36 from under his longcoat, aimed through the strap iron, and fired. His bullet struck the third man in the back of the head. The man's skull seemed to come apart in a spray of pink mist. The corpse slumped forward, and the one who said he would betray Archuleta squirmed out from under the dead weight and flung himself at the cell door, gasping for air, his face streaked with blood, his eyes wide with fear.

"Get me out of here or I am a dead man!"

The lieutenant and one of his men had rushed into the cell block upon hearing the gunshot.

"Let this man out," said Grail.

The lieutenant didn't like Grail's peremptory tone, but he complied. Once freed, the Mexican clung to Grail.

"You have saved my life, senor. I am forever in your debt."

Grail shoved him roughly away. "Your life means less than nothing to me. You have saved yourself if you tell me what I need to know."

"I will. I swear it."

"If you lie to me, I'll throw you back in there with your friends. I doubt you will live long enough to hang."

"No, senor! I will not lie."

"Traitor!" snarled one of the prisoners.

"Let's go." Grail grabbed the Mexican's arm and took him into the small, spartan office adjacent to the cell block. Delgado followed. As much as he wanted Diego Archuleta to answer for the death of his father, he regretted now having taken part in this business.

4

"Archuleta is hiding out in the village of Truchas," Delgado told Hugh Falconer later that night. "Grail is leaving in the morning. I have decided to with him."

Falconer finished off his whiskey and poured himself another as he glanced at Delgado, seated in a chair by the fireplace, elbows on the arm of the chair, chin resting on clasped hands. Delgado was gazing moodily into the flames of the fire roaring in the big stone hearth.

"Just the two of you?" asked the mountain man.

"No. Colonel Doniphan is sending a company of men under the command of a Captain Cooper. Grail didn't want any soldiers along, but there was nothing he could do about it. The lieutenant in charge of the prisoners heard everything and informed Doniphan."

"Archuleta's probably not alone. Did this man Grail think he could do the job by himself?"

"Apparently. He's a killer, Hugh. I don't think

human life holds any value as far as he is concerned. And his job is to kill Archuleta. That might not be easy if the soldiers take him prisoner, and I have a feeling Colonel Doniphan wants him taken alive. He wants the people to see Archuleta get a fair trial. If you can call the kind of trial he will get fair."

"I don't think you should go, Del."

"I must."

"If something happens to you, what will become of your mother? I don't know that she could take the shock of losing you so soon after she's lost her husband."

Delgado allowed that Falconer had a valid point. His mother had seldom ventured out of her room since Angus McKinn's death. She was under a doctor's constant care. It was as though a big part of her had died with Angus, and Delgado didn't know if she would ever fully recover.

"I have to go," he decided. "I have to make sure Grail doesn't murder Archuleta."

Falconer folded his lanky, buckskin-clad frame into a chair facing Delgado.

"You're not really worried about Archuleta."

"No, I guess not. But if he is gunned down in cold blood, the revolution will have another martyr. I know, it seems now as though the rebellion has failed. But all that is needed to revive it is one spark. Remember that dragoon, Fitzgerald, shot down El Tomacito. One more incident like that and it could start all over again."

"Well," said Falconer, "I admire your motives."

"But not my methods?" Delgado smiled. "You said that very thing to me once before. Do you recall?"

"Sure I do. On the levee in St. Louis. You were

going to try to prevent Brent Horan from buying that slave girl."

"You stopped me then. You won't be able to stop me this time, though. My mind is made up, Hugh."

"I can tell." Falconer drank some more whiskey, contemplating the situation. "Truchas is up in the high country. On the divide, with no cover in any direction. Nothing but open ground and deep snow. Archuleta will see you coming for miles. You won't catch him by surprise, so you'll be in for a fight."

"If he dies fighting for what he believes in, that's better than being hanged as a traitor."

"I just don't want to see you die fighting for what you believe in, Del."

"So I guess that means you're coming along."

Falconer nodded.

"Not just for my sake , I hope."

"For your mother's sake, Del."

Again Delgado had to smile. "I know you'll be glad when Jeremy and I stop getting into trouble, won't you?"

Falconer sighed. "I wonder if that day will ever come?"

Chapter Ten

"The difference between murder and justice"

1

Truchas was a small collection of adobes that seemed to be perched on the top of the world. Up here, above the timberline, the snow lay deep and blinding white in great expanses. And, in spite of being clad as warmly as humanly possible, Delgado winced every time that wicked north wind came howling along the divide—which was often.

The Missouri volunteers suffered as much as he. Thanks to the legendary foresight of General Kearny, who had planned for every eventuality prior to marching out of Fort Leavenworth, including winter campaigning in the high country, they were each provided with a blue woolen longcoat. Most of them wore a scarf, muffler, or piece of cloth around their heads and knotted under their chins to keep their hats from being carried away by the capricious wind, and to keep their ears from freezing. They sat huddled in their saddles, some suffering in stoic silence, others cursing the snow, or the cold, or New Mexico, or President Polk, or themselves for being so foolish as to ever set foot out of Missouri.

Only Hugh Falconer appeared immune to the new elements. Wearing a heavy white capote—perfect camouflage on the snowfields—over his buckskins, he didn't even seem to notice just how cold it was. Delgado reminded himself that this man had survived for many years in the mountains. The life of a trapper was one of constant hardship and general privation.

Although he didn't think he required a nursemaid, Delgado was glad to have Falconer along. No one was sure quite what to expect once they reached Truchas, but the frontiersman was one of those men who somehow knew exactly what do do in every eventuality. This came, Delgado supposed, from experience. There probably wasn't much Hugh Falconer hadn't seen. And danger was nothing new to him.

Having left Taos at daylight, they reached their destination about noon of the following day. They paused on the backside of a ridgeline, out of sight from the town. Falconer, Delgado, Grail, and Captain Cooper moved in a crouch to the rim and scanned the adobes a long rifle shot away. Smoke curled from a few chimneys. Several horses in a cedar-post corral pawed at the snow, trying to find some grass beneath the frozen crust. There was no one out in the open. Truchas, from what little Delgado knew of the place, was home to a handful of sheepherders and their families.

"Looks peaceful enough," mumbled Cooper. He forced the words out through clenched jaws, trying to keep his teeth from chattering.

Delgado had learned that Cooper—like Doniphan, a lawyer in civilian life—had seen some action as a volunteer during the Black Hawk War ten years ago. This experience had led to his election as a company commander in the First Missouri Mounted Rifles. His outfit had been one of the companies that had not been converted to infantry by Stephen Kearny. By all accounts, he and his men had acquitted themselves very well during the recent campaign against the revolutionaries. But Cooper, a capable man who had earned the loyalty of his men, knew his limitations. He was not accustomed to independent command, and had evinced a genuine interest in listening to good advice. For this reason he was as glad as Delgado that the legendary Hugh Falconer had consented to come along on this expedition.

True, the mountaintop village looked peaceful, but they all knew that looks could be deceiving. Delgado wondered, though, if Diego Archuleta was really here. Perhaps he had never been. Perhaps they had come all this way for nothing. Delgado hardly cared at this point. His one goal in life right now was to get warm again. *I would like to have some feeling in my hands and feet just once more,* he thought as he gazed longingly at the chimney smoke and imagined the cheerful little fires that produced it.

"Captain, maybe we should move in from two sides," suggested Falconer.

"That's a good idea. I'll take half the company around to the south."

Falconer nodded. "You do that. And keep below the skyline. If Archuleta *is* there, no point in letting him know we've come calling until we have to."

"Right," said Cooper.

"He had damn well better be there," said Langdon Grail.

"When we see you break cover," Falconer told Cooper, "we'll come in."

"Good."

"Luck, Captain."

"Let's hope we don't need too much luck." Cooper left them, returning to his men. Illness and injury had decimated the ranks of his company in the four months since Fort Leavenworth; there were only thirty-nine recruits fit to ride. Cooper took twenty of them and started his flanking maneuver around Truchas.

"Maybe I should ride in alone," said Delgado. "If Archuleta is there, he might be willing to give himself up."

"Doesn't matter if he's willing or not," said Grail.

"We could possibly save a few lives if we give him a chance to surrender," said Delgado.

"No," said Falconer. He glanced at Delgado with an apologetic smile. Delgado thought he resembled an Indian on the warpath; beneath his eyes he had daubed streaks of tobacco juice mixed with mud—this was an old trick designed to prevent snow blindness. "Too risky, Del," he added, sensing that his young friend was inclined to debate the issue. "Archuleta doesn't know you the way I do. He might not trust you. You can't tell what a man on the run with his back to the wall will do. Besides, Diego Archuleta isn't likely to give up without a fight."

Delgado didn't argue the point. He left the ridgeline and went back down the slope to where the nineteen Missourians stood by their horses, using their mounts to block the wind and moving around to try to encourage the circulation in their arms and legs. Delgado did likewise. Falconer and Grail remained up above, watching for Captain Cooper.

Ten minutes crawled by, followed by ten more.

Finally, the mountain man and his companion rejoined Delgado and the volunteers.

"Time to go," said Falconer, swinging into the saddle and removing the fringed buckskin sheath from his Hawken rifle.

As they rode over the ridgeline into view from the village, Falconer instructed the volunteers to speak out to left and right and to keep well apart. Delgado rode to the right of the mountain man while Grail kept to his left. Grail didn't carry a rifle; he drew the Colt Paterson from under his buffalo coat.

Grail had told him that the Paterson was one of the new revolvers created by Samuel Colt. The five-shot, .36 caliber, holster-size pistol had been used by the Texas Rangers for five years. One of the gun's strongest advocates, Ranger Captain Sam Walker, was now working for Colt to secure a military contract for the .44 caliber pistol, the Walker Colt, with which the United States Army wanted to arm all its mounted troops. Delgado could well understand why. Colt had revolutionized firearms; his pistol possessed greater accuracy and range than the old flintlock, and it could fire five bullets in less time than it could take someone armed with a single-shot pistol to fire once and reload.

For his part, Delgado carried only the little over-and-under derringer his father had given him. The weapon was practically worthless at a range of more than twenty feet, but Delgado had not come to Truchas to kill people.

As they neared the village, they still saw no sign of activity around the adobes, and Delgado began to get nervous. Surely, by now the occupants of those houses were aware that blue-coated American soldiers were closing in from north and south.

Falconer, Delgado, and Grail entered the village's single street, holding their horses to a walk. The soldiers began to pass between the adobes on either side of them. Every door and window shutter was tightly shut. At the other end of the street Captain Cooper was coming toward them, flanked by several of his men. A dog barked, and Delgado almost jumped out of his skin. Then he heard an infant squall from inside one of the adobes. So there were people here! Maybe they were afraid to venture out of their homes, thinking that the American barbarians had come to slaughter them.

He was opening his mouth to share this thought with Falconer when he heard the creak of a door opening and looked over his shoulder to see that the door to an adobe they had just passed was open enough to permit a rifle barrel to protrude.

"Look out!" he shouted.

The rifle spoke. A soldier who had passed between two of the houses and reached the street right behind them was struck in the back. He cried out, slumped forward, and then slipped sideways out of the saddle as his spooked horse jumped away.

At that instant a man with a rifle popped into view on the roof of the house to Delgado's right. Heart lurching in his chest, Delgado fumbled with the derringer beneath his coat, snug against his belly under his belt. Grail was faster. The Colt Paterson barked twice, and the man on the roof somersaulted to the ground, landing with a sickening thud so close to Delgado's horse that the animal shied sharply to the left, colliding with Falconer's mount. Falconer swept Delgado out of the saddle with one arm as he himself cleared the saddle, swinging a leg over the saddlehorn. They dropped down between the two horses. Like a cat, Falconer landed on his feet. Delgado's bad ankle turned at an awkward angle beneath him, and he fell to one knee. Langdon Grail rode on down the street. Falconer's horse, and Delgado's, followed him. The mountain man's Hawken boomed like thunder. Delgado caught a glimpse of a man in a doorway, and then Falconer's bullet punched the man back into the darkness of the adobe's interior.

Picking himself up out of the mud and snow of the street. Delgado whirled as a man charged out of the house directly across from the one occupied by the rebel Falconer had just shot. A snarl on his swarthy features, the man came straight at Delgado with a cane knife brandished over his head. *Just like that terrible night in Taos,* thought Delgado. The panic was gone; suddenly he was quite calm and deliberate. He raised the derringer at arm's length and waited until he could fire at point-blank range. The rebel's legs ran out from under him, and he sprawled on his back in the blood-splattered snow, dead.

The action seemed to shift farther down the street, toward the middle of Truchas. Another soldier toppled from his saddle. Galloping past an adobe, Grail fired twice into a window where a rifle barrel jutted out between the shutters, and then he made a running dismount that spoke volumes about his youthful agility. Kicking in the door, he entered the adobe with the Colt Paterson blazing. He appeared a moment later, framed in the doorway, methodically reloading the revolver. That took guts, marveled Delgado—to go charging into the adobe with only one cartridge left in the Colt's cylinder.

Two houses down the street from Grail, the door of another adobe hut opened and a man emerged using a young woman as a human shield. He held a knife to her throat. Captain Cooper, trying to keep his prancing horse under control, shouted at his men not to shoot. The Colt reloaded, Grail started in that direction. Delgado broke into a run. He was afraid for the woman's life. If one of Cooper's Missourians didn't kill her trying to shoot the rebel, then Grail was perfectly capable of doing so. The rebel was yelling at Cooper, but the captain did not understand what he was saying. "He wants your horse!" Delgado yelled. Cooper glanced along the street at him, a befuddled expression on his face. He didn't know what to do. Delgado thought it was a good trade—the rebel might spare the woman's life for the horse and at least a slim chance of escape.

Grail was still walking toward the rebel. There was an almost casual air about the way he moved, as though he were taking a stroll along a quiet boulevard. The rebel saw him, screamed at him to keep his distance or he would kill the woman, but Grail didn't even break stride, and Delgado thought *My God, he is going to shoot*, and even as the thought came to him, he watched in horror as Grail began to lift his gun arm.

A pistol spoke. The woman screamed. But she wasn't hurt. The rebel who had been hiding behind her pitched forward, knocking her to her knees. The knife slipped from his lifeless fingers. His dead weight bore the woman to the ground. She got out from under him and scrambled to her feet, intent on running, but the street was full of soldiers, so she stayed where she was, frozen in terror.

Diego Archuleta came out of the adobe, a pistol in his hand. Standing above the man he had just shot in the back, he spat on the corpse.

"Bastard!" he growled. "Coward, to hide behind a woman's skirts."

Grail walked right up to him and pointed the Colt at the spot between Archuleta's steely eyes. "Drop that pistol."

Archuleta smirked and let the empty single-shot, percussion pistol slip from his hand. "What's your name?" asked Grail pleasantly.

"He is the man you've come all this way to kill," said Delgado as he pressed the derringer against Grail's spine. "Only you're not going to kill him."

Delgado was aware that Archuleta was staring at him over Grail's shoulder, but he kept his gaze firmly fixed on Grail's trigger finger.

"Lower your gun, Mr. Grail," said Delgado.

"What the hell is going on here?" bellowed Cooper.

"Pull that trigger, and you will die right along with him," said Delgado.

He was bluffing—he very much doubted if he could backshoot Grail, even if the man did blow Diego Archuleta's head off—and he could only hope Grail wouldn't call his bluff. Not just for Archuleta's sake, but his own, as well. It seemed likely that Grail, if he killed Archuleta, would spin around and pump a couple of bullets into him, if only out of principle. Grail was not the kind to let someone who had pointed a gun at him just walk away. And then what would happen? Delgado decided that Falconer would probably kill Grail. So they would all be dead, and for what?

Grail lowered the Colt Paterson, turning slowly as he eased the hammer down. He looked at Delgado with a fairly insolent smile on his lips.

"What difference does it make," he asked, "if this man dies here or on the gallows?"

"The difference between murder and justice."

Grail shook his head. "You're a fool, McKinn. That's a fine distinction in this case. You think he'll get justice in Beaubien's court?"

"You're right," allowed Delgado. "The real reason I'm doing this is that I just don't like you."

"Well, now, I can understand that. Not many people do."

He walked away. Archuleta glanced at the derringer in Delgado's hand. The little pocket pistol was now aimed at him.

"He is correct," said the rebel leader. "Judge Beaubien will make certain I pay with my life for the death of his son, Narciso."

"And you should."

"You make no sense, McKinn. I would just as soon die here. Go on. Kill me. I am responsible for your father's death."

"I know. He didn't deserve to die."

Archuleta shrugged. "Perhaps not. But you do. You are a traitor, Delgado McKinn. May you burn in the fires of Hell for betraying your own people."

"You will not be made a martyr," said Delgado flatly, knowing that Archuleta was trying to provoke him into shooting. "Not today."

At Captain Cooper's command, two soldiers dismounted and flanked Archuleta, pointing their guns at him. Delgado pocketed the derringer and turned away. The shooting had stopped. Delgado wondered bleakly if any more innocent people had lost their lives this day in the little town of Truchas.

Falconer was coming up the street, leading his horse and Delgado's. As he handed over the reins, the mountain man said, "You reckon this means the revolution is over, Del?"

"I pray that it is." Delgado sighed as he swung wearily into the saddle.

2

It was a Thursday morning when a man came to the McKinn house and informed Delgado that Diego Archuleta wished to see him. Delgado reluctantly agreed.

He had been busy all week making arrangements for his mother to be looked after and his father's business to be handled by reliable associates during his absence. His father's business? No, it was his own now. That would take some getting used to. He did not feel competent to run such affairs. In his youth—those golden, simpler days before he had gone off to Oxford—Delgado had always managed to avoid becoming too involved in the business, although Angus had wanted to show him the ropes. Time enough, Delgado had argued, in the years to come. He was young and had made an art out of shunning responsibility. His mother had been his willing accomplice. She would tell Angus not to rush things, that their son needed to enjoy his childhood. Now Delgado's lack of interest had come back to haunt him. Fortunately, Angus McKinn had employed trustworthy subordinates who knew the value of an ingot of silver, or a hundredweight in wool, men who were expert when it came to tariffs and the buying and selling of commodities, and who were adept at making a profit in the process.

Delgado's plan had been to leave tomorrow, Friday; he had no desire to watch Diego Archuleta swing on the gallows in the square. For all intents and purposes the rebellion was over, and he was more than ready to put it all behind him. He was ready, also, to see Sarah again, his beloved Sarah, to hold her in his arms and taste her lips again. He still carried, at all times, the tea rose she had given him at the moment of their parting.

Falconer was going with him. So was Jeremy, much to Delgado's surprise—until he learned that Jeremy had received a letter from his sister informing him that their father was gravely ill and pleading with him to come home at once. So Jeremy was turning his back on war and glory because he had read between the lines and feared that Jacob Bledsoe's days were numbered.

Delgado procrastinated until that afternoon. It did not seem right to keep a dead man waiting, but Delgado could muster no enthusiasm for the task. He did not want to see Archuleta again. What did the man want to say to him that had not already been said? Delgado was in no mood to be called a traitor again. Finally, he steeled himself and crossed the square, beneath the naked trees, turning his collar up against the bitter blasts of cold wind that rustled the dead leaves across the old paving stones. The sky was overcast, as gray as lead. Archuleta had been condemned to die at sunrise; Delgado wondered if he would feel the warmth of the sun on his face, one last time, before the hangman covered his head with the black hood. Before the noose was placed around his neck, pulled tight, and the hangman's knot laid just so across his left shoulder. Before the trapdoor dropped away, and he made that last, long descent into eternal sleep. It did not seem right to kill a man without letting him have one last look at the sun. Delgado shuddered—it was not entirely due to the weather.

Archuleta was the only prisoner in the cell block where, a fortnight ago, Delgado had seen Grail kill a man who, in turn, had been trying to strangle the life out of the rebel who was willing to sacrifice Archuleta to save his own life. Delgado wondered what had become of that man, the betrayer of the rebellion's heart and soul? Judge Beaubien had kept his word, releasing him as soon as Archuleta was brought in, though it had galled the judge to let live one of those he held responsible for his son's death. Did that make Beaubien an honorable man? Delgado couldn't decide. He had been thinking a lot about honor of late; what man so often labeled traitor would not? He wasn't sure anyone had come out of this bad and bloody business with his honor intact. *I least of all can stand up to such scrutiny.* Of one thing Delgado was fairly sure. Archuleta's betrayer would not live long. He had the mark of Cain upon him now, and before too many more days had passed his corpse would be discovered in the gutter.

"You wanted to see me?"

Archuleta was sitting in the corner, a blanket over his shoulders, knees pulled up tight against his chest as he tried to contain his own body's heat—the only source of heat in this cell block. He looked up upon hearing Delgado's voice. Lost in his own thoughts, he had not heard Delgado coming. Delgado wondered what he was thinking. About his family, perhaps? Archuleta had sent his wife and children to safety—relative safety—in Mexico before the arrival of the Army of the West. Quite possibly they did not even know their husband and father was about to be executed for murder. And, oh yes, treason. Or was he thinking about his country? Or about what lay on the other side of that long drop on the scaffold? What *did* a condemned man think about in those last precious hours of life?

"Yes. Thank you for coming."

He rose, shedding the blanket. His face was gaunt and bearded, the cheeks hollow, the eyes dark-rimmed with sleeplessness. But there still burned a fierce flame of pride and courage in those eyes. Delgado had heard that some of the men executed last week had not met their fate too well. A few had begged for mercy. One had been carried up onto the scaffold. Another had voided himself, whimpering like a puppy, as the hangman slipped the black hood over his head.

Delgado knew that Diego Archuleta would meet his death with dignity.

He came to the cell door, and Delgado had to make a conscious effort to stand his ground, within Archuleta's reach if the man put his arms through the strap iron; he was afraid of Archuleta and didn't mind admitting it to himself. Still, he did not want Archuleta to know.

"What do you want from me?" he asked.

"I want to know why."

Delgado said nothing.

"Why did you betray your country, McKinn? I want to hear it from your own lips."

Delgado sighed. "I don't care about politics," he replied. "I only wanted to prevent bloodshed."

Archuleta nodded. "The blood of your people? Or American blood?"

"It's all the same."

"You care about your people. So do I. I believe you were misguided. You were never truly one of us."

"I don't know. I am willing to concede that you are a true patriot, and that I am not, if it will make you feel any better."

Archuleta made a dismissive gesture as he turned away, walked to the back of the cell, and then spun on his heel to face Delgado again.

"I have known about you for many years," he said. "Before you went away, I believed you to be a young fool, a knave, who cared only about his own pleasures, and gave not a thought to more important things."

He paused, waiting perhaps for Delgado to defend himself. But again Delgado remained silent.

"I see that you are still such a man, McKinn. That makes you well-suited to become an American. Your father was the same way. Concerned only with himself."

"Is that why he had to die?" Delgado shook his head, disgusted. "Men like you are all the same. It has nothing to do with patriotism. It's power. You have the power to make other men kill for you, or die for you. You held sway over these people, and you didn't want to give that up. Without that power, you felt you were nothing. That's why you were willing to die to keep it. If you couldn't lead the people, you would just as soon see them dead. That's the way you think, Archuleta."

"I fight for the people!" snapped the rebel leader.

"No. The people fought for you. But no longer. Not after tomorrow."

"You will see," sneered Archuleta, coming to the cell door as Delgado turned to go. "You will regret having taken the side of the Americans. The people will know who betrayed them when the Americans make slaves of them."

"That won't happen," said Delgado, "and you know it. That's just your excuse, your way of playing upon the fears of others to make them do your bidding. This has nothing to do with race, or nationality. I have met Americans who are just like you. Englishmen, too, for that matter."

He left the cell block. The same lieutenant he had met before was on duty.

"Stay alert," Delgado advised. "I would not be surprised if an attempt is made to free Archuleta tonight. And he must die tomorrow. If he is freed somehow, more innocent people will lose their lives."

"You can count on us, sir."

Delgado nodded and stepped out into the cold and wind and snow. He caught a whiff of tobacco smoke. A figure cocooned in a long buffalo coat was inclined against the outer wall of the jailhouse. Painfully aware that he was unarmed, Delgado recognized Langdon Grail.

"You saw Archuleta," said Grail, pushing away from the wall with a shrug of his shoulders. "Was he seeking absolution for his sins?"

"Not at all."

"You have to admire the man. He sticks to his principles."

"He has no principles, any more than you do."

Grail was smoking a cigarillo. His black smile formed around it. "You don't like me. That's a shame. You're a big augur in these parts now, McKinn. Someday you might have need of my services. You know, if there's anything that troubles you. Or anyone. I can deal with it."

Delgado thought of Brent Horan. If he paid this man, he would go to St. Louis and do away with Horan. Simple as that and no questions asked. The right or wrong of it didn't matter to Langdon Grail. How could one so young be so twisted? Grail was barely more than a boy, and yet he was a killer, a killer without compunction or remorse, and he was very good at what he did—he'd proven as much in the Truchas fight.

"I'll take care of my own problems," said Delgado.

"Maybe." Grail scanned the empty, windswept plaza. If anything, the day was darkening. There would be more snow tonight. "I'll be headed for Bent's Fort tomorrow. Are you staying to watch Archuleta hang?"

Delgado said he was not, watching Grail closely, not daring to take his eyes off the man. It was like standing next to a rattlesnake coiled to strike.

"I am. That way I can tell William Bent that I've seen him dead with my own eyes."

"Even though you weren't the one to kill him. I'm sure Mr. Bent will be grateful. Thanks to you, he was captured."

Grail shrugged. "Better that than nothing, I suppose. Guess I'll be going now. Maybe we will meet again, McKinn."

God forbid, thought Delgado as he watched the slender shape of Langdon Grail angle across the plaza, the angry, bitter wind obliterating his footprints in the show. It was as though he had never passed this way.

3

That evening, when he visited his mother for the last time, Delgado was encouraged to see with his own eyes that her condition, however slowly, was improving. The doctor had told him that what Juanita McKinn needed most of all was a reason for living. She had lost that the day Angus died. Delgado was afraid his mother would try to talk him out of returning to St. Louis so soon, perhaps telling him that she needed him to stay. To her credit, she did nothing of the sort, though she could not deny that she was concerned for his safety on the Santa Fe Trail in the dead of winter.

"I just can't wait until spring," he said. "But don't worry. Hugh Falconer will ride with me, and Jeremy, as well."

"You must love this girl very much."

"I want to spend every day of the rest of my life with her."

"You will bring her here so that I may meet her?"

"Of course I will." Delgado was relieved that she did not ask him if he intended to bring Sarah to Taos to stay. Where they made their permanent home would be left entirely up to Sarah. He would go anywhere, do anything, just as long as he was with her.

"I am happy for you," said Juanita McKinn, stroking his cheek with a trembling hand. "Your father and I often wondered if you would ever settle down. Now you will have a wife and a family. You must promise to give me many grandchildren so that I may spoil them."

Delgado took her hand and raised it to his lips. "I have taken care of everything here, Mother. You need not concern yourself with anything. Just rest and get well. I'll expect to see you up and about when I return."

As he was leaving her room, there came a knock on the front door. Falconer, who had been warming himself by the fire, reached the door first. Delgado noticed that the mountain man had a hand resting on the yellowed bone handle of the Green River knife sheathed at his hip. *I hope the day will come here in Taos,* thought Delgado, *when a man can open his own door without fear of violence.*

Three men entered. One was Donaciano Vigil, who had succeeded Charles Bent as territorial governor. He had been on Manuel Armijo's staff, but switched his allegiance to the Americans, and Bent had rewarded him with an appointment to the position of secretary of the territory. As a soldier Vigil had commanded several successful campaigns against the Navajos, and as a politician he was trusted by Americans and most New Mexicans alike.

With Vigil was Ceran St. Vrain and Francis Blair, Jr. A former partner of the Bent brothers, St. Vrain had led Santa Fe volunteers in the recent campaign against the insurgents. Blair, of course, had prosecuted Diego Archuleta and the other ringleaders; it was he who had constructed what Delgado believed were the unwarranted charges of treason against the defendants.

"Senor McKinn," said Vigil, "pardon our intrusion at this late hour, but we wished to speak with you before your departure."

McKinn gestured toward the chairs closest to the roaring fire in the big stone hearth. "Please, gentlemen, make yourselves comfortable. Drinks?"

Vigil and Blair declined, but St. Brian gratefully accepted a brandy.

"We have today received startling news," said Vigil. "Santa Anna has seized power in Mexico City."

Delgado glanced at Falconer. He wondered if these men knew that Santa Anna's return had been accomplished with the connivance of the President of the United States. He turned to Blair. "Does this surprise you, sir?"

Blair seemed to realize what Delgado was getting at. "No, sir, it does not. As you know, my father has many important friends in Washington."

Not least, mused Delgado, a man named James Knox Polk. Frank Blair, Sr. had been one of Andrew Jackson's most trusted advisers. The current president was Old Hickory's protégé. The connection was obvious. The prosecutor's father would always be welcome in the White House while Polk resided there, and would be privy to important matters of state. It had seemed likely to Delgado that Frank Blair, Jr. would be kept appraised of noteworthy events by his father.

"In my opinion," said St. Vrain gruffly, "this means a prolonged war. Santa Anna considers himself another Napoleon. He will never give up the northern provinces of what he believes to be his empire. Not without a stiff fight." The French-American frontiersman finished off his brandy and, with a nod from Delgado, poured himself another.

"I fear he will try to reconquer New Mexico," said an anxiety-ridden Vigil.

Delgado was aware that Donaciano Vigil had good reason to be fearful. If Santa Anna did retake the province, men who had gone over to the American side would surely forfeit their lives—and Vigil would be one of the first to stand before a firing squad. Delgado sighed. President Polk had been a gullible fool to trust Santa Anna, to actually believe such a scoundrel's guarantees that he would make peace the moment he again ruled Mexico. And that was what he would do—rule. Santa Anna was a tyrant, a dictator, the worst of the lot.

So it wasn't over, after all.

"What is it that you gentlemen want from me?" he asked.

"We want you to stay, Senor McKinn," said Vigil. "I will appoint you secretary of the territory."

Which was, in effect, the second highest position in the new territorial government, making Delgado, if he consented, the governor's successor.

Delgado was dumbstruck.

"We are fearful of what the people might do once they find out about Santa Anna," said Blair. "There might be another rebellion."

"What could I possibly do about that?"

"Perhaps you don't realize how much influence you actually have over the people," remarked St. Vrain.

"Yes, I do. I have absolutely none."

"On the contrary," said Vigil. "Many people on both sides of the conflict profess to have the interests of the people at heart. Yet the people can see that this is not true. With you they know it *is* true. You have always done what you believed to be first for them, without consideration of your own interests. A case in point is your intervention at Truchas to prevent the murder of Diego Archuleta, even though he is responsible for your father's death. The people know of these things. They aren't blind. And they aren't stupid. There are precious few leaders whom they trust anymore. You are one of those leaders, whether you know it or not."

"And," added Blair, "whether you *like* it or not."

Delgado shook his head. "Santa Anna will have his hands full holding onto Mexico. He poses no threat to us here."

"Perhaps not," conceded Blair. "But you must admit it is possible—it would be just like him—to send agents provocateur into the territory in order to foment unrest."

"You would have a calming influence upon the populace," said Vigil. He seemed on the verge of dropping to his knees and begging Delgado for his help.

Delgado made up his mind. "I am sorry, gentlemen, but I am bound for St. Louis. I have . . . very important business to attend to there."

"But your country needs you, sir," insisted Blair.

Delgado's temper flared. "And what country is that, sir?"

"Why, the United States of America, of course."

"At the risk of facing the charge of treason," Delgado fired back, "I feel, sometimes, like a man without a country."

Falconer stepped forward. "Ceran," he said, addressing St. Vrain, whom he knew best of the three visitors, "you and your friends will just have to make do without Del. We're going to St. Louis in the morning, and that's final."

St. Vrain nodded. There was a layer of steel beneath Falconer's affable demeanor, and he knew better than to test that steel.

"Forget it, Frank," he told Blair, finished off his brandy, and turned to Delgado. "Have a safe journey, Mr. McKinn. See you around, Hugh."

He led the other two men out.

"They want to use you," Falconer told Delgado after the door had closed on the trio. "Vigil's a turncoat of sorts, or so some will say. And Blair isn't too popular in certain circles because of his behavior at the trials. They're scared, right down to the ground, and they wanted to use your popularity as a shield."

Delgado nodded. "I suppose that was their thinking. But I can't believe I have such influence."

"Better get used to it. You're going to be an important man in these parts. As Blair said, whether you like it or not."

Chapter Eleven

"The idea is to make peace."

1

Delgado gave what Hugh Falconer had told him about the drastically altered circumstances of his life a great deal of thought during the first portion of their long and arduous journey back to St. Louis. He decided he didn't like being an important man. Not at all. It was an albatross around his neck, inherited from his father, who had carved a niche and made a name for himself. Delgado preferred obscurity, anonymity. Of course, what he wanted didn't matter.

What he really wanted was to live, happily ever after, with his beloved Sarah, doing what he had to do to keep the business Angus McKinn had built turning a profit, so that he could provide not only for Sarah's every need, but her heart's every desire as well. What Falconer had been trying to tell him was that, try as he might, he would not be able to divorce himself from the politics of the situation. His pedigree—half Anglo and half Hispanic—made him a valuable asset to both sides in this new and in some ways uneasy relationship between New Mexico and the United States of America.

The journey was not without its hazards. Game was scarce, and by the end of the trail Delgado was convinced that he and Jeremy would have starved to death were it not for Hugh Falconer. The mountain man sometimes had to go to great lengths to provide them with fresh meat every other day or so. Often his catch was a solitary rabbit, or a couple of fish harvested from a half-frozen creek with a makeshift spear, or a scrawny sage hen or prairie dog flushed out of nest or hole. They subsisted the rest of the time on hard biscuits and strips of dried venison. For emergency rations they had the one pack horse, but the situation never got that serious.

Falconer seemed virtually oblivious to the hardships they were forced to endure. It was manifest that his first concern was the survival of his two younger companions. "I have to admit," he told them, "that after everything we've been through, I kind of think of you two as my own sons."

This was a startling revelation from a man like Falconer, who seldom aired his innermost feelings, and it brought Delgado up hard against the realization that he admired, respected, and depended on Falconer to the degree that one might expect of a son.

Nine weeks after departing Taos, they arrived, haggard and hungry, at Falconer's cabin a few miles west of St. Louis.

It was the middle of the afternoon, and Lillian urged Jeremy and Delgado to stay the night before going the rest of the way. The fire in the hearth was alluring, but neither of them was inclined to tarry for even an hour, now that their destination was so near at hand.

"I must get home," explained Jeremy. "That last I heard, my father was very ill. Do you have word of him, ma'am?"

"I have been to see him on several occasions,

the last time three days ago," replied Lillian. "He is bedridden, and while I cannot truthfully say he is doing better, he is no worse, at least."

"What does the doctor say is wrong with him?"

Lillian glanced at Falconer, surprised, and then back at Jeremy. "You do not know?"

"My sister gave no specifics in her letter."

"I'm truly sorry, Jeremy, to be the one to tell you this. But your father is stricken with consumption."

All color bled from Jeremy's face. He rocked back on his heels, and Delgado put a steadying hand on his friend's shoulder. There was no cure for consumption. Jacob Bledsoe would never recover.

"I must go," said Jeremy, striving to keep himself together.

"We will leave immediately," said Delgado.

"I think you should wait here, Del, at least until tomorrow."

"For what reason?"

"Let me test the water, so to speak, where my father's feelings about you are concerned."

"There's more to it than that."

Jeremy forced a smile. "I should know better than to try to pull the wool over your eyes."

"You're worried about Brent Horan, aren't you?"

"I doubt that he has forgotten, or forgiven."

"A thousand Brent Horans could not keep me away from Sarah one more hour."

"You don't know him as I do," persisted Jeremy. "You're a brave man, Del. I've seen you in action, and there are none braver. But you're still no match for Horan."

Delgado bit his tongue, stifling a retort born of

wounded pride. In spite of the anguish he suffered over the condition of his father, Jeremy could still think of Delgado's best interests. He was, thought Delgado, a true friend. A strong bond had been forged between the two of them since that summer day when they'd departed St. Louis together, bound for adventure at the other end of the Santa Fe Trail.

"I can't stay," said Delgado. "I just can't, Jeremy. Sarah has occupied my dreams, my thoughts, my every waking moment for nearly six months. Six long months! I must see her. I can't come this close and stop."

Jeremy drew a long breath. "To care so much for someone can be a dangerous thing. Love can make fools out of wise men."

"Perhaps you have never loved anyone as I love your sister. If you had, you'd understand why I must go on."

Jeremy turned away, but not before Delgado saw the pain twist his features. "Don't be too sure of that. Well, if you must, come on. Let's get going."

Delgado clasped Falconer's hand in his own. "I'll be back to visit in a day or two."

"You're welcome under our roof anytime, Del."

They reached St. Louis as the sun dipped below the horizon, and twilight gave the snow on the streets a blue translucence. After many weeks in the barren, wintry wastes of the high plains, where the only sounds were the howling of wolves above the moaning wind, the noises of civilization were to Delgado very welcome indeed. The barking of dogs, the sound of laughter from one of the houses they passed by, the rattle and clatter of a carriage, the clang of a blacksmith's hammer, the faint, merry tinkle of piano keys, the distant clamor of ship's bells and steam whistles along the waterfront—it was all music to his ears.

When, finally, they arrived at the stately manor at the corner of Laurel and the Rue St. Eglise, Delgado's heart was beating like a trip-hammer in his chest. Sudden, bloodcurdling fear seized him. For six months he had dreamt of this moment—and now that it was here he could scarcely refrain from turning tail. Jeremy saw the look on his face and had to laugh.

"What's come over you, Del? Got cold feet all of a sudden?"

"No. No, of course not."

Still, he couldn't help but worry. What if something had happened to change Sarah's mind about him? He couldn't imagine what that something might be, and yet . . . The problem was that he did not think he could face life without Sarah Bledsoe. He needed her as he needed breath itself and, try as he might, he knew he would not feel secure until she was his bride. Only then would he know for certain that life would be worth living.

Steeling himself, he dismounted and followed Jeremy to the front door.

When they entered the house, Clarisse was just turning the corner into the hall, leaving the gallery, having come down the stairs carrying a tray—Delgado surmised that this had been Jacob Bledsoe's evening meal, and it didn't look like it had been touched. The Creole Negress stopped dead in her tracks and stared, and for the first time Delgado realized in horror that he must look a sight. He hadn't bathed or shaved in weeks. In his rush to see Sarah again he hadn't given his appearance a thought. What a fool he was! He should have at least lingered long enough at Falconer's cabin to make himself presentable.

"Clarisse!" Jeremy stepped forward, smiling.

She put the tray down on a taboret and went to him, giving him a maternal peck on the cheek as they embraced.

"How is Father doing?"

"He is in his room. Go on up, Jeremy. It will do him good to see you again."

"Clarisse? Is someone here?"

Delgado's heart skipped a beat, for this was Sarah's voice, coming from the gallery staircase.

"Your brother is home at last, child," called Clarisse. Then she smiled at Delgado. "And there is someone else you will want to see, I think."

He heard her racing down the stairs. Jeremy met her at the end of the hall, and she gasped at the sight of him and flowed into his arms.

"Jeremy!" she cried out in delight. "Jeremy, I'm so glad—!"

She saw Delgado then, and Jeremy, grinning, let her go and stepped away and said. "Wasn't easy, Sis, but thanks to Hugh Falconer we've managed to bring your man back safe and sound."

Sarah stood there a moment, gazing at Delgado. She was, he thought, the most beautiful woman in the whole world, with her big hazel eyes and ruby lips in a heart-shaped face framed by chestnut brown curls, her slender figure complemented by a pale yellow muslin dress.

"Del?"

"Sarah." His voice was a hoarse travesty of its usual self.

"Oh, Del!" She ran to him, and he wrapped her in his arms, and she kissed him with all the love and passion in her soul. Tasting the salt of her tears of happiness, Delgado knew at that moment that all was well. His doubts fled. The world was a wonderful place, and life would be worth living after all.

"It seems as though you've been gone forever," she said, breathlessly happy. "I missed you every minute you were away."

"And I missed you, Sarah. More than I can say. I'll never leave you again."

"You'd better not!" She turned to her brother while clinging possessively to Delgado's arm. "Promise you won't tell Father how I greeted my future husband, Jeremy. He'd think I was a shameless hussy."

"Don't worry. I wouldn't dream of telling him." Jeremy went up the stairs, eager to see his father.

"Del, you're so thin!" exclaimed Sarah. "Can we fatten him up, Clarisse? Not too much, of course."

"I think we can manage that, child." Clarisse headed for the kitchen.

As soon as Jeremy and Clarisse had gone and they were alone, Delgado took Sarah by the shoulders and held her at arm's length and looked her in the eyes and said, "Sarah, you called me your future husband. I guess that means you'll marry me?"

"Don't be silly. Of course I'm going to marry you. I knew we would be man and wife the moment we first met."

"You did? I think I did, too. As for setting a date, I suppose we'll have to suffer through a proper—that is to say, long—engagement."

"It had better not be too long, Mr. McKinn," she said and, curling her arms around his neck, gave him another heart-stopping kiss. When it was over, she slid him a look that Salome might have envied. "We're going to have lots and lots of children, Del, so we had better get started soon."

"Sarah!"

"Oh, did you think you were marrying a prim and proper young lady, sir?"

He laughed. "No—and thank God I'm not!"

"Come along. I'll heat some water for your bath. You smell like . . . like the Santa Fe Trail in all its pungent glory. And I'll get you a nice sharp razor. You must look your best when you go in to ask my father for his little girl's hand in marriage."

2

Having his son safely home again put some life into Jacob Bledsoe. He insisted on being moved downstairs, complaining that the walls of his bedroom, where he had been incarcerated for weeks, were beginning to close in on him. Sarah didn't think it was a good idea; the doctor had recommended that his patient remain in bed, warning that activity would only aggravate his condition. Jacob waved her protests away. "Just humor a dying man's few simple requests."

"Don't say such things, Father."

"Why shouldn't I? I'm reconciled to my own mortality, and you should be, too, my dear."

Delgado and Jeremy carried him downstairs and placed him in his favorite chair in the front parlor, over near the fireplace, where a warm, cheerful blaze popped and crackled. Delgado was astonished by Bledsoe's appearance; the man had been hearty and robust six months ago, and now he was pale, haggard, and much thinner. His eyes were bloodshot, with dark rings around them.

Sarah had told Delgado that her father suffered from fever, weakness, loss of appetite, and a persistent cough that grew progressively worse. She knew there would be no improvement. All they could do was make him as comfortable as possible and wait for the end. Delgado felt sorry for his beloved Sarah. How difficult it had to be, to watch someone you love die by inches before your very eyes, and all the while your job was to present a sunny disposition in hopes of keeping the patient's spirits up. Delgado was glad, both for his mother's sake and for his father's that Angus McKinn had died suddenly. Better that, by far, than this.

"I relish a bit of brandy," said Bledsoe.

"Father, you know the doctor said you could not indulge in strong spirits," said Sarah.

"To blazes with what the doctor said!" Bledsoe wheezed and hacked sputum into a handkerchief.

"Allow me, sir," said Delgado. With an apologetic glance at Sarah, he moved to the sideboard and poured Bledsoe a dollop of brandy. Sarah didn't approve, but she kept silent.

"Thank you, my boy. Thank you." Bledsoe accepted the glass gratefully, sipped, and closed his eyes in ecstasy. "The sad news of your personal tragedy has preceded you, Del. Angus was more than a business associate to me. He was my true friend, and I mourn his passing."

"Thank you, sir."

"I understand the leader of those murderous rebels was caught and hanged. A man by the name of . . . of . . . oh, what was that blasted man's name?"

"Archuleta. Diego Archuleta."

"Yes, yes. Archuleta. That's the one. I'll warrant you were glad to see him pay for his crimes."

"But they called him a traitor, and I don't think treason was one of his crimes. He was just fighting for what he believed in. And rebellion is, after all, very American."

"Well, at least the killing has stopped," said Bledsoe. "And you and my son are safe. What of Hugh Falconer?"

"He is well. He saved my life on more than one occasion."

"Extraordinary man. Extraordinary."

Delgado related how he and Falconer had been the only two to have escaped Turley's Mill alive. Jacob Bledsoe was visibly impressed by the courage Delgado had displayed by riding to warn the Americans, even though Delgado played down his role in the affair. Sarah, on the other hand, appeared shaken by the realization of how close she had come to losing the man of her dreams.

"Don't worry, Sarah," said Delgado, trying to lighten the mood. "I don't intend to get caught in the middle of any more insurrections."

"I hope this damnable war is over soon," growled Bledsoe with a sidelong glance at his son, Jeremy. "Unfortunately, we've invaded Mexico. Generals Taylor and Wool are moving south from the Rio Grande, and General Scott will soon strike westward for Mexico City from either Tampico or Vera Cruz." He shook his head dolefully. "It is a mistake to press the issue. A ghastly mistake, I tell you. We have California now, and that is what President Polk really wanted all along. Who knows how much more American blood will be spilled. And to what end? Should we take the better part of Mexico proper, we shall never be able to hold on to it. The North would never let that happen."

He began to cough again, his whole body racked with the violence of the seizure. Clarisse materialized with a cup of hot honey tea and bade him drink. The tea seemed to help.

Delgado glanced at Sarah. She nodded, and Delgado, trying to dislodge the lump in his throat, stepped forward.

"Mr. Bledsoe, there is something of great importance I want to discuss with you."

"Oh?" Bledsoe also glanced at Sarah. "I wonder what that might be?"

"I have asked your daughter to marry me, and she has made me the happiest man in the world by consenting to do so. I . . . we . . . would like to have your blessing."

"My blessing. Not my permission? If you had waited a few weeks, I would be in my grave, and you wouldn't have to worry about my blessing."

"Father!" exclaimed Sarah. "What a horrible thing to say!"

Bledsoe relented. "My apologies to you both. Of course you have my blessing. I am a sick and crabby old man, so please make allowances. You see, I am very afraid. Afraid of dying." He stared pensively into the fire. "But to know that my daughter's happiness—not to mention her security—is assured is a great comfort to me." He looked up at Delgado and smiled. "Do you intend to live here in St. Louis?"

"I'm not sure, sir. Whatever Sarah wishes to do."

Bledsoe nodded. "Perhaps in keeping a home and raising a family my daughter will discover that she has little or no time to pursue her crusades—abolitionism and all those other troublesome notions."

"Don't count on that, Father," said Sarah.

"Naturally, I leave my business to Jeremy, although he is not in the least interested. However, my daughter's dowry is nothing to sneeze at, I can promise you. Oh, I realize you are a quite well-to-do young man, Del, and you will have no difficulty in maintaining Sarah in the style to which she is accustomed, but you understand that a father feels a duty to do what he can to secure his daughter's future."

"Yes, sir."

Bledsoe sipped at his tea. "There is one other matter. Well, two, actually." He looked at Clarisse. "I want Clarisse to stay with Sarah. But I suppose I should manumit her, and leave that decision up to her, as well."

"Oh, Father, that would be wonderful," said Sarah, delighted. She went to Clarisse and gave her a hug. "You'll be free, Clarisse. I have long prayed for this moment."

Delgado thought Clarisse was taking her emancipation rather somberly.

"You're more than welcome to stay with us, naturally," he told her. "But the choice is yours. Perhaps you have something else in mind." He was thinking of the man, Stephen Maitland, at the St. Louis *Enquirer*.

"This child," said Clarisse, referring to Sarah, "is like a daughter to me. I had my own flesh-and-blood girl once. She die of the yellow fever down New Orleans way. Then I come here, and watch Sarah grow up into a fine young woman, and I think sometime I would have wanted my own daughter to be just like Sarah, had she lived."

"I love you so, Clarisse," said Sarah and kissed the Creole Negress on the cheek.

"I go where you go, child."

"That's settled, then," said Bledsoe. "Last but not least, Del, there is the matter of Brent Horan."

Jeremy shot out of his chair. "I hope for his sake he has not insulted my sister again during my absence," he snapped, truculent.

"Calm down, Jeremy. Calm down. He has done nothing of the kind. Nothing at all. If the truth be known, Brent has had his hands full with other things. Daniel Horan passed away a few weeks after you two boys left for Santa Fe."

"Passed away?" scoffed Jeremy. "Murdered, you mean, by slow poison."

"There is no evidence of that," said Bledsoe sternly. "In fact, whatever the mysterious ailment was that finally took Daniel, it must be congenital, for now it seems that his son suffers the same affliction."

"What?" Jeremy was incredulous.

Bledsoe nodded. "Brent Horan is dying by inches."

"But why," asked Delgado, "especially if he is dying, is Brent Horan a matter of concern to me?"

"Sarah didn't tell you?"

"Tell me what?"

"The day after you and Jeremy left, a Mr. William Darcy called. He said he was representing Brent Horan in an affair of honor. Darcy is a notorious character. A riverboat gambler by trade, and a duelist of some note, besides. He had come to make arrangements for a duel. It is to be done on Bloody Island."

Delgado shook his head. "That was six months

ago. Surely Horan's temper has had ample time to cool."

"Brent was very much in love with my daughter before she went away to the academy. In fact, that was one of the reasons I sent her away. She was sixteen then, and much too immature to marry, in my opinion."

"Marry?" echoed Delgado. He looked querulously at Sarah.

"He was a handsome, dashing cavalier," she said. "Or so I thought of him that way. Perhaps I'd read too much Walter Scott. I was foolish, and flattered by his attentions. It was just a childish infatuation on my part, Del. I didn't know the kind of man he was."

"I should hope not." Delgado remembered that day on the levee when he had watched Brent Horan in the process of purchasing the pretty octoroon—what had she been called? He couldn't recollect her name. But she had obviously been destined to become the object of Horan's pleasure.

"Please don't be upset with me, Del."

"I'm not. Believe me, Sarah, I'm not. It's just that I had hoped, by now, that this business with Horan would be water under the bridge."

"It may very well be," said Bledsoe. "But I think we should resolve this right away. Put it behind us, once and for all."

Delgado stared at him. He had a pretty good idea what Jacob Bledsoe meant. *"Right away" means before I marry his daughter. He doesn't want Sarah to become a widow.*

"Then maybe I should pay Brent Horan a visit," he said, knowing that was what Jacob Bledsoe wanted to hear.

Bledsoe nodded, pleased.

"I'll go to Blackwood with you," said Jeremy.

"That's not a good idea," said Bledsoe.

"No, it isn't," agreed Delgado. He put a hand on the scowling Jeremy's shoulder. "The idea is to make peace."

"You can't mend fences with a man like Brent Horan."

"*You* can't. Perhaps I can. I'm certainly willing to try."

"There is a risk," said Sarah. "He could have forgotten what happened before, but seeing you might make him remember. He might challenge you."

"I doubt that he's forgotten, because you were involved, and you're not easy to forget, Sarah. No, I'll go." He turned to Jacob Bledsoe. "I will send my card to Blackwood tomorrow and await his earliest convenience."

3

Early the next morning, Delgado went to the livery where he had purchased the four-stockinged bay the night he'd left St. Louis, the horse who had carried him down the Santa Fe Trail only to die—valiantly, he liked to think—running a gauntlet of insurgents in ambush at the Arroyo Hondo. He hired the owner's son, a twelve-year-old boy, to deliver his card to Blackwood, promising the eager lad a dollar when he brought Horan's answer back to the Bledsoe house. Delgado had written *At Your Earliest Convenience* on the back of the card. That was all. He was sure it would be enough.

The eternal optimist, he hoped that Brent Horan's ardor to see him dead would have cooled in six months' time. If not, so be it. Delgado had no intention of fighting a duel, and nothing would make him change his mind. No matter how hard Horan hated him, the man still considered himself a gentleman. He would not dream of shooting Delgado down in cold blood. So there was no harm in taking Jacob Bledsoe's suggestion and going to Blackwood, while there was a chance the whole matter might actually be amicably resolved. It was the least Delgado could do for Bledsoe; Sarah's father deserved a little peace of mind.

His next stop was the offices of the St. Louis *Enquirer,* which were located in a two-story brownstone on Market Street. This stretch of cobblestoned road between the levee and the square was the heart of the St. Louis business district. There were mercantiles, milliners, haberdashers, bootmakers, gunsmiths, land agents, doctors, dentists, and most of all lawyers; Delgado thought that there were more lawyers per capita in the United States than in any other country in the world. Every politician he could think of had started his professional life before the bar. He supposed this plethora of barristers was a perfectly natural byproduct of a democratic society where the people enjoyed the liberty to handle their own affairs without governmental interference. On the other side of every blessing lurked a curse.

Most of the ground floor of the *Enquirer*'s building had been given over to the production of the city's foremost penny press. A pair of steam-operated printing presses were making a deafening racket, and Delgado had to shout at the top of his lungs to be heard by the ink-stained apprentice whom he asked about Stephen Maitland's whereabouts. The boy pointed skyward, indicating the second floor, and Delgado ascended a steep, narrow flight of stairs, and found Maitland at his cluttered kneehole desk, scribbling furiously.

Maitland was a thin, gawky man in a rumpled tweed suit. A dour expression on his pale, angular face, he looked up at Delgado, with a pair of spectacles perched precariously on the tip of his nose; he was annoyed by the interruption. There was no heat in this big room filled with desks except that produced by a coal-burning stove at the far end; Maitland's grip was limp and cold as he took Delgado's proffered hand. He recognized Delgado's name immediately, and the annoyance turned into alarm as he looked about him like a conspirator who has just heard menacing footsteps behind him.

"What . . . what do you want, Mr. McKinn?"

"I wanted to thank you for your part in getting my letters to—"

Maitland put a finger to his lips, then crooked a finger, and Delgado leaned closer over the desk.

"No one here knows about this, Mr. McKinn, and I would very much like to keep it that way if you don't mind."

"I don't mind," said Delgado, mystified.

"You must realize that my . . . my relationship with Clarisse is . . . is a secret. Sterling was the only one who knew."

"I see. It might interest you to know that she will soon be a free person. Jacob Bledsoe has pledged to provide her with manumission papers."

Maitland stared at him, as though he had suddenly lost his ability to comprehend the English language. "I . . . I think you must misconstrue me, sir."

"Perhaps I do."

"You see, our relationship is a clandestine one not because she is a bondwoman, but . . . but because I am . . . I am a married man."

"Ah," said Delgado. He didn't know what else to say.

Maitland folded his spectacles, stowed them away in a drawer, and got to his feet. "Please come with me, Mr. McKinn."

"Certainly."

Delgado followed him downstairs and out onto the crowded sidewalk. They started walking in the direction of the levee, where the smokestacks of dozens of riverboats resembled a forest of tree trunks in the city's haze. Now that he was away from the *Enquirer,* Maitland seemed much more relaxed.

"She's a wonderful woman, isn't she, Mr. McKinn?" He sighed.

"Clarisse? Why yes, I suppose she must be. I don't know her all that well, but . . ."

"She is very . . . very passionate. My . . . my wife is not. You might say Helen is just the opposite, if the truth be known."

"Ah," said Delgado again, suddenly wishing he was elsewhere. He wondered what Clarisse could possibly see in this nervous beanpole of a man. She was an exotic and attractive woman in her own right, and she could have had her pick of men—especially if she was content to play the role of mistress. He wondered, too, why Maitland was confiding in him, a total stranger. Perhaps because he had no one else to talk to.

"If it ever got out that I, that we . . ." Maitland

shuddered, and it wasn't the cold January wind that made him do so. "It's not that she is a Negress. No, not at all."

Maitland's tone of voice convinced Delgado that the man was lying; Clarisse's race was at least part of the problem. In this place, and in this day and age, Maitland would be ostracized if it became known that he had a black mistress. He might have gotten away with it in New Orleans, but then the Crescent City was very cosmopolitan.

Maitland came to an abrupt halt and clutched Delgado's arm. "I . . . I love her, you know. Have no doubt of that." He blushed and looked away. "The fact that Mr. Bledsoe intends to free her is not good news, actually. No, not good news by any means. She might decide to leave St. Louis now. She might go north. Dear God, I could lose her. I . . . I know it's terribly selfish of me to think that way, but . . . but I'd just as soon she remained a slave. I mean, it's not as though Mr. Bledsoe mistreats her."

Delgado grimaced. He was beginning not to like Stephen Maitland.

"Clarisse is devoted to Sarah Bledsoe," he said. "And Sarah will soon be my wife."

Maitland blinked his owlish eyes at Delgado, slow to comprehend. "You don't approve, do you, Mr. McKinn?"

"Frankly, no."

"I have no right to ask this of you, but I . . . I am, you might say, a prisoner of my own desires. Where Clarisse is concerned I do not seem to have a will of my own. She has bewitched me."

"I don't know where my wife and I will reside," said Delgado, anticipating precisely what Maitland was about to put to him.

"If . . . if it's here in St. Louis . . . ?"

Delgado thought, *How did I get myself into this?* Grimacing, he nodded. "As far as I am concerned, what Clarisse does is none of my business, and never will be. Your secret will be safe with me."

Overwhelmed with gratitude, Maitland clasped his hand.

"Thank you!" he gushed. "Thank you, Mr. McKinn! If there is ever . . . I mean, if I can ever be of any service to you . . ."

Delgado nodded wearily. He could not imagine how Maitland ever could be of service to him.

They continued walking east, toward the river. "I owed Sterling my job at the newspaper," explained Maitland. "He was my . . . my friend. I don't have many friends."

Brows knit, Delgado was the one to stop in his tracks this time. Maitland took several steps before he realized that he was walking alone, then turned.

"Twice you've used the past tense when referring to him," said Delgado.

Maitland's eyes got bigger. "You didn't know? You haven't heard?"

My God, thought Delgado, suddenly cold to the marrow of his bones.

"We . . . we only just got the news a few days ago," said Maitland. He pressed his lips tightly together, and his eyes watered up. "Sterling was killed in California."

Delgado looked beyond Maitland, at the riverboat smokestacks, remembering the occasion aboard the *Sultana* when he had first made Sterling's acquaintance.

He took a deep breath. "How did it happen?"

"Come back to the office with me. I've kept all

his dispatches. Would . . . would you care to see them?"

"Yes, I would. Thank you."

They returned to the *Enquirer.* Maitland removed the dispatches from a locked desk drawer, handling them almost reverently. They had been folded and creased and stained and in some cases torn—Delgado felt sure they had come a long way over rough terrain under usually poor conditions.

"I'll leave you alone," said Maitland. He could tell that Delgado was deeply moved. "Feel free to take as long as you like."

"Thank you."

The dispatches were in order according to date, and Delgado settled back with a deep sigh and proceeded to read them through.

General Kearny left Santa Fe near the end of September with three hundred dragoons, Lt. Emory and his topographical engineers, a battery of mountain howitzers, and one very witty and observant reporter. After ten days on the trail they met the famed mountain man Kit Carson, who, with twenty other adventurers, were also bound for California. They had heard tell of the Bear Flag Revolt by the American residents and were looking for some excitement. Kearny persuaded Carson to act as his guide.

The terrain soon became too rough for wagons, so Kearny packed his supplies on mules and pressed on. His men were often short of food and water as they crossed first the desert and then the mountains. But Kearny's dragoons were tough characters, hardened by long months of patrolling and campaigning on the high plains, and they were well-trained, highly disciplined troops. Sterling was full of praise for them. He heaped many superlatives upon these soldiers, and upon their commanding officer.

Finally, reaching California in early December, Kearny paused at a ranch owned by a man named Warner, where he learned that Commodore Stockton had seized the port of San Diego. Frémont and the Bear Flag rebels controlled Monterey to the north. That left the Mexican loyalist under Captain Juan Flores at Los Angeles with the enemy above and below him. By all accounts the Californians were in dire straits. Flores could muster only four hundred men, and had less than a thousand rounds of ammunition to distribute. It seemed, wrote Sterling, that California was destined to become part of the United States of America, and there was precious little the Californians could do about it.

Kearny sent a message to San Diego, informing Commodore Stockton of his whereabouts, and Stockton promptly dispatched Captain Archibald Gillespie with forty men to rendezvous with the First Dragoons. Kearny met Gillespie on the road and discovered that a detachment of Californian lancers had been tailing the Americans from San Diego. The general ordered an attack at dawn, December 6th. He was confident of victory. Too confident, wrote Sterling, for his men were exhausted, and their mounts were on their last legs. Still, Gillespie and Carson were all for battle, and the numbers were stacked heavily in favor of the Americans.

The dragoons roused themselves at two A.M. and mounted their motley assortment of mules and horses. Because of the condition of their mounts, the dragoons reached the position of the lancers in a piecemeal fashion, only to discover that the dampness of the bitterly cold morning had wet the powder in the firearms. The Californians struck back with a bold countercharge, and put their lances to good use. The saber-wielding dragoons could not withstand their charge, and only the arrival of Kearny's artillery saved the day. The lancers retired in good order, and Kearny, reported Sterling, was left with one very bloody nose. Eighteen Americans were dead, including a pair of captains, Moore and Johnston, with whom Sterling had often enjoyed a round or two of whist. Of the seventy-five Californians engaged in the battle, only one lost his life.

Though left in possession of the field of battle, Kearny knew it had been a Pyrric victory. He also knew his troops were in no condition to pursue the enemy. As it turned out, he didn't have to. Moving slowly westward, Kearny found himself besieged by the lancers at Rancho San Bernardo. The arrival of a relief force sent out by Commodore Stockton drove the pesky Californians away. On December 12th, wrote Sterling, he arrived at San Diego with the First Dragoons and got his first look at the Pacific Ocean.

Right away sparks flew between Kearny and Stockton. The former claimed to have orders from Washington that made him supreme commander of American forces in California. Stockton, having gotten there first and conquered San Diego and a large chunk of southern California, refused to cede authority. He did not question Kearny's orders, but argued that they had been rendered inoperative. The plans for a campaign against the Californians at Los Angeles was his, and by thunder he would lead it.

Toward the end of December the Americans moved north, six hundred strong. Sterling had enjoyed his fortnight in balmy San Diego and was sorry that the war had to interfere with his sightseeing. Still, he had a job to do, and he rode north with the army.

Captain Flores made plans to ambush the Americans when they crossed the San Gabriel River. Although aware of the presence of the enemy, Stockton tried to force the crossing without waiting for artillery covering fire, as Kearny advised. By sheer weight of numbers the Americans forced the Californians back. Flores reluctantly ordered a withdrawal. Stockton urged his men to press their advantage and drove the Californians before them. While Stockton's battlefield judgment left something to be desired, wrote Sterling, the man's courage was beyond reproach; he had been in the thick of the action from start to finish.

That night, according to Sterling's final dispatch, the Americans camped in the hills north of the San Gabriel. Spirits were high, because in the morning they would push on to Los Angeles, and no one expected Flores to put up much of a fight. Surely, tomorrow the Stars and Stripes would fly over Government House, and President Polk would finally have California, his heart's desire. The United States would stretch from coast to coast, and America's "Manifest Destiny" would be realized. *As a good Whig,* wrote Sterling, *I suppose I should not feel quite so exhilarated.*

Those were his last words.

Delgado rubbed his eyes and looked up to see Maitland approaching.

"How did he die?"

"Some of the Californians slipped back to the river that night," explained Maitland. "They fired a few shots at the campfires. A bullet struck Sterling at the base of the skull and killed him instantly. I'm told he probably never knew what hit him."

Feeling drained, empty, Delgado muttered his thanks, left the dispatches on Maitland's desk, and walked out of the building.

He aimlessly wandered the streets of St. Louis for several hours, missing his friend terribly. Poor Sterling, killed in a war he had opposed, and so far from home.

Chapter Twelve

"You will meet me on Bloody Island."

1

That evening the boy from the livery brought Brent Horan's answer to the Bledsoe house. On the back of Delgado's card Horan had written: *Tomorrow.*

The next morning Delgado rented a horse at the same livery and rode alone to Blackwood.

To the very end Jeremy insisted he was a fool to go in the first place, a bigger fool to go alone, and finally an even bigger fool to go unarmed. Delgado was certain he was in no danger.

"Honor means everything to Horan," he said. "He may still want to kill me. I suppose that's why I'm going, to find that out. But he won't shoot me down in cold blood."

"At least take your derringer along."

"No."

"You're too stubborn for your own good, Del."

"I'm not going to give him any excuse."

"Brent Horan doesn't need an excuse. I know him better than you do. He is unpredictable. And I would not stake my life on his honor."

"Why do you hate him so much?"

Jeremy's lips thinned. "It is something that happened a long time ago. Maybe I'll tell you about it. Someday."

Delgado didn't press. Whatever secret Jeremy

was guarding, it had obviously been a turning point in his friend's life, an event that had colored the rest of his days, and not for the better. And Delgado had a feeling that as much as Jeremy blamed Brent Horan for whatever had happened, he blamed himself as much or more.

The morning was cold and clear, but the sun felt warm on Delgado's frozen cheeks as he rode out of St. Louis, past the great clearings where the snow was piled high enough to conceal the unsightly tree stumps. Soon he came to the old dark woods marking the perimeter of the Horan estate. Passing down the green tunnel of trees, he shuddered involuntarily as he passed the spot where, six months ago, he and Jeremy had found Talbott, the slave catcher, bringing the runaway field hand he had just killed out of the forest.

At long last he came to the Horan mansion. A black youth loped around the side of the house to hold his horse, and an old, white-haired house servant greeted him with grave reserve at the door. Delgado introduced himself and said that Brent Horan was expecting him. The old man nodded, appropriated Delgado's hat, coat, and gloves, and led him to the doors of the front parlor. The house was as cold and silent as a tomb.

Horan was sitting in a wing chair near the hearth, clad in a brown riding suit, his feet, encased in knee-high black boots polished to a high sheen, extended toward the fire. The drapes were pulled closed over the windows, and the fire provided the only illumination in the room, and without the sunshine the room seemed colder than it really was.

"Mr. McKinn's here to see you, suh," said the old man.

"Get out."

The old man slipped back, pulling the door gently shut.

Horan didn't look around. He continued to stare into the fire. A gentleman would have risen to greet his guest, but Delgado hadn't expected cordiality, so he crossed the room to stand near enough to the hearth to thaw his frozen limbs.

"What do you want from me?" asked Horan.

Delgado turned to face him—and was shocked by the man's appearance. Clearly, it was true. Whatever mysterious ailment had leeched the life, little by little, out of Daniel Horan now had Brent in its grasp. In six months Horan appeared to have aged ten or fifteen years. He was gaunt, his cheeks hollow, his eyes sunk deep in their sockets. His skin had a grayish, translucent quality. His hair was streaked with white at the temples. Deep lines bracketed a mouth etched in pain.

Horan smiled thinly at the look on Delgado's face. "I'm sure you've heard that I am ill. No condolences are necessary."

Even though this was Brent Horan, Delgado hated to see anyone consumed by disease and dying by inches, especially someone so young.

"What do the doctors say?" he asked.

Horan shrugged, winced, and turned his attention back to the flames. "The slaves say it is voodoo. That someone has put a curse on me. They are not, I might add, brokenhearted."

"What do you think?"

"I don't think. I know. I am being poisoned."

Delgado recalled Jeremy telling him that Brent was slowly poisoning his father. If that was true, then this was surely justice in the Old Testament sense of the word.

"But I would think," said Delgado, "that it would be extremely difficult to poison a man who suspects he is being poisoned."

"Pull the sash."

Delgado saw the bell pull on the wall beside the mantelpiece and gave it a tug.

"Once more, for Naomi," hissed Horan.

Delgado pulled the sash a second time. Very faintly, he heard a bell jangle in some distant corner of the big house. A moment later, the octoroon slave girl Delgado had last seen on the levee on the day of his arrival at St. Louis entered the room. She was barefoot, and instead of the plain calico dress one might expect a slave to wear, she was clad in a scarlet dress, daringly low cut and adorned with black lace. It was the type of garment, garish and suggestive, that a woman of easy virtue might wear. Her tousled hair fell in abandon to her ebony shoulders. There was an almost feral gleam in her dark eyes. She looked at Delgado, and he could tell she recognized him.

"This is Naomi," said Horan. "She is a whore. That is why I insist that she dress like one. She is my murderess."

Delgado got the impression he was an actor in a bad dream. What exactly was going on here? This scene was almost too macabre to be real, and he began to wonder if Brent Horan was mad.

He looked at Naomi, waiting for her reaction to Horan's accusation, but her expression was inscrutable and told him nothing.

"Oh, yes, McKinn. The bitch is murdering me," continued Horan. "But I don't know precisely how. I make her taste all of my food. She takes the first sip of any drink that is placed before me. As you can see, she does not seem to be similarly afflicted. I have no proof, therefore. Nonetheless, I am certain."

"Surely, a man like you doesn't need proof to act," said Delgado dryly.

Horan grinned like a fox, without mirth.

"You mean why don't I just kill her and be done with it?"

"You are certainly capable of such a thing."

"Quite so. And I *will* kill her, in my own good time. Oh yes, she will die before I do. You see, McKinn, we have a peculiar situation here. Naomi knows she is doomed, and yet she doesn't try to run away. What does that tell you? That she is willing to die in order to accomplish her purpose. Which is my death."

"And you? You're evidently willing to play the game through to the end."

"Oh course."

Fascinated by this morbid situation, Delgado shook his head. "Let's say, for the sake of argument, that you're right—that she is poisoning you. If you did away with her now, you might recover."

"But then I would be deprived of going to her every night, of taking my pleasure as I watch the hate unmasked in her eyes, of having my way with my own executioner."

Delgado stared at him. "You have a twisted mind, Horan."

"Thank you. I think, perhaps, that day on the levee, you wanted to prevent me from buying her, if only to spite me."

"That's true, in part. It wasn't to spite you, though."

"Indeed? You wanted her for yourself, perhaps?

Well, I can't blame you. Look at her. She is beguiling, isn't she? And she is a wildcat in bed."

"That's not why, either. I wanted to save her from you."

"Ah. The truth is out. You're another one of those crusaders, aren't you? This country is full of them. You wanted to save her from—what? A fate worse than death?"

He is mocking me now, realized Delgado. *He is insane. That means I was wrong—I* am *in danger here.*

"Something like that," he said.

"You wanted to, and yet you didn't. That's your problem. You lack the courage of your convictions. I'll give you a second chance. Life doesn't often give us second chances, McKinn, so consider my offer carefully before you let another opportunity slip through your grasp."

"I'm listening."

"One round of whist, McKinn. If you win, you can take Naomi away from here, saving her life in the process. What do you say? Come on, man. You're a gambler, aren't you?"

"And if I should lose?"

Horan struggled to get to his feet, a mask of pure hate on his face.

"Then you will meet me on Bloody Island."

"You mean a duel."

"That is precisely what I mean. You won't accept a challenge issued in the conventional way, will you? You have nothing to gain by it, since you have no honor to protect, and since you know I will prevail. So what do you say? You could save this nigger wench's life."

Delgado glanced at Naomi. As impossibly bizarre as it sounded, he believed that Brent Horan would kill this woman. Was she really poisoning him? Perhaps so. Not that it truly mattered. She would die, and she knew it, and Delgado actually flirted with the idea of accepting Horan's offer. After all, he'd had the chance to rescue Naomi from this evil man once before, and failed. Failed her—and failed himself, as well. Could he walk out of here and leave her to a terrible and certain fate?

Then he thought of Sarah, and the bright promise of their future together, and knew that, yes, he could. He had to. Bitterly, he realized that perhaps Horan was right. Perhaps he did lack the courage of his convictions—if he had any convictions. But he had too much to live for to throw his life away.

And it was clear that Naomi did not want to be rescued.

He looked Horan straight in the eye and said no.

Fury stormed across Horan's ravaged features, and Delgado suspected that, had he been possessed of a weapon at that moment, Horan might have killed him on the spot, and the gentleman's code of honor be damned.

"One day," snarled Horan, "you will face me on the field of honor."

"Horan," said Delgado coldly, "I came to tell you that Sarah Bledsoe and I are to be married. I had hoped you would realize that while there may have once been something between the two of you, there is nothing now. Sarah changed while she was away, and she despises everything you represent."

Horan sank back into his chair. The effort required to rise and stand for a few moments had completely exhausted him.

"You will never marry her, McKinn," he said

confidently. "If I can't have her, no one will. Now get out of my house, you gutless bastard."

With a stranglehold on his flaring temper, Delgado walked out of the room. In passing Naomi he forced himself to look her way, but it was as though he did not even exist for her; she was gazing at Brent Horan with such malevolence that Delgado believed Horan was telling the truth—that she was, somehow, killing him by degrees, and was perfectly willing to die if it meant ridding the world of his shadow. Horan's will was strong, but no more so than Naomi's. The two of them were locked in a deadly embrace, and both were too proud to let go. Delgado wished he had her courage.

He collected his hat, coat, and gloves from the old servant in the main hall, then his mount from the boy outside, and urged the horse into a gallop as soon as he was in the saddle, eager to be gone from this wicked place.

2

Jacob Bledsoe was anxious to hear all about Delgado's visit to Blackwood, and that afternoon he had Delgado and Jeremy carry him down to the parlor from his bedroom; now that he had two strapping young men to transport him, he expressed his intention to come downstairs on a daily basis. With Jeremy and Sarah present, Delgado related the whole story, leaving nothing out.

"So you see, sir," said Delgado in conclusion, "I failed in the endeavor. There still exists bad blood between Brent Horan and me."

Bledsoe shook his head. "Incredible. Simply incredible. The man must be stark raving mad. As long as he lives, Del, your life is in jeopardy."

"Which is why Brent should be killed," said Jeremy.

"You stay away from him," said Bledsoe. "Give me your solemn word that you will, son."

"Very well, Father. I will avoid him. If possible."

"It's possible—just steer well clear of Blackwood. Horan rarely leaves that place these days."

Jeremy just nodded unhappily.

"Please understand, Mr. Bledsoe," said Delgado, "that this doesn't change anything. I still intend to marry your daughter."

Bledsoe nodded. "Of course you do. I think the two of you should be wed as soon as possible. And then, Del, I want you to leave St. Louis. Go back to Taos and take Sarah with you."

"I will not leave you, Father," said Sarah firmly. "I cannot."

"You will both be safe in Taos. Horan cannot harm you there. Please, daughter. Do this one last thing for me. Del, do you concur?"

"I leave that decision up to Sarah." In fact, what Jacob Bledsoe suggested had already occurred to Delgado during his ride back to town from Blackwood. It had also occurred to him that Sarah would never leave St. Louis as long as her father lived, so he had reluctantly decided not to even broach the subject.

"Not like you, Del, to run," said Jeremy.

"Jeremy, you're a fool!" snapped Bledsoe.

Sarah went to her father and kissed him on the cheek. There were quiet tears in her eyes. "If it is your wish, Father, I will go away."

Delgado couldn't believe his ears.

"Good! Good!" Bledsoe rubbed his hands together. "That's settled then. The two of you decide on a date. Make it soon. The sooner the better."

"What about appearances, sir?" asked Delgado. "If we seem to rush into this, tongues may begin to wag, you know."

"And there are vicious tongues in this town," said Jeremy.

"To hell with appearances," grumbled Bledsoe. "Good God, man, I have lived my whole life for the sake of appearances. Now that I am about to cast off this mortal coil, I realize how wrong I have been to do so. Besides, I have my heart set on giving the bride away, and a long engagement could be fatal to my plans." He smiled at the small joke he had made.

"I wish you wouldn't say things like that, Father." Sarah sighed.

Bledsoe patted her hand. "I find it rather ironic that the two of you are suddenly preoccupied with keeping up a good appearance in this matter. If memory serves me, you are the same two hotheads who helped a prisoner escape from jail and then smuggled abolitionist propaganda into the house of a prominent slaveowner." He chuckled. "Now, suddenly, you're worried about what people think?"

Delgado smiled. "It's what *you* think that matters most, sir."

"Well, I'll tell you what I think, young man. I think my daughter has made a very wise choice for a husband."

"Thank you."

"No, it is I who should thank you, Del. And God help you. You'll have your hands full with this one, I promise you. She is full of surprises."

"Oh, Father," said Sarah, trying bravely to sound light of heart. "Admit it. You wouldn't want me to be any other way."

"Hmph! What about a best man, Del?"

"I thought I would ask Jeremy."

"Splendid!" said Bledsoe.

"Of course," said Jeremy without much enthusiasm.

"What's wrong with you?" asked his sister.

"Nothing. I would be pleased to be your best man, Del."

"Fine. I think I'll ride out and tell Hugh Falconer. I want to make sure he's going to be at the wedding."

The next day Delgado rode out to the Falconer cabin to do just that. The mountain man was chopping firewood when he rode up, and invited Delgado in for some hot coffee. The day was sunny but cold, and Delgado gratefully accepted the invitation. He told Falconer and Lillian that he and Sarah had decided to be married in two weeks' time.

"We'll be there, of course," said Lillian, delighted.

"Wouldn't miss it," said Falconer. "So, Del, why don't you tell me what's bothering you?"

Delgado was taken aback. "Is it that obvious?"

"We've been through quite a lot together, you and I, in the last six months. I think I can read you pretty well, and right now I'd say you're worried sick about something. Maybe I can help."

Delgado proceeded to tell him about yesterday's visit to Blackwood. "The man is obviously insane," he concluded. "He is obsessed with the idea of doing away with me. But why? It makes no sense. He isn't rational. I stopped him from committing murder aboard the *Sultana.* He should thank me for that. And I am marrying a girl who wouldn't have anything to do with him even if I had never entered her life."

He stopped and looked sheepishly at Falconer, realizing he had given himself away.

"Yes, Hugh, I'm scared. Brent Horan scares me."

"Me, too."

"Would I stand a ghost of a chance against him in a duel?"

Falconer shook his head. "Even if you did, would it make any difference?"

"No, I guess not."

"I didn't think so."

"I will not fight a duel. It's one thing to kill a man in the heat of battle. But dueling is . . . is cold-blooded murder, any way you look at it. Don't you agree?"

"Doesn't matter what I think, Del. It's what you believe, and you have to live your life according to your beliefs."

Delgado sighed. "I just don't understand why Horan is so set on killing me."

"Pride."

"What do you mean?"

"You keep getting the best of him, Del. You beat him at cards. You made him back down from lynching that abolitionist. Then you helped Rankin escape. Don't think those men you saw outside the courthouse weren't there with Horan's blessing. There are probably twenty, thirty men in these parts who would drop everything to do his bidding. They feel beholden to Daniel Horan for helping them through the hard times, and that carries over to his son, without question. It's an obligation, of sorts."

Delgado nodded. "Jeremy told me."

"As for Sarah, you'll never be able to convince Horan that you didn't steal her away from him. He doesn't like to lose, Del, and he loses every time with you. But on Bloody Island he knows he wouldn't lose."

"Do you think Sarah is in danger?"

"No way of telling. Horan isn't rational, as you said. Who knows what he might do?"

"But he is deathly ill. He couldn't do much."

"Don't be too sure."

"What do you suggest?"

"Leave St. Louis as soon as possible and take Sarah with you. Sounds to me like Horan will be dead before summer. Then you can come back if you want to."

"Running away." Delgado grimaced. "Smacks of cowardice, don't you think?"

"Put pride aside and concern yourself with Sarah's safety."

"Yes, of course. Well, Jacob Bledsoe made the same suggestion. I guess I'd better be getting back."

"Won't you stay for supper?" asked Lillian.

"Thank you, ma'am. Maybe some other time. I'm grateful for the coffee."

Falconer walked outside with him.

"If you need help," said the mountain man as Delgado mounted up, "you know where to find me."

Delgado nodded and rode away. It was a comfort to know that a man like Hugh Falconer would back him if matters took a turn for the worse.

He was wending his way through the hustle

and bustle of the St. Louis streets when a covered surrey rumbled right by him, and he caught a glimpse of Blackwood's white-haired doorman handling the reins. There was someone in the rear seat, beneath the calabash roof, huddled in blankets, and though Delgado didn't get a clean look at the passenger, he knew it had to be Horan. A vague but disquieting premonition prompted Delgado to wheel his horse around and follow the surrey. He was confident Horan hadn't seen him, and he was curious to know what his nemesis was up to. Whatever it was, Delgado felt sure he wouldn't like it.

The surrey came to a stop in front of the Planter's House hotel. Delgado angled his horse to the opposite side of the street. Dismounting, he tethered his mount to one of the iron hitching posts and climbed up onto the sidewalk. Across the street Brent Horan emerged from the surrey and was met by a man Delgado had never seen before. He was obviously a man of breeding. He was clad in a well-tailored frock coat in hunter's green, fawn-colored trousers, polished boots, and a silk hat. He carried a malacca cane. The man gestured to the Planter's House barroom as he talked to Horan, and a moment later they entered that establishment together.

Delgado hurried across the street, dodging a horseman in a hurry and a dray wagon loaded with casks, and headed in the direction of the river. He approached the old slave, who was standing beside the surrey.

"Good afternoon," said Delgado. "Do you remember me?"

"Yessuh. Good afternoon to you, suh."

"Could you tell me, who was that man who was just speaking with Mr. Horan?"

"Dat's Mistuh William Darcy, suh. He's a long time friend of the massuh's."

Darcy! The man who, according to Jacob Bledsoe, had tried to deliver Horan's challenge the day after he and Jeremy had left St. Louis. A notorious character, Bledsoe had said. A riverboat gambler by trade, and a duelist of some note, besides.

Why had Horan come to town to meet Darcy? Perhaps just to have a friendly drink or two in the Planter's House barroom. But supposedly Horan seldom left Blackwood these days. And he was certainly in no condition to make the trip. Delgado admitted to himself that he had felt relatively safe knowing that Horan was essentially confined to the plantation by his illness. That sense of security was now proven false. Delgado felt he needed to know what Horan was up to.

"Thank you," he told the old man and followed Horan and Darcy inside.

The barroom of prestigious Planter's House was no ordinary saloon. Dark polished wood, gleaming brass, maroon and dark green upholstery, a thirty-foot pier glass above the back bar, ornately framed oils of seductive nudes, the best labels, the aroma of the finest cigar tobacco—even the spitoons were kept at a high polish. Only gentlemen were allowed in this establishment, and there was quite a few of them present at this hour, enough to keep four bartenders hopping behind the fifty-foot mahogany bar. Delgado had been here before, with Jeremy, who frequented the place when he wasn't off fighting in a war.

Delgado found a spot for himself at the end of

the bar near the street entrance and scanned the room, locating Brent Horan and William Darcy at a table beneath one of the stained glass windows depicting a white plantation house at the end of a tree-lined drive. They were staring at someone farther down the bar, unaware of Delgado's presence. Delgado hoped he could keep it that way.

"Name your poison, sir," said a barkeep.

"A cognac."

The man nodded and poured a dollop of the amber liqueur into a glass.

"Are you a guest in the hotel, sir?"

"No." Delgado paid for the drink.

"My good man, have you heard the news?" A middle-aged gentlemen had bellied up to the bar next to Delgado. He was flushed and bleary-eyed; obviously he had overindulged.

"What news are you referring to?" asked Delgado pleasantly, trying to scan the faces along the bar.

"Why, about General Winfield Scott, of course. Ol' Fuss and Feathers himself. He's captured Vera Cruz. Why, by this time, his army must be on the march for Mexico City. He'll whip that devil, Santa Anna. Mark my words, sir, the war will soon be over."

"Splendid," said Delgado. "Now, if you will excuse me . . ."

He stepped away from the bar, studying the men collected at the far end of the mahogany. If he moved deeper into the room for a better angle, Horan and Darcy could not help but see him. Quite possibly, Horan would let him alone in this public place. But Delgado didn't want to take that chance. If it was at all possible, he wanted to avoid the man altogether.

Then he saw Jeremy Bledsoe separate himself from a crowd at the far end of the bar. A belligerent cast on his features, he moved, unsteadily, toward Horan's table.

"It has come to my attention that you two gentlemen are staring at me," he said, putting a caustic slur on the word *gentlemen*.

Smiling coldly, Darcy glanced at Horan.

"We were discussing your sister, sir," said Horan. "We have heard she is involved with a ring of criminal abolitionists who help slaves escape their rightful owners. The rumor is that she does not charge a fee for the nigger bucks, as long as they consent to sleep with her."

The silence started at the tables adjacent to Horan's and spread like a highly contagious virus across the room.

"Did you hear that?" one man near Delgado whispered to another.

Delgado moved. "Jeremy!"

Jeremy glanced at him. So did Horan. But Darcy was watching Jeremy like a hawk.

As he neared the table, Delgado said, "Jeremy, don't do this. Remember the promise you made to your father."

Jeremy looked at him as though he did not know who Delgado was. Then he leaned over the table and backhanded Brent Horan.

Darcy shot to his feet. Horan remained in his chair, touching his jaw where Jeremy's knuckles had left a red welt. Triumph blazed in his eyes. He glanced at Darcy.

"Would you do the honors, Mr. Darcy?"

"I consider it a privilege, Mr. Horan," replied the gambler.

"Any time, any place," hissed Jeremy.

Darcy turned to Delgado. "Am I to assume that you will represent Mr. Bledsoe in this affair?"

Sick at heart, Delgado nodded. He wanted no part of this madness, but Jeremy was his friend, and he could not forsake him now.

"Bloody Island," said Darcy. "Tomorrow at dawn. Pistols will be Mr. Horan's weapon of choice. Is that understood?"

"Perfectly," said Delgado.

Horan got to his feet.

"Why are you doing this, Horan?" asked Delgado. "Is it because I refused to fight you?"

"Oh, you will, McKinn, you will. No, this is unfinished business between Jeremy and me. It has nothing to do with you. I don't want to leave any loose ends. Good day, gentlemen."

He walked out of the barroom.

"Bloody Island, at dawn tomorrow," said Darcy and followed Horan.

Delgado realized everyone in the place was staring at him and Jeremy. "Let's get out of here," he said.

They reached the crowded sidewalk as Horan's surrey pulled away. Darcy was seated beside Horan. Neither man looked around.

As he watched the surrey go, Delgado said, "You're a fool, Jeremy. They planned this whole thing."

"Horan is right. We have unfinished business."

"What kind of business? Damn it, Jeremy, what will I tell Sarah? And what will you tell your father?"

"You didn't have to involve yourself."

"I'm as big a fool as you are."

"Fine. I'll find someone else to serve as my second."

He started to walk away. Delgado caught up with him, took him by the arm, and spun him around.

"I haven't forgotten how you stood at my side that night in Taos, when Archuleta's men were after me and my family. I'll stand by you tomorrow. But I want to know why. I want the truth, Jeremy. Why is this happening?"

"Darcy's been watching me ever since we got back. Every day I've come here at this hour. I established a routine so Horan would know where to find me. I didn't want this to happen at my own house, in front of my father."

Delgado shook his head. "How considerate! So you never meant to keep that promise."

"It had to happen."

"But I want to know why. Why this bad blood between you and Horan?"

"I'll tell you in the morning. On the way to Bloody Island."

Delgado let go of his arm. "Jeremy, my friend, he will kill you."

"Probably. If *I* don't get him, though, it will be up to you, Del."

"I am not going to fight a duel. I have too much to live for to throw my life away."

"I don't," said Jeremy, and turned away.

3

Early the next morning before dawn, Delgado found himself in a surrey rattling through the sleeping streets of St. Louis. They had slipped out of the Bledsoe house, walked a couple of blocks along Laurel Avenue, and found the rented conveyance waiting for them, as Jeremy had arranged. The driver was perceptive enough to know that something was afoot that he would be better off knowing nothing about, so he kept his mouth shut and attended to the business of delivering his passengers to Maple Point, which Jeremy informed him was their destination. Delgado still wanted to know the reason for the long-standing feud between his friend and Brent Horan, but Jeremy did not want to talk in the presence of the driver, so Delgado was forced to bide his time.

They had left Jacob and Sarah ignorant of the dark mission upon which they were now embarked. Jeremy insisted that no good could come from telling his father in advance, and on that score Delgado had to agree. But he had wanted to tell Sarah the whole truth. Most of all he wanted to explain to her, before the fact, why he was involved in an affair which in all likelihood would result in the death of her brother. He was afraid she would hate him for it—and hate him all the more for keeping it a secret from her. But Jeremy begged him not to speak to Sarah, and in the end Delgado agreed not to. How could he refuse Jeremy this? It would be like refusing the last wish of a dying man. Through it all ran Delgado's strong conviction that nothing on earth could deter Jeremy. This was the moment Jeremy had been living for. The question remained—why?

At Maple Point, north of the city, a boat was to be waiting for them. Jeremy had made this arrangement, too. Here they would also be met by a Dr. Loveless. According to Jeremy, Loveless was one of the few St. Louis physicians whose discretion could be relied upon by duelists. Not surprisingly, the good doctor was a Southerner who believed devoutly in the validity of the affair of honor for the settlement of differences between gentlemen. Loveless had made numerous excursions to Bloody Island. Apart from this, he was a capable physician whose presence on the dueling ground had saved more than one life. Loveless, however, had not yet arrived at Maple Point, and Jeremy took this opportunity to finally share his secret with Delgado. Suddenly, he seemed almost eager to do so.

"Not too many years ago," he began, "I developed a real friendship with Allan Horan, Brent's older brother. The two of them were as different as the moon and the sun. Allan was a decent fellow, well liked by all who knew him. He would go out of his way to help a person in need, be they acquaintance or complete stranger. He never had a harsh word for anyone—except Brent. They were usually at odds.

"It happened that Allan and I fell in love with the same girl. Her name was Annabel—Annabel Christophe. Her father was a merchant. He's dead now. Annabel was as beautiful as . . . as an angel." Jeremy paused. His voice was trembling, and he took a moment to collect himself, staring past Delgado at the river where the dark shape of Bloody Island was silhouetted against the gray eastern sky.

"Allan and I both courted Annabel, but eventually she had to make a choice, and she chose me. Allan accepted her decision with good grace. He bore me no ill will. Our friendship was strong enough to withstand even this strain. Annabel agreed to marry me. But I ruined everything. I was an impetuous fool, then."

Delgado smiled. "I'm afraid you still are, my friend."

"Yes, yes, I suppose I am. You see I . . . we . . ." Jeremy shook his head, his features twisted with powerful emotions. "We made love, Annabel and I. She became pregnant. Needless to say, she was distraught. If her father found out, he would be outraged. He would forbid her to marry me. I would not be allowed even to see her again. Annabel's reputation would be ruined. I begged her to run away with me. We would be married and live where no one would be aware of the truth. But she wouldn't do it. The poor girl . . ." Jeremy's voice broke.

Delgado put a hand on his friend's shoulder. "Did your father know?"

"Certainly not. I dared tell no one. Not even Sarah. Well, that's not exactly true. I did tell one person—Allan Horan. I knew I could trust him. He agreed that Annabel and I should leave St. Louis and promised to help us in any way he could. But then . . . then Annabel took matters into her own hands. She was in a fit of despair, Del. She wasn't thinking straight. She went to an old woman who lived on the Creve Couer. The woman gave her a potion that would cause her to miscarry. Only something went wrong, and . . . and Annabel died."

"My God. Jeremy, I'm truly sorry."

Jeremy nodded and took a moment to compose himself before continuing with his story.

"Naturally, the rumors began to spread like wildfire. And this is where Brent Horan comes in. He spread the word that Allan was the child's father. You see, Brent was always jealous of Allan. He didn't like it that Allan was the eldest and stood to inherit Blackwood. And he knew his brother too well. Knew he wouldn't deny the charge and wouldn't point the finger at me. Of course, I admitted everything. But, oddly enough, almost everyone thought I was just trying to protect Allan, when, in fact, he was the one protecting me. I pleaded with him to tell the truth, to defend himself, expose Brent for the liar that he was. But he was too proud. He wouldn't do it. Instead, he disappeared. He did it for me, you know. He realized that his running away would convince everyone that he was, indeed, responsible for what had happened to Annabel. You have to understand, Del that her death hit him very hard. He loved her as I did. Perhaps even more than I. He went to Europe a broken man. Nothing seemed to matter to him anymore. Nothing except friendship and my good name. He sacrificed everything for me."

"I see."

"One other knew the truth—Sterling, the newspaperman. I don't know how he found out, but Allan made him swear not to tell a soul. He never did. He admired and respected Allan. Everyone who knew him did."

"So that must be why Sterling disliked Brent Horan so."

"He was a very good judge of character."

"Did you hear from Allan again?"

"He wrote to me a couple of times. I was the only one he wrote to, apparently, and he made me promise not to tell anyone where he was. I kept that promise. And then, for a long while, I received no word from him. I became concerned. Finally, I heard from a woman who had worked as his housekeeper in Paris. Allan was dead. His body had been found in the Seine. His death was ruled a suicide. I suppose he'd never gotten over Annabel. So you see, he died, alone in a strange land, for my sake."

"And you blame yourself as much as you blame Brent Horan. Or more."

"Of course I do," said Jeremy bitterly. "I was a coward. I should have taken responsibility from the very first, but I didn't, and things got out of hand, and once Brent made his accusations, it was too late, because Allan would never back down from Brent. Never give Brent the satisfaction. It was between the two of them. Do you see what I mean?"

Delgado nodded. It all made sense to him now. Not just Jeremy's hatred for Brent Horan, but also his friend's compulsion to place himself in jeopardy on the field of battle. And, soon, on the field of honor. Jeremy did not want to live. The deaths of Annabel Christophe and Allan Horan burdened his soul.

Doc Loveless had still not arrived. Jeremy was getting anxious, constantly glancing at the eastern sky, trying to calculate the precise imminence of dawn. "We will wait ten minutes more," he told Delgado, consulting his keywinder. "Then we will have to go on without the good doctor." Delgado nodded. A gentleman was not late to his own execution. That would be exceedingly bad form.

Loveless arrived in the nick of time, driving a buggy at breakneck speed. Jeremy introduced him to Delgado. The physician was perfunctory in his courtesy. "Let's get on with it, shall we, gentlemen?" he asked, fishing his own timepiece out of a vest pocket. Jeremy stared at the black medical grip Loveless removed from the buggy. Wondering, assumed Delgado, if the neatly rolled bandages and astringents and steel instruments contained therein would have to be employed this morning in a desperate battle to save his life. The arrival of the doctor seemed to have a sobering effect on Jeremy. But Delgado knew his friend wasn't going to back down. Not after all these years of being haunted by two ghosts.

They got into the rowboat, and the boatman pushed off, then settled down with the oars. He obviously knew this stretch of river well, for he managed to negotiate the tricky currents with almost contemptuous ease and landed them at the northern tip of Bloody Island. Chunks of ice, some bigger than the boat, as well as dead animals, uprooted trees, and other flotsam provided obstacles in the swift main current, but the boatman deftly avoided all hazards. No one uttered a word during the crossing. Delgado tried to keep his teeth from chattering. The morning was bitterly cold and seemed colder still on the river. Besides that, his nerves were frayed.

Bloody Island was approximately two hundred yards at its widest point, and nearly a quarter of a mile in length. Most of it was thickly wooded. The dueling ground was a clearing along the eastern shore, out of sight of St. Louis. There was a law on the books in both Missouri and Illinois against dueling, and though it was not strictly enforced, men engaged in affairs of honor preferred secluded spots where no one was likely to witness the activity. Bloody Island fit the bill perfectly, and had been used for the purpose for more than thirty years, although Delgado had learned that it had acquired its name as a result of a fight back at the turn of the century between Indians and keelboatmen.

Another boat was beached on a sandy spit at the northern tip of the island, and the boatman sat on a nearby log, puffing phlegmatically on a corncob pipe. His attitude was one of a man who had not a care in the world, and, unreasonably, Delgado resented him for it. Their boatman joined the other after Jeremy had given him payment for the passage over. It was simply sound business practice, mused Delgado, to require cash on the barrelhead from a customer who was on his way to possible death.

Jeremy led the way along a footpath that twisted and turned through the dark, silent woods. Just as they reached the clearing, golden shards of sunlight began to pierce the overgrown verdure. Immediately, a mockingbird launched into song. The mighty river murmured as it rolled by. The wooded hills of Illinois made a pretty picture a quarter mile to the east. But the bucolic pleasantness of the scenery was lost on Delgado. Brent Horan and William Darcy stood together in the clearing, and his undivided attention was focused on them. Darcy came forward.

"Gentlemen," he said with a curt, barely civil nod.

"We are here on a solemn and unhappy occasion," said Dr. Loveless gravely. "Is there any possibility of reconciliation?"

Jeremy shook his head. Loveless turned to Darcy, brows raised in a silent query.

"Mr. Horan requests that we proceed," said the gambler. "Unless Mr. Bledsoe wishes to withdraw."

Jeremy glanced at Delgado, who realized he

was expected, as Jeremy's second, to speak for his friend.

"Mr. Bledsoe has no intention of withdrawing," he told Darcy.

"Then," said Loveless, "it becomes the duty of the seconds to see to the loading of the weapons."

Delgado drew two pistols from the pockets of his longcoat. He carefully measured powder, rammed home the bullets, and affixed the percussion caps. Having rejoined Horan, Darcy was similarly employed. Delgado offered both pistols to Jeremy. Jeremy selected the one he wanted, and Delgado slipped the other back into a pocket.

"Thank you, Del," said Jeremy, his voice without emotion.

"God bless you, Jeremy." There was much more that Delgado wanted to say. He wanted to plead with his friend to refrain from going through with this madness. He wanted to convince Jeremy that as a young man he had his whole life ahead of him. That there was no point in living in the past. One had to live for tomorrow. Everyone made mistakes. That his death would break his ailing father's heart. That he, Delgado, would miss him terribly. But he said nothing else, knowing it would all be quite fruitless.

"The time has come, gentlemen," said Loveless.

Delgado helped Jeremy shed his heavy cloak. Jeremy shuddered and smiled at Delgado. "Quite cold this morning."

Delgado nodded. Across the clearing Brent Horan was suddenly doubled over and racked by coughing. Darcy supported him, or he might have fallen to the ground. Delgado watched hopefully. Perhaps Horan would become too ill to continue. Maybe God would spend a miracle. But Loveless was marking off five paces, and when he was done, Horan had straightened up and was no longer coughing.

"Five paces—fifteen feet," said Loveless. "Is that agreeable?"

Delgado was horrified. At such close range there was bound to be bloodshed. He had hoped the two principals would stand at either end of the clearing. That way, with luck, Horan might miss Jeremy. A fragile hope, but Delgado was clinging to slender threads.

"Quite," said Darcy.

After glancing at Jeremy, who nodded, Delgado sighed and said, "Yes."

"The principals will take their places." Loveless had made two distinct marks in the frosty grass with the heel of his boot. Jeremy and Horan stood at these marks. Loveless had paced off his line at right angles to the rising sun so that neither man would have it in his eyes. Suspended just above the Illinois shoreline, the sun was directly in Delgado's eyes, but he didn't move. He felt the sun's meager warmth on his face and listened to the mockingbird progress rapidly through its astonishing repertoire.

"Gentlemen," said Loveless, "you may cock your pistols. You will hold them pointed at the ground until I give the signal. When I say *Fire*, you will have to the count of four to discharge your weapons. I will count out loud, slowly, and then give the signal *Stop*. You may not fire before or after the count of four. If you do, Mr. Horan, Mr. McKinn will be obliged to shoot you. If *you* do, Mr. Bledsoe, Mr. Darcy will be within his rights to shoot you. Is that understood?"

"Yes," said Jeremy.

Horan nodded.

"Gentlemen, are you ready?"

"Ready," said Jeremy.

"I'm ready,"said Horan.

Delgado thought, *I could draw this pistol from my coat and kill Brent Horan where he stands.*

And then what would happen? Darcy would shoot him, and Jeremy would shoot the gambler Darcy. In that scenario, at least Jeremy might survive.

But, Delgado reminded himself, Jeremy does not want to survive. Then, too, there was Sarah. *You selfish, cowardly bastard,* Delgado thought bitterly, hating himself so much at that moment that he could taste bile. As had happened at Blackwood, when Horan gave him an opportunity to save the slave named Naomi, Delgado found himself unwilling to sacrifice himself.

"Fire!" said Loveless. "One—two—three—"

Jeremy and Horan raised their pistols simultaneously, fired as one. They stood so close that it seemed to Delgado that the muzzles of their weapons almost touched. He saw the blossoms of flame, shrouded in acrid white powder smoke, saw Horan rock back on his heels, thought for one brief instant that by some miracle Jeremy had actually won the day—and then watched in horror as his friend pitched sideways to lie on his face in the grass, unmoving.

He rushed forward, reaching Jeremy just as Dr. Loveless did. Gently, they rolled him over. A patch of blood was growing on the front of Jeremy's white shirt. Delgado watched Loveless tear the shirt open, examine the wound, feel for a pulse at Jeremy's wrist, then at his neck, and finally close Jeremy's sightless eyes.

"He is dead," said Loveless. "Shot through the heart. May God have mercy on his soul."

The doctor rose and glanced at Darcy, who was supporting Horan's weight. Horan was pressing his right arm against his side.

"Are you hit, sir?"

"Just a scratch," said Horan hoarsely.

Greatly shaken, feeling numb, Delgado stood and turned to face Brent Horan, very much aware of the weight of the pistol in his coat pocket.

"Well, then," said Horan with an infuriatingly casual smile as Loveless bent to examine his wound. "That's finally settled. Now there remains the business between us, McKinn."

Delgado shook his head. "You fool. You didn't win anything today. Whether he killed you or you killed him didn't matter to Jeremy. He got what he wanted."

"And what was that?"

"Atonement."

He turned away from Horan, picked Jeremy up, and walked back through the dark, silent trees with the body of his friend in his arms, while the mockingbird continued to sing somewhere in the branches overhead.

Chapter Thirteen

"Dying for the wrong cause"

1

That day and all the next, Jeremy Bledsoe's mortal remains lay in an open casket in a downstairs room, and the macabre rituals of death were carried out. He was attired in his Regular Army uniform. Delgado was nearly certain that Jacob would not survive to see his son laid to final rest; the old man refused to leave the chair that he had positioned at the head of the casket. When friends of the family came to pay their last respects, they would offer him their sincerest condolences, but most of the time he did not seem to even be aware of their existence. He kept staring at Jeremy's face as though he expected his son to open his eyes at any moment.

Dr. Lowry and his wife came, as did Joshua Pilcher and his wife. Jessie Benton made an appearance, representing her father, Senator Thomas Hart Benton. Old Bullion was in Washington, trying to put a stop to a war that had raged long enough. There were others—many others—that Delgado had never met. He did not care to meet them now, either. He watched their coming and going from the window of his upstairs room, from which he seldom strayed, not wishing to intrude upon Jacob Bledsoe's grief, or Sarah's. And feeling a good deal responsible for that grief, besides.

"I suppose I should have tried harder to stop him," he had told Sarah. "But I didn't. Not really. If you hate me, Sarah, I will understand. I wouldn't blame you if you did."

"Hate you? Don't be silly. I love you, Del. You mustn't blame yourself. There was nothing you could have done. Don't you think I know how Jeremy was? I remember Annabel Christophe. I was a few years younger than she, but I remember quite well when she died. And even though Father tried to shelter me from the rumors that were flying about, I heard them. Like everyone else, I thought there must have been some truth in what Brent Horan said about his brother. Allan's disappearance seemed to confirm it. Jeremy never told me what really happened."

"In part that is what he couldn't live with," said Delgado. "Perhaps I shouldn't have told you the truth, either." He had told her everything Jeremy had said, thinking she had the right to know.

"No, you were right to do so. In fact, I think everyone should know the truth. People should know Brent Horan for the liar he is."

"Maybe you're right," conceded Delgado.

He wrote down, to the last detail, Jeremy's version of what had happened to Annabel Christophe and why. The next morning he called on Stephen Maitland at the offices of the St. Louis *Enquirer.*

"I would like you to print this in your newspaper," he said.

Maitland took the letter. "What is it, Mr. McKinn?"

"You might say it is the confession of a man who knew he was about to die."

As he read, Maitland turned more pale than

usual. "Good heavens! I . . . I don't know that I can do what you ask, sir."

"What's the matter? Are you afraid of Brent Horan?"

"He is a . . . a very powerful man."

Delgado was in no mood to play games. "So am I, Mr. Maitland. I have a good deal of power over you, now don't I?"

Maitland's owlish eyes blinked rapidly behind the thick lenses of his spectacles. "You mean . . . you mean Clarisse, of course," he whispered.

"Perhaps I should bring the matter up with your superior. I believe the owner of this newspaper visited the Bledsoe house this very afternoon. He has long been acquainted with Jacob Bledsoe, hasn't he?"

"What . . . what matter are you referring to?"

"This letter, of course."

"Oh, yes. Of course. Well, I . . ."

Delgado remorselessly pressed his advantage. "You once said that if ever you could be of service . . ."

"Yes, yes. I remember." Maitland sighed in pure anguish. He folded the letter and with resignation put it in his pocket. "I will see that it is printed, Mr. McKinn. You can rely on me."

Delgado wagged a stern finger at him. "In the next edition."

"Yes."

When he got back to the Bledsoe house, he learned that during his absence Jacob had finally collapsed. He was resting quietly in his bed.

"Did you tell him?" Delgado asked Sarah.

"I didn't have the chance to."

They had agreed it would be better if Jacob heard the truth about Jeremy's connection with

Annabel Christophe's death from one of them before he read it in the newspaper.

"I hope we are doing the right thing," said Delgado. He had been assailed by doubts all the way back from the *Enquirer.*

"I'm sure we are, Del. The people who matter will not think less of Jeremy, for he has done the honorable thing, and tried to set matters right. Or, at least, that's what we're doing for him. I think he would have done the same had he been clear-headed. But his hatred for Brent Horan clouded is judgment. His self-hate, too. Yes, I truly believe we are doing the right thing. It is Brent Horan who will be exposed as the scoundrel he is."

"Question is, how will Horan react?"

"Who cares?"

"I do, for one. So should you. Aren't you afraid of him, Sarah? Of what he might be capable of doing?"

"No, I most certainly am not."

"Well, I am. And just because you are a woman, don't think for a moment that you aren't at risk."

"He is an evil, wicked man, and if I can become the instrument of his downfall, then I shall consider myself a very fortunate person."

Delgado wasn't quite sure what she meant by that, but he was too preoccupied with his own thoughts to ask her.

Early the following day, Stephen Maitland personally delivered the morning edition of the *Enquirer.* Without seeming to, Delgado watched him and Clarisse slip lovers' glances at one another as he pretended to look at the paper, which Sarah had eagerly grabbed out of Maitland's hand. Delgado couldn't get used to the idea of Maitland and Clarisse being lovers; they were an odd couple, indeed. But there could be no denying that the Creole Negress had strong feelings for the pale, gawky newspaperman. Truly, mused Delgado, love was blind.

"I hope this is what you wanted," said Maitland.

"Yes, quite," replied Sarah with a quiet kind of triumph.

"I suppose I ought to be getting back." Maitland gave Clarisse one last, longing look and took his leave.

At noon Jeremy Bledsoe was laid to rest in a churchyard, beside the grave of his mother. His father could not attend. Jacob was still unconscious, in a coma from which, according to the doctor, he might never emerge. Delgado was proud of Sarah. Through it all she bore up bravely. At least a hundred people showed up. Hugh Falconer was present, along with Lillian and Johnny. When the service was over, the mountain man found an opportunity to take Delgado aside while Lillian spoke with Sarah. Falconer looked as grim as Delgado had ever seen him.

"I know what you're trying to do," said Falconer. "You and Sarah."

"I don't know what you mean."

"You're striking back at Brent Horan. But it won't work. He doesn't care about his reputation. Not anymore. The man's dying."

"We just wanted the truth to be known."

"You're stirring up a hornet's nest."

"What do you suggest I do?"

"Either get out of town or kill him, Del. Before he kills you."

"That's what Jeremy told me."

"I know the two of you had become close

friends. I'm glad you agreed to serve as his second. At least he had a friend there when he died."

"I thought about shooting Horan. But I just couldn't bring myself to do it. I wasn't willing to give my life to save Jeremy's. What kind of friend is that? I'm a coward, Hugh."

"No," said Falconer firmly. "You're just too damned civilized for your own good. This was something Jeremy felt he had to do. Whether you thought it was right or wrong, you had to let him go through with it."

"Would you have?"

"You know how much I thought of him. But yes, I would have."

"I'm not going to run," said Delgado. "I feel as though I've been running away from something all my life. From the responsibilities that my father wanted me to shoulder. From everything that was going on in New Mexico. I didn't want to take a stand. Well, I'm going to this time. A person has got to be willing to fight for what he thinks is right, no matter what the cost."

"That's what it's all about in this country, Del."

"I know." It was all quite clear to Delgado now. America was a vision, a goal not yet attained, and being one of its citizens meant being blessed with an opportunity that most people in the world would never know—an opportunity to transform vision into reality. A reality of equality and prosperity for all. To pursue this dream was not merely a right, but the responsibility, of every American.

Diego Archuleta had said that all Americans were concerned only with themselves. But Delgado knew that wasn't true. He thought about Brent Horan and Langdon Grail, and, yes, to an extent even Jacob Bledsoe and his own father. Such men proved that the idea of America, the *promise,* was more than the sum of its parts. And some of those men, like Horan, stood in the way. Delgado knew it was time he tried to right the wrongs he saw all about him. That was what his beloved Sarah was trying to do. America had its shortcomings, but they could be overcome, and he was ready to do his part.

True, this final reckoning with Brent Horan was in large measure a personal affair. But it was more than that. It was not the end of anything, but just the beginning. . . .

"Beware, then," said Falconer. "Keep alert. Horan is running out of time. He'll have to make his move soon. When he does . . ."

"Yes. I know where to find you. But this is something *I* have to do."

Falconer nodded. "But you may need to even the odds. Horan won't come for you alone. He's afraid of you."

"Of me? Don't be ridiculous."

"It's true. You see, he knows you're not a coward. And he knows you've beaten him at every turn. So I'm pretty sure that this time he'll have help."

Delgado took Sarah back to the house on Laurel Avenue. She said not a word, and seemed very tied and careworn. Delgado could think of nothing to say that would comfort her. He turned her over to Clarisse, who took her upstairs to her room, and went into the parlor to pour himself a stiff drink, which he badly needed. Clarisse had built up the fire in the hearth, and he settled in a chair near it and tried to relax. He found that to be a very difficult proposition. He kept thinking about Brent Horan, hating the man more than he had hated anyone in his life. In fact, he was sure now that he had never really hated anyone or anything before.

Clarisse came downstairs. He called her into the parlor.

"Horan thinks he is being poisoned by one of his slaves," he told her. "He makes her taste his food and drink, and yet she has no ill effects. Still, he is convinced she is killing him."

Clarisse just stood there, inscrutable, watching him.

"Do you think that's possible?" asked Delgado. "*Could* she be poisoning him?"

"*Oui.* It is possible, I think."

"But how?"

Clarisse shrugged. "There are a number of ways. She is perhaps using belladonna, a plant that grows wild in the marshes."

"Yes. The nightshade. I remember from my chemistry class at Oxford. Extracts of the leaves and roots were used in ancient times by women to dilate the pupils of the eye, which they thought made them look more desirable. Belladonna means 'beautiful lady' in Italian. But if she puts it in his food, why isn't she affected?"

"Perhaps she has built up a resistance to it. This can be done by taking small quantities over a long period of time. She would still become ill, but not as ill as he."

"I see."

"Or perhaps it is not poison at all. I know of this woman. She is called Naomi, *n'est-ce pas*?"

"That's right."

"Her previous master sold her to the slave dealer because she practiced voodoo."

Delgado shook is head. "Voodoo or poison, whichever method she is using, she hasn't worked quickly enough to suit me."

"If that is all, I must go now to the kitchen."

Delgado nodded. The brandy conspired with the warmth of the fire to make him drowsy, and he soon drifted off into a fitful sleep, only to awaken with a start to find Clarisse touching his shoulder.

"She wishes to see you."

The clock on the mantelpiece told him he had slept for hours. He hurried upstairs, tapped on Sarah's door, and entered at her bidding. Sarah had not changed out of her dress of mourning black. She stood at a window, and he went to her. He could tell she had been crying, but she was calm and composed now.

"It's getting dark," she said. "I don't want to be alone."

Poor Sarah! She had lost her brother, and at any moment her father might succumb. He could not blame her for fearing the darkness, and for the first time Delgado became fully aware of the responsibility he now bore upon his shoulders. He was all Sarah Bledsoe had left.

He took her in his arms and held her close, and later he sat up on the bed while she slept with her head on his chest. He stayed awake through the night, holding her, protecting her, making her feel secure, and only when the first shreds of daylight came stealing through the windows did he leave her, still sleeping soundly. He went downstairs to find Clarisse, wanting coffee for himself and a nice breakfast tray for Sarah when she woke.

Reaching the bottom of the stairs, he turned the

corner into the hall and, hearing a telltale rustle of clothing behind him, began to turn around, catching a brief glimpse of a man wearing a white hood over his face, with holes cut out for the eyes—and then something hard hit him at the base of the skull, and he fell in an explosion of sweeping pain and blinding white light. The light faded to black, and he fell, and kept falling, falling, falling into oblivion. . . .

When he came to, he was momentarily disoriented. Sitting up, a moan escaped him as the walls began to spin and the floor beneath him felt as if it were tilting sharply one way and then the other. His skull felt as though it had been split in two. His vision slowly cleared, and he looked around and remembered where he was and what had happened, and the sudden fear nearly strangled him. He got to his feet, then stumbled and fell to hands and knees and got up again with Sarah's name on his lips, and somehow half ran, half crawled up the stairs to her room, her *empty* room. He ran next to Jacob's room and found Bledsoe in his bed, and his first thought was that *My God they've killed him.* But Jacob was still alive. These men weren't Diego Archuleta's rebel killers. No, Brent Horan was behind this. Delgado was sure of it. Jacob was still lost in the coma. Delgado thought bitterly that perhaps now that would be for the best if he never came out of it, because Sarah was in Brent Horan's hands.

He checked every room upstairs, even though in his heart he knew Sarah was gone. He found Clarisse downstairs, bound hand and foot and gagged, on the floor in the kitchen, and he untied her, removed the gag, and she told him what he already knew, that two men had grabbed her and bound her, two men wearing white hoods with holes for the eyes cut out.

"They took Sarah," he said, his voice hollow, as though it reached his ears from the black depths of a bottomless pit.

"Horan," was all she said.

Delgado nodded and went up to his room and put on his coat. He made sure the derringer was in the pocket. Then he left the house. He borrowed a horse from the nearby livery and nearly rode it into the ground getting to Falconer's place.

As the two of them rode for Blackwood, snow began to fall. Delgado was oblivious to the cold. He was numb with fear. Fear for Sarah, for she was at the mercy of a man gone mad.

"He won't be alone," Falconer told him. "I reckon we'll have four or five men to deal with."

"Who are they?"

"Backwoodsmen, mostly. Men who've been beholden to the Horan family for years."

"How could they stoop so low as to do this for Brent Horan?"

"In one way or another they feel they owe him."

"Owe him enough to kidnap Sarah? Perhaps to die for him?"

"We'll find out soon enough," said Falconer.

2

They checked their horses where the road emerged from the dark old woods to angle across the cultivated fields toward the big white house. Delgado was inclined to go charging straight in, and when he saw the house, the urge was nearly too strong to resist because he was sure Sarah was in there. In there, with Brent Horan, that dangerous lunatic, and Delgado was afraid of what he might do to her. Or might have already done. He still could scarcely believe Horan had sent his minions to abduct her. After all, that wasn't a very honorable thing to do—something a gentleman would never even contemplate—and Delgado realized he had been relying too much on Horan's carefully nurtured self-image. The facade had crumbled. Horan didn't care anymore. He could let his true self shine because he was dying, and because of the letter printed in the *Enquirer*, and because he would go to any lengths to destroy Delgado before he died. Which meant there was no telling what he would do.

But Falconer was wise in the ways of war, and Delgado curbed his impatience and waited while the frontiersman carefully surveyed the house and the approach to it. Delgado didn't see anything moving. The house was dark and seemed lifeless. Not even any smoke came out of the chimney. But Falconer could see things the average man would miss. Of this Delgado was convinced, and he waited, putting his trust, and Sarah's life, in Falconer's capable hands.

Finally, Falconer drew a deep breath, flexed the tension out of his shoulders, and turned to Delgado. "I knew a man once," he said, "who kidnapped a woman and staked her out to draw his enemies into the open where he could get a shot at them. It worked, too. They rushed out to rescue her, and some of them got killed. That's what this is all about, Del. Horan doesn't want Sarah. Not really. It's you he's after. And here you are."

"He is accustomed to getting what he wants,"

said Delgado bitterly. "Had I known he would go this far, I would have accepted his challenge."

"Now he's got help."

"So much for honor. How much help do you think he has?"

"That's the problem. We have no way of knowing in advance."

"So what do you suggest we do?"

Falconer was gazing at the house again. "An old Indian trick might work." He told Delgado what he expected of him. "Are you game?"

Delgado nodded. He was surprised to find himself so calm, and deliberately began to check the loads in his over-and-under derringer.

"I've got something for you that has a little more sting," said Falconer, and he drew a .36 Colt Paterson from under his capote. It was just like the pistol Langdon Grail had used to such devastating effect in Truchas.

"Where did you get this?" asked Delgado as he took the revolver.

"I bought two of them just the other day. One for you, and one for Jeremy." Falconer took a second Colt from under the capote. "I'm sorry I didn't have a chance to give this to him."

"We've evened up the odds," said Delgado with grim satisfaction, testing the balance of the revolver in his hand.

Falconer gave him a long, solemn look. "Don't go getting yourself killed."

"You either."

Falconer smiled and nodded approvingly. "You'll do," he said and with a tap of his heels put the horse under him into motion.

They rode out of the woods stirrup to stirrup, holding their mounts to a walk, going up the road between the snow-covered fields toward the Horan house. The only sound Delgado heard was the crunch of snow beneath the hooves of the horses. No birds were singing. Thank God, he thought, I don't hear a mockingbird. It was a sound he would always associate with death.

The distance between the house and the woods was about four hundred yards. It seemed like four hundred miles to Delgado. He watched the darkened windows, but still there was no movement, no evidence that anyone saw them. But someone was bound to be watching. *Here I am, Horan, you bastard,* he thought. *This is what you've wanted all along. Ever since that day on the* Sultana. *So what's keeping you?*

Three hundred yards. Two hundred. They were halfway to the house, and still nothing, and Delgado began to entertain doubts. Maybe the house *was* as empty as it looked. Maybe Horan had taken Sarah somewhere else. Maybe, God forbid, he was having his way with her at this very moment, using her the way he used Naomi. Delgado tried to drive the maddening thought from his mind.

One hundred yards—and then Falconer shouted at him to look out. The mountain man had seen something he had missed, but Delgado didn't waste time looking for it. He steered his horse sharply right while Falconer cut left and kicked the animal into a gallop across the field. The gunshot rolled across the open ground and bounced off the line of trees behind them, echoing in the brittle winter stillness. Delgado bent low in the saddle, knowing Falconer was galloping hard in the opposite direction. More gunfire. Delgado glimpsed blossoms of flame from two of the downstairs windows, but still he had no idea how many men stood between him and Sarah, or even why they would. Not that it mattered anymore. If they tried to stop him from reaching the woman he loved, then he would kill them.

Suddenly, his horse stumbled and went down, and Delgado thought at first that the animal had been hit. The deep snow softened his fall. He managed to hold onto the Colt Paterson as he rolled and came up on one knee. The horse got up, shook itself and trotted off. Not hit—it had only lost its footing among the furrows of hard frozen ground concealed beneath the snow. Delgado saw Falconer circling his house on the far side, clinging to the side of his pony so that the men in the house had no clear shot at him, and firing the Colt Paterson that had been meant for Jeremy Bledsoe beneath the horse's neck; the Hawken, in its fringed and beaded buckskin sheath, remained tied to his saddle. Delgado caught just a quick look, and then the mountain man disappeared round the house, the snow flying up from beneath the hooves of his hard-running horse.

Steeling himself, Delgado got up and ran for the corner of the house.

A gun barrel protruded from a window and swiveled toward him. Delgado blazed away with the Colt, sending three bullets through the partially closed wooden shutters. Splinters flew. He heard a man cry out in pain. The gun barrel disappeared. Reaching the house, Delgado threw open the unlatched shutters, stepped back, and then plunged headlong through the glass.

He fell over the body of the man he had shot. The room was dark, and Delgado didn't get a good look at him. Didn't want to. The man was writhing on the blood-slick floor. Delgado doubted that he was a threat any longer, but he knew it would be foolhardy to leave an enemy behind him, even a semiconscious and badly wounded enemy. He brought the butt of the Colt down hard on the man's skull and the movement ceased.

As Delgado got to his feet, a door on the other side of the room swung open. He saw the shape of a man, then the blossom of flame that was a muzzle flash, and realized he was silhouetted against the window. Then he gasped as the bullet grazed him high on the left arm. The gunshot was deafening in the confines of the room. The bullet slammed into the wall behind him. He dived for cover behind a pair of chairs bracketing a small table, fired once lying on his side, and knew the shot was wild. But it drove the man back out of sight.

Delgado's first instinct was to stay down, but he thought of Sarah and, leaping to his feet, overturned the table and one of the chairs as he ran full tilt at the door, hurling himself through, hitting the floor and sliding across the slick marble of the main hall, seeing the man clearly in better light—a rough-hewn character in homespun, his back to a wall, reloading his single-shot rifle. Still sliding across the floor, Delgado fired once, and the bullet slammed the man against the wall. A look of surprise on his bearded face, the backwoodsman let the rifle slip from his hands and pitched forward to the floor. Delgado knew he was dead.

To the sound of splintering wood Falconer crashed through the door at the far end of the hall. At that instant a man emerged from one of the rooms opening onto the hallway. Seeing Delgado, he turned and raised a flintlock pistol, and Delgado's heart lurched in his chest as he pulled the Colt's trigger and heard the hammer fall on an empty chamber. But before the man could fire, Falconer's Colt spoke once. The man sprawled forward. His pistol hit the floor and discharged, the bullet drilling harmlessly into the wall. He rolled over, clutching at his shattered shoulder and hissing at the pain through clenched teeth. He looked up to see Falconer standing over him.

"Nothing's worse than dying for the wrong cause," said the mountain man.

"Reckon," said the man.

"You've paid your dues to Horan. Now go home."

With Falconer's help the man got to his feet. He looked bleakly at Delgado. "Right glad I didn't kill you."

"Where's Sarah Bledsoe?" snapped Delgado.

"Upstairs. She ain't been harmed. Not a hair on her head. Mr. Horan promised, or I wouldn't have done what I done."

"Get," said Falconer. "And don't look back."

The man nodded and went out the way Falconer had come in.

Delgado didn't wait to see the man leave; he was bounding up the staircase. He tried every door he came to, and the one door that was locked he kicked open. Sarah was standing over by a window, head bowed, hands clasped together. She looked up with a gasp as Delgado barged in, and then she smiled.

"I was praying that you would come through unharmed," she said calmly.

He took her in his arms and embraced her so tightly that it took her breath away.

"Did he . . . did he hurt you in any way, Sarah?"

"No."

"Thank God."

"Clarisse. Is Clarisse all right?"

"She's fine. Where is Horan?"

"I don't know."

"Come on." He took her by the hand and led her out of the room and down into the main hall. She stared at the man Delgado had shot to death. "I'm sorry," he said. "I had to do it." He wondered if the man had a family. Probably. *Which means I've made some poor woman a widow. And how many children would never see their father again?*

The doors to the room where Delgado had met with Brent Horan a few days earlier stood open, and Hugh Falconer straddled the threshold.

"Is he in there?" asked Delgado.

Falconer was staring at something, or someone, in the room, and he didn't look around, just nodded.

"Wait here," Delgado told Sarah and started to sip past Falconer into the room.

The sight that greeted him stopped him in his tracks.

Brent Horan sat in the same chair as before. The room was dark and cold; the fire in the hearth had burned down to orange embers in a mound of gray ash. Horan's head was slumped forward on his chest, and Delgado wondered if he was unconscious or dead. He glanced at Falconer.

"Is he . . . ?"

"I don't know. I thought you'd want to handle it."

"Yes. Yes, of course." He had admitted to Falconer that he was scared of Horan. It wouldn't do for someone else to resolve the bitter feud that had developed between the two of them. Falconer was right. He had to be the one to deal with Horan.

With a hand in his coat pocket, gripping the loaded derringer, Delgado entered the room and crossed to stand in front of Horan's chair. Even this close he couldn't tell if the man was breathing.

"Horan?"

No response. Delgado leaned closer, reached out with his left hand, and shook Horan's shoulder.

Horan's eyes snapped open. He clutched Delgado's extended arm, making an incoherent, animal-like sound. Delgado withdrew the derringer from his pocket and thumbed the hammer back. Seeing the gun, Horan laughed, an unpleasant, wheezing sound.

"You're too late, McKinn."

He threw aside the blanket that covered him from the chest down—and Delgado saw the knife. A big kitchen knife. It had been thrust to the hilt into Horan's belly. His clothes were soaked with blood.

"She couldn't wait," hissed Horan.

"Naomi?"

Horan nodded. "Poison was too slow. She knew she was out of time. She put this blade in me and ran. But she . . . she won't get far. Talbott . . . Talbott is on her trail. By now the bitch is probably dead."

Delgado pulled his arm free. Horan's grip was weak. He was bleeding to death, and he had very little strength left. Lowering the hammer on the derringer, Delgado pocketed the pistol and drew a ragged breath.

"Why the long face, McKinn? You can watch me die. That should please you."

Delgado shook his head. "But I'm glad you won't be hurting any more people."

"I have no regrets."

"Then I am truly sorry for you."

"I don't want your pity!" rasped Horan, and then a spasm of pain contorted his face. His skin, noticed Delgado, was white as alabaster. Looking under the chair, Delgado saw a pool of blood. He couldn't believe Horan had held onto life this long. No doubt he had known that to keep the backwoodsmen at their posts he had to conceal his condition from them.

"McKinn? McKinn, are you still there?" Horan's eyes were open, but he could no longer see.

"I'm here."

"Damn you, McKinn," he whispered. "You win again."

He slumped forward, and Delgado heard the death rattle in his throat.

Falconer was waiting with Sarah in the hall. The mountain man had kept her out of the room.

"He's dead," said Delgado flatly. "That slave, the one called Naomi, knifed him, and he bled to death. But he held on, hoping his men would kill me. They didn't know he was dying. They wouldn't have stayed to fight had they known. Dead, he had no power over them."

"Let's go home," said Falconer.

They went outside. Falconer's horse was standing nearby, and the mountain man rode out to collect Delgado's wayward mount, which had strayed down to the edge of the trees that marked the course of the creek running behind the Horan mansion. Delgado climbed into his saddle and helped Sarah on behind him, and they took the road across the snow-covered fields and into the woods.

A hound was standing in the lane and bayed at them as they drew near. "That's one of Talbott's dogs," said Delgado and checked his horse. A moment later, the slave catcher emerged onto the road, leading his horse, with several other hounds following in his wake. A body was draped over the saddle. Seeing them, Talbott froze. A shotgun was racked across his shoulder, and he brought it down as though he was thinking about using it, but Falconer already had the Hawken mountain rifle out of its buckskin sheath, and Talbott wisely tossed the shotgun aside.

"I didn't have nothing to do with it," he said gruffly, glancing at Sarah.

"Did you hear the shooting?" asked Delgado.

"Sure, I heard. But I didn't want no part of that business. I'm just the overseer here. I catch a few runaways. I take care of my own job and that's all."

"You're out of business," said Falconer. "Your boss is dead."

"Is that a fact? Well, I always knew he'd come to a bad end." Talbott shrugged his indifference. "There's other plantations."

Delgado was out of the saddle now, and Talbott watched him warily as he approached, but Delgado moved past him to the body draped over the slave catcher's saddle. A closer look confirmed Delgado's fears. It was Naomi.

"I think she was sick," said Talbott, as though that was a good excuse for killing her. "Leastways, she didn't go far."

The look Delgado gave him made Talbott take a step back.

"Look here, mister," said the slave catcher. "Don't go gettin' riled at me. I was just doing my job."

"One day soon," predicted Delgado, "they'll call this murder. And I will do everything in my power to bring that day about." He returned to his horse.

Emboldened now that he was reasonably sure Delgado would do him no harm, Talbott lifted Naomi's head by grabbing a handful of her hair. "She was right purty, for a nigger. I was halfway sorry I had to shoot her."

"Halfway isn't good enough," said Falconer.

"Look at that," said Talbott, disgusted. "Nigger blood all over my saddle."

"That's American blood," replied Delgado curtly. "As American as yours. Or mine."

He swung back up in the saddle behind Sarah, put his arms around her, and, taking up the reins, urged the horse into motion. Giving Talbott a final, steely look, Falconer followed, and soon the lane took them out of the dark old woods and into the cold sunlight.

We invite you to preview a new novel of adventure and war on the Western frontier:

The Black Jacks
by Jason Manning
Coming soon from Signet Books

CHAPTER ONE

Patience had never been Sam Houston's long suit. As he stood on the porch of the weathered one-room cabin on Cedar Point and gazed bleakly through the evergreens at the shimmering blue expanse of Galveston Bay, he wore without realizing it a ferocious scowl on his craggy face. Trials and tribulations beset him at every turn. He was a man of action, predisposed by nature to tackle problems quickly and aggressively. Yet here he stood, forced by circumstance to bide his time, at present powerless to act.

Restless, he stamped his feet and pulled the brightly colored Indian blanket closer about his brawny shoulders. This infernal weather didn't help matters. Texas weather was notoriously unpredictable, but never more so than in the month of February. Following two balmy weeks of false spring, when the redbuds began to decorate the woodlands with splashes of pink, and the dogwood put on their new buds, a blue norther had blown in yesterday, all gray and raw.

Though the sun was out today, the wind was still strong out of the north, and the chill caused him pain in the ankle which had been shattered by a musket ball at the Battle of San Jacinto. A pair of prominent Louisiana physicians—one of whom was his old benefactor, Dr. Ker, who had treated the grave wounds he'd received at Horseshoe Bend while fighting the Creek Indians with ol' Andy Jackson—removed twenty pieces of bone from his leg a month after the victory at San Jacinto. But by that time many weeks had passed without proper medicine or poultices, and Houston was resigned to the fact that his ankle would never be wholly recuperated.

If only he could have a drink! A nip of Old Nash would smooth his troubled brow! But no. He had promised his beloved Margaret that he would abstain. An old Texas formula of orange bitters helped a little, but it was really a poor substitute for genuine Oh-Be-Joyful. Still, his fiancee had made him swear, and a man's word was his bond. But, by the eternal, it was damnably hard to do the right thing sometimes.

By the eternal. Houston smiled. How many times had he heard his mentor, his idol, and his friend, Andrew Jackson, roar those words when riled. Old Hickory had gone into retirement at his plantation near Nashville, Tennessee, after eight glorious and tumultuous years as president of these United States, an old man whose rail-thin body was worn out by seventy-three years of travail, but whose mind was still sharp as saber steel.

These United States? Houston shook his head. A mental slip of the tongue. Despite his best efforts, Texas was still an independent republic. Annexation had eluded him. And that was a shame, because Texas *needed* to become part of the United States. There was ample cause to wonder if she would long survive on her own.

A magnificent destiny had aligned Sam Houston's life with Jackson's, and as he stood there watching the bitter cold wind ruffle the surface of the bay, Houston reminisced. Virginia-born forty-seven years ago, he had moved to Tennessee with his mother and siblings following the death of his father. Finding farm work distasteful, Houston had run away from home and lived among the Cherokees for three years. Adopted by Chief Oo-loo-te-ka, he was called The Raven. Later, to pay his debts, he was forced to find work as a school-teacher, though in large measure he was himself an unlettered frontiersman.

Then, in 1813, Regular Army recruiters had come to Maysville, and by taking a silver dollar from a drumhead Houston had pledged himself to military service. His mother gave him a musket and his father's ring, the one inscribed with the word HONOR. She had enjoined him never to disgrace the family name. "I had rather all my sons should fill one honorable grave than that one of them should turn his back to save his life. My door is open to brave men. It is eternally shut against cowards."

With the rank of ensign, Houston had distinguished himself at the Battle of Horseshoe Bend. Wounded twice—once by arrow, the second time by a musket ball—his heroics came to the attention of General Jackson. The shoulder wound was still a running sore to this day, and bothered him with nearly as much consistency as the ankle.

Following his military service, Houston had become a lawyer and entered Tennessee politics with Andrew Jackson as his sponsor. Before long, Jackson was president, and Houston was governor of Tennessee. The Raven's future shined with almost blinding intensity.

But then he married Eliza Allen. He was thirty-five, she was nineteen and unsure of her feelings. Emotionally still a child, Eliza was unprepared for the role of wife, and three months after their marriage, the Houstons separated.

Pacing the length of the cabin's porch, Sam Houston frowned. Those days had been the most bleak and bitter of his life. He had resigned the governorship and sought refuge among his old friends, the Cherokees, forsaking a promising future. *Sic transit gloria mundi!* Fame was indeed fleeting. A thousand rumors were circulated; his political enemies claimed he had acted in a ungentlemanly fashion toward poor Eliza, and when he refused to answer these charges they "posted" him as a coward, after a custom of the day. He did, however, chivalrously defend Eliza. "If any wretch ever dares to utter a word against the purity of Mrs. Houston I will come back and write the libel in his heart's blood."

Everyone acquainted with Sam Houston knew this was no idle threat.

With a sigh, Houston moved to an old rocking chair at the end of the porch. The *Telegraph and Texas Register*, dated February 18, 1840, was anchored against the caprice of the wind by a hickory cane sporting a staghorn handle. Houston picked up the newspaper and cane and sat down. Sitting in this rocking chair made him feel old and useless. Almost as useless as he had felt after that debacle in Tennessee. He had never told his side of the story to anyone. Honor would not permit him to do so, for the truth would sully poor Eliza's reputation, and that he would never do, not even to save his own good name.

At that time he had been so consumed by despair that he had even contemplated suicide. Aboard the steamboat *Red River,* bound for the mighty Mississippi by way of the Cumberland River, he had been standing on deck one day, giving serious thought to hurling himself into the murky waters below, when he saw an eagle soaring against the blazing yellow orb of a setting sun. The eagle swooped low over his head and screamed defiantly. Suddenly he had known, with a pure conviction, that his destiny lay to the west. The next day he made the acquaintance of Jim Bowie, the legendary knife fighter and adventurer. Bowie's tales of Texas had filled Houston with wonder and excitement.

Billy Carroll, his political foe, who replaced him as Tennessee's governor, had been heard to say, sarcastically, "Poor Houston! Rose like a rocket, and fell like a stick." But Houston had risen again, like a phoenix from the ashes. After a sojourn with the Cherokees, he had gone to Texas as President Jackson's agent to report on Indian affairs. To Texas Sam Houston hitched his star. He had led a ragtag army of volunteers to stunning victory at San Jacinto, defeating Santa Anna, that self-styled "Napoleon of the West," and an army of veterans who had recently—and brutally—suppressed rebellion in Mexico's southern provinces. Houston had gone on to serve as the first president of the Republic of Texas.

But now it seemed as though his star had waned yet again. Shakespeare was so right—there most certainly was a tide in the affairs of men. His tide had ebbed. He had served his term as president. Texas law forbade him to serve two consecutive terms. Now, God forbid, Mirabeau Bonaparte Lamar held the reins of state in his completely inadequate grasp. And Houston, nearly destitute, had resorted to the practice of law in a country burdened with a surfeit of "cornstalk lawyers." Finally, and worst of all, his beloved Texas was in dire straits. The Panic of 1837 which had ravaged the economy of the United States was now having its doleful effect on Texas. Currency was worthless, land could scarcely be bought or sold, and debts remained unpaid. On top of everything else, the republic was threatened by Mexican and Indian aggression.

But Sam Houston would not give up. He had learned from Andrew Jackson that a real man never did. No, he was going to resurrect himself once more, with the Almighty's help and Margaret Lea's love, and he would save Texas from disaster. Therein lay the reason for his impatience. So much to do in so little time!

His body servant, Esau, came out onto the porch. "You want I should bring you some orange bitters, Marster Sam?"

"No."

"Some hot coffee, then? It be almighty brisk out here."

Houston glowered. "By God, no, Esau. What I need are a few brave men to rescue this republic from certain destruction."

Esau blinked and went back inside. The Old Chief was in one of his earth-shaking moods, and it was best to leave him at such times.

Houston's blue eyes swept the tree-covered point of land which he had purchased three years ago. He had planned to build a summer cottage at land's end, where the breeze off the bay would keep the heat, mosquitoes, and black "eyebreaker" gnats under control. He would name the place

Raven's Moor. Unfortunately, he lacked adequate funds to start construction. All he had now was his law practice. Ordinarily, fradulent land claims and old Spanish grants made the Texas real estate business a bonanza for lawyers, but the republic was in such severe economic doldrums that precious few clients could pay an attorney's fees in cash. And besides, Houston readily admitted that he was an indifferent lawyer at best. His preference was politics. But soon he would have a wife to support.

Thoughts of Margaret softened the grim lines of his craggy face.

In May of '36, a month after the victory at San Jacinto, Houston had sailed into New Orleans aboard the trading schooner *Flora*, and among the hundreds who gathered at the levee to see the bigger-than-life Texas hero were young girls from Professor McLean's School, who had traveled by stage all the way from Marion, Alabama. One of McLean's pupils was seventeen-year-old Margaret Lea. Slender and fairly tall at five-foot-seven, Margaret was a beauty, with violet blue eyes and light brown hair streaked with gold, and a serenity that made her seem more mature than her years.

Her family was one of the most distinguished in the South, her ancestors had fought in the American Revolution. Soldiers and lawyers and politicians inhabited her family tree. Her father managed a prospering plantation on the Cahaba River in Alabama. A pious and proper young lady, Margaret was also clairvoyant, and on that day in New Orleans she confided to her closest friends that she had a very strong feeling that she would meet Sam Houston again.

After his term as president of Texas expired,

Houston visited the United States to drum up investors for the Sabine City Development Company, of which he was a major stockholder. Townbuilding was all the rage in Texas, and Houston was confident that a community located at the mouth of the Sabine River would flourish. He also wanted to buy some blooded horses, and visit Andrew Jackson during his travels. The last thing on his agenda was finding the woman of his dreams.

At Mobile, Alabama, he called on a prominent local businessman, Martin Lea. Lea invited Houston to his country home, Spring Hill, where his wife was entertaining his sister, Margaret, and their mother Nancy. When he saw Margaret, Houston fell in love at first sight.

That night, a thoroughly beguiled Sam Houston sat and stared at Margaret, clad in a beautiful tartan dress, soft candlelight gleaming in her hair as she played the piano. Since leaving the McLean School, she had attended the new Judson College for young ladies, becoming an accomplished piano and harp player and impressing everyone with her gift for poetry. Late that evening, Houston walked with Margaret in the azalea garden. He picked a pink carnation and presented the flower to her. She put it in her hair. The moonlight filtering through the pecan trees, the romance in the air—even now Houston could vividly recall that evening stroll.

He was forty-six years old, she was only twenty, and yet she fell in love with this gallant adventurer. For his part he had given up on achieving personal happiness. Ten years had transpired since his disastrous marriage with Eliza Allen. During his exile among the Cherokees he had carried on a tempestuous relationship with Tiana, daughter of "Hellfire Jack" Rogers, the Scots trader, and his Cherokee wife. But that, too, had ended poorly, due in no small measure to his fondness for ardent spirits, an affliction that prompted the Cherokees to call him *Oo-Tse-Tee Ar-dee-tah-Skee*—Big Drunk.

To the dismay of Nancy Lea, Houston courted Margaret for a week, all business forgotten. Houston was charming—this much Nancy would concede. But he was a drinker, a profane man, a duellist, an adventurer, and there were those rumors about his former wife and that Indian princess. Houston was completely candid with Margaret regarding his many faults, and Margaret decided it was God's will that she should be His humble instrument in saving Houston's life. Not to mention his immortal soul. At the end of this week-long whirlwind romance, Houston asked Margaret to marry him and she accepted.

She was his *Esperanza,* he declared, the "one hoped for." "My heart is like a caged bird," she wrote him, "whose weary pinions have been folded for months. At length it wakes from its stupor, spreads its wings and longs to escape."

Sam Houston sighed and rose restlessly from the rocking chair. Before long Margaret would be here in Texas with him—and what did he have to offer her? A ramshackle cabin, a mountain of debts, and a few practically useless redback dollars in his pocket. Something had to happen, and soon.

Tom Blue, his other servant, came trotting around the corner of the cabin.

"Rider comin', Marster Sam."

Houston walked to the edge of the porch and peered up the lane at the three horsemen coming through the cedars. He squinted to identify them, but his eyes weren't what they used to be. *I am just a broken-down old war horse,* he thought bitterly. One of the horsemen was leading a riderless pony. A fine-looking colt. Then Houston recognized the gray hunter beneath the saddle of the man in the lead, and his heart soared. Only one man in Texas rode such a splendid thoroughbred.

As the riders drew near, Houston saw that he was right. The man on the gray was Captain John Henry McAllen. And that was Dr. Ashbel Smith with him! Houston smiled. He had told Esau that he needed a few brave men to save Texas. Well, by the Eternal, here were two who fit that bill perfectly!